Praise for Michelle W............

"Well written, aptly conveying a strong sense of family among the sisters, the quartet shows great promise."
—4 stars, *RT Book Reviews* on *Undone by the Duke*

"A tender, exquisitely romantic tale . . ."
—Connie Brockway, *New York Times* bestselling author on *Undone by the Duke*

"Rich with historical detail and insightful characterization, *Unraveled by the Rebel*, the second in Willingham's intriguing Secrets in Silk series, is a lushly sensual treat."
—John Charles, *Booklist*

"This genuinely funny and thoughtful third Secrets in Silk Regency romance is a delightful addition to the series. The elements of blackmail, vengeance, and forbidden love weave their way into the story, making this an outstanding page-turner."
—*Publishers Weekly* on *Undressed by the Earl*

"Willingham successfully draws readers into an emotional and atmospheric new tale of the Clan MacKinloch. Allowing a gentle heroine to tame a hero who has lost his ability to speak draws readers into the story and keeps them enthralled to the very end. Well-crafted, brimming with historical details and romantic from beginning to end, this is Willingham at her best."
—4 stars, *RT Book Reviews* on *Tempted by the Highland Warrior*

"Two wounded souls find hope and redemption in *Surrender to an Irish Warrior,* a richly detailed and emotionally intense medieval romance."

—*Chicago Tribune*

"Memorable characters and exciting plot twists make this one worth hanging on to."

—4.5 stars, *RT Book Reviews* on *To Sin with a Viking*

Unlaced by the Outlaw

Also by Michelle Willingham

SECRETS IN SILK SERIES (REGENCY SCOTLAND)

Undone by the Duke

Unraveled by the Rebel

Undressed by the Earl

Unlaced by the Outlaw

MACEGAN BROTHERS SERIES (MEDIEVAL IRELAND)

Her Warrior Slave

"The Viking's Forbidden Love-Slave" in the *Pleasurably Undone* anthology

Her Warrior King

Her Irish Warrior

The Warrior's Touch

Taming Her Irish Warrior

"Voyage of an Irish Warrior"

"The Warrior's Forbidden Virgin"

Surrender to an Irish Warrior

"Pleasured by the Viking" in the *Delectably Undone* anthology

"Lionheart's Bride" in the *Royal Weddings Through the Ages* anthology

Warriors in Winter

Unlaced by the Outlaw

A SECRETS IN SILK NOVEL

MICHELLE WILLINGHAM

Montlake
Romance

Text copyright © 2014 Michelle Willingham
All rights reserved.

Published by Montlake Romance, Seattle

www.apub.com

Amazon, the Amazon logo, and Montlake Romance are trademarks of Amazon. com, Inc., or its affiliates.

ISBN-13: 9781477826010
ISBN-10: 1477826017

Cover design by becker&mayer! LLC

Illustrated by Judy York

Library of Congress Control Number: 2014908858

Printed in the United States of America

For Kathy Tobin, a wonderful sister-in-law and a friend. Thanks for all of your support over the years.

Chapter One

Her sister was missing.

Most older sisters would leave such a terrible problem in the hands of their parents. Or possibly alert the authorities. Margaret Andrews did neither.

For one, she knew exactly who had kidnapped Amelia. Second, she knew that the blackguard intended to force her sister to wed him. And third, Margaret had suffered untold humiliation when that same awful man had abandoned her only days before their wedding, three years ago. Lord Lisford might have shattered her girlish dreams, humiliating her in the face of society, but Margaret would never let the same thing happen to her baby sister. This was more than a dangerous situation—this was her opportunity for vengeance.

It didn't matter that it was the middle of the night or that she was the daughter of a baron. The man who had wronged her was about to destroy Amelia's life, and Margaret was *not* about to stand aside and let it happen. She'd beg the devil himself, if she thought he could help her.

Cain Sinclair was the next best thing.

A flutter of nerves caught her stomach as her coach pulled to a stop in front of the inn where he was staying. It was nearly midnight, and she'd left Lady Rumford's ball the moment she'd learned of Amelia's disappearance. Margaret was still wearing the sage-green silk gown with white gloves, for she'd not taken the time to change.

This was a very bad idea. What was she thinking, venturing into a public inn while wearing a ball gown?

But it couldn't be helped. *Please let him be here,* she prayed. The Highlander was a man she'd known for ten years. From the moment she'd laid eyes on him, she'd sensed that he was the sort of man her mother had warned her about.

Taller than most men, he had broad shoulders and lean muscles. His piercing blue eyes and black hair gave him the look of a fallen angel. He wasn't a gentleman and he didn't care what anyone thought of him.

Ruthless was the best word to describe him. And when he wanted something, he never stopped until he got it.

Unfortunately, what he wanted was *her.*

She took a deep breath and stepped out of the coach. Her footman eyed the inn and shook his head. "Miss Andrews, I think you should wait inside the coach. I'll go and find Mr. Sinclair on your behalf."

That was the sensible thing to do. It was what her mother would want. But she knew, without a single doubt, that Sinclair would ignore the footman and do whatever he wanted to. Whereas if she pleaded with him, there was a chance he might help her.

With every moment she sat in this coach, Lord Lisford was taking her sister farther north, toward Scotland. Time was critical, and what did she care if it was not an establishment a lady would dare to enter? She was already ruined. After five Seasons, Margaret knew what the ton thought of her. They believed she was to blame for Lord Lisford abandoning her before her wedding day.

The familiar ache of bitterness stiffened her spine. It was high time the viscount paid the price for what he'd done to her. And if he thought he could hurt her sister without serious consequences, he was sadly mistaken.

Margaret ignored her servant and marched straight toward the door. For a moment, she paused with her hand upon the doorknob. *Go back,* her conscience ordered. But instead, she gathered her courage and opened the door.

The haze of tobacco cloaked the room, while the scent of ale filled the space. Men were playing cards in one corner, while others busied themselves with getting drunk as soon as possible.

She stared at each of the men until at last she located Sinclair. He didn't move, but his mouth tightened when she stepped closer. Her presence was as out of place as a pig in a ballroom, and every male eye fastened upon her.

Her conscience was still screeching at the idea. *Get out of here! Ladies do not associate with men at an inn. You cannot be here.*

Cain Sinclair's icy blue eyes regarded her as if she'd lost her mind. And perhaps she had, since she'd gone to such lengths to seek his help.

"You don't belong here, lass," he said.

"Amelia's been taken by Lord Lisford. You have to help me find her." Margaret crossed her arms, staring coolly at a drunkard whose attention was fixed upon her bosom.

How did you think these men would react to your presence? her common sense chided. *They're nothing but rogues and vagrants. Any one of them would attack you, and then where would you be?*

The Highlander leaned back in his chair, his long black hair falling past his shoulders. He wore a brown-and-green kilt and a brown coat that revealed white shirt sleeves rolled against his forearms. A matching length of plaid was draped across the shirt, fastened at the shoulder with an iron brooch. At his waist, he wore a leather sporran. A faint scar edged his lower arm, a reminder that he'd been in many fights. Somehow, it made her feel safer, knowing that Sinclair could protect her far better than the elderly footman who had accompanied her.

"Come with me, and I'll tell you more about what happened," Margaret urged. The sooner she left this place, the better she would feel. The question was whether or not he would help her.

"Do your parents know?" he asked softly.

She shrugged. "I didn't tell them. I want to find Amelia before any harm is done."

They would find out soon enough. But more than that, she felt a sense of responsibility. *She* was supposed to have chaperoned Amelia at the ball. If she'd remained at her sister's side at every moment, this wouldn't have happened.

Her guilt was a hair shirt against her conscience. This was her fault, without question. And she had to atone for it, no matter the cost to her own reputation.

Sinclair took a slow drink of his ale, studying her. She couldn't guess what he was thinking, but he needed to hurry up.

"Why did you come to me, lass, instead of the police?" His lazy tone held a hint of wickedness, and she faltered.

"Because I—"

Because I know you'll find her. I know you won't let any harm come to her, and I trust you more than any man.

She drew closer and reached for his hand. It felt as if she'd thrown out every shred of decent behavior. A wildness thrummed in her blood as her fingers laced in his.

"Because I need your help," she whispered.

His thumb brushed the edge of her palm in a silent caress that echoed deep inside. His rough hands were callused, but his touch was light enough to set her senses on fire. What did that say about her, that she would be so attracted to a man so inappropriate?

She was a good girl. She obeyed the rules, listened to her parents, and never wore a gown with a daring neckline. All her life, she'd been a model of proper behavior.

And yet, right now, she realized that she was asking this man to come with her. To be alone with her in a coach for hours on end.

Don't do this, her sense of propriety begged. *You cannot behave in this way. It's not right.*

But she met his gaze steadily and said, "Please."

There were a thousand reasons why he should tell her no. Cain Sinclair knew that Margaret wasn't thinking clearly. She was upset and angry that her sister had been taken by Lisford. Her pleas had naught to do with common sense, and they were born of desperation.

"I'm no' the man who can help you, lass," he said, keeping his voice low. She was the daughter of a baron, while he was the son of nobody. Even now, she wore a ball gown that cost more than his income for a year.

Once, he'd been foolish enough to believe that he could reach above his station to a woman like her. Beautiful and full of grace, Margaret held enough spirit to challenge him. Every time she lifted that chin of hers, it made him want to loosen up her good-girl manners to find the woman underneath it all. "You don't ken what you're asking of me."

"I know precisely what I'm asking of you." She regarded him as if she were the Queen of England and chose a seat across from him. "I want you to find my sister. Lord Lisford is trying to compromise her and force her into marriage. Use your knowledge of the roads leading toward Gretna Green. You'll take me with you, and we'll find Amelia before that man can ruin her."

He couldn't believe she was serious. "You're wanting to take a long journey with me, all the way to Scotland?" he said slowly. "Do you no' realize how far that is?" It would take at least a week, if not a fortnight, depending on the condition of the roads.

"We'll find her long before that," she said. "I believe it."

"And you don't care what others will say about this?" he asked, gentling his voice. "'Twill harm your own good name, lass."

She took a deep breath and squared her shoulders. "For one, I'm already ruined. After five Seasons, I believe it's clear that no one wants to marry me. Aside from a few men whom I would never consider marrying." She stiffened as if she didn't want to think of it. "Therefore, I am little more than a spinster. Moreover, this is about Amelia, not me."

He touched her fingers again, disbelieving what she'd said. She was speaking as if all her prospects were ruined. "You don't have to go yourself," he insisted. "Your father could alert the authorities."

"And then everyone would know what Lisford did to her. Amelia would be forced to wed him, even if they rescued her." Margaret shook her head. "No one must know of this. We have to find her quickly, before anyone discovers the truth."

He steepled his hands together. "But why do *you* want to go?" There was no reason for it. She would only get herself into trouble, dragging him with her.

She hesitated before answering the question. "I promise you, I won't get in the way. I just . . . need to see that she's all right. It was my fault she was taken. I should have watched more carefully."

Before he could refuse again, she leaned in. "You would do the same for your brother."

And there, she had played her trump card. She knew him too well. The shadow of guilt crossed over him, for he hadn't taken care of his younger brother as well as he'd wanted to. He'd spent the last few years fighting to keep Jonah out of trouble.

"I'll pay you for your time," she offered quietly. "Enough money that you could send Jonah away to school. Not Eton, perhaps, but he would get an education and have a better life."

Damn her for offering something like this. She *knew* he couldn't walk away from the chance to give his brother a future. Although he had a little money of his own, he lacked the connections to enroll Jonah in the right school.

"And what makes you think I'm a safe traveling companion?" he demanded. She had to enter this agreement with her eyes open, to fully ken what she was asking. They would spend days and nights together.

"N-nothing would happen between us. You'd be driving." She stood up from the table, offering her hand. "If you find Amelia, it will all be worth it. I can't let Lord Lisford take advantage of my sister. Not after what he did to me."

Cain didn't ask questions, for he'd tried to stop Margaret from marrying the viscount years ago. She'd stubbornly refused and had been humiliated when Lisford had abandoned her.

It was the best thing that could have happened to the lass, though she'd never admit it. The viscount would have driven Margaret mad within a few months.

"I'll help you," he said at last. "But in return, you'll see to it that Jonah is accepted at a good school. And they canna throw him out, either." He didn't doubt that his younger brother would break every rule in existence.

Cain dropped a few coins on the table, and Margaret took his arm. "I promise, I will ensure that he has the best education possible."

He guided her outside, and her footman followed. The older man eyed Cain as if he suspected the worst. "Miss Andrews, might I ask what this . . . gentleman's intentions are? I presume he is the Mr. Sinclair of whom you spoke?"

"He is, yes. Mr. Sinclair has been a friend of my family's for many years now. I've hired him to help search for my sister."

The footman's expression grew pained. "Miss Andrews, truly, this is unwise. Your father would never—"

"My father will not know of this. Not if you wish to keep your position," she warned. "Now, Mr. Sinclair, do you have a coach you would prefer to use, or will this one suffice?"

Normally when he'd traveled between Scotland and London, he went on horseback. It was rare that he had the luxury of a coach at all. He sent Margaret a sidelong glance. "And here, I was wanting a coach made of gold."

She sighed. To the footman, she said, "Mr. Primrose, that will be all. You may return to my father's house on foot."

The footman appeared aghast at her orders. "But Miss Andrews, I cannot let you go off with this man alone. Your father would have me dismissed immediately."

Cain eyed the man. "Tell Lord Lanfordshire the truth. Tell him that Miss Andrews asked me to help her search for her sister. He is welcome to send his men along with us." To the driver he added, "If you're wanting to go with us, Miss Andrews will pay you for your services. Or if you'd rather no', you can leave us now."

She gaped for a moment, for Cain knew she'd expected *him* to do all the driving. Truthfully, he was hoping she would abandon this wild goose chase and stay at home where she belonged. She was fully unprepared for such a journey.

The coachman appeared uneasy. "I'll drive you to the edge of the city, Miss Andrews. No farther than that."

Margaret shrugged. "It doesn't matter to me, so long as we find Amelia."

"And if we don't?" Cain wanted her to be prepared for the worst, but she seemed oblivious to that likely reality.

"Our friend, the Earl of Castledon, is searching the main roads," she continued. "I want us to travel along any other roads Lord Lisford might have taken. One of us has to intercept her."

Her determination rivaled a warrior woman, like Boudicca. He tried to imagine Margaret with her hair cropped short, wielding a sword against the enemy as she charged into battle.

The image didn't fit, for she'd sooner die than get a wrinkle in her gown or let a single strand escape that topknot. Even so, it was . . . interesting. Beneath her polished surface, he'd glimpsed the defiant spirit of a rebel. Aye, she wore gowns and bonnets. But any woman who would demand help for her sister, at the cost of her own reputation, was a woman of courage. She'd always cared about others more than herself.

Cain ordered the driver to take them through the Tottenham Court gate leading out of London. Margaret gave the man half a crown in payment, before she entered the coach. She adjusted her white gloves, smoothing the edges of her ball gown. Around her throat, she wore a strand of pearls, while a jaunty ostrich feather perched in her blond chignon. Beside her on the seat rested a green bonnet.

In the shadowed darkness of the vehicle, Cain sat across from her. "This is foolish. And dangerous, you ken?" He wanted her to understand the risks before she traveled with him.

"I have to find her," she whispered. She reached out to grip his palms while the coach rumbled along its journey north. "I can't let Lisford hurt Amelia. He humiliated me in front of everyone, and I won't let her become his next victim."

A dark tension pulled at him. Aye, the viscount had made Margaret into a laughingstock when he'd abandoned her before their wedding. Cain had tried to warn her away, but she wouldn't listen to him. He'd already bloodied the viscount's nose once, when he'd had the chance to fight against Lisford in a boxing match. But now that the viscount had targeted Margaret's sister, he'd gone too far.

"I am glad you didna marry him." He released one hand and reached up to touch her cheek. "He would ne'er have been man enough for you." The moment his roughened palm slid over her bare skin, she shivered.

He had no right to touch her, but she didn't deny him. Over the years, he'd watched her transform from a prim and proper lady into a strong-willed woman.

"It ne'er had to be that way," he reminded her. "You could have been married by now, with a bairn to hold in your arms." He stroked her cheek, drawing his palm down to her throat. He wanted her to remember the night he'd asked her to wed him.

Margaret's gaze fixed upon the floor of the coach. "We weren't suited." Gently, she pulled his hand away from her face, reminding him of the boundaries between them. She reached into her hair and withdrew the feather, before covering her dark blond hair with the bonnet. Cool green eyes stared into his.

"Because you're too good for the likes of me, is that it, lass?" He stared hard at her. "I'm no' a prince or even a baron. I've little more than two coins to rub together." The words sounded bitter, even to him, but she'd wounded his pride. Aye, he lacked a large house and servants. But he would have taken care of her.

Her spine went rigid again, and she stared out the window. "You wouldn't like being married to a woman like me, Mr. Sinclair. We're too different."

He knew she'd said that to push him away, but he didn't believe it at all. To ease her melancholy, he teased, "Ah, but you'd like being married to a man like me, lass." He sent her a lazy smile, but she didn't respond to it. Her face was pale with worry, and she continued to stare out the window.

"We have to find Amelia," she insisted, in an effort to change the subject. "That is of utmost importance."

"We'll try." But his mind was not upon finding Amelia Andrews. Instead, he was wondering how long it would take Margaret to realize what a mistake she was making. This was the most impulsive thing she'd ever done—leaving in the middle of the night with him. Even now, she wasn't prepared for a long journey. Every hair was tucked into place within the bonnet, and not a smudge of dirt marred her face. She looked as if she were about to set foot within a palace instead of taking a journey north.

"We'll have to stop for supplies at the edge of the city," he reminded her.

She frowned at that. "We've no time to stop. Already Lord Lisford is over an hour ahead of us. We have to move swiftly before he gets too far."

"And you believe he avoided the main roads?" he asked, settling back in his seat.

She nodded. "The tolls and turnpikes would slow him down. If he's trying to force her to elope, he'll want to reach Scotland as quickly as possible."

Cain wasn't so sure of that. Lisford struck him as a baw-headed fool, one who acted without thinking. "Did you say Lord Castledon is searching the main roads?"

"Yes. I want to go in a different direction, in case the earl doesn't find her first." Grimly, she added, "If Lord Lisford has hurt Amelia in any way, you have my permission to kill him."

"Bloodthirsty, aren't you?" he murmured. Though he suspected she didn't truly mean it, there was no question that if Amelia's virtue had been compromised, Margaret would want the man's head.

"When it comes to the viscount, yes." She rubbed at her bare arms, and it was then that he noticed she had no wrap. Cain took off his coat and handed it to her. Margaret accepted it gratefully and drew the edges around her shoulders.

He didn't blame her for her anger. She'd endured public humiliation from the man and was determined to protect her sister from suffering the same fate.

"Thank you for agreeing to accompany me," she said after a time.

"What would you have done if I'd said nay?"

"I would have hired someone else." She rested her head against the side of the coach, adding, "But I'm glad you agreed to come. I feel safer with you."

The words dug into him like a dull blade. He knew that she felt nothing for him, aside from friendship. She believed he was acting out of Jonah's interests, nothing more.

The truth was, he'd never have let her go alone. She had damned near ripped his heart out of his chest a few years ago. She got beneath his skin in a way no one else did. It burned him to know that she held such power over him, even now.

"You shouldna feel safe with me, lass. You ken what I want from you." He leaned forward, resting his wrists upon his knees.

"You might pretend to be wicked, Cain Sinclair," she said softly. "But I know you too well. There is honor in you, whether you want to believe it or not."

He insisted upon stopping for a few supplies before they continued north. Personally, Margaret believed it was unnecessary. This journey wouldn't last more than a day or two, and she felt certain that they could stop for food at an inn, if needed.

"These roads are in the middle of nowhere," he countered. "And the towns along the way are no' places where I'd want to stop, lass."

He'd left her no choice and bought enough food for over a week. With every minute the men spent loading the supplies into the coach, her frustration level grew. Though she knew her anger was born from the need to protect Amelia, she found it impossible to remain calm.

Her sister could be in trouble at this very moment. That ruffian had taken Amelia against her will and was trying to force her into marriage. It was appalling.

But when Cain dismissed her driver and hired another coachman, Margaret grew uneasy. She'd known that her driver had wanted no part in this, but hiring a stranger seemed dangerous. She trusted Sinclair to help her follow Amelia . . . but no one else.

"Are you certain you'd rather not drive?" she asked Cain. She was beginning to wonder if he was deliberately stalling to keep her from making this journey.

"This was your idea, no' mine," he said. "And your driver is going to alert your father."

Which meant that Lord Lanfordshire would send even more men after her, once he discovered that both daughters were gone. "Why? We're losing so much time, and now my father will be furious with both of us."

Cain helped her back inside, and only when he'd shut the door behind him did he answer. "You're daft if you think we can do this alone, Miss Andrews. We need his men, and Lord Lanfordshire will want to find his daughter."

"We shouldn't have stopped," she countered. "Amelia needs us, while we've wasted so much time. We didn't need so many supplies."

"And what do you ken about traveling to Scotland?" he shot back. "You're used to riding in your comfortable coach along the main roads, and it takes longer than a week. You've ne'er taken these roads, lass. I have. There's a reason why men don't travel these roads. There's naught to be found. It willna do your sister any good if we starve to death before we reach her."

"Do you think I can even touch a bite of food, knowing that Lisford has her?" Margaret insisted. Her stomach clenched at the thought of Amelia suffering.

"You will after two days," he predicted. "These roads are no' comfortable, lass. And he mightn't have gone this way."

"I'll endure it if I must." Though she could tell already that her teeth would rattle out of her head by the time they reached Amelia. These back roads were rough and filled with holes.

For the next few hours, she stared outside at the midnight sky, hoping that they would intercept Lisford. But with each mile that passed, she grew more worried that Sinclair was right. The viscount wasn't a man who would endure this kind of discomfort. Her backside was bruised, and she'd been jostled so many times, she doubted if she would sit comfortably for a week.

They had stopped at a few turnpikes, but they had already veered off the main pathway and had taken a different route that she'd never traveled.

Cain Sinclair sat with his hands on his knees, staring out at the darkness. He'd made no effort at all to sleep, and she was deeply conscious of his presence.

He was a tall man, and she'd be lying if she didn't admit to herself that he was handsome. His black hair hung down past his shoulders, but it looked smooth, like a raven's wings. She doubted he'd ever worn a waistcoat in his life. This was a man who knew nothing about her way of life . . . and yet, she couldn't take her gaze from him.

"You're staring at me, Miss Andrews," he accused, turning to face her.

She looked away immediately. "I apologize, Mr. Sinclair. My thoughts were wandering, and I was paying little attention to anything, I fear."

The lie slipped easily from her lips. She'd wanted to touch that dark hair, to run her fingers along the edge of his strong jaw. Curiosity made her even more intrigued by the idea of exploring the hard ridges of his shoulders. Because he was forbidden.

To distract herself, she closed her eyes, trying to sleep. But in her imagination, other visions tormented her. This man tempted her and always had. And now she was traveling alone with him, where anything might happen.

Her inner voice was horrified by the idea, while another part of her didn't care. She'd made this decision to save Amelia, and whatever consequences arose from that, she would face without hesitation. But she sensed that the carefully crafted distance between them was starting to crumble.

"Why did you ask for my help, lass?" he asked. "When you wanted naught to do with me?"

"Because you know these roads better than anyone else."

A twisted smile came over his face. "I think you had other reasons for asking."

She didn't know what to say to that. How could she say that she trusted him, that she believed he could help her when no other man could? Other men would give up the search if they didn't find Amelia. Sinclair wouldn't.

He leaned in closer. "If you were wanting to be alone with me, all you had to do was ask."

Margaret stiffened. "That was never the reason, Mr. Sinclair." She met his gaze squarely. "I intend to find my sister, no matter how long it takes. I was responsible for her, and it was my fault that this happened." She folded her arms and stared out at the darkness once again. Though she supposed he was only trying to get a reaction from her, the teasing made her angrier. She *did* blame herself for this. Her stomach ached with fear, and she was holding back all her emotions.

What if the viscount had hurt her sister? What if, at this very moment, her sister was suffering from his unwanted attention?

"It wasna your fault," came Cain's answer.

"It was," she argued back.

"Torturing yourself is no' going to help." He reached out and took her gloved hand. "We *will* find her. I promise you that."

She risked a glance back at him, and in his deep blue eyes, she saw a man who intended to stand by her, no matter what happened. It should have reassured her, but instead, her emotions knotted up inside her. She might have brought him on this journey to find her sister . . . but Cain had his own intentions.

"Get some sleep," he said quietly. "You're going to need it."

Margaret closed her eyes, though she wasn't tired at all. How did he even think it was possible to sleep, with such jarring roads? Her teeth were clenched together, as if she could still the rattling of her body.

And it didn't stop. Mile after mile, she fought to remain in her seat, despite the jostling. Eventually, she gave up the pretense and opened her eyes. Sinclair kept his stare fixed out the window, searching for a sign of something.

"How much longer do you think we'll have to travel before we catch up to Amelia?" Margaret asked.

Sinclair said nothing at all, which wasn't a good sign. But possibly he hadn't heard her.

"Mr. Sinclair, I asked you—"

"I know what you asked." He crossed his arms. "And I don't think she went this way, Miss Andrews."

Before he could say another word, the coach hit a large hole in the road, and Margaret struck her head. An involuntary cry of pain escaped her.

Sinclair was at her side immediately. "Are you all right, lass?"

She touched her hand to her temple, wincing at the tender spot. "It's not bleeding." Even so, she would have a terrible bruise. "Is the driver *trying* to go along the roughest part of the road?" This journey was nothing at all like she'd imagined it would be.

You shouldn't have left London, her common sense reminded her. *This is no place for a lady.*

Sinclair glanced outside, but there was little to see. "It's been raining, and the mud makes it harder to travel."

Margaret swallowed hard, and the seeds of doubt began to take root. What if all this travel had been for nothing? But then, she'd wanted to ensure that Lisford was pursued on every road. Her discomfort didn't matter, if Amelia had endured the same or worse.

"Will we stop for the night, if we don't find Lisford?" she asked furtively, almost afraid of what he'd say. It seemed unlikely that Cain Sinclair would stop for any reason.

"We don't have to, except to change horses," he admitted. "It's why I brought our supplies. We can eat along the way."

Margaret nodded in agreement. That was what she'd wanted, though she hadn't expected the roads to be this terrible. In her mind, she'd imagined overtaking the viscount within the hour and rescuing her sister. The reality was far different.

"Or we can turn back," he said softly. "You're no' used to traveling like this."

In other words, he thought she couldn't endure the hardship. Well, he was wrong about that. "I want to find my sister," she informed him, adjusting her gloves. "No matter how long it takes."

Cain removed his hat and folded his arms behind his head. "Try to go back to sleep, lass. The journey has only begun."

That was what she feared. They had been traveling for miles, and there was no sign of anyone on these roads. She might be following a wild trail with no end in sight.

Sinclair had his eyes closed, and his muscled forearm rested across his lap. The cool night air didn't seem to bother him, and she huddled inside his coat. It was warm and smelled of whisky and male skin. Wearing his clothing made her feel as if she were in his embrace, and it warmed her in a different way.

You're too good for the likes of me, lass, he'd accused.

That wasn't it at all. It was simply that they came from opposite worlds. From the moment she'd laid eyes upon Cain Sinclair, she'd known exactly the sort of man he was. Rough-mannered, overbearing, and confident in himself.

Even when she'd first met him, he'd been proud. He'd refused to take help from anyone, and she respected that. His parents were dead, and he'd had a younger brother to care for. Cain had been hot-headed, rebellious, and he was the sort of young man who secretly fascinated her.

She closed her eyes, burrowing into his coat. Sleep would not come, but she took comfort where she could.

Hours later, a loud cracking sound woke her. The coach swayed violently, sending her flying across the space. She gasped when she fell against Cain, her knees striking the floor of the coach. He gripped her tightly, shielding her. "Hold on, lass."

"What's happening?" she blurted out, terrified when the motion sent them both against the door.

Her question was answered when the coach swerved. She was battered and flung against the interior, and Cain landed hard on top of her.

He shielded her with his body, but none of that mattered. Seconds later, the coach overturned.

Chapter Two

C ain Sinclair stared at the young woman, who was wearing a white frothy gown that resembled whipped cream. She held up her skirts, struggling to keep them out of the mud, while the good Scottish rain poured down over her.

"Of course, this would happen to me." The young woman sighed and stared up at the sky. "Why won't it ever stop raining?"

Her voice held the cultured accent of Britain, marking her as an outsider. He didn't know why she was here, but he suspected she was wealthy.

Women like her didn't exist here. Not only did her clothing proclaim her riches, but she was tiptoeing across the grass as if trying to avoid any speck of mud. The dirt road was sodden from the rain and would be slippery to walk upon. At the far end, the land shifted into smaller hills, where a manor house stood. Undoubtedly the young woman was now living there.

"You're in Scotland, lass," Cain answered. "It rains most every day." He stepped out from behind the oak tree where he'd been watching.

The young woman glanced around, frowning to herself. She eyed him as if she wasn't certain whether she should speak to him.

"I am Cain Sinclair," he told her. "I suppose you'd be one of the Sassenachs who arrived just yesterday."

"You make that sound as if I have a dreadful disease," she remarked. Wincing slightly, she took careful steps through the mud. When she drew closer, she tucked a strand of blond hair back into her creamy bonnet. Every inch of her was delicate and composed. She was easily the most beautiful girl he'd set eyes upon.

With another glance around, she said, "It's not proper for us to speak together without a true introduction, but I don't suppose there's anyone around to do the honors. I am Margaret Andrews. My father is a lieutenant colonel in the army, and his brother is the Baron of Lanfordshire." She raised her chin and added, "And yes, we do live at Ballaloch in the stone house. It's a smaller estate that belongs to our family."

The manor house was large enough to give homes to over a dozen crofters, Cain thought to himself. From her curious gaze, he grew self-conscious of his appearance. He was wearing the same kilt and plaid he'd owned for three years, and the colors were faded to a dark green and brown. His shirt was too large, for it had belonged to his father. Mud and water seeped through the holes in his shoes, and he stiffened as if she'd passed silent judgment on him.

Pride made him walk closer. It didn't matter what she thought of him. She was naught but an English lass, fair enough to look at. Yet he suspected she viewed him as one beneath her.

He wasn't. This was his homeland, and the blood of his ancestors had watered the fields. They had fought for their freedom, and damned if he'd let her look down on him.

"The rain's going to get worse," he told her. "You should go home before that gown is ruined."

She wrinkled her nose. "I was trying to escape the house. I don't suppose it worked very well."

"Escape from what?" He stared back at the large manor, wondering if she had cruel parents.

"Lessons," she admitted. *"Mother is training all of us to be ladies. We have to spend hours on embroidery, watercolors, and music. Sometimes dancing."* She winced at the idea. *"I would rather be outside where I can walk without a book on my head. Where I don't feel so imprisoned."* Lifting her face skyward, the rain spattered against her cheeks. *"Only, I didn't think it would start raining this early."*

"You shouldna wear your best gown when you go walking," he advised. *"Save it for cèilidhs and fancy balls."*

She sent him an apologetic smile. *"Unfortunately, I didn't have time to change my gown whilst I was making my great escape. My mother will be furious with me if it's ruined."*

"Will she thrash you?" He wondered exactly what this woman would endure as a punishment.

"Worse. I'll likely have to sew a new gown. I'll be trapped inside for days on end, sewing until my fingers bleed." She shuddered, but he detected a note of humor in her voice. *"I should prefer the sound thrashing, actually."*

Cain was beginning to wonder if she was even real. In all of his seventeen years, he'd never met a woman like her.

"Do you know this land very well?" she asked.

"Aye. Since I was a wee lad."

Her face brightened in a smile. *"Well, then. If you were trying to escape, where would you go?"*

Cain pointed toward the grove of trees in the distance. *"There are many oaks and rowans over there. Some are good for climbing, and the leaves are so thick they'll shelter you from the rain."*

Her green eyes held a glimmer of mischief. *"I'll remember that, Mr. Sinclair."* She took a deep breath, smoothing back her wet hair. *"One day, I hope to wed a prince or a duke. Someone who is so busy with his own affairs, he won't care if I want to walk in the rain or climb trees."*

"I wouldn't care," he heard himself say.

Miss Andrews laughed. "Well, I suppose I'll just have to wed you, then, won't I?" The words were spoken in jest, but they startled him.

"Aye, lass," he responded. "One day you might." It had never occurred to him that he would encounter someone like her. But beneath her gown and mannerisms lay a girl who wanted freedom as badly as he did. Her prison was made of rules and restrictions. His was being responsible for his four-year-old brother, Jonah, ever since their parents had died.

Miss Andrews didn't respond to his answer but adjusted her white gloves and eyed the sky once more. As soon as she did, the skies transformed from a light rain into pounding drops.

"Have you an umbrella, Mr. Sinclair?" she inquired, trying in vain to shield herself from the rain.

Cain unpinned a length of the wool plaid wrapped around his shirt, and he raised it over his head. "I've only this. You can share it with me, if you wish."

He could tell from the hesitant expression that she didn't want to.

"I'm afraid that isn't proper," she informed him. "To be so close to you . . . my mother would not like it."

"As you like."

He started to walk along the path leading home, but she called out, "Wait, if you please!"

He turned back, and she hurried toward him. She reached out for the other end of the plaid, shielding her head from the rain. "I said it wasn't proper. But that doesn't mean I don't want to escape the rain. I do need the shelter."

Standing this close to her, he could smell the enticing vanilla scent of her skin. Her gown was soaked, and though they didn't touch, he was entranced by her.

Cain escorted her back toward her home, and she grew strangely silent. Once, her footing slipped on the wet grass, and he caught her by the waist, steadying her before she could fall.

"Thank you." The plaid fell from her fingertips, and she lowered her gaze. "I suppose I should be going now." Without waiting for a reply, she began to hurry up the hillside to her house. He stood watching, and when she reached the door, she turned back and waved. "It was good to meet you, Mr. Sinclair!"

Her insistence upon proper manners struck him harder than the rain. He'd never met anyone like Margaret Andrews. And likely never would again.

⚜

Cain's skull was pounding with pain. The image of Margaret faded from his mind, the forgotten memory disappearing the moment he opened his eyes. It was pitch black outside, and he couldn't see anything. A dampness upon his forehead revealed that he was bleeding, and his head was swollen from where he'd struck it hard. Dizziness passed over him, and he took a steadying breath.

"Margaret." He tried to call out, but his voice barely broke a whisper. Was she alive? He vaguely remembered the coach tipping over, before they'd rolled down a hillside. The faint odor of lamp oil seeped into the space, but it was the silence that made him uneasy. He used his hands to feel his way around the coach, and when he touched a pile of silk, he realized that Margaret was lying motionless against one door. The other door was now the ceiling, from where the coach had tipped on its side. He tried to reach up to the window, but his fist met with jagged glass. If they tried to fit through it, they'd be cut to ribbons.

"Margaret," he repeated, reaching down to touch her. She made no sound, and fear ripped through him at the thought of her being dead. *Let her be alive*, he prayed silently. For a moment, he couldn't breathe.

He carefully felt his way downward until he found her neck. Her skin was warm, and beneath his fingertips, he felt a slow pulse. A rush of relief flooded through him, that she was still alive. He managed to pull her onto his lap, trying to determine if she was bleeding in any way. The moment he touched her arm, she let out a moan of pain.

"Lass, we need to get out of this coach," Cain told her. "Can you hear me?"

She didn't respond, but at least she was breathing. His eyes adjusted to the darkness, and he saw that her eyes were still closed. Her face tightened with pain when he removed her bonnet, searching for a head wound. When he found none, he breathed a little easier. She remained unconscious, and he held her close, hoping that she would awaken soon.

Margaret was the saint, while he'd sinned at every chance he had. It was little wonder that years ago she'd spurned his offer of marriage. But he hadn't stopped wanting her. Even now, with her fragile body lying against him, he wanted to claim her lips, tempting her into ruin.

She stirred against him and moaned. "What happened?"

"The coach overturned," he told her. "How badly are you hurt?"

She didn't answer, and he realized that she'd fainted again. Gently, he laid her back while he tried to determine the best way to get them out. Likely he would have to force the door open at the ceiling and try to lift Margaret up. Or else break the remaining glass and hope they could squeeze through the small opening.

But as he stood on one of the seats, reaching for the door handle, a strange scent caught his attention. It was a blend of burning oil and smoke.

Fire.

The lantern must have shattered and ignited the oil when the coach overturned. Damn it all, he had to get them both out fast.

The sound of a man screaming broke through the stillness, as if the driver was trapped in the flames. Cain reached up to open the door, but it wouldn't budge.

He let out a foul curse and tried to ram against it with his shoulder, but he suspected the metal handle had bent when the vehicle had rolled. There were no tools, no means of forcing the door open.

What could he do now? The only other exit was at the bottom of the coach, and that door couldn't open farther than a few inches.

The driver's screaming suddenly ceased, and God help them both, Cain knew what that meant. When he peered through the crevices of the window, the bright flare of flames illuminated the space. The fire was spreading toward them, and if he didn't get them out, both of them would die, trapped inside.

"Get up!" he shouted, shaking Margaret. There was no time for gentleness now. "Lass, we have to get out of here."

"C-Cain?" she murmured, her voice sounding sleepy. "What's happening?"

"The coach is on fire," he said. "And we're going to be burned alive if we don't force the door open."

She went silent, and he pointed toward the roof. "The door at the top willna open, and the fire is approaching swiftly. Is there aught we could use to pry the door open?" he asked. "A shoe or . . . anything?"

She stared at the obstructed door, and he sensed the horror dawning within her. "I've nothing. I'm so sorry." Her voice held back her terror, as if she were a pane of glass, about to shatter.

"Ne'er you mind it, lass." He would put all of his strength into breaking the door, even if he broke his own bones in the process. Once more, he turned the door handle and rammed his upper body against the wood and shattered glass. Pain reverberated through his shoulder, and it didn't budge.

Again, he worked at the door, praying to God he could force it open. Fear and energy coursed through him as he fought to save them.

"Cain?" Margaret whispered. "Are we going to die?"

"No' if I can help it." Over and over, he smashed his weight against the door, while the heat of the fire raged closer. The choking smoke tainted the air, and he dreaded the approaching flames.

"There's another way," Margaret whispered. "Below me. The fire isn't there yet."

"We canna fit through that," he argued. "It's no' possible."

She eased the other door open and lowered her legs. "You're too big," she admitted, "but I might be able to get out beneath the coach. Then I could let you out from the top."

The space was barely large enough for her, and it was only a frail hope that she could wedge herself beneath the coach.

"Try," he ordered. She slid her legs through the opening, and eased herself lower.

"I'm sorry." Hysteria edged her voice, and she struggled to force herself through. "It's smaller than I thought. I can get through the coach door, but it's too narrow beneath the coach to get out."

Her idea made him consider another possibility. "Stay there, lass. There's something else we could try."

She obeyed, and he slipped his legs through the doorway.

Although the door provided only a narrow opening, he believed he could use his strength to help get her out. Gingerly, he bent his knees and tried to see underneath the coach. It seemed that one of the wheels had broken off and was balancing part of the weight. Though it was unlikely he had the strength to lift the vehicle, he could try to raise it enough for her to escape.

He gripped the edges of the door frame. "I'm going to ask you to get underneath the coach as far as you can. When I tell you to go, I'm going to lift it up, and you'll get out."

God, let him have the strength to do this. If she didn't move fast enough, or if his grip slipped, the weight of the vehicle would crush her skull.

He shut the thought down, for at least that was a better fate than burning to death.

"When I get out, what shall I do next?" Her voice revealed terror, and she reached out to him. "How can I get the door open?"

"Try to climb to the top of the coach and force the handle with whate'er you can find."

"And if I can't get it open?"

He gave no answer to that, for both of them knew what would happen. The fire was spreading quickly, and there was little time left. Already the air was hot, the smoke searing his eyes. "Get out and try."

He wouldn't blame her if she was incapable of saving him. The chances of him surviving this were slim. But if he could save her, at least his soul could rest easy.

It was strange, knowing that death was staring him in the eyes. He reached out to touch her face. "Take care of Jonah, if the worst happens."

"You're going to get out," she insisted. "I promise you that." Her hand covered his, and she squeezed it gently. "I won't let you die."

He wanted to kiss her, to steal one last taste of the woman he wanted. But there was no time for it. Instead, he marked the memory of her fragile skin, and promised himself that he would use every last reserve of strength to save her.

She eased herself through the door, and when she had gone as far as she could, he braced his legs in the opening and grabbed the frame. "Are you ready, lass?"

"Yes."

From deep inside, he drew upon all the strength he possessed. He seized the sides of the open doorway and bent his knees, slowly straightening while he bore half the weight of the coach. Thankfully, he was able to lift it a few inches. He could only pray that it was enough.

"Go!" he shouted. His muscles burned with exertion, the cords of his veins straining as he lifted. It was excruciating, and he felt his hands slipping.

Steady, he urged himself. Seconds ticked by, and he fought with every last fiber of his being to keep the weight aloft.

"I'm out!" she called to him. With that, he released the weight, the jarring burden falling from his hands. He struggled to catch his breath, leaning his head against one of the seats. Relief poured over him, and he hardly cared what happened now.

Margaret would survive this, and it was enough.

His breathing was labored, his heart pounding with the exertion of lifting the weight. But strangely, he was at peace with himself.

The fire would continue its path toward him. The flames would consume the wood and metal, and Margaret might not save him. But there were no regrets. He might have made a thousand mistakes in his life, but he would never regret giving up his life for hers.

He kept his head low, waiting for death to claim him.

Margaret was horrified by the sight of the overturned coach. Fire raged where the oil lantern had struck the wood, and it was steadily overtaking the vehicle. The driver was already dead, the flames turning his body into a blackened corpse. The horses had scattered, their terrified neighs breaking the stillness.

And Cain was going to die if she didn't get him out.

Nausea swelled up in her throat, but she couldn't let herself become sick. She had to find a way to open the door. Cain had risked everything to save her, and she could do no less for him.

Margaret gripped her skirts and moved toward the vehicle. Flames licked at the wooden wheels, and the body of the coach was already hot. She didn't know how much time she had to get the door open, but she hoped it would be enough.

The door was well out of her reach, but she thought she could climb up. *You're not strong enough,* the voice of doubt taunted. Margaret gritted her teeth, ignoring her fears. Cain would die if she stood by and did nothing.

She reached up as high as she could, struggling to pull herself up the side of the coach while she avoided the fire. "Hold on, Mr. Sinclair!" she called out to him. "I'm almost there!"

She crawled on her hands and knees, gasping at the smoke until she reached the top. Once she reached the twisted door handle, it became clear why Cain had been unable to get it open. It was badly bent, and when she tried to turn it, the metal wouldn't move. Through the jagged glass, she could see him holding a length of plaid across his nose to avoid the choking smoke. Her eyes burned, and she found a handkerchief in one pocket to cover her own nose.

Her mind blurred with panic while she tried to find something to use as a lever. Anything.

The spokes of a wheel might work. She climbed back down, trying to break one free, but it held fast. From inside the coach, she heard the sound of Cain trying to smash the remaining glass. But even then, she didn't know if he could fit through the window.

He would die if she didn't work quickly. The fire was burning faster, and soon enough, it would destroy the coach. She couldn't let that happen.

Determination drove out the fear. Using her foot, she kicked at the wheel spokes, until the wood cracked. At last, she was able to wrench one of them free.

Her muscles burned with pain, but she ignored the vicious ache as she climbed back to the top. Right now all that mattered was getting him out alive. Margaret wedged the spoke against the twisted door handle and leaned back. Beneath her feet, the coach was growing hotter, as if she were trying to stand upon a wood stove.

"Hold on!" she called out to Cain. "I'm trying to pry open the door."

He said something in reply, but his words were muffled amid his coughing. She pulled as hard as she could, struggling to straighten the bent metal.

It wasn't enough.

Frustration and fear consumed her as she leaned her body weight against the handle. Giving up wasn't an option. The aching fear intensified as she twisted the wood, trying in vain to pull the door open. With every second that passed, her fears taunted her.

You're too weak. He lifted this coach to save you, and you're not strong enough to help him.

No. She couldn't give up so soon. Somehow, she had to get this door open, no matter how much it hurt.

Her arms ached as she bent her knees and pulled with all her strength. Cain rammed his shoulder against the door once again, and the sudden momentum sent her flying backward. She tried to grab something to catch herself from falling, but she hit the ground hard, her head striking the grass. The coach door swung open, and Cain hoisted himself up. Dizziness made her vision swim, and Margaret couldn't understand the words he was shouting at her.

She blacked out for a few moments, and when she regained consciousness, she saw that Cain's clothing had caught fire. His own roar of pain mingled with her scream, but he dropped to the ground and rolled. Within moments, it was out.

He was curled up on his side, trembling, while his clothes were blackened and burned.

"W-we have to get out of here," she stammered, but he wasn't moving. Oh dear God. He had to get up. Why was he still lying there?

Her head was pounding as she got to her hands and knees, moving toward him. The scent of burned flesh was enough to make her stomach twist. It had happened all too fast. She couldn't understand how it was possible.

"Are you all right?" she asked him. But although his shoulders revealed that he was indeed breathing, his eyes were tightly closed, as if he were holding back the agony. Blood soaked the back of his head—he must have struck it when he hit the ground.

"Can you get up?" she asked him, but he gave no answer.

The shaking came over her then, with the terror of being alone. She had to find a doctor, to get help for Cain . . . but they were stranded in the middle of nowhere. His earlier claim, that there was nothing along these roads, had proven to be correct.

A faint lavender and rose color edged the horizon, revealing the coming dawn. Her first instinct was to sit down and weep, but she knew it would do no good. And if she left him here to seek help, he might die in the meantime. Her hands were trembling, but she reached out to touch him. Beneath the shirt, his skin was angry red and blistered, blood covering his back.

"You must get up, Mr. Sinclair," she told him. "We can't stay here." She reached beneath his arms and tried to pull him. The moment she touched him, he let out an unholy shout of pain. She dropped Sinclair immediately, realizing that he was worse off than she'd imagined.

Think, Margaret, her brain urged. He needed someone to help with his injuries. But how could she move him? She stared out into the darkness where one of the horses was standing back from the fires. Though she needed two, with Cain wounded, she could only handle one.

She knew next to nothing about animals, but if she could get him on the mare, it was their best hope. Slowly, she rose to her feet, and when she tried to take a deep breath, she coughed against the smoke.

Her composure was hanging by a single thread, and she was afraid if she allowed one teardrop to fall, she would become a sobbing mess. She walked slowly toward the horse, hoping the animal would not rear up or panic. The mare let out a whinny, moving away as she approached.

"Hush now," Margaret murmured. "I'm going to need your help. And if you do as I ask, I'll try to find carrots or an apple for you."

Although the animal couldn't understand a word of her conversation, it was the best she could do. She moved sideways, trying to reach the reins. The leather was burned, and there was no saddle, since the mare had been harnessed to the coach. Thankfully the bridle was intact, and Margaret seized it, leading the animal toward Cain. Though she had no idea how she would get him on top of the horse, she had to try.

Her brain turned over the problem, and although she thought of a way to get him on the animal, it still might not work. And if she did secure him to the mare's back, it meant she would have to walk.

Sinclair was a tall man, and in this instance, it was a godsend. One of the wooden crates containing food had been thrown from the coach before the fire had started. It was tall enough to stand upon, and she picked it up along the way.

When she reached Sinclair, she set the crate down and placed the mare's reins atop it, which would let her step upon them to prevent the animal from moving. All she had to do was lift Sinclair high enough to push him onto the animal's back.

Inwardly, she worried that she wasn't strong enough. Cain Sinclair was a heavily muscled Highlander, and she doubted if she could manage his weight.

He still had not regained consciousness, except for the time she'd touched him. Undoubtedly, she would hurt him again, and she braced herself for the prospect.

You must lift him, she reminded herself. *You have no choice.* No matter how heavy he was, no matter how weak she was, she had to save him.

This time, she braced herself for his reaction. She seized him under the arms and lifted him quickly over her shoulder, struggling to stand up. He didn't respond at all, which frightened her even more. His head was still bleeding, and she knew she had to bind the wound.

Margaret shoved back her rising panic, her muscles burning as she held him and stepped atop the crate. He was slipping down, his knees buckling.

The threat of failure was so strong, she could taste it. But Cain had done everything in his power to save her from burning to death. She had to get him out of here, no matter how weak she was.

Straining hard, she bent her knees and shoved him upward as hard as she could. His face and torso slid over the horse's back, and when at last his body hung across the mare, she let herself cry.

Tears streamed down her face as she tore a strip of fabric from her gown and used it to bind his head wound. She wept as she gathered the reins and drew the horse away. Their supplies had been thrown from the coach when it had overturned, and she gathered up whatever food she could find, stuffing it into the crate. It would serve as a basket, and she tied it across the mare's back. Carefully, she covered the supplies with her petticoat, forming a makeshift pillow for Sinclair's face. It was better than him lying prone, she decided.

Hot tears burned at her eyes as she stared at the wreckage and the darkness all around them. Her body was numb with the knowledge that they were stranded here together. They could no longer help Amelia tonight, if her sister had indeed traveled this way.

The tears continued to roll down her cheeks, and she wept openly, knowing that all chances of finding Amelia were lost. She could never catch up to her sister like this—not with Cain wounded and both of them without a coach.

Margaret picked up a fallen piece of wood to use as a torch to light their way. Her shoes sank into the mud as she trudged forward, praying that she would find a town or an inn within the next hour or so. Behind her, the fire raged against the fallen coach, burning the wreckage. And now, they were stranded in the middle of nowhere.

Cain had been right. There was nothing at all ahead of them, and apart from the fire and the barest traces of sunrise in the distance, she saw no other lights. Her hands shook, but she forced herself to walk onward.

You're alive, she reminded herself. For now, it was all that mattered.

Chapter Three

There's no doctor, not for miles," the vicar apologized. "But you and your husband can share our house until we can send word to him."

Margaret stood at the doorway to the village church, her feet blistered and bleeding within her leather shoes. It had taken nearly three days to reach this small parish, and Cain's wounds had worsened during that time. He'd hardly spoken a word, and she'd barely managed to get him to drink or eat. All of their food was now gone, and she had reached the end of her strength.

"I would be grateful for a place to stay," Margaret said, "but I would be even more thankful if we could have privacy." The last thing she wanted was to be living in such close quarters with strangers. Even worse, how could she answer their questions? No—they needed to remain on their own.

When the vicar hesitated, Margaret straightened. "His wounds need tending, and I would not wish to inconvenience you. If there's another cottage nearby or some other shelter—"

She let her words drift off, touching the pearl necklace she wore. The vicar's eyes widened at the sight of the pearls, and she knew that neither he nor his wife had much to call their own. But her pearls would bring in enough income to support them for quite a while.

In her other hand, she held the torch aloft to light the way. Cain was still resting atop the horse, and though they had endured several days of traveling, she would go farther if necessary.

"My wife and I can stay with my brother," the vicar offered. "I know he won't mind, especially if we are well compensated for our trouble."

"We would be most grateful," Margaret said, holding her chin up. "And we do pay our debts." She reached into her reticule and offered the man a guinea. "After my husband has recovered, you may have the necklace. Perhaps more, if we are comfortable."

She kept her tone rigid, not wanting the man to believe he could take advantage of them. Inwardly, she was terrified of what lay ahead. She was accustomed to servants who would meet every need, and what did she know about tending wounds? This was going to be a living nightmare.

You could leave him behind and continue your search for Amelia, the darker side of her conscience warned.

But when she glanced back at Cain, her heart plummeted at the thought of leaving him. She couldn't. He had given so much to her, leaving London on this fool's quest and saving her life. Though she didn't understand the muddled feelings inside her, the idea of walking away was impossible. She cared for this man, and he was her friend.

Margaret turned around, walking a few paces back toward the horse, while the vicar started down the pathway toward his house. He was telling her about the dwelling, but she didn't hear a word of his explanation. She was too concerned with the prone man beside her.

For the next few days, she would have to tend his wounds and pray that she could help him recover.

She held the torch, being careful as she ducked inside the small cottage. The fire had nearly burned out, and the vicar added more peat. Margaret tossed her torch on top of it and went back to Cain. "Will you help me get him off the horse?" she asked the vicar.

The older man agreed, and the two of them lifted Cain down, Margaret holding his legs. She ordered the vicar to lay him face-down upon the bed, so as not to hurt him any more than was necessary.

"There's water in the bucket," the man offered. He glanced at Cain's burned shirt, adding, "And he can have one of my old shirts from the trunk over there. I'll send my wife in tomorrow morning to help you, if she's needed."

"Thank you," Margaret said quietly. When the man had left, she stoked the fire and lit one of the oil lamps. The dim amber light revealed a bed just large enough for two people. Cain lay sprawled across it, and his face was tight with pain.

God help her. She knew nothing about what to do now, though she had tried to clean his wounds in the past few days. The plaid had not caught fire, thankfully, but his shirt was ragged and full of dried blood. The wounds were starting to heal, but she was more worried about how he had drifted in and out of consciousness. And then, too, it felt so intimate to be here with Cain . . . almost as if they truly were married.

His long black hair was covering part of his face, and she smoothed it back. Gently, she began unfastening his plaid and shirt, lifting the garments away until she revealed his wounds.

His back was bleeding and raw, the skin terribly burned. Blisters covered his back, and she strongly suspected he was suffering a fever. Near his shoulders, the skin was an angry red color.

Margaret found a handkerchief and soaked it in cool water. Then she brought it over and laid it upon his burned skin. He shuddered a moment but didn't awaken. She couldn't even imagine the pain he must have endured, suffering in such a way.

She ran her fingers over the base of his neck, and he stirred slightly. The last time she'd touched him like this was when he'd stolen a kiss. And though men had kissed her hand a time or two, Cain Sinclair's mouth was the only one she'd ever tasted. He kissed like the Highlander he was, demanding and fierce. She'd never forgotten the recklessness he provoked or the way he'd coaxed her to surrender. A man like him would never court a woman or ask permission to touch her hand. No, he knew just how to steal her senses, how to push away the edges of propriety to reveal a very different woman within.

Margaret touched his hair, so afraid that she wouldn't be able to save him. She didn't want him to suffer or die because of her. Regardless of the past between them, they were friends.

Or at least, they had been once.

Within the cottage, she found a wooden cup, and she filled it with water from the bucket. She helped turn him slightly, supporting his head with her arm. Guiding the cup to his lips, she tried to get him to drink. Though his eyes remained closed, his body seemed to instinctively know what she was offering.

It occurred to her that she would have to cook for both of them. She knew nothing about preparing food, but she supposed she'd have to learn how. They were already in the vicar's debt, and she didn't want to see his wife looking down on her as if Margaret were incapable of caring for herself.

Her stomach was growling, so she decided to find something to eat. She found a bag of oats, unsure of whether they were meant for people or the horses. But perhaps she could make porridge or a gruel from it.

Surely there couldn't be much more to it than boiling the grain and water together. She didn't know how much to use, but she guessed at the amount of oats and poured two handfuls into a pot of water, setting both over the fire to cook. While the water heated, she pulled a stool beside the fire and thought of her sister. Trying to find Amelia was the most impulsive decision she'd ever made. She hadn't considered that she might not find her or that she might be stranded out here.

In her heart, she feared that there was no hope for either of them. It had taken nearly three days to reach this place, and she'd had to walk alongside the horse, only stopping for a few hours of sleep. Cain had been barely conscious, unable to get on or off the horse without her help. And now, it was too late to go after Amelia again. Surely by now, her sister had been rescued or ruined. She prayed it was the former.

Margaret turned back to Sinclair and pulled a stool beside his bed. Gently, she touched his cheek. "I do hope you awaken soon."

And she prayed that she could take care of both of them.

⚘

ONE WEEK LATER

Beatrice's heart was breaking.

Although she knew that a wedding was meant to be a day of joy and celebrating, she felt like a brittle shell. Thank the good Lord, her youngest daughter Amelia had been brought back safely.

But all she could think of was Margaret.

Why, oh why had her daughter gone off to search for Amelia that night? Why hadn't she told them the truth and sought their help? Her heart was sick at the thought of Margaret being gone for so long.

Her husband, Henry, reached over and took her hand. The ceremony had begun, and Beatrice tried to put aside her sadness. There was much to be thankful for. Not only had Amelia been rescued by the Earl of Castledon, but it seemed that the pair of them were well matched. Her youngest daughter was talkative and often gushed her feelings. At first, Beatrice had worried about the earl being too quiet and stern. Instead, he appeared charmed by Amelia, and he spoke his wedding vows with sincerity. His bride looked up at him with shining eyes, and in them, Beatrice saw the promise of love.

She was happy for them—truly she was. And yet, the tears in her eyes were not only a mother's tears of joy. They were also tears of grief that another daughter was lost, unable to share in this moment.

Henry squeezed her fingers in a silent reminder of their own wedding day. He was trying to reassure her, to offer his support. Even so, she was numb inside. Despite a week of searching, there was no trace of Margaret or the Highlander, Cain Sinclair.

Once, she had trusted Sinclair, believing that he, of all people, could keep Margaret safe. He would move Heaven and earth on her behalf. But he, too, had disappeared. He could be dead, for all they knew.

Beatrice's imagination conjured up all sorts of horrid visions, of her daughter being left alone, lost with no one to help her. She frowned at the thought, then dimly became aware that the wedding was over. The guests were clapping, and she forced herself to do the same.

"You look despairing," Henry whispered in her ear, as they stood from their chairs. "Try to smile for Amelia's sake. I believe this will be a good marriage."

She forced a false smile onto her face, offering a congratulatory embrace to her youngest daughter and her new husband. They went into the dining room, where a wedding feast had been prepared for all of the guests. Her other daughters, Victoria and Juliette, were getting food for their children, and Beatrice saw her chance to slip away for a good cry.

She hurried up the stairs, hoping no one would see her. As soon as she closed her bedroom door, she gave in to the tears. But her solitude was short-lived, for Henry had followed her upstairs.

"It's expected for a mother to cry at a wedding," he said slowly. "But this is about Margaret, isn't it?"

She tried to dry her eyes with a handkerchief and waved him away. "Go back and celebrate with our girls. I just need a few moments to myself."

Henry ignored her, coming to sit upon the bed beside her. "It's going to be all right, Beatrice. We will find Margaret, no matter how long we have to search."

She didn't look at him, so afraid that he would try to console her. Sure enough, he reached out to touch her face. "Dry your tears and come back with me." He leaned in, and she turned her face at the last moment so his kiss caught her cheek instead of her lips.

"Later," she said.

He stared at her and warned, "Don't shut me out, Beatrice. I know how you're feeling."

She knew she was being hurtful to him when he was trying to comfort her. But for so many years her husband had been away at war. The distance and time had forced her to be more independent, to rely on no one but herself. And ever since he'd returned, it was like being married to a stranger. For over twenty years, Henry had known the old Beatrice, who couldn't manage an estate or do much more than ladylike pursuits. He knew nothing of the woman she was now, one who had fought to save her girls from poverty. One who now realized that she was no longer a silent statue in her marriage.

She had a voice of her own, opinions of her own, and she needed Henry to recognize that.

"You have a duty to our wedding guests," he reminded her, "as their hostess. If you busy yourself with the necessary tasks, you won't think of Margaret anymore."

She gaped at him. "Do you honestly believe that? Henry, you were away for years. You never saw our girls growing up the way I did."

His silence hung over both of them, before he admitted, "It wasn't by choice."

No, but when he'd had the chance to return, he'd gone to London instead. He claimed it was to settle the details of the inheritance after his older brother's death, but it had felt like he was avoiding her. Their marriage had slowly deteriorated over time, and now she didn't know how to repair the torn seams.

Beatrice took a deep breath and forced herself to meet his gaze. In his eyes she saw sympathy and a trace of grief. "I'm sorry. It's just been a difficult day for me."

He stood and straightened, looking more like an officer than her husband. "You're not alone in this, Beatrice. But for one day, you must put aside your melancholy and try to be happy for Amelia. She needs both of us to stand at her side."

She knew he was right, but she asked, "Give me a few minutes more, and I'll return."

After he'd gone, she touched her cheek where he'd kissed her. He was trying so hard to mend the differences, but she didn't know if that was possible anymore. The heartache inside her was more than grief over Margaret. It was loneliness and years of regret. She wasn't the sort of wife Henry needed anymore, and she was struggling with the words she wanted to say. The marriage she had and the marriage she wanted were two different things.

You have to try again, her conscience urged. *Allow him to kiss you and comfort you.*

But she didn't know if she had the strength to try again.

The days and nights blurred and were impossible to count. Cain was only aware of each breath and the agonizing fire upon his back. He vaguely remembered the accident and that he'd somehow fallen against the surface of the coach, his shirt catching fire.

A cool, damp cloth rested across his shoulders, and there was a pillow beneath his cheek. He didn't know where they were or what had happened to Margaret, but the vague memories suggested that she'd fed him and given him water during the past few days.

It took a moment for his eyes to adjust, but as he opened them, he saw Margaret seated on a stool, warming her hands before a fire. Her hair was down around her shoulders, and her sage-green ball gown was ragged and torn. Despite her unkempt appearance, he'd never been so glad to see her face.

"Good morn to you, lass." His voice came out raw, hoarse from all the smoke he'd inhaled.

She spun, and her eyes revealed a blend of shock and relief. "You're awake." A fragile smile bloomed upon her face, and it warmed him to see it.

"Where are we?" he managed to ask.

Her shoulders lowered, and she admitted, "I found this village, and I made arrangements for us to stay here."

His suspicions sharpened at that. "How?" No one would willingly give up a cottage without a good deal of money. Had she found the coins he'd hidden within his plaid? He'd deliberately kept very little in his sporran, for it was too easy for thieves to steal.

Margaret's gaze turned downward, and she flushed. "I told them you were my husband. I offered to pay them with my pearl necklace so we could stay here until you recovered."

The necklace was far too much to offer. It was a wonder someone hadn't stolen it from her at night. It bothered him even more to think that if anyone had tried to harm her, he couldn't have lifted a hand to stop them. "That was too dangerous, lass. They could have taken the necklace and killed both of us."

"No, this is the vicar's house," Margaret explained. "He and his wife agreed to stay with his brother while you recovered."

So far as he knew, there were no villages near the location of the accident. Which raised another question in his mind. "How did you bring me here?" Surely she must have had help. Margaret was tall but slender, and he doubted if she had the strength to lift him.

"On horseback. You were unconscious and in a great deal of pain from the burns. We had to travel for several days before we reached Wickersham." She turned, adding a brick of peat to the fire, as if it were no matter at all.

"Did anyone help you?" Somehow, from the look on her face, it didn't seem so.

Margaret faced him and shook her head. "It was very hard to lift you and get you out of there. The hardest thing I've ever done."

Though she spoke the words in a soft tone, he sensed the hardships she'd endured. Most women would have crumbled and wept at such a situation. Instead, she'd saved his life.

"How long has it been since the accident?" he asked.

"Nearly a fortnight now."

A fortnight? Cain couldn't believe it could possibly have been that long. And yet, the agony of his burn wounds seemed to have lessened somehow. A thousand questions tangled up inside him, of how he could possibly have remained unconscious for that long. How had she fed him and taken care of him?

"I gave you laudanum for the pain," she admitted, answering one of his unspoken questions. "The vicar's wife had some, and I paid her for it with the last of my coins. You were hurting so badly, I had no choice."

It explained why he hardly remembered anything from the past two weeks. But there was more he needed to learn. "What happened to your sister? Was there any sign of her?"

Margaret shook her head. "I don't know." Though she kept her expression neutral, he knew she was disappointed. "I can only hope that my father or Lord Castledon found her in time." She went to pour water into a basin, as if she needed the distraction. After sitting beside him, she lifted the cool cloth from his shoulders and replaced it with another.

"You should have returned home and left me, lass," he said quietly. "You could have used your necklace to pay for the journey."

She remained at his side and didn't answer at first. "I wasn't going to leave you here to die."

Her words held a trace of softness that he'd not heard in a long time. He didn't know what to say, for he knew too well that she deserved better than a man like him.

"As soon as you're strong enough to travel, we'll go," she told him. She was about to stand up, but he caught her wrist.

"How badly was I hurt?" Though it wasn't nearly the fiery ache he'd remembered, he could feel the weakness lingering.

She pulled back her wrist, as if he'd tried to accost her. Her voice was cool, but she answered, "It was a wonder you lived, Mr. Sinclair."

There was fear within her, and he questioned whether she blamed him for losing Amelia's trail. Before he could ask, she brought him a bowl of soup. "You must be hungry. It's only simple fare, made with barley and vegetables. And there's a bit of bread."

"Thank you." He took the bowl from her, his fingers brushing against hers. "Have you eaten?"

She nodded, adding, "My cooking is not very good, I'm afraid. It's the first time I've tried to make soup. The porridge and other meals weren't much better."

"You've no' cooked before this? Even at Ballaloch?"

She sent him a wan smile. "Do you think Mrs. Larson would let any of us set foot in her kitchen?"

"I suppose she wouldna allow it." Their housekeeper had the personality of a war general, but he liked Mrs. Larson well enough. She'd always made sure he had a full meal before he'd left the Andrews household.

He tasted Margaret's soup and resisted the urge to spit it out again. There were boiled vegetables and barley, but the broth itself was little more than water.

"It's terrible, I know." Margaret sent him a twisted look. "I could hardly tolerate it myself."

He forced himself to take another spoonful, pretending that there was flavor there. "It's no' so bad."

"And you're lying, Mr. Sinclair." She grimaced as she put the pot of soup near the hearth once more. "I would gladly eat anything else. But I didn't want the vicar's wife to cook for us."

He didn't ask why, but Margaret rolled her eyes. "The woman was insufferable. She took one look at my gown and decided that I was a useless young lady of the ton who couldn't even boil water. And worst of all, she's right."

Cain knew this was one of those conversations where any word he spoke would get him into trouble. To avoid an answer, he took another bite of the terrible soup.

"I can't do anything," Margaret admitted. "I was raised to marry a duke or a marquess. I can plan menus and organize a dinner party. I can host a society event, but when it comes to surviving here, I'm useless."

"You're still alive," Cain felt compelled to point out. "You built a fire and tended my wounds. That's no' so verra useless, lass."

She sent him an incredulous look. "The only reason we have a fire is because I kept a torch burning from the coach accident. I couldn't dare let it go out."

He took a deep breath and forced himself to move his legs to the side of the bed. It hurt like hell, but he wanted to sit up and face her. "You saved our lives, Margaret Andrews."

"I only returned the favor. We both would have died if you hadn't helped me get out."

"We're even then," he told her. "And if you're wanting to go and look for Amelia, that we'll do."

She sobered at that. "I fear it's too late to find her now, Mr. Sinclair. Even if she did come this way."

He didn't like the defeated tone in her voice. This was the woman who had climbed atop a burning coach to save him. She'd already risked everything to save her sister, and he wasn't about to give up. "We willna stop searching until we ken whether or no' she's safe. I promise you that, lass. We can leave in the morning, if you wish it."

When she didn't answer, he offered, "Or I could take you back to London." He wondered if her parents knew what had become of them. They'd been gone for so long, it surprised him that no one had come after them.

"No, I don't want to go back," she said.

"Does anyone ken where we are?"

Margaret shook her head. "I should have sent word, but I didn't want—" She let the thought drift away, but he pressed further.

"You didna want what?"

She took the bowl of soup from him, turning her back. "I didn't want to face them yet. I should never have gone after Amelia, and I just . . . wanted to stay until you were better."

In other words, she was hiding from her family. But it was surprising that she wanted to remain with him. He leaned on one elbow, waiting for her to sit beside him once more.

"Have you been tending me all this time? Alone?" His memories were vague, and he recalled little of what had happened.

Margaret nodded. "I had no choice." She sat on a stool beside him, her posture rigid. "But you *are* getting better."

"Then you've seen me naked, have you no'?" Given how long she'd cared for him, it was inevitable.

"We do not need to discuss that." But Cain didn't miss the pretty blush upon her cheeks. She *had* seen him.

"It doesna seem verra fair that you've seen all that God gave me, when I've seen naught of you," he teased.

He expected an indignant response, but instead, Margaret sent him a narrowed gaze. "Life isn't fair, now, is it?"

"Nay, lass. And now I'm beginning to wonder what else you did to me while I was asleep." He studied her, wondering if those hands had touched his bare skin.

She folded her arms across her chest. It appeared that she was about to snap at him, but then a sudden mischievous look crossed her face. "Wouldn't you like to know?"

Cain choked back a laugh. "Aye, Margaret. I would."

She leaned back, and he noticed that her blond hair was carelessly pulled back, several locks framing her face. He liked seeing her in this way, with her hair unbound, her hands bare of gloves. In this place, she appeared like any other woman—a woman he wanted to touch. "I fed you. I helped you drink water."

He suddenly grew aware that she must have also taken care of more personal needs as well. It shouldn't have embarrassed him, but it was strange to realize that this woman had taken care of him in ways only a wife would know.

"It wasna my intention to burden you like that, lass," he admitted. He enjoyed teasing her, but more than that, he was grateful for her help.

"And I washed you," she said with a wry smile. There was a glimmer of wickedness in her tone, and he reached out to take her palm.

"Did you?" He'd suspected that, but it startled him that she was playing along with his game. "Now *where* did you wash me, lass?"

"I washed every last inch of your . . ." She let the words hang, allowing his mind to wander toward sinful thoughts.

". . . back," she finished.

"How disappointing. There are other more interesting bits of me," he pointed out. And damn it all, but he wished he'd been awake while she'd bathed him.

Margaret's smile turned smug. "I had to tend your wounds, didn't I?" Her face was relaxed, and she tucked her feet up beneath her skirts.

"Aye, you did."

She closed her eyes for a moment, resting her face against her palm. Cain watched her resting and added, "I like you better this way, lass."

"What way?"

"You're more like the girl I knew back in Scotland. The one who wanted her freedom."

She opened her eyes, and met his gaze with her tired one. "Sometimes I grow weary of being a proper lady. With you, I can say whatever I like."

"Aye, you can." Cain saw the exhaustion lingering upon her face. He doubted that she'd slept much in the past week. "After this, where do you want to go?"

Margaret yawned and said, "I want to continue searching for my sister. But we won't go anywhere until you've regained your strength. I've no wish for us to continue our journey until you're able to defend me from anyone who might attack a lady."

He didn't want to admit she was right, but it was true enough that he could do little to protect her. "Another day or two, then."

"A week," she corrected. "At the very least."

"It willna take that long, lass." Although the burns still hurt, he believed he could endure the pain. "And you should send word to your family that we're both safe."

"I will later," she agreed.

Cain couldn't understand why she would hesitate, but he suspected it was embarrassment that she had not found Amelia and that they'd been stranded together.

"Will you heat a bit of water for me?" he asked her a few minutes later. "I would like to shave."

"Of course."

Margaret brought him a linen cloth and a small basin of warm water. Cain reached for the cloth and washed his face. His beard had grown in, and he asked her to find a razor for him.

At that, she began searching the cottage until at last she found what he needed. "Here." Margaret held out a leather case containing a Sheffield razor, a strop, and a stone. "I think this will do."

He unfolded the bone handle from the blade and sharpened it using the stone and strop. Then he soaped his face and beard with the warm water, acutely aware of how she was watching him.

The blade cut easily, and he kept his gaze fixed upon her. "Have you no' seen a man shave before?"

She shook her head, her cheeks reddening. "I suppose I shouldn't really be watching."

"You could help, lass. If you'll shave the parts that I miss." Without a mirror, he could only shave by touch. He worked with the blade, and left a portion of the mustache over his upper lip.

"Will you shave that for me?" he asked, handing her the razor.

Margaret frowned, though she accepted the blade. "I've no idea what to do, Mr. Sinclair."

He lifted his face toward her and pointed to his upper lip, shifting his tongue beneath it to make the surface easier to cut.

A smile escaped her. "You look like a chipmunk when you do that."

"It's so you won't be cutting any of my skin," he explained. He reached for her hand and drew it toward him. Guiding her, he showed her how to cut away the hair.

She stood between his legs, her face flushed as she studied the work before her. Her hands were gentle as she held his chin with one hand. He didn't speak, not wanting to distract her. Instead, he studied the curve of her cheek and the dark green eyes that were so intent upon him. She revealed her emotions in those eyes, and right now, she was being careful not to cut him.

"How is your back?" she asked.

"It still hurts." Though he didn't want her to think him weak, the effort of sitting up was starting to intensify the pain.

When she'd finished, he said, "Run your fingers over my face and tell me if I've missed a place."

Her fingers were gossamer as she slid them over his cheeks and chin. He closed his eyes, imagining her long fingers moving over his flesh. When her hands stopped, framing his face, he pulled her down to sit on his knee.

"Cain, I can't," she murmured. "It's not proper."

"Where have you slept these past nights?" he countered. "On a chair?"

"That's none of your affair, Mr. Sinclair." She was growing more flustered, and he pressed her further.

"Or did you sleep beside me?" he suggested, keeping her trapped upon his lap.

She stood and pushed back from him, her face crimson. "I slept on the floor, mostly. I would never dare to sleep beside you."

She turned her back on him, and he decided it was time to retreat. "You saved my life, Margaret. That's no' something I'll be forgetting."

She took a poker and pushed at the peat upon the fire. He could read the embarrassment in her demeanor, and finally she admitted, "I'm sorry I forced you to help me search for Amelia. The wounds you suffered . . . they were my fault."

Why would she believe such a thing? "'Twas an accident and you're no' to blame for it."

"But if you hadn't come with me, none of this would have happened." She finally faced him, and he saw the shame upon her cheeks.

He stared at her. "I don't regret any day spent with you, Margaret Andrews. No matter what the cost."

⚔

Jonah Sinclair paced across the tiny space of their thatched cottage. His older brother had warned him to stay out of trouble, but he was itching to leave. He'd never left Ballaloch—not once in his fourteen years.

He knew every rock, every blade of grass in this region. He'd spent his days exploring every inch of the land, and he envied the Baron of Lanfordshire's manor and the Earl of Strathland's estate. He dreamed of owning a house like those, of having servants and wealth. But more than all else, he wanted to leave the Highlands. His brother, Cain, traveled all the time, and Jonah longed for that freedom.

He dreamed of traveling beyond the boundaries of Scotland, whether that meant sailing across the Irish Sea or going south to

England. The thirst for adventure burned inside him, and he was old enough to look after himself.

Only fear of the unknown held him back. But . . . maybe he could find Cain. He knew his brother traveled regularly to London. Jonah was certain that if he followed the roads and took enough supplies, surely he could make it there. And Cain wasn't here to stop him.

He had a little money saved, enough to get by. Surely he could make it far enough south. And if the money ran out, he could work until he earned more. He flexed his muscle and felt it with his hand. No, he wasn't as strong as his brother. But he *was* growing, and he could manage the journey south.

Jonah gathered a few things into a bundle, along with a second bundle of food. Though he wanted to take more with him, it was already heavy with the potatoes he'd stored. He could make his way toward Glen Arrin and then continue on.

The door swung open without warning, and he saw Joseph MacKinloch standing there. "Going somewhere, lad?"

The man was older than Cain and had once worked for the Andrews family as a footman. He'd left a few years ago, after the manor house had burned in a fire.

"What are you doing here?" Jonah asked. "Cain isna here, if you're looking for him."

"It's no' him I came to see." MacKinloch stepped inside the house and closed the door behind him. "Aren't ye supposed to be living with Rory while Cain is away? He's a friend of yer brother's, isn't he?" Jonah didn't meet his gaze and MacKinloch continued, "I came to be sure ye weren't going to do something foolish." His gaze passed over the bundles. "Like run away from home."

"I'm no' running. I'm traveling," Jonah said. "Cain asked me to meet him in London." He tried to make the lie sound plausible by keeping his voice even.

"Did he, now? And who would be driving ye there?" MacKinloch's expression held amusement, as if Jonah were behaving like a child. It irritated him, for he was old enough to make his own decisions.

"I'm walking." Jonah lifted his chin. "I can get there on my own."

"'Tis forty miles to the nearest coaching inn, lad. Why don't ye try telling the truth?" MacKinloch crossed his arms and regarded him.

Jonah's face colored, but he refused to admit anything. "I've heard that one of my kinsmen is traveling that way. I'll ask if I can ride along with him."

"As it happens, I'm going toward London," Joseph said. "I've business there of my own. If ye're wanting me to take ye to your brother, that I can do."

Wariness coiled in the pit of his stomach. "And why would you help me?"

MacKinloch rubbed at his brown beard. "Ye may not remember my sister, lad, but she was all I had. I didna look after her the way I should, and now she's gone. Yer brother shouldna be leaving ye alone so much."

"I'm fourteen. Old enough to look after myself," he said. "It's what I always do."

"Aye, ye do. But London is a far sight different than Ballaloch. A lad like yerself would fall into trouble fast."

He shook his head. "I wouldna get into trouble." It was adventure he wanted, above all else.

"Am I wrong that ye helped the others set the Earl of Strathland's wool on fire that night, a few years ago?"

Jonah froze, for he'd never thought anyone had seen him. After Lord Strathland's men had shot several of his kinsmen, it had been an act of vengeance that he'd committed with his friends. It had been both terrifying and thrilling, watching the wool go up in a blaze of fire.

Aye, he'd done acts of mischief before, but nothing quite like that night. And since then, Cain had kept a closer watch upon him, forcing him to live with Rory and Grania when he had to be away.

"They ignored ye, because ye were just a boy," MacKinloch said. "But I saw ye there."

Again, Jonah said nothing. Though if MacKinloch had seen him, then he'd been involved, too. At his questioning look, Joseph nodded. "Aye, lad. I set some of the fires, too, and I've no regrets for doing so. Strathland deserved to lose his income, after what he did to my sister." His face darkened, and he added, "But that's over now. The earl paid the price for his misdeeds, and he's locked away where he can harm no one."

"Why are you going to London?" Jonah asked.

"I was asked to leave Ballaloch, and since then, I've no' been able to find a way to make my living. I thought I'd try being a footman in London. There are more people, more chances to make my way."

"You need references," Jonah pointed out.

MacKinloch patted his coat pocket. "I have those." With a smile he added, "My mother taught me to read and write when I was young. No one will ask questions, since I've come from so far away."

Jonah wasn't sure about that, but he didn't bother to contradict the man.

"If ye're wanting to leave for London, I can take ye there," MacKinloch promised. "We'll travel by mail coach, and ye won't be alone on the journey, lad. That is, if you've enough money for the fare."

The uneasy feeling in his stomach wasn't quite gone, but he knew the man was right. Forty miles was a goodly distance to travel on foot. It would take him far too long.

But he only had a little money—not nearly enough. Beyond that, he had only the clothes on his back. Nothing even to sell.

He knew his brother had money of his own, but Cain had never told him where it was hidden. Last night, Jonah had turned the house upside down, but there was not so much as a single coin. Clearly, his brother had a different hiding place.

"In two days, then," he suggested to MacKinloch. "I want to gather a few more things. If that's all right." It would give him time to search for his brother's money and question Cain's friends. He would take what he needed and pay it back later.

A sense of excitement pushed back the fear. Perhaps it wasn't a bad thing to go with someone. It didn't matter if he found Cain or not—this was his moment to find adventure.

His friends had claimed that London was a place where anyone could become wealthy. If a man was willing to work hard enough, he'd have enough coins to do anything he wanted. But more than the money, Jonah craved the independence.

"I'll return for ye then," MacKinloch promised, before he left.

Two days to search, Jonah thought to himself. He had to find the money somehow.

Chapter Four

ONE WEEK LATER

It was nearly dawn. The fire had dwindled down to embers, and Cain couldn't sleep. Margaret had kept a firm distance between them, and he suspected she'd continued to sleep in a chair simply for propriety's sake. It was ridiculous, for there was no one to care about it. And he wanted her to be comfortable. There was room enough on the bed for both of them, and there was no reason for Margaret to suffer because she was too embarrassed to share the space.

Silently, he got up, placing his pillow as a divider. His limbs were stiff, but he could move easier now than a few days ago. He saw Margaret twisted in the chair with her head resting upon her arm. Without asking, he reached out and lifted her up. She stirred, murmuring, "What's wrong, Sinclair?"

"Naught, lass. Go back to sleep." He laid her down on the other side of the bed with the single pillow between them. She wasn't conscious of anything, but the moment she stretched out on the mattress, he covered her with the blanket. Then he lay down upon the opposite side.

The delicate scent of her skin ensnared him, making him want to pull the pillow aside and touch her. Over the past few days, he'd been acutely conscious of Margaret's presence, even though she'd kept herself apart. He'd savored the last few nights, knowing they were as close as he'd ever get to her. Despite the rare kisses he'd stolen over the years, he knew the invisible boundaries between them. Yet, Fate had handed him an opportunity. Here, there were no ballrooms or silks. The stark isolation of northern England was familiar to him, and he knew how to survive in the middle of nowhere. He'd be a fool not to savor this time with her, enjoying whatever moments he could. In a matter of hours, they would leave this place.

He turned to his side, but Margaret didn't move. The dim glow of the fire revealed goose bumps rising over her bared arms.

She was still awake; he was certain of that. And whether or not she was feigning sleep, he reached out to touch her arm. Her skin was cool beneath his fingers, and he caught her involuntary flinch, as if he'd set her on fire. But she didn't pull away.

Cain slid his hand over her arm in a silent caress. Damn the pillow between them. He removed it, setting it out of the way, and curled his body against hers. The sensation of her hips pressed against him caused a fierce arousal. She'd always had this effect on him, like a confection he wanted to devour . . . but wasn't allowed to taste.

God, he wanted to peel away that gown, to run his mouth and teeth over her flesh. He wanted to cup her soft breasts, nuzzling them until she puckered for him.

His erection was straining against the sheets, and he drew his hand to her waist. "I know you're awake," he murmured in a deep voice. "But keep on pretending you're asleep, lass."

He gave in to impulse and pushed her fallen hair off her neck. He needed to taste her, to remind her of what there had once been between them.

His breath warmed her skin, and she spoke at last. "Please . . . don't."

"There's no one here to see. No one would know." He lowered

his mouth to her neck, brushing his lips against her pulse. She shuddered, her hand reaching back to grip his knee.

"If I were your husband," he continued, "do you know what I'd do?"

"You're not my husband," she responded. Her voice was the barest whisper, and there was no denying her apprehension. But her hand remained upon him, as if she wanted to hear his answer.

"I'd awaken you in the morning by moving in close." He kept his mouth on her throat, letting her feel the hard length of his arousal against her backside. "I'd reach over and cup your breast in my hand."

He moved his palm higher, keeping it just below the swell of her bosom. Beneath his hand, he could feel the constricted lines of her corset. "I'd touch you there, rubbing your nipple until it was tight, wanting my kiss."

Margaret tried to break away from him, but he held her fast. "I'd use my tongue against your bare skin, teasing your breast until you craved more." Her breathing had shifted, and he could feel the telltale trembling of her body. "I'd take you in my mouth, lass, and suckle you until you were ready for me."

"Mr. Sinclair, please," she begged. "Let me go."

But he'd already relaxed his hand. She could leave any time she wanted to.

"I'd move on top of you and enter your body with my flesh," he said. He moved against her, as if he were already doing so. "I'd fill you and thrust inside, until you begged me no' to stop."

Abruptly, Margaret broke free, and scrambled to her feet. She didn't look at him, but she blurted out, "Stay away from me."

Cain got up from the bed and faced her. "You felt it, didn't you, lass? You're afraid of me, no' because you think I'll harm you. But because you fear you'll like it."

Her chin jerked up, and she glared at him. "How dare you? Do you think I'll fall prey to your whims, behaving like a woman of loose morals?" She reached forward and snatched a knife from the table, pointing it toward him. "If you *ever* try to touch me again, I'll bury this in your black heart."

Her face was crimson, but he suspected it was embarrassment more than anger. She hadn't pulled away at first, making him wonder if there was a trace of guilt.

"I'll go and prepare our horse while you get some food ready," he informed her, letting her keep the knife. If it made her feel safer, he didn't care. 'Twould be easy enough to take it from her before she hurt either of them.

Margaret said nothing as he went outside, but he knew she was seething over what he'd done. And yet he held no regrets. He'd never made it secret that he desired her, and he wasn't the sort of man who spoke gentle words or behaved like a gentleman.

He was more like an outlaw. Rules didn't matter to him, and he'd broken the law more than once. Though he supposed he should have regretted touching Margaret Andrews, it only left him wanting more. He wanted to pleasure her, to take her over the edge until she cried out with ecstasy.

When he returned to the vicar's house, she served him a watery gruel. Vengeance in the form of food. He choked it down, and she packed up their meager belongings.

"I'm going to see the vicar and his wife and give them this necklace," she informed him. "After their hospitality, I owe them that."

He gave a shrug, but it bothered him that she would give up her jewelry on his behalf. Margaret ought to keep her baubles, and he didn't like the idea of her handing over a necklace that might have been worn by her mother or grandmother.

"Meet me by the horse when you're ready," he told her, before she departed.

The morning horizon was a pale rose creased with clouded light. Cain didn't doubt that it would rain again, likely within the hour, from what he'd glimpsed of the gray skies. Though his back was still sensitive to the fabric of the shirt Margaret had given him, he could endure the pain. The burns had healed enough for him to travel, and that was all he needed.

Margaret was busy packing supplies for their journey, and he went to pay a visit of his own to the vicar's wife. He found the older woman inside the church. She was holding Margaret's pearls, examining them in the morning light.

"I'm wanting those back," he interrupted. "You canna have her necklace."

"She promised it to us," the vicar's wife insisted. "We gave you our house and supplies for nearly three weeks."

Cain moved forward, letting his height intimidate her. "And where will you find anyone to buy the pearls? No' here." From inside a hidden seam of his plaid, he withdrew a handful of coins. "These are of better use to you now."

"The pearls are worth more," she argued back.

Cain stepped even closer, forcing her to crane her neck to look at him. He took her empty hand and pressed the coins into them, holding her wrist firmly. "I wouldna advise you to keep the pearls. Especially when I could take them from you now."

A shadow of fear crossed her face as she understood his meaning. Cain reached for the pearls, never taking his gaze from her face. "The coins will compensate the both of you." He pocketed the necklace and added, "Margaret has lost enough during the past few weeks. She doesna need to lose her pearls."

He stared hard at the vicar's wife to ensure that the woman wouldn't do anything foolish. No, the coins weren't as much as the pearls were worth. But they were a generous offer for using their house for a fortnight.

Cain left the church and returned to Margaret, who was busy tying belongings onto the horse. He helped her mount the animal and then swung up behind her. "Are you certain you want to continue north, lass?"

"I do, yes. Though I know it's too late to help my sister, I can go toward Juliette's estate at Falsham, south of Edinburgh," Margaret said. "I can stay there until I decide what I want to do."

He detected a slight note of uncertainty in her voice. "What about your parents? I could take you to their home in Ballaloch."

She stiffened against him. "I'd rather not face them. Not after what I did and how long we've been together. They will suspect the worst of me."

He sensed that a good part of her frustration was directed toward herself for acting on impulse. This journey had been her idea, not his. And now that it had resulted in disaster, she blamed herself.

"You've done naught wrong," he insisted.

"That isn't true." Her voice was a whisper, as if in memory of what had happened between them earlier.

"Are you *wanting* to do something wrong?" he asked, letting his hands rest against her waist.

"Of course not." She pushed his hands away, straightening her posture as if to remind herself that she was still a lady. But there was a rebellious side to Margaret Andrews, beneath the white gloves and stiff corset. She could have protested the moment he'd lifted her out of the chair and laid her down on the bed beside him. Instead, she'd allowed him to lie beside her. And he had no doubt that he'd tempted her.

Cain guided the horse to the top of the hillside, shielding his eyes as he searched for his bearings. He was torn between wanting to take Margaret back to Ballaloch and allowing her to continue toward Falsham. Although he could leave her behind at her sister's estate, he questioned the wisdom of it. So far as he knew, Juliette was still in London. He didn't want to bring Margaret to Falsham without a family member there to protect her.

A moment later, the clouds opened up and began to pour down the rain. Margaret let out a sound of dismay, and he unpinned the brooch from his shoulder, freeing a length of plaid so she could shield herself from the downpour.

"Don't you need something to cover up from the rain?" she asked, glancing back at him.

"I'm used to it, lass. It doesna bother me." Thankfully it was summer, when the weather was somewhat warmer. Autumn rain was terrible, so cold it could freeze a man's blood.

He led the horse through the open land, following a silvery stream north. After a few hours, he stopped to get water. He filled a small flask that he'd taken from his sporran and brought it back with him. Margaret had pinned up her sodden hair and was waiting calmly for him.

Cain handed her the flask and said, "Have some water."

She took it and ventured a slight smile. Glancing upward at the rain shower, she offered, "I believe I have more water than I need, thank you." But even so, she drank. "Is there any food?"

"Did you bring any of the gruel?" he teased.

Margaret grimaced. "I will be glad when I never have to cook again. I haven't any talent in the kitchen, it seems."

In response, Cain handed her some bread that he'd taken from the cottage that morning. He suspected it might not be very good, for Margaret had made it out of flour and water, cooking it in a cast-iron pan near the hearth. The bread was flat and hard, but Margaret accepted the small loaf. She tried to break it in half, but it was like trying to break a rock apart.

"I don't have any faith in this," she admitted.

"Soak it in water and see if that softens it."

Margaret poured water from the flask and eventually was able to separate the two halves. Cain took his, waiting for her to take the first bite.

The moment she did, Margaret spat it out. "Ugh! It's like eating paste." She tried to offer some to the mare, but even the horse wrinkled its nose and turned aside.

He decided that now was a good time to keep his opinions to himself. "I could try to get fish, if you're wanting more to eat."

Margaret took a small sip of water, then another. "A fish luncheon would be welcome right now, if you could manage it. My bread tastes like mortar."

"You tried." He walked toward the stream, trying to decide the best way to trap fish for them. Margaret followed him through the meadow, still clutching at her skirts. Even caught in the midst of the wilderness, she was every inch a lady. But she was walking with her arms crossed over her torso in a way he didn't understand.

"Is something wrong?" he asked. "You're walking strangely."

She shook her head. "It's just that I have no spencer or shawl to cover my gown. I should have brought a wrap of some kind, but I forgot, since we were in a hurry."

Cain stared at her, realizing that the rain had soaked her bodice, revealing every curve. The gown she was wearing clung to her skin, but the green shade had grown discolored over the past few weeks. "You can wear my coat," he suggested.

"Please," she agreed. "It's cold from all the rain." Margaret pulled the coat closed before lifting her skirts and stepping toward the stream. When her back was turned, he spied shapely calves and tiny bows on the back of her stockings.

Interesting.

Shielding his eyes, Cain studied the stream. It appeared that the water widened farther out, and it was possible that one of the rivers fed into it. On the opposite side, several trees hung low over the water. If he was going to find something for them to eat, it would be there.

"Look around and see if you find anything else to eat," he instructed her. "Berries or fruit. In the meantime, I'll see if I can get fish."

Margaret nodded and crouched down beside the stream, uncorking the flask with one hand. While she busied herself refilling it, she asked, "How far are we from Scotland?"

"A day or so longer. You must have strayed off the main road when you brought us to Wickersham, for we're closer than I'd thought. We'll keep on this road and go as far as the border."

Once she was safely at her sister's estate, he could continue west toward Ballaloch to look after Jonah. In the past, Cain had given the boy into the care of Rory and Grania MacKinloch, but the woman had died a few weeks ago. He worried about whether Rory was able to take care of Jonah, now that they were both alone.

Cain had been able to support his brother over the years by working in secret for Margaret and her sisters. The young women had created a secret business of their own, selling women's unmentionables. He had delivered them from Scotland to London, traveling every month back and forth as he'd returned with fabric and materials. They had named the business Aphrodite's Unmentionables.

Margaret's reclusive older sister, Victoria, had gotten the idea to sew scandalous corsets and chemises made of silk and satin. Some of the garments revealed a great deal of female flesh, which made them quite popular among the London women.

But after so many years, he'd made up his mind to put an end to the traveling. Jonah needed someone to keep him out of trouble.

Margaret corked the flask, and handed it back to him. "I'll get food for us," he told her, "and then we'll leave."

"How far is it until we reach the next village?" She struggled to pin back her wet hair, trying to restore order to the dark blond mass.

"Nightfall," he predicted. "Our horse canna get far carrying both of us."

Margaret removed her gloves, trying to wring out the excess water. "Do you believe Amelia went this way, Mr. Sinclair?"

"No," he admitted. "I don't think Lisford would ken how to travel these roads." He unsheathed his dirk from his belt, wondering if she was having second thoughts. "Are you certain you're wanting to go to Falsham, lass? I canna understand why you don't wish to return to your parents."

Guilt flushed in her cheeks and she stood up from the stream. "I know I ought to go back. And I will send word soon, I promise. It's just that . . . I don't want to become a prisoner in my parents' house. If I return to London, then that is exactly what will happen."

"They willna make you a prisoner," he argued. Margaret made it sound as if they intended to shackle her to the wall.

"I will not be allowed to leave the house or go anywhere. I've damaged their trust in me." She stepped closer to the stream. "If I stay with Juliette, she won't blame me for what I've done, the way my parents will."

Cain supposed that was reasonable enough. Since it was farther to London than Falsham, it made sense. He gripped his dirk and eyed the water.

"How are you planning to catch the fish?" she asked, studying his dirk. "Will you stab them?"

He almost smiled. "If I find one close to shore, aye." Truthfully, he was searching for a means to trap one. He glanced at her a moment, and an idea occurred to him. "Take off your petticoat."

Margaret blinked. "I'm sorry, what did you say?"

"You heard me, lass. Take it off and hand it over. Our fishing will go much faster if we have it to use as a net."

She started to back away, holding on to her skirts as if she believed he would tear them off. "Mr. Sinclair, that isn't proper at all."

"Are you hungry or no'?"

She nodded. "But is it truly necessary to use my undergarments? We could use a piece of your plaid instead."

He moved toward her, catching her around the waist. "The plaid is to keep us both warm, lass. You won't be needing the petticoat." He kept his hands upon her spine, watching the troubled emotions cross her face.

"I know you're right," she said, putting her hands up against his chest and stepping back. "I do. But it's just that . . . no man has seen my undergarments before. It feels shameful."

Her cheeks were burning, but she closed her eyes. "If I do this, promise me you won't think badly of me."

Cain had no idea what to make of that, but he agreed.

"I willna think less of you," he said. "And if it brings us food, 'twill be worth it."

He turned his back to her, giving her privacy while she removed her underskirt. A few moments later, she handed him a petticoat made of fine lawn, edged with lace and ribbons. It was not at all sensible, but he realized that she did enjoy beautiful undergarments. He sent her a dark smile, and she held up her hand. "Do not say anything about my petticoat."

"I said nothing at all."

"I could read your thoughts." She closed her eyes and waved her hand at him. "Get on with it, then."

He took the petticoat and knotted the waist closed. "Stay here and keep your feet dry." He removed his shoes and socks, stepping into the icy water. Then he found a narrow end of the stream where it flowed rapidly over the rocks.

He stood with the petticoat billowing through the water like a net, hoping the fish would swim inside. While he waited, he glanced back at Margaret. This journey had been difficult enough, and they had to have sustenance. He'd endured hunger before, as a lad, but he doubted if Margaret had. Her face was peaked, and he suspected it wouldn't take much to send her into a faint. "When was the last time you ate food that you didna cook yourself, lass?"

She shrugged. "Almost three weeks ago."

Which meant she was as starved as he was. "I hope we'll catch fish soon." The water was frigid around his legs, but he would not give up until he'd found something for her.

Margaret was already too thin, and he was beginning to suspect that she was punishing herself for what had happened to Amelia. Worry creased her face, along with shadows beneath her eyes.

Eventually, he felt a slight movement against the petticoat, and he closed it swiftly, trapping the fish inside. He kept his hands fastened around the top, letting out a little water at a time until he managed to bring the catch to shore.

"Let's see what we've caught." He opened the petticoat, revealing two fish the size of his hands.

Margaret eyed them and sent him a sidelong look. "They aren't very large, are they? And how does one clean a fish exactly?"

"I'll take care of it, if you'll gather wood for a fire." He gutted the two fish, and though it wouldn't be much, it was better than nothing. Margaret did as he asked, and in time, he had a fire going, with both fish spitted.

"I could eat them raw," she admitted. "I can't remember the last time I was this hungry." She turned her stick and added, "I'm sorry I couldn't find berries or anything else."

"It doesna matter." They sat in silence, cooking their fish over the fire. When the food was ready, he ate his own portion, but was surprised to see Margaret using two sticks to cut and eat her portion. Somehow she'd managed to create silverware out of twigs.

"Still proper, I see."

"Always." Margaret had her knees tucked beneath her gown, and she glanced over at the soaked petticoat. "I suppose I'll have to leave that behind, or my undergarments will smell like fish. I wonder what anyone will think when they find it."

Oh, he knew exactly what a passerby would think, and he sent her a knowing look.

Margaret bit back a laugh. "Well, they would be wrong, wouldn't they?"

"Would they?" Cain studied her, silently letting her know that he wanted far more from her than friendship. He moved in, setting her makeshift silverware aside. "Come here, Margaret."

Her smile faded, and she appeared troubled. "Cain, nothing can happen between us. We're friends, I know, and we've been through a great deal of turmoil these past few weeks. But you must understand that—"

He cut her off, capturing that talkative mouth in a kiss. Her lips were soft, and he held her face between his hands while he took what he'd been wanting. "You talk too much, lass." He had a better idea for that mouth, and he coaxed her to kiss him back.

She was reluctant, but he persisted. "There's no one here to see us. No one to pass judgment upon you."

Her green eyes held apprehension, and she whispered, "I'll pass judgment upon myself."

He paid no heed to her words but gave in to the urge he'd been holding back. He slid his tongue against the seam of her mouth, and she opened to him, her fingers trembling against his shoulders.

He slid the coat away, revealing the green ball gown. It was still damp from the rain, and he took both of her hands, drawing them around his waist. He claimed her mouth again, and a soft sigh escaped her. She started to kiss him back, and the tentative response only deepened his desire. He nipped at her lips, and she slid her own tongue inside his mouth. The moment she did, he grasped her hips, drawing her closer. He needed to feel her body beneath his, to spend time learning the taste of her sweet skin.

Abruptly, Margaret turned her cheek, resting it against his. "I shouldn't do this, Mr. Sinclair." Her voice was shaky, as if she didn't trust herself to speak. Neither did he.

Reluctantly, he pulled back. "Finish your food and we'll go." His body was raging, but he knew he'd pushed her too far. Margaret stood waiting for him, her face crimson.

Cain brought the horse back to her and helped her up. She shivered slightly from the damp gown. It did seem that she had fewer layers beneath her clothes, beyond the petticoat she'd lost. He suspected she had traded her corset to the vicar's wife for one she could fasten herself.

Although she was still wearing his coat, it wasn't enough to keep her warm. He swung up behind her and unpinned the brooch, wrapping his plaid around her shoulders. Though it was wet, at least it offered another layer.

Her shoulders were tense, her mouth tight as he gripped the reins. He kept the pace of the mare steady, not wanting the journey to be even more difficult.

Cain urged the mare back onto the road, and when the animal began walking, Margaret's backside pressed against him. The motion reminded him of how she'd felt in his arms, and the more he remembered her softness, the more aroused he became. He couldn't have stopped the reaction if he'd wanted to. This was likely going to be the most uncomfortable journey he'd ever endured. His traitorous body reveled in the feeling of her warm body so close.

She smelled good, like the sugar biscuits Mrs. Larson had made from time to time. He wanted to lean in and devour her skin, bringing his hands against the silk until she felt the same arousal he did.

"Mr. Sinclair?" she whispered. "Y-you're too close to me."

He felt her body stiffening, and he knew she was well aware of his response to her. Though likely she wanted to ignore their circumstances, he believed that honesty would be best. "It can no' be helped, lass." She tried to scoot forward, and he held her in place. "I'd have to be dead no' to be affected. You needn't worry that I'll do anything at all." Whether or not she believed him, it was true. He'd die before hurting her.

Margaret went motionless, her hands digging into the horse's mane. "I am sorry about all of this, Mr. Sinclair. It's my fault that we're stranded here."

He moved one hand back to her waist, keeping the reins in his other palm. Leaning in against her neck, he murmured, "I canna say that I mind being stranded with you so verra much, lass."

A tremor broke over her, as if she wasn't at all unaffected by him. Right now he wanted to tilt her head back, to claim her mouth and kiss her again.

"Did you say we'll reach the next village at nightfall?"

He recognized it as a means of changing the conversation. "Aye, lass. If we keep a good pace and don't stop again."

Her shoulders slumped down, but she gave no word of complaint. It was as if she was having an inner argument with herself, and eventually she straightened and lifted her chin. He could have balanced a mug of ale upon her head, if he'd had one. The mare kept to an easy walk, and Margaret rested one hand upon the horse's neck to balance herself.

"Do you ken any good songs?" he asked her. If they were to ride for several hours, it might as well be entertaining.

"You want me to sing?" She turned back to him in disbelief. "At a time like this?"

"You could. 'Twould entertain both of us." It was also better than the painful arousal of his groin at the constant motion of her hips as the horse walked.

"I'm in no mood to be entertaining. I would rather enjoy the silence."

"Silence is dull. And I do ken a few songs, but you might no' like them." Mostly they were bawdy tavern songs he'd overheard.

"You could sing a hymn," she offered. "Perhaps 'Love Divine, All Loves Excelling.'"

"Go on, then," he bade her. But instead of complying, she kept her back ramrod straight.

"As I've told you, I have no desire to sing."

"Perhaps you canna sing," he said. "And you're no' wanting me to learn that your voice is worse than a crow's."

"My voice is perfectly respectable," she countered. "Although I choose not to perform publicly. If you're so intent upon singing, why don't you carry the tune?"

A smirk crossed his face. He had a mind to ruffle those stiff feathers and get a rise out of her. In a deep baritone, he sang:

> *In Edinburgh, there was a lass,*
> *Her face as pale as milk*
> *Every man longed to pinch her—"*

"Stop!" Margaret interrupted. "You were *not* about to sing such a vulgar song before me."

He didn't bother to hide his grin. "Well, 'tis the only song I could think of. And it's a common term for a woman's—"

"Don't say it," she moaned. "You're just trying to embarrass me."

"Nay. I'd hoped you'd laugh." At least it would keep their minds off the journey. But when she turned to look at him, he caught a glimpse of merriment in her eyes. Her mouth pressed tight as if to hold back a laugh.

The mare continued her ambling walk forward, across the green meadows sparsely dotted with trees. Cain kept his arms around her, both for balance and because he wanted to.

"My parents are going to lock me away for the rest of my life," Margaret admitted at last. "I've brought the most horrid scandal upon them, even worse than what happened to Amelia. I won't be able to show my face in London, and everyone will believe the worst of me."

"That you've sinned with a Highlander?" he murmured against her ear. The heat of her hips pressed between his legs.

"No one will believe I'm innocent." Once again, she straightened in the saddle. "And as I said before, I'll have to go into isolation until the talk dies down."

"How long?"

"A few years," she admitted. "Even then, I might not be received anywhere."

"Your friends willna turn their backs on you," he said. "If they're true friends."

"Oh, but they will. They'll have no choice, for if they received me, it would bring shame upon them. I cannot see anyone or speak to them. And I can't say that's something I'm looking forward to."

She turned back to him. "I will send word to my family, I promise. But I'll ask them to meet me at Falsham."

She was stalling the inevitable. And yet, the rules and intricacies that she lived by were impossible for Cain to believe. "You don't think trying to save your sister's virtue will matter to them?"

"Not when I've compromised my own."

She spoke as if her life had ended, that all was lost. He cared naught for what anyone thought of him, but he knew she would be hurt by the cruel words. And he wanted to protect her from that.

"What will happen to your sister, once she's found?" he asked.

"She'll have to marry quickly." Margaret glanced back at him. "And honestly, I do pray that Lord Castledon found her. He might be a stern widower, but I've seen the pair of them together. Amelia makes him laugh, and I think he cares a great deal for her."

"I thought she was trying to match *you* up with him." Cain remembered the way her meddling younger sister had kept trying to bring Margaret and the earl together.

"Oh, he was kind enough. But he's not for me."

"I'm glad to hear that I won't have to be killing him, then." He tightened his grip around her waist, and she stared back at him.

"You wouldn't do something like that."

"Well, I might no' kill him. But aye, if any man tried to claim you, I'd take you away from him." He saw no reason to hide his intentions. "But we were talking about your sister. If she weds Castledon, will he protect her?"

"There would be talk, but the earl could shield her from it. His actions would silence those who would seek to hurt Amelia."

He thought it strange that marriage would solve nearly any indiscretion, whether the bride was at fault or not.

"Would marriage save you?" he asked quietly.

She bowed her head and admitted, "No man would have me. Not after this."

"I'll have you, lass. You ken that already." He kept her close, resting his mouth against her nape. It didn't matter to him what any of them thought. Margaret had saved his life, and he'd do what was necessary to protect her.

She remained in his arms, leaning her head back against him for the barest moment. But when he nipped at the soft skin of her shoulder, she tensed immediately and sat up straighter. "You're a good man," she murmured. "And if it were that simple, I know we could come to an arrangement. But we both know that I have to wed a titled lord. Someone with enough power behind his good name that it would overcome my faults."

Aye, he was penniless, without a drop of blue blood. But he could protect her far better than any man with "Lord" in front of his name. And it was beginning to irritate him that she couldn't seem to move past the need for a title.

"Thank you for your offer, Mr. Sinclair," she said, tilting her head back to face him. "It was kind of you."

She might have been thanking him for opening a door or helping her onto a horse. "Save your good manners, Miss Andrews. Especially when you'd rather go into isolation for years, ne'er showing your face, than wed a man like me." His words found their mark and she turned away.

"You wouldn't understand."

"Aye. I don't ken why you care so much about what others think. What kind of life is that, lass?"

"It's the way I was raised." Her voice was heavy, as though she was fighting back tears. "I've made my mistakes, and I'll accept the consequences for them."

Although they were as opposite as coal and diamonds, he didn't like the idea of her being punished for trying to help her sister. "Damn them all, Margaret. They're no' worth it."

She didn't deserve to become an outcast for this. And would to God he could stand at her side to defend her. If any man dared to speak lies against her, Cain would shred the man apart.

"Even if none of this had happened," she continued, "if I did marry a man like you, it would be an even greater scandal."

Anger took hold inside him like a hot coal searing wood into smoke. "Don't worry, lass," he said. "I won't be asking you again."

Margaret jerked the reins from his hands, pulling the mare to a stop. She turned to face him. "I *am* grateful to you, for all that you've done. You went on this journey with me, and you protected me at every turn. I could not ask for anything more."

Then she touched his cheek with her left hand. "You're an honorable man, Mr. Sinclair. But we both know that a marriage between us would be nothing but a mistake."

⚔

She'd wounded his pride. Margaret knew it, just as she knew she'd thrown down a gauntlet. She hadn't meant to be that blunt, but Cain Sinclair frightened her. He seemed to reach past her years of good breeding, finding another woman inside. Around him, she rebelled against all that was right and proper. She climbed atop burning coaches and allowed him to take far more liberties than he should. With every moment she spent at his side, she felt herself becoming someone else—a wicked woman who cared nothing about propriety or what was right. A woman who reveled in the freedom he'd given her.

"I'm sorry," she murmured.

Before she could pull her palm away, Sinclair caught it and covered her hand with his own. The heat of his skin warmed her hand, and her face flushed at the contact.

He had saved her life, and she didn't want him to believe she was disdaining him. She couldn't put into words the way she felt about him, but fear and desire were tangled in a knot. She'd been raised in a world where marriages were forged upon uniting families with noble blood. All her life, she'd prepared for an ambitious union, one where she could be useful to a husband. She knew the intricacies of good manners and could host a dinner party in the same way a general could plot out a battle strategy.

And the first time she'd chosen a man to marry, it had ended in disaster. *Poor Margaret, left behind before her wedding day. The viscount only asked her to marry him because of a wager. He never intended to go through with it.*

"Don't pity me, lass." His voice held a dangerous edge, and she didn't know how to calm the rigid anger within him.

"It wasn't pity," she protested. "I was only trying to thank you for what you did. I apologize if you thought it was."

"That's no' a verra good apology," he said, touching her nape. His deep blue eyes caught hers, holding a warning. "I think you need to apologize again."

She tried to avert her face, but he wouldn't pull back. Instead, he tilted her chin up, forcing her to look at him. His blue eyes were burning with sensual intent.

"This is a better apology," he told her, as he leaned in and captured her lips. His mouth moved against hers lightly, and it sent a wave of warmth rippling over her skin. It was a gentle kiss, inviting her to lean in. He coaxed her, making her want to surrender every last inch of propriety. It was as if invisible hands were touching her, stroking secret places deep inside. She couldn't have pulled away if she'd wanted to.

This man was, and always had been, forbidden to her. He was raw, untamed, and didn't care a whit about what anyone thought. In his kiss, she tasted sin and temptation.

And God help her, she wanted him badly. He made her want to throw her life away, seizing the pleasure he could bring. His tongue probed at her, entering her mouth. Her imagination conjured up visions of his hands moving over her bare flesh. Heat shot through her, and she couldn't catch her breath. Cain was kissing her boldly, his hands moving to rest upon her waist.

"What are you doing?" she managed to ask against his mouth.

"I'm showing you what you're giving up, by refusing to wed me." He moved his mouth close to her ear, capturing her earlobe. "If you were mine, lass, I'd stop right this moment. I'd lay you down upon the grass and take you until you cried out my name."

Against her hip, she felt the hard length of his arousal, and she knew he meant what he'd said.

"But you won't," she reminded him. "Because you promised to keep me safe."

"I ne'er promised no' to tempt you, lass."

Her lips were bruised from his lips, but he'd made her feel alive. "You think to compromise me in truth, don't you? Everyone will believe it anyway." Frowning, she added, "That isn't the woman I want to be."

"I asked you to be a wife, no' a mistress," he reminded her.

She knew that. But even so, she suspected that Cain Sinclair would not relent in his pursuit. And despite her protests, he'd awakened a part of her that was hungry to learn more.

God help them both.

Chapter Five

They reached a village when it was nearly nightfall. There was no inn, but Cain arranged for them to stay in a farmer's barn. Margaret wasn't at all eager to sleep amid the straw and animals, but the only alternative was to sleep outside.

It was freezing cold at night, even wearing Cain's coat. She wished that she'd had the foresight to bring a spencer or a cloak to cover her dress. Not only to push back the cold, but also to avoid the stares she'd received from the villagers. They'd eyed her as if she were mad. Perhaps she was, to make such a journey in a torn ball gown.

But Cain had suffered more. After the long distance they'd traveled, his mouth had been set in a tight line when they'd stopped. If they were to continue, he needed something to ease the wounds on his back.

For that reason, she'd sought the help of an apothecary to look at his burns. She'd slipped out when he wasn't looking and asked a few of the villagers before she found the right man. The apothecary was younger than she'd expected, nearly her age, and she wondered if he would know how to treat Cain's wounds.

"I've a salve that will ease the burns," the man had answered. He eyed her torn ball gown. "If you've a means of paying for the medicine."

Margaret nodded. "I have, yes." She twisted the ring on her finger. "We won't be staying long. We actually came in search of my sister Amelia, who might have come through this village a few weeks ago." She described the young woman to the apothecary. "Did you happen to see anyone who looks like her?"

He shook his head. "The pair of you are the first visitors we've seen in weeks. Though I must say, you're not like the travelers we normally see. A few shepherds, some peddlers. Not ladies."

Her mood dimmed. If Amelia had not come this way, then likely Lord Lisford had taken the main roads. This impulsive journey had been for nothing at all. It was what she'd suspected, but she'd needed to ask. "Bring the salve with you, and I'll take you to my husband."

She led him back to the barn, but before she could enter, Sinclair was already outside searching for her. There was immediate relief on his face when he saw her, and she could tell he was angry that she'd left.

"What's he doing here?" Sinclair demanded, as soon as she walked forward with the man.

"This is Mr. Snow, the village apothecary," Margaret explained. "He's here to look at your back."

"My back is fine," he said. "'Twill heal well enough."

Which was a lie. She knew how badly he was hurting. "Take off your shirt," Margaret demanded. To the apothecary, she apologized, "I fear my husband is in a great deal of pain. We survived a fire on our journey here, but his burns have not healed well."

Cain moved toward her, using his height as intimidation. She tilted her neck back to meet his iron stare. "I don't need your help, *wife*."

Margaret smiled at the apothecary. "Isn't it just like a man, not to know when he needs help?"

Cain's expression held frustration, and she didn't doubt he wanted to rage at her for embarrassing him like this. His blue eyes darkened like gunmetal, and he crossed his arms in front of his chest. "It's no' necessary."

"If you don't want the salve, I can be on my way," Mr. Snow offered, holding up the container. He looked as if he didn't want to get involved in their quarrel.

"We do," she answered.

"He's no' touching me," Cain snapped. "Leave it be, Margaret."

She glared at him, for this wasn't his decision to make. "I'll take the salve and apply it myself. We're also in need of food and supplies for the rest of our journey," she told the apothecary. "Bring us enough to last another week, and you may have this ring."

The man agreed, hurrying out while Cain turned to her. "We don't need those things, lass."

"We have no food left," she reminded him, leading him inside the barn. "And I, for one, am quite hungry." She suspected half of his ill temper was due to a growling stomach. A good meal would help both of them. "Now take your shirt off, so I can put your medicine on."

"What makes you think I'll do what you say, lass?" His voice held a tangible threat, but she ignored it and unpinned the plaid, pushing it off before she unfastened the top button of his shirt. The moment she touched him, his eyes flared with heat.

Standing this close, she was aware of his male scent and how easily he could overpower her. Her finger passed over his bare chest and she tugged at the linen to lift it over his head.

Though she had seen him without his shirt before, it suddenly struck her that this was not a man accustomed to being ordered around. He rested his hands upon her shoulders, one hand curling around her neck. Gooseflesh rose over her skin, and she suddenly remembered what it was to lie beside this man, to feel his warm breath against her throat.

She broke free of him and opened the jar of salve. "Sit down, please." Her voice quavered, and she wanted to curse herself for it.

Instead, he caught her waist and leaned down until his mouth was a breath away from hers. "If I let you do this, I'm claiming a boon of my own."

"This is for your own good," she protested. "I don't want you to suffer."

"You're being verra demanding." He rested his forehead against hers.

"I'll be gentle," she promised. She didn't ask what boon he wanted, for she suspected it was a kiss. And although everything within her warned that this was a bad idea, she knew the pain he was enduring.

Margaret took a deep breath, while he sat down. She smeared her hand within the ointment and detected an herbal aroma. Cain's back was still raw and inflamed, and she began on the edges where the burns weren't quite as bad. He flinched the moment she touched him but said nothing.

"Mr. Snow told me that no one passed through this village in the past few weeks. Amelia wasn't here at all." She smoothed more of the ointment across his back, trying not to hurt him as she did.

"I thought as much." Cain let out a hiss when she touched another tender area.

"I'll try to hurry up," Margaret said. "I know it stings."

"I'll be smelling like a garden," he complained. "And it's going to get all over my shirt."

"Does it feel any better?" she asked, dipping her hand back into the salve.

"I'm no' certain it's worth the price you paid," he said. "You could have kissed me to make it better."

"I cannot say as I have any desire to touch my lips to your back," she admitted. It would take a few more weeks, months even, for it to fully heal.

"I wasna talking about my back, lass. If you kissed my mouth like you did earlier, I'd be forgetting all about any pain."

She gave no reply and finished applying the salve, covering up the jar once more. "There. I think that should help."

Cain took her hand and led her to stand before him. "Thank you, lass." He held her hands lightly, but she didn't pull away. A moment later, Mr. Snow returned. Upon one arm, he held a basket.

"Mr. and Mrs. Sinclair, I've brought the supplies you requested." He walked inside, and he was followed by another man. "There's food for a few days." It was clear that he'd brought the other man to ensure that Margaret kept her word.

"Show me what you've brought," she bade him, twisting off the amethyst ring. She wanted to be certain that it was indeed food within the basket.

He did, and while she examined the contents, he asked, "You came up from London, then?"

Before Margaret could speak, Sinclair intervened. "That's no' your concern." He began pulling his shirt back on, and then he came to stand beside her.

The apothecary sent her a look and asked, "Are you all right, my lady?"

At that, she realized that her clothing made the man believe she had been abducted. "Of course I am," she insisted. "As I told you, we were looking for my sister when we left London. There was a coach accident, and it took us longer to travel this far."

The apothecary seemed as if he didn't quite believe her, and he exchanged a look with the other man. "I'll take the ring now, my lady. Since I've done as you asked."

"You have," she agreed. But before she could pass over the ring, Cain stopped her.

"You willna be giving over any jewelry, lass." Instead, he withdrew a handful of coins from a hidden fold of his plaid and passed them over to the men.

Now where had that come from? He'd had money all this time and had never said a word about it? When she sent him a questioning look, he answered it with his own stare. He wasn't going to offer an explanation.

Before the apothecary and the other man could leave, Margaret blurted out, "I must ask . . . is there anyone in the village who might be willing to drive us to Scotland in the morning? There would be a greater reward once we reach my sister's house. She married the Viscount of Falsham, and I would be glad to pay the cost of the journey."

Once again, the two men exchanged silent glances, but the apothecary paused, staring at Cain. "If you paid in advance, I might find someone."

"We don't have enough for that," Cain interrupted. "But even a blind man could see that she is from a family of wealth."

A slight smile curved over the taller man's face. "Is she?" His tone made it clear that he didn't believe them. "Nay, Snow, they should pay beforehand. If they've no more coins, then we can't help them."

"But my family *does* have money," she argued back. "Can't you see this gown is made of silk?"

"It could have been stolen," the taller man said. Shaking his head, he escorted the apothecary out. "Come now, Brother. Let them go on their way."

Frustration welled up inside Margaret. She wasn't accustomed to being treated like a pauper. Exactly what did they believe of her?

Cain took her shoulders and guided her back. "You look as if you want to go after those men with a blade, lass."

She wasn't about to be coddled. "And where exactly did you get any money? Have you had it all this time?"

"Aye. Did you no' think I'd come prepared?"

"But . . . my necklace." She reached up to her throat, wishing she hadn't given it away. Especially since he'd had money to pay for their stay.

"Don't be worried about that, lass." An enigmatic look crossed his face, but he only said, "Sit down and have something to eat."

She supposed he was right. Despite the slight meal they'd had for luncheon, she was utterly starving. At this moment, she was ready to begin gnawing on the wood.

He opened up the basket and offered it to her. It took an effort not to dive at the food and begin stuffing herself. Margaret waited for Cain to break the bread in half, and the moment she took the first bite, she couldn't eat fast enough. Her stomach was roaring for food, and even the cheese he gave her wasn't enough to sate her hunger.

"I believe I would trade this gown for a hot meal right now," she admitted. "And I would eat every last bite."

In silent response, Cain handed her his remaining cheese.

Margaret paused, startled at his actions. The Highlander was larger than she, with broad shoulders, and undoubtedly he needed more. "I don't need to take your food, Mr. Sinclair. I'll manage until we can get more."

He pressed it into her hand. "Do you think I could eat it, when I ken how hungry you are?"

She stared at the cheese again. Such a small portion would hardly fill either of them, but the gesture was too much. "I'll take some of it," she said, breaking the cheese in half.

Margaret couldn't help but taste the guilt as she finished the rest. Her throat grew dry, and she asked, "Is there any water?"

"I wouldna drink any water from this place," Cain said. Instead, he pulled out a bottle of spirits from the basket. "We can share this."

She wasn't at all keen on the idea of drinking whisky or wine. Though she had tasted the occasional glass of sherry, she usually drank lemonade.

"A wee dram willna hurt you, lass. You can take a sip, and if you don't like it, I'll drink the rest."

Judging from the size of the bottle, he could easily become drunk. And that wouldn't do at all—she needed him to help her on the journey. She held out her hand for the bottle and decided to take the slightest taste.

She expected a harsh, throat-burning liquor. Instead, there was a sweetness to the drink, rather like summer raspberries.

"This isn't whisky," she remarked. "Somehow I thought the apothecary brought something of that nature."

"It tastes like raspberry wine." Cain took it from her and drank another swallow before handing it back.

Truthfully, it was the most delicious concoction she'd ever tasted. A warmth flooded through her, relaxing her until she hardly cared that they were staying in a barn.

"Don't be drinking it too fast, Miss Andrews," Cain warned, taking a small sip of his own, before he passed it to her.

"It's not at all like the sherry I've tasted. It's lovely." She drank out of the bottle where his lips had rested. Her head felt light, and she viewed Cain Sinclair as if from a distance. The raspberry wine was not at all intoxicating, as she'd feared. Instead, it was a welcome drink on a day that had not started out well at all.

My, but he was handsome, she thought. His long black hair hung around his shoulders, and she wondered what it would be like to touch it again.

She stared at his lips, remembering the earlier kiss. She wouldn't mind kissing Cain Sinclair again. It was quite nice. If that was the boon he'd mentioned, she could give it now.

"Lass, you shouldna be watching me like that," he warned. "You look as if you're wanting something from me."

"I was thinking about kissing you," she said. The words came out of her mouth without warning, and she was startled to realize that she'd spoken her thoughts aloud.

"You've had too much wine," he said, taking the bottle back. But not before he took a deep swallow, corking it and setting it aside.

"I like that wine," she said. "And I can't think that I've had more than a glass of it. You needn't put it away." Dismay filled her that he would take it from her.

"If you were sober, you wouldna say things like that," he countered. "It's time that you got some rest."

How could he think that she could ever become intoxicated? Margaret prided herself on temperance, and she would never consider allowing spirits to interfere with common sense.

"I am not at all inebriated," she informed him. "And furthermore, you needn't dictate to me as if I were a young child in need of sleep."

There was a smirk on his face that irritated her. "As you say." He shrugged and leaned back against one of the horse stalls.

"Where do you plan to sleep, Mishter . . . that is, Mr. Sinclair?" she corrected. My, but she couldn't seem to speak clearly. Her head felt light and fluffy right now.

"In the loft."

"That's good," she agreed. "You should not sleep beside me. You might tempt me into sinning. And I am a good girl." Narrowing her gaze, she wagged her finger. "Don't come into my bed."

"Only when you ask me to," he agreed.

There was an amused smile on his face that made him even more handsome. She really did like him when he wasn't scowling at her or telling her what to do. She blinked a moment and dizziness washed over her.

"Not tonight," she said. Though it would be quite cozy to snuggle in his arms. There were no blankets, but if they lay next to one another, she imagined it would be comfortable.

"And what if your feet get cold?" he asked. "Shall I stay in the loft, even then?"

"They won't get cold," she said. "I do have your coat, after all." She took a step forward, surprised when the ground swayed beneath her. Sinclair was reaching toward the loft ladder, and she decided to warn him.

"The ground is crooked," she informed him. "You'd best be careful or you might fall."

"I'll remember that." He was fighting a laugh, which she couldn't understand. It wasn't funny at all, when she was trying to offer a warning.

Sinclair caught her by the waist and guided her toward a soft pile of hay. It didn't look like a good place to sleep, but she supposed she'd have to make herself a nest and do the best she could.

"I was wrong about you, you know," she told him. "You are a very good man."

"I'm no' a good man at all, lass."

She stumbled again, but he kept her from falling. This time, she drew her left hand up his chest. "You *are*. Even if I do find you exasperating."

"It goes both ways." He kissed her forehead and tried to send her away. But she was feeling bolder right now, wanting another kiss like the one he'd given her earlier. Even if she was never going to marry any man, Cain Sinclair had the best kisses.

"Wait," she said to him. She stood on tiptoe and pressed her mouth to his. When he didn't move, she demanded, "Aren't you going to kiss me good-night?"

"You're no' wanting to start this. Believe me when I tell you that it's no' a good idea." He was like a mountain, fierce and forbidding as he stared down at her. A man of ice, who would not surrender another soul-stealing kiss.

Margaret thought about the way he'd held her close while they were riding north. His strong arms had never let her fall, and she'd been well aware of how badly he wanted her.

She rested her palms against his chest, and beneath his shirt, she felt the harsh beating of his heart. His eyes burned into hers, and she swallowed hard. "Sometimes I wish I could marry you."

Without another word, Cain deposited her in the hay and climbed the ladder up to the loft.

ॐ

Cain slept like hell. His back itched, the barn was cold at night, and he couldn't stop thinking of Margaret. The woman couldn't handle spirits, and the raspberry wine had addled her mind. She'd not been herself at all.

Nor had he. This was one of those days when he cursed himself for possessing a shred of honor. Aye, he'd kissed her many times, but it had always been wickedness on his part. Leading the good girl down the pathway to sin, that was what he'd done.

But if he'd given her more kisses last night, he wouldn't have stopped there. He'd have unbuttoned her gown, kissing the bare skin revealed by each button. He'd have touched her until she was pleading for more. She knew just how to push him to the edge, and she'd haunted him for years now.

Given a single chance, he'd have—

"Mr. Sinclair?" came her voice from below. "Are you awake?"

Awake, aye, and craving the touch of her. But he cursed the thought away and answered her. "I am." He swung down to the ladder and climbed down from the loft.

Margaret stood against one of the horse stalls, waiting for him. Her white gloves appeared pristine, despite the stable filth. Her hair was tucked up in a neat chignon, but her eyes were shadowed, as if she'd not slept at all.

"Good morning to you," she began. Her voice held a no-nonsense tone that reminded him of a governess. "I want to continue our journey as soon as possible."

He studied her a moment and asked, "How are you feeling?" After the wine she'd drunk last night, it wouldn't surprise him if she was feeling poorly.

"I've a headache, if you must know. But it will pass."

"You should eat," he advised her. "'Twill settle the sickness in your stomach, lass."

She winced. "No, food doesn't sound very appetizing at the moment." Steeling herself, she added, "The basket is over there. Eat what you wish, and I'll wait for you."

She went to stand by the door, and he noticed the way she closed her eyes against the light.

"Eat something before we leave," Cain ordered, "and I'll prepare the horse."

He brought their mare out from the stall, fastening the animal's bridle. He'd given the farmer payment for feed and water for the mare, but he'd been telling the truth when he'd admitted to the apothecary that they hadn't enough money to pay for the journey to Scotland.

He no longer cared. Traveling on horseback with Margaret was far more interesting.

She picked at the food while he readied the horse. "How is your back this morning? Should I put more of the salve on it?"

"You can do that at night," he said. It had been torment with her hands upon him, not only because of the pain, but also because of her proximity. He desired her deeply, and having her touch him only reminded him of what he couldn't have.

Margaret packed up the basket of supplies and straightened her posture. "I am ready to leave whenever you think it's best."

But as soon as she'd spoken the words, a cold gust of wind blew through the doorway, causing her to shiver. Cain walked past her and glanced upward. Once again, the skies were clouded with the threat of rain. She wasn't ready to leave—not dressed as she was. After all the weeks she'd spent caring for him, she needed proper traveling attire.

"No' yet," he told her. "There's something I must do first."

She started to ask questions, but he only said, "Wait here. I'll be back in a moment." He wanted to see if any of the women had a warm woolen gown they could sell. He believed there were enough coins for that.

"Are you planning to rent another horse?" She suddenly started after him. "Or ask about a coach, even?"

"Just stay here." He didn't want to spoil the gift.

"I'll go with you," Margaret insisted, walking beside him. Cain stopped immediately and turned to her.

"Nay, lass. I said to stay here, and that you'll do."

"Why? Don't you think I'd rather—"

"I don't care what it is you're wanting. You'll stay here and be surprised at what I'm hoping to give you." He'd nearly snapped at her, but honestly, the woman was far too stubborn.

She looked utterly bewildered by what he'd said. "You don't have to give me anything, Mr. Sinclair."

He took her by the shoulders and gently turned her to face the barn. "Go back and wait."

This time, she obeyed. When she risked a glance back at him, he nodded and pointed to the barn. Let her believe what she wanted. There were many days of traveling ahead of them, and she would grow colder, the farther north they rode.

He walked toward the center of the village, hoping to find someone he could ask. There was a younger woman, near Margaret's size, who agreed to sell him a simple long-sleeved gown. He sent her back with a few coins, asking her to help Margaret change, and the woman was happy to agree.

Before he could follow, he spied a landau near the edge of the houses. Now what was such a coach doing here? It was too fine a vehicle for any of the village folk, and he hastened his step to reach it.

The moment he saw Viscount Lisford's crest, he wanted to curse. Cain waited a moment to see if anyone was watching, and he quickly opened the door to the landau. No one was inside.

But Cain fully intended to find out exactly what had happened to Margaret's sister.

***

"Mrs. Sinclair?" came a young woman's voice.

Margaret turned around and saw a girl standing there, one not much older than herself. "Yes?" she answered.

"Your husband sent me to help you get dressed. He said you needed a new gown?" The young woman held out a dark green bundle of wool. Had she handed Margaret a thousand pounds, she could not have been more surprised.

She accepted the bundle and unfolded it to reveal a simple, unadorned gown that was the color of pine needles. It had long sleeves and buttoned in the front. Not the gown a lady would wear, but it was sensible enough that she could dress herself. Cheered by it, she asked, "Did he send you to help me change my gown?"

"Yes, he did," the girl said. "And when he told me you were wearing a ball gown, I knew you would not be able to undress yourself."

It wasn't entirely true. During the time she'd spent at Wickersham, she had traded with the vicar's wife for a corset she could fasten by herself. She'd worn the ball gown day and night, since there was no other choice, but at least she could breathe easier when she slept.

"Did my husband already give you enough coins to pay for it?" she asked.

"He gave me enough," the young woman said. "If you'll turn around, I'll help you change. There's also a cloak."

She unbuttoned Margaret's gown, leaving the corset and chemise while she lifted the old gown away.

The new gown was slightly loose, but Margaret hardly cared. The wool would keep her warm, and she would no longer feel so exposed at her shoulders. Last, she fastened the cloak around her, and she smiled. It didn't matter that she was dressed like a village girl—she was comfortable for the first time in days.

"Better?" the young woman asked, tucking a stray pin into her chignon.

"Much." Margaret smiled at the girl. "I'm so grateful to you. I can't even tell you how much I appreciate it."

"I was glad to help. Men don't realize how difficult it is to get dressed in a formal gown." With an answering smile, the girl departed.

Margaret tucked away the remnants of the old gown, not knowing if they could be salvaged. She waited for half an hour, and finally

Sinclair arrived. His gaze passed over her, and he nodded with approval. "I see you got the gown and cloak I sent. They aren't new, but at least you willna be cold when we travel."

She sent him a grateful smile. "Thank you, Mr. Sinclair."

Though he acknowledged her thanks by lowering his head, the look in his eyes held her motionless. His blue eyes were studying her as if he wanted so much more from her. And the dress seemed to remove another boundary between them.

She took a breath and asked, "Are you ready to go?"

He hesitated. "Nearly."

Something was wrong. She could see it in the tightness around his eyes, in his barely-contained frustration. "What is it?"

Cain crossed his arms. "There's someone here whom you've been wanting to see. Someone you've been searching for."

Margaret's heart pounded, and she hurried toward the door. "Is it Amelia? Have we found them?"

"No' exactly," Sinclair answered. "Lord Lisford is here."

Chapter Six

Having an adventure wasn't what Jonah had thought it would be. It had been several days since they'd traveled across the Highlands, moving southeast. MacKinloch had led the way, and Jonah was beginning to realize how unprepared he'd been for such a journey.

It had rained endlessly, and he couldn't remember the last time he'd been dry. Even at night when they stopped to make camp, he'd shivered beneath the tent MacKinloch had set up.

"Have ye changed your mind about going to London?" the man asked. "If ye'd rather turn back, just follow the road back toward Ballaloch."

Jonah wanted to. His feet were covered in blisters from his thin-soled shoes, and he was hungrier than he could remember. After several days of searching, he'd not found any of Cain's money. He'd searched everywhere, even digging near some standing stones, but he'd found nothing at all. He'd given MacKinloch the only thing of value he owned—a pistol that had belonged to his father. Cain would be furious when he learned of it, but Jonah supposed he could buy it back.

"Well, lad?" MacKinloch prodded.

"I'll keep going." He wanted to prove to himself that he was as strong as his brother. Why, if he could make this journey once, he could go back again. And perhaps he could get work delivering things between England and Scotland, like his brother. He wanted people to look up to him, the way they respected Cain.

"'Twill take a fortnight at least," MacKinloch told him. "Longer, until we can get horses." His gaze narrowed upon Jonah. "Are ye certain your brother had no coins in safekeeping? How was he expecting ye to pay for aught?"

Jonah said nothing about the few coins he'd saved. He might need them in case MacKinloch abandoned him.

"Cain left me food," he told the man. "And he said I wouldna need anything else." Which was true, since he had potatoes and grain for gruel. He caught fish in the loch, and sometimes he traded them for bread or stew. Mrs. Larson had brought him a pudding on a rare occasion, but mostly if he wanted something, he had to steal it.

He'd stolen a lot from Lord Strathland over the years. His friends had showed him how to slip inside the large manor house and take food or small valuables no one would miss. A pair of shoes or a linen handkerchief. Things an earl wouldn't notice.

His stomach had twisted with guilt, but after a time, he'd dulled himself to it. Because of the earl, he and his brother had lost their home. Lord Strathland had also been merciless to their friends and neighbors, using his influence with the authorities to bring down anyone who opposed him.

Paul Fraser was Cain's best friend, and he loathed the earl more than anyone. Not only because Strathland had ordered his father's hanging, but also because the man had held an interest in Juliette Andrews, the woman Fraser had loved for years. It was Cain who had stopped Fraser from killing the man.

Jonah had sometimes stayed up late, eavesdropping on them at night.

"He has his eye on Juliette. I swear to God, if Strathland dares to bother her, I'll—"

"Juliette doesna like him," Cain had said. *"You've naught to fear, Fraser."*

But something *had* happened to Juliette Andrews, though Jonah had never learned what it was. Cain had spent several nights drinking heavily. The shadow of the earl's deeds hung over all of them, even though the man was now locked away in an asylum.

No one had forgotten the death and madness. Jonah shivered at the thought. And now he was on his way to London, where the earl happened to be locked away.

He trudged behind MacKinloch, feeling as if his legs were going to drop off at any moment. He took a drink from his flask of water and reminded himself that this was his way out of Ballaloch. Even if his feet were raw and bloody in another day or two, it was better than the alternative.

"We'll have to find a horse and a wagon," the Highlander said. "Your brother will owe me for yer share, once we reach London."

"I've given you the pistol," Jonah said. "That should be enough."

"The pistol's no' worth the cost of taking ye with me. I'll be needing more." Again, the threatening tone in MacKinloch's voice made Jonah uneasy. He wouldn't abandon him out here alone, would he?

"My brother will pay you," Jonah promised, though it wasn't true at all. He didn't actually know *where* Cain was, but by the time MacKinloch learned the truth, he hoped it would be too late. There were a thousand places he could disappear to, in the middle of the city.

"What will you do when you reach London?" Jonah asked. The Highlander had dwelled in Ballaloch for many years, until his sister had died. No one would tell him what had happened to the girl, but Jonah knew Strathland had been involved somehow. It was why MacKinloch loathed the earl.

"Well, lad, there's someone I've been meaning to visit," he said.

"Family?" Jonah ventured.

But the man's eyes held a dangerous glint. "Nay, I've no family left."

"My parents are dead, too," Jonah offered, though of course MacKinloch already knew that. "They drowned." He hardly remembered what had happened that day, for the memory was blurred, almost as if it had happened to someone else. And yet, he offered the remark, hoping that MacKinloch would tell him more of his plans. "Who will you visit?"

The man remained silent, but his hand moved to the pistol he'd taken from Jonah. "Don't be worried about that, lad. I won't be leaving ye alone until we've found Cain."

Perhaps that was meant to make him feel better, but it would be worse for him if they actually *did* find his older brother. Cain treated him as if he were four instead of four-and-ten. But all of it would change, once he began earning money for himself.

Jonah would steal again, if he had to. His fingers were light, and it couldn't be that difficult to cut a reticule from a rich woman or lift valuables from a waistcoat. If he couldn't find work, he'd do what he had to in order to survive.

But his stomach churned at the thought. Unbidden came the sudden image of his mother's face, her eyes staring at him with disapproval.

She won't ever ken what you're doing, he told himself.

And yet, he couldn't let go of the sense that he was traveling down a path from which there was no return. He was torn by the thought of his brother finding him.

Or worse, if he didn't see Cain again.

Margaret had never considered herself a violent sort. Yet, the moment she set eyes upon Lord Lisford, her temper erupted. He deserved to bleed for what he'd done to Amelia. Heedless of her long skirts, she barreled forward until she crashed into him.

"I say, what—" His words broke off when he saw her. The moment he recognized her face, the viscount went deathly white.

Good. He had many reasons to be afraid, the least of which was being beaten senseless by Cain. That is, if she didn't wallop him first.

It didn't seem that Cain was going to let her, for he'd emerged from the stable and was approaching both of them. "Are you wanting my assistance, lass?"

"Only if this blackguard tries to run." Margaret gripped Lisford with her left hand to prevent him from going anywhere. Her right arm was throbbing from when she'd collided with him. "Where is my sister?"

The viscount cleared his throat. "Sh-she's in London." He risked a glance at Cain, who had cut off his escape from the opposite side.

Lisford tried to extricate himself from her grasp, but Margaret hung on. He wasn't going anywhere—not until she knew precisely what had happened. And if he was alone this close to Scotland, it was possible that he'd gotten away with his misdeeds.

Not anymore. Her hand curled into a fist, and she struck him hard across his nose. Lisford winced with pain, and Margaret felt a primal sense of satisfaction.

"What did you do that for?" he demanded, raising his hands to fend her off.

Was he that daft?

"For stealing Amelia away in the middle of the night and trying to ruin her." Never before had Margaret felt such a rage. Not only because of what he'd done to her sister, but also for the way he'd left her behind only days before her wedding. Thank goodness she hadn't married him.

"I ought to cut your heart out with a spoon," Margaret said to Lisford. "You deserve far more than a broken nose." He was a man who took advantage of innocent women, and he ought to be hung, drawn, and quartered for what he'd done to Amelia and herself.

Cain's shoulders were shaking, and she strongly suspected he was laughing at her. Laughing! How did he dare?

With great effort, she forced herself to lower her fists. "Let us begin again," she said, trying to feign a calmness she didn't feel. "I want to know exactly what happened that night."

"I've no wish to harm a lady, Miss Andrews. But I must ask that you back away and let go of me." Lisford's voice was steady, despite the blood trickling from his nose.

"Not until I know what you've done with my sister." She gripped his cravat with one hand, to prevent him from leaving.

"She is safe. I promise you that." He wiped his nose with a handkerchief.

"And how do I know you're telling the truth?" Margaret demanded. "You tried to ruin her with your idiotic scheme to marry her. My sweet sister, who never did anything wrong."

He tried to step back, but Sinclair crossed his arms as if to assure her that the viscount was going nowhere. "Go on, then, Lisford. I'd like to be hearing what you have to say about this." The Highlander gestured for him to continue.

"I thought she would see it as a grand romantic gesture," the viscount confessed. "I was wrong, and she's now safely back with her family, I assume."

"You assume?"

"Lord Castledon took her back." His face reddened, and he

winced at his swollen nose. "I, ah, was asked to spend time away from London. I have a country estate not far from here."

Margaret frowned. "I thought your estate was in Wales."

He faltered again. "It was. I mean, it is. There's another property that requires my attention. It's . . . well, it's in need of some work." His gaze passed back to Mr. Sinclair. "What brings you north with *him?*"

"I thought I'd bring him along to kill you when we found Amelia," Margaret lied. She curled her left hand into a fist. "That could still be arranged."

Lisford's face was the color of chalk, and she added, "How do I know she isn't still with you?"

"She isn't. I swear to you both, I let her go." The viscount wiped again at his bleeding nose with a handkerchief. "I knew she wouldn't come with me willingly, but I thought she would change her mind once she realized how badly I wanted to wed her. I thought she would love the adventure of an elopement."

Fury boiled inside her as Margaret confronted the man. "You never deserved a woman like Amelia."

He didn't deny it, but he said only, "It was a misunderstanding. And I, ah, won't be visiting London for some time."

"You're despicable," Margaret told him. "I hope to never lay eyes on you again, after what you did to me. Us," she amended. For so long, she had suppressed her anger, telling herself that to unleash it would not change anything. She had tried to begin again, but the truth was, no gentlemen were interested in her after that. They assumed that if Lisford had cried off, she was somehow to blame. And oh, it was impossible to swallow.

Years of dark anger came roaring out. "I wish I'd never agreed to marry you."

The viscount tugged at his cravat. "Our betrothal was never real. Surely you knew that." He looked embarrassed and cast a look back at Sinclair. "It was nothing but a wager, and I'm only sorry I let it go too far."

"Because of you, no man wanted to marry me." Margaret glared at him. "My good name was ruined, though I never did anything wrong."

"No," the viscount said softly. "You pushed anyone else away. It was your own bitterness that caused men to avoid you." He took a step backward, and his silent retribution struck her down. "And now, you've brought on your own ruin, by traveling with this lout."

Margaret stood motionless, for there was truth in his words. Even so, she would not allow him to speak against Cain. "This 'lout,' as you call him, is a trusted friend. He protected me on my journey. And if you'll recall, last month he defeated you in a boxing match."

Lord Lisford acted as if she hadn't spoken, though she knew he well remembered his swift defeat. He had wagered that he would win the fight, and Cain had volunteered to be his opponent.

The Highlander had beaten him into the ground. And he'd done it for her.

She met Cain's gaze, and his narrowed expression toward the viscount suggested that he would gladly fight again.

But Lord Lisford was already backing away. "I should be going now. Be assured, I will not trouble your sister or your family any longer. I intend to continue my travels." The viscount bowed and hastily made a departure.

Before he could leave, Cain caught him by the arm. He gripped the man hard, reminding him that his strength was far greater. "If you're no' telling the truth, I will hunt you down. You'll wear your entrails as a necklace, Lisford."

Though it was a gruesome prospect, Margaret couldn't help but be grateful to Cain for intimidating the man. But it startled her when he continued. "I think you should be apologizing to Miss Andrews," he said. "No' only for what you did to her sister, but also to her."

Lisford hesitated and took another step backward. There was more fear on his face than regret, but he did relent, saying, "My apologies, Miss Andrews." Eyeing Sinclair, he added, "I suppose you'll be happier having a man to reform than one who is already respectable. And the ton will be surprised at your choice."

His words felt like a blow to the stomach. She knew that her decision to find Amelia would have repercussions, but she hadn't considered that Lord Lisford would spread rumors and idle gossip. She should have known better—he would do anything to bring attention to himself, even if that meant bringing her down even further.

Sinclair's fist struck the viscount hard across the jaw, and the man crumpled. Lisford's hands curled against the mud, and he remained on his knees.

"Don't say a word against her." The Highlander withdrew the dirk from his waist and jerked the man up, pressing the blade to the viscount's chin. "If I cut out your tongue, you willna be able to spread lies about Miss Andrews. 'Twould no' be hard."

"Please," the man whispered. He was trembling violently, and from the dark look on Sinclair's face, Margaret wondered if he was considering it. Her own thirst for blood had abated, and she didn't doubt that Lisford was terrified of the Highlander.

"Please what?" Cain taunted. "Please cut out your tongue to prevent you from speaking? Or did you mean that you'll ne'er speak a single word against Miss Andrews or any of her family?"

"Yes," the viscount blurted out. "I won't talk. I promise. Ever."

Sinclair turned back to her, as if waiting for an answer. There was no trace of mercy in his eyes, and for the first time, she wondered precisely what the man was capable of. He appeared furious with the viscount. "I could nick the tip of his tongue, as a reminder, if you think that would help, Miss Andrews."

No, she wouldn't go that far. "Let him go, Mr. Sinclair. I don't think he'll bother us again."

He kept the knife close to the viscount's mouth. "Oh, I'll be letting him go. But know this, Lisford—" He jerked the man's head backward. "If you do anything foolish, I'll ken what you've done. And you'll regret it."

He pulled back the knife, and Margaret breathed a sigh of relief. It was then that she noticed a small group of people had gathered around. They appeared uneasy by what they'd witnessed. "Go," Cain ordered. To Margaret he added, "Gather your things. We're leaving now."

Margaret didn't argue, but retreated into the stable. She'd never seen this side to him, so cold-blooded and violent.

But oh, it felt good to have her vengeance against Lisford. Her fist was sore, but she'd never felt such a rush of satisfaction, punching a man. It was unladylike . . . and glorious.

When he returned, Cain spoke not a word to her but seized the mare by the reins and lifted Margaret onto the horse. There was tension in every part of him, in the way he swung up behind her, and in the way he gripped her waist. He urged their mount onward, taking them north.

They rode swiftly, and Margaret leaned back into him. Her mind was spinning off with both exhilaration and worry. She ought to be ashamed of herself and feel awful about the way others would gossip about her misdeeds.

And yet, she couldn't quite be sorry for it. She had faced that horrid worm of a man and now she understood why men fought. There was something quite satisfying about facing one's nemesis and bringing him down.

True, she still had to be concerned about what everyone would say about her being alone with Cain Sinclair all these weeks. But strangely, it was too easy to put the matter aside and let it be for now. She would handle those consequences later.

She murmured to Sinclair, "Thank you for allowing me to face Lisford. I know it's inappropriate, but I rather enjoyed hitting him." She smiled at him, feeling her mood strangely lightened by the violence. Beneath her, the skirts were twisted, and she attempted to straighten them. Her hands brushed against Cain's inner thighs, and he jolted at the touch.

"Easy, lass."

"I'm sorry." But she was in such a jubilant mood, she hardly cared. "On days like today, I envy you. Men have so much freedom. You never have to obey rules about proper behavior, and if you're angry, you can tear a man apart."

She waited for him to agree with her, but instead, Cain said, "Women have power too, lass. In their own way."

She didn't believe that. "Hardly. From the moment I was born, my mother taught me how to speak, how to dress. I was expected to marry a lord and be a respectable wife. There were hardly any choices at all for me. And you saw how it turned out with Lisford." She shuddered. "What a horrible, cowardly man he was."

"But you agreed to marry him when he asked you," he pointed out.

She heard the edge of anger in his voice, and decided to tread carefully. "That was years ago. I made a mistake and didn't see him for who he was."

"You saw his title and his wealth, and that was enough for you."

The words wounded her, for it made her sound terribly selfish, when that wasn't it at all.

"That's not entirely true," she said, feeling her good mood dissipating. "I thought he was handsome and kind. I believed we could have made a good match between us." She'd been trying to be the obedient daughter, marrying a man of whom her parents would approve and one who had seemed like the perfect gentleman. But . . . some of what Cain had said was right. She wouldn't have considered Lisford, if he had lacked the qualifications she'd been seeking. And perhaps that *did* make her deserve the humiliation.

"Did he ever kiss you?"

She didn't understand where this was leading, but she grew more conscious of the tension in Sinclair's arms. It was as if she were sitting in front of a block of stone. Something was bothering him. "No, he only kissed my hand."

Whereas she had kissed Cain on several occasions. He'd taken apart all her rules and shattered all semblance of propriety. She liked kissing him far too much.

She suddenly grew aware of his hardened body surrounding her. The heat of his thighs pressed against her own legs, and he held the reins with his arms against her shoulders. "You're angry with me for saying yes to Lisford, aren't you?"

"He wasna worth the ground you walk upon."

She grew motionless at that, not realizing that he'd seen it that way. Her choice of Lisford had never been right, but now, she was glad that the viscount had cried off. What a mistake that would have been, to marry such a wastrel. She never could have endured years of marriage to a man who gambled constantly and who had no sense of honor.

Margaret rested her hands upon Cain's legs, snuggling in. It felt comforting to be this close to him. The rhythm of the horse's pace could easily put her to sleep.

But then she grew conscious that he was deeply aroused by her proximity. She'd been startled the first time it had happened, and she knew she ought to move forward in the saddle to prevent their bodies from touching.

Yet strangely, this time she wasn't quite as shocked by the feeling of his body pressed to hers. Instead, she felt herself responding to him. As the horse walked, the movement bumped her backside against him, and she heard him let out a quiet curse.

But she kept her hands where they were. His thighs were iron-hard muscles, as were his arms. He was so strong, so bold. She closed her eyes, remembering what it was like when he'd lifted her into his bed, whispering wicked words of what he wanted to do to her.

She ran her hands gently over his legs, from thigh to knee, feeling the rough plaid between them. Her own boldness surprised her, but he made no move to stop her. Instead, he took the reins in his left hand and used his right arm to pull her closer. His palm rested beneath her breast, as if asking a silent question.

He leaned in to murmur in her ear. "Touch me again, lass, and I willna be responsible for the way I'm touching you in return."

A shiver rocked through her, along with the desire to allow it. The good girl, Margaret Andrews, would never ever do such a thing. She would slap his hand away with her fan and tell him to stop.

But then again, she'd just punched a man in the nose. Breaking the rules had felt so good, so liberating. What harm could there be in experiencing a simple touch? Cain would never hurt her.

Tentatively, she stroked his leg with her palm, leaning back as she did. In answer, his hand moved to her breast, caressing her nipple.

You were warned, she could imagine him saying.

Unexpected sensations slammed into her. The dark, delicious pleasure ached as he tempted her with his hand, bringing her dormant feelings to life. Between her legs, she felt an answering echo, and her fingers dug into his thigh. The moment her hand stopped touching him, he, too, stopped his caress.

God help her, she wanted him to continue.

Once again, she ran her hands over his legs, using her fingers to stroke his muscled thighs. He answered by gently pinching her nipple, his wicked fingers stroking her pliant flesh.

She didn't know what had come over her. It was as if the chains of propriety had suddenly broken, bringing rebellion in their place. Or perhaps it was because her time with Cain was growing short. Soon, she had to return to her old life, and she didn't know where he fit in.

A hushed moan broke forth from her, and abruptly, Cain drew the horse to a halt in the middle of a field. He swung down and lifted her off the mare.

"Why have we stopped?" she asked. Her cheeks reddened, and beneath her gown, her breasts were tight.

"You ken exactly why we stopped, lass." He drew her hips to his and kissed her hard, claiming her like a starving man. Heat and desire poured over her, turning her knees weak. She'd never imagined she would push him over the edge by touching him. He was devouring her, his hands moving down her spine and clasping her hips.

And she realized exactly why women would give in to temptation.

"Wait," she tried to interrupt, using her palms to push him back. "I-I don't think we should do this."

He tipped her chin up, and in his blue eyes, she saw a need so great, it staggered her. "I told you what would happen if you touched me, lass." His hands remained locked around her waist, and she could feel the length of his erection pressed against her skirts.

He brought his mouth to her throat, and his warm breath sent shivers through her. "I'm no' a gentleman like Lisford. When you offer, I take."

"I didn't offer my innocence," she whispered back. It had been curiosity and an unexpected desire to feel his body. She should have known better than to cross that boundary.

Every part of him was strung tightly, but he didn't let go of her. "You ken what you do to me, lass. You drive me to madness with any touch at all."

"I'm sorry," she said. "I won't do it again."

The darkness in his gaze was enigmatic. She knew he wouldn't harm her, but neither would he let her go. Her breathing was ragged, and she wished she could go back and undo her actions.

And yet, she didn't regret the way he'd made her feel. It was as if he was transforming her, stripping away her white gloves and drawing her down into delicious decadence.

"You can touch me any time you want, lass. But you must ken that there's a price for it." He ran his thumb along the edge of her jaw in a silken caress.

"And what price is that?"

He stripped her gloved hand, placing it against his cheek. His breath warmed her palm. "Temptation, lass. And that is a verra big problem for both of us."

Cain saw the worry in her eyes, but he wanted her to understand that she was playing with fire. Despite her being cloaked from throat to ankle, he craved her. With each day he spent at her side, he wanted her more, and he didn't trust himself to leave her untouched. From the moment she'd touched him openly, it had taken apart his good sense.

He lifted her onto the mare and took the reins, walking beside her. The physical distance was necessary to regain control.

"You don't have to walk," she said. "If you do, we won't reach Scotland by nightfall."

"We won't reach Scotland by nightfall if I ride, either," he said, though she wouldn't understand. He glanced up at her while keeping pace with the mare. With a dark smile, he asked, "Exactly how much control do you think I have, lass?"

She sent him a wry look. "I should have brought my fan to rap your knuckles. Or perhaps you could find a stick. I could poke it in your ribs if that would help."

"It might." He signaled the horse to go faster, running alongside the mare. Although he didn't speak to Margaret, the exercise helped to clear his head.

Soon enough, she reached out her hand to him, concern upon her face. "You shouldn't be running so hard. You're still recovering from the burn wounds."

Aye, he knew that. But he'd not expected her to voice worry for him, especially now. The understanding moved beneath his repressed desire, and he realized that here, in the wilderness, there was only the two of them. She had to rely upon him for survival, and in this place, he had an advantage.

Cain reached up and squeezed her palm in answer. Margaret pulled back on the reins, and he stood a moment to catch his breath. On the ground at his feet, he spied a small twig, and he handed it to her. "You might need this, lass."

She held it out like a dagger when he swung up behind her. "Don't try to touch me, or I'll jab you." But there was a smile on her face.

Cain kept one arm around her waist and urged the animal faster. He changed the direction of their path, leaving behind the road and taking them across the meadow. If they rode westward, they would reach the main road and one of the coaching inns by nightfall. It was their best hope for shelter.

"Where are we going?" she asked. "This doesn't look like the right way."

"We're no' going to Falsham," he told her. "I've decided we'll go to Ballaloch instead."

She stiffened against him. "And just what gave you the right to make that decision? I want to stay with my sister. Why would I want to go all the way to the western Highlands?"

Because he wasn't ready to let her go yet. If he took her to Falsham, he suspected he'd never see her again. And he couldn't let himself grasp that reality. He had a true chance of winning her heart while they were alone. Whether or not she knew it, Margaret had sealed her own fate by touching him. It was the first time she'd ever initiated a caress, in all these years. If a beautiful woman showed interest in him, he'd be daft to leave her behind.

"My brother has been alone for many weeks," he told her. "I went along with your wishes, but now that Amelia is safe, you're going to follow mine."

She stared back at him in disbelief. "What makes you believe that I'll listen to your dictates?"

"Because you don't know the way," he said. "And I do."

"Why are you doing this?" Her face grew indignant. "I thought you were going to protect me and escort me back."

"And that I'll do, lass. But my brother's well-being has importance, too. And it's my turn to make decisions."

For nearly an hour, she kept silent, holding her posture erect, trying to maintain distance between them. Her anger was palpable, but he supposed she'd get over it soon enough.

He kept his arm around her waist, but she was trying to avoid touching him. It made the journey easier, not having her backside rub up against him. Even so, her presence was alluring. He remembered, too well, the scent of her hair, the touch of her lips.

In the late afternoon, he stopped near a stream to let the horse drink. He brought her a bit of leftover food, but Margaret only picked at the bread. Her thoughts seemed troubled, and she said at last, "Where will we stay tonight?"

"I'll find a coaching inn." It shouldn't be too far now, he guessed.

"We are *not* sharing a bed," she reminded him.

"If that's what you're wanting." He finished his own food and reached down to drink from the stream. "But you ken that I willna harm you, lass."

"I do know that," she admitted. "But I wish you weren't trying to tell me what to do. If you'd wanted to go to Ballaloch that badly, you could have asked me. I am not an unreasonable woman."

"Admit it, lass. You were wanting to be rid of me sooner, and that's why you wanted to go to Falsham."

She let out a breath and shook her head. "I wanted to go to Falsham, because I'll have a little more freedom before my parents come to shut me away."

"You'll have far more freedom with me," he pointed out.

She leveled a gaze at him. "Hardly. Your idea of freedom is telling me that I may eat bread or cheese. If I'm lucky, perhaps you might let me choose whether to ride in front of you or behind you."

He didn't argue with her. "I prefer in front. That way, I can hold you, lass."

A pained expression crossed her face. "I made a mistake when I touched you earlier. It was idle curiosity, and I am very sorry for it."

"I'm no' sorry at all." Cain walked back to her, sliding his hands around her waist. He drew her close, his hands resting on her hips.

"But if everyone believes you're ruined, lass, you might as well do it properly."

He said it in teasing, but the troubled look didn't leave her face. "No. That's not what I want at all."

Cain pulled a pin from her hair, and a long blond lock tumbled to her shoulders. Though he had no intention of forcing her to do anything against her will, he wanted her to know what it would be like if they were together. "Whate'er we do in this next week is between us, Margaret." He didn't want to think about afterward.

"I know what you're offering me. But I can't," she whispered. "I may have ruined my reputation and everything else. But inside, there's a part of me that doesn't want to be what everyone else thinks I am. I don't want to hold regrets for a moment's pleasure."

His hands slid into her soft hair. "It would be a great deal longer than a moment, lass." He nipped at her lower lip, adding, "I could spend all night touching you." He couldn't let go of the thought of lying beside her, of seeing her tousled hair in the morning.

"But you won't." She raised a hand to hold him back and returned to the horse. "Keep your hands to yourself, Mr. Sinclair."

Her glare warned that she meant every word. He'd overstepped, pushing her too far too soon. "It was an invitation, no' a demand, lass."

But he should have known better. She wasn't about to throw away twenty-five years of proper behavior. Without asking, he lifted her back on the horse and took the reins.

Instead of riding with her, he began walking beside the mare, leading it through the meadow, as he'd done before. Margaret had fallen quiet, but she soon relented. "Both of us know that you can't walk to the inn. Ride behind me, if you must, else we won't reach shelter before dark."

Cain swung up onto the mare and increased the pace. "As you will."

Some of the landmarks had changed since he'd gone this way in the past. He kept the setting sun in front of him, knowing it would lead him to the western roads. But he'd expected to come through one of the smaller villages by now.

A suspicion took root that perhaps they'd gone farther north than he'd thought. If that was true, then they could not reach the coaching inn by nightfall. But he would not say anything to Margaret, since he didn't want her to believe that they were lost. That couldn't be true—he knew this region well.

But when the sun crept steadily lower, she asked, "Where are we, Cain?"

"I ken where I'm going. Or have you forgotten how many times I delivered garments for you and your sisters?"

"No, I haven't. But you haven't answered my question."

And that was because he wasn't entirely certain. There ought to be a river running parallel to the road, but he'd not seen it. If that was so, then there was only one remaining alternative where they could spend the night—at a large manor house only a few miles from the border of Scotland.

"We'll be there soon," he lied. To change the subject, he asked, "Have you chosen a man to replace me and make the deliveries for Aphrodite's Unmentionables?"

"Not yet. You were the one man we trusted to keep our secret." She leaned back against him as they rode.

Inwardly, Cain wondered if Margaret had ever worn such sinful unmentionables. Over the years, she'd tried repeatedly to convince her sisters to give up the business. Yet, it was a hard fact that the money they'd earned was enough to transform their lives.

It had changed his, as well. He'd put aside money of his own, though even after saving for four years, it would never be enough for what he wanted. He was chasing an impossible dream, of having a good home and giving Jonah the life he'd never had.

The sun rimmed the edge of the horizon with rose and gold, sinking steadily lower. In time, Margaret turned to him.

"We're not going to reach the inn tonight, are we?" Within her voice, he heard the uneasiness.

"No. Perhaps in the morning."

She turned slightly in the saddle. "I was afraid of that. What will we do, if we have no shelter?"

"I'll find something." Though he wasn't certain if they would reach the manor house in time, it was the best hope they had.

Chapter Seven

Being so close to Cain Sinclair was unsettling. There was a caged power in him, of a man who was restless and tense. He wanted more from her, and his very words had slid beneath her defenses, making her desire him. But Margaret knew better than to give in to temptation. It would only bring about greater problems.

By dusk, there was no village in sight. She was beginning to wonder what Sinclair intended to do—set up a place for them beneath a tree?

"Where will we stop?" she asked.

His grip tightened upon the reins. "If I havena found what I'm searching for, then when we reach the next stream, we'll make camp."

"And what is it you're searching for?"

He didn't answer but kept moving the horse at a steady trot. She doubted if he would find anything at all, but to her surprise, he drew the horse to a stop at the top of a hill. "I was looking for *that,* lass."

Below them was a manor house larger than the stone house her parents owned in Ballaloch. From the size of the dwelling, there was no question that it belonged to a nobleman and his family. A sudden tightness clenched in her throat at the sight of the residence. "Was that where you thought we could stay?"

"Aye. Perhaps in the stable or among the servants."

She hesitated. "No, we could do better than that." The thought of sleeping in a warm bed with a hot brick at her feet was entirely too tempting. If she presented herself as a lady traveling with her cousin, it might be that the family would allow them to stay inside the house. Perhaps the gentleman might even be acquainted with her father. She could only hope that he would overlook her common gown and appearance, recognizing her breeding.

Margaret touched her hair and ensured that every last pin was in place. "We're going to knock at the front door and ask to pay a call upon the lord who owns this estate."

"And if he's no' there?"

"There are lights ahead," Margaret reminded him. "The servants would not light the main rooms if no one was there." She squared her shoulders. "After we knock at the door, let me speak to them. Do not say a word, I beg of you. If they learn you're a Scot—"

"They'll throw us out," he finished. "Or worse."

"Yes, well, if you can imitate an Englishman, it would be to your benefit."

"I'm wearing a kilt and plaid," he pointed out. "It's no' as if my clothes help matters. They'll ken who I am."

He was right about that. Thinking for a moment, she said, "I suppose you have no choice, then. I'll say that you're related to the Viscount of Falsham. With any luck, they won't know any differently."

"It's no' a bad idea," he admitted.

Margaret could only hope so. Paul Fraser was a Scottish viscount, and his estate was south of Edinburgh. The nobleman who lived here might believe they were related.

They continued down the hillside until they reached the gravel driveway. Cain helped her to dismount, and Margaret steeled herself against what lay ahead. She knew how to present herself, how to play this role. She could only hope that whoever resided here would take pity upon them and grant them shelter for the night.

With her heart pounding, she strode up to the front door, beckoning Sinclair to stand behind her. She rapped the brass knocker and waited, silently praying that they would find what they sought.

A thin older man answered the door, and his expression revealed surprise. "We were not expecting guests at this hour. May I inquire as to who you are and why you are here?"

"I am Margaret Andrews, daughter of Baron Lanfordshire," Margaret began. "My cousin and I were traveling to Ballaloch. However, our coach overturned and my maid died in the accident." She lowered her gaze, trying to keep to the truth as much as possible, though some lies were unavoidable—an imaginary maid among them. "We were hoping to seek shelter for the night, until we can travel to a coaching inn on the morrow."

"Your father is Colonel Lord Lanfordshire, I believe," came a man's voice. Margaret glanced behind the footman and saw a tall gentleman approaching. His dark blond hair held a streak of gray, and his eyes were a warm brown. He sent her a kindly smile. "I am Lewis Barnabas, of Hempshire."

The name sounded somewhat familiar, but she couldn't place it. The man was older than herself, and he had strong features. Though he wasn't handsome, Margaret couldn't quite stop staring at him.

Suddenly, she managed to recall her manners, and she curtsied slightly. "I am pleased to meet you, sir. My father is Henry Andrews, Lord Lanfordshire. And yes, he did serve in the army during the war."

"I don't travel to London often, but I've had the pleasure of meeting him. Your sister is the Duchess of Worthingstone, I believe."

"She is, indeed." Margaret breathed a sigh of relief that the man did seem acquainted with her family.

"But I have not had the pleasure of meeting you, as of yet, Miss Andrews." His eyes gleamed, and her attention went directly to the man's mouth. She found herself comparing his clean-shaven face with Cain Sinclair's beard stubble. The two men were opposite sides of a coin, dark and light.

Mr. Barnabas reached out his hand, and Margaret placed her left palm in his. He raised her hand to that mouth, and she felt her cheeks flush.

"I've no' had the *pleasure* of meeting you, either," came Sinclair's voice from behind her. His brogue had thickened, and when he held out his hand, there was a warning in his eyes. "I am Cain Sinclair."

Though his words were polite, Margaret knew full well that he didn't like Mr. Barnabas. The threat in his expression was unmistakable.

"You are both welcome in my house," Mr. Barnabas said. He added, "And I am glad that Miss Andrews has a cousin to look after her. A woman of her beauty could fall into danger without someone to protect her."

Margaret was taken aback by his words. He thought her beautiful? Even at the age of five-and-twenty? Instinct warned that this man possessed a golden tongue and was speaking the words she wanted to hear, rather like Lord Lisford. Even so, she wished for a moment that she was still wearing the green silk, despite how impractical it was.

"Will we be meeting Mrs. Barnabas?" Cain asked pointedly.

"There is, regrettably, no Mrs. Barnabas." He smiled at Margaret, his gaze lingering enough to make her look away. "At least, not yet."

Cain's hand pressed to the small of her back in an unmistakable warning. He also insisted on keeping his coat after the footman took hers. It was almost as if he was afraid he wouldn't get it back.

"I fear we've intruded upon you at an inconvenient time," Margaret apologized.

"Not at all." Mr. Barnabas's voice was warm, disarming in the way he watched her. "Would you care for a small repast? I could have my cook prepare something for you."

Margaret was about to decline, for it was yet another way to trouble their host. But before she could reply, Cain interjected, "Aye, that would be lovely."

Lovely? He'd never spoken such a word for as long as she'd known him. She strongly suspected he was mocking Mr. Barnabas or even herself. But when she turned to him, his expression was shielded. Something had him on edge, and she couldn't tell if it was wariness of their host or jealousy.

"I'll have my groom see to your horse," Mr. Barnabas offered. "In the meantime, follow me into the dining room, and you can tell me more about what happened."

He led the way, but before Margaret could follow, Cain said, "Keep up your guard, lass. Something is wrong in this place."

"Mr. Barnabas has been nothing but polite," she whispered, hastening her step. She couldn't think of what he'd possibly noticed that could be wrong. They'd been granted shelter by a gentleman, and she'd caught nothing untoward in their interaction.

"He has his eye upon you."

That was what this was about. He didn't like the thought of any man being kind to her or paying attention. Margaret relaxed somewhat, for she could easily handle this situation.

"What if he does?" She shrugged, giving it little importance. "Am I not permitted to speak with a respectable man?"

She was baiting him and knew it. For Heaven's sake, they were only staying a single night. After this, it was doubtful she'd see the gentleman again. And once he learned about her scandalous past, that would be the end of that.

Sinclair stiffened at her words, but leaned in to her ear. "Have a care, Margaret. I'm no' going to leave you alone with him."

Now that was going too far. It wasn't as if Mr. Barnabas had any intention of accosting her. Whether it was jealousy speaking or whether Sinclair genuinely had a reason to doubt the gentleman, Margaret couldn't say. But his domineering behavior was back, and she wasn't about to let him tell her what to do. Rather than argue, she quickened her step until she caught up with their host.

The dining room boasted a mahogany table that would seat ten. Two silver candelabras rested on each end, and the Oriental rug was thick beneath her shoes. Before Mr. Barnabas could do so, Cain chose a chair and pulled it out for her. She accepted the seat, and Mr. Barnabas sat to her left. Sinclair sat across from her, no doubt so he could kick her beneath the table.

Margaret tucked both legs beneath her chair, just to be safe.

"Tell me how I can be of help to you," their host urged. "I could lend you my coach in the morning to take you to the next coaching inn."

Though she wanted to thank him and agree that yes, she did want to borrow the vehicle, she caught a sudden frown on Sinclair's face. His mouth was set in a firm line, his eyes holding a dark anger. Honestly, this was going too far.

"I would be most grateful to you for your assistance, Mr. Barnabas. My father will recompense you for any expenses or perhaps, I could—"

But the gentleman was already shaking his head. "No, it would be my pleasure to help a stranded lady in distress." He sent her a smile, but beneath it, she detected a note of insincerity. It was the proper answer to give, but did he mean it?

She studied him more closely, trying to understand what it was that Cain Sinclair saw. The dining room was lovely and inviting, with flowers on the side buffet, and the footman stood at the far end of the room, his posture immaculate.

Perhaps that was it. Everything was *too* perfect.

She studied the silverware and the china pattern. Every plate was turned so that the bird pattern was facing in the correct direction, and there was nothing out of place. Not a single crumb marred the surface of the tablecloth. Which was as it should be. It demonstrated an attention to detail that many servants lacked.

"We can talk about our journey in the morning," Cain said. "You should eat something, lass, and rest."

The butler, whom they learned was John Merrill, poured wine for them, while a footman served them a thick vegetable soup. Their host made conversation, telling them about how many acres of land he owned and the estates he would one day inherit. In a way, it reminded her of the Viscount Lisford—as if Lewis Barnabas was trying to impress her with the promise of a different life. Lord Lisford had invented tales of his own wealth, stories that had turned out to be false.

Not that it mattered. But Barnabas's voice did hold a trace of boasting, and it made her question why he would bother telling her this. Was he trying to gain her attention?

The second course arrived, and the footman served them roasted pheasant and creamed spinach. There was also warm bread and butter. When she glanced over at Cain, he was staring at his pheasant as if wondering how to eat it. He studied the cutlery for a moment before he met her gaze. He shot her a wicked smile, then picked up the fowl with his hands and bit into it.

Margaret wanted to groan. Mr. Barnabas eyed Sinclair as if he were a barbarian. But she strongly suspected that Cain was playing his own game. He knew he ought not to use his hands with the food. She nudged his foot beneath the table, and he responded by touching his foot to her calf.

When he ignored her silent command to use better manners, she asked, "Was there something the matter with your fork and knife, Cousin Cain?"

"Aye." He picked another piece of pheasant off the bones and demolished it. "'Twas an inconvenience."

"Please forgive my cousin's manners," Margaret apologized. "He has been living in the Highlands recently, and I fear he's falling back on bad habits."

But Cain only smiled and wiped his hands upon the tablecloth. Margaret winced and took a sip of the wine. *Look at who I am,* his eyes seemed to say. *I willna change the man I am. No' even for you.*

She sobered, tracing the stem of her wineglass. He was doing this on purpose, to remind her that he wasn't a man who followed any rules but his own.

"This is some of the best food we've had since the accident," Margaret told Mr. Barnabas, by way of changing the subject. "I am grateful for the meal."

She enjoyed every bite, savoring the delicious flavors. The pheasant was rich with a red wine sauce, and she ate slowly to enjoy the food. Mr. Barnabas was telling her more about his family and the estate, but Margaret was hardly listening. Her attention was caught by Sinclair, who was staring at her. For a moment, she couldn't think why, until she realized he was mimicking her table manners, buttering a small piece of bread with the correct knife. There was a covert smile upon his mouth.

He was indeed mocking her, there was no doubt. A man like Sinclair cared nothing for fine manners, and likely he was proving to her that he could behave himself when he wanted to. Had he ever dined at a table as fine as this one? Would he know how to manage the different pieces of silver or whether to let the footman serve him at table? But he seemed to adapt easily, making her wonder how she'd misjudged him.

"I wasn't aware that Lord Lanfordshire had a Scottish cousin," Mr. Barnabas began. "Or is it on Lady Lanfordshire's side?"

"We're distant cousins," Cain remarked. "My family lived in Edinburgh for a time."

Though Margaret knew it was a lie, there was no trace of untruth in Sinclair's voice. He spoke about the city, talking about it as if he'd been there before. He might have, for all she knew. But she found herself entranced by the lilt in his voice, while he described the clouded skies and how Edinburgh Castle stood above the rest of the city atop a hill.

"And where were you escorting Miss Andrews?" Mr. Barnabas inquired. "Back to London?"

Cain shook his head. "She has asked me to take her to Ballaloch, her father's estate in the western Highlands." The warning look in his eyes asked her not to argue. It wasn't as if she had a choice, anyhow. They both knew she could not travel on her own.

"That's quite a long distance for you," Mr. Barnabas remarked. "It might be easier to take her to your family in Edinburgh than to travel so far north."

"I'll be visiting my cousin Beatrice whilst I am there," Cain countered, with a mocking smile. "It's no trouble at all." He folded his hands across the table. "Thank you for the food, Mr. Barnabas. 'Twas quite good."

"I'll admit I am pleased that our paths crossed this night," Mr. Barnabas said. "And now that the weather is turning, I imagine you will both be glad to have shelter."

Actually, Margaret was most looking forward to clean sheets and a bed, but she nodded, suppressing a yawn. Then, too, it would be strange having a private room after she'd spent all of her nights with Cain. She'd grown accustomed to having him near, and his presence comforted her.

"I will have a maid escort you to one of the rooms, Miss Andrews," Mr. Barnabas said. "And in the morning, I look forward to having the pleasure of your company." To Cain, he added, "If you don't mind, I should like to speak with you a little more, Mr. Sinclair. We can discuss your forthcoming journey."

"As you like. But I'll be wanting a room close to my cousin's," he insisted. "For her safety."

"You will be a few doors away from her," Mr. Barnabas promised. "Now, I shall bid you a good night, Miss Andrews."

Margaret started to follow the maid but was surprised when Cain shadowed her. He glanced back at Mr. Barnabas. "I'll return, as soon as I see her to her room."

It wasn't entirely proper to leave their host like that, but she knew Cain would only cause a greater scene if she refused. They had nearly reached the stairs when he leaned in. "Don't be getting too comfortable here, lass. I saw the way he was watching you."

"Whether or not he was watching doesn't matter a whit. We're leaving in the morning."

He walked beside her, taking her hand in his. "Aye. But I don't believe he'll lend us a coach. You, perhaps, but no' me."

"After the way you ravaged your food with your hands, I shouldn't wonder."

His hand tightened over hers. "I only behaved as he thought I would, lass. There's something I'm no' liking about this man, and I want no help from him. We'll go on as we have."

Margaret freed her hand from his. "But we *need* his help, Sinclair. Aren't you weary of traveling on horseback?"

"I've done it many a time, lass."

"I'm not accustomed to such travel," she admitted. "And I would be grateful for another means of getting there." She stopped at the top of the stairs. "And whether or not you believe it, I think we should accept Mr. Barnabas's offer."

When the maid turned around, her expression was unreadable "Here is your room," she told Margaret, opening the door.

To Cain, the maid added, "I'll show you to your own place, after the master has spoken with you." She walked a short distance to the landing and waited.

Margaret stepped inside and saw that the bed was turned back and a fire glowed on the hearth. Right now, she wanted to drop into bed, snuggling beneath the coverlet until she fell into a dreamless sleep.

"Rest well, lass," Cain said. "We'll leave in the morning."

She stole another look at him, and in his deep blue eyes, she saw the look of a man who would never let anything happen to her.

ꭤ

BALLALOCH, SCOTLAND

SEVEN YEARS EARLIER

Margaret walked through the glen, her skirts brushing the edges of the damp grass. The sky was dreary, like an old woman who couldn't be bothered to smile. But it did nothing to discolor her spirits, for she was enjoying the time alone, with no one to tell her what to do. Over one arm she held a basket filled with bread for the crofters. Many were struggling to feed their families after the Earl of Strathland had increased their rents.

Behind her, a voice called, "Wait! I'm coming with you!"

She repressed the urge to sigh when she saw her youngest sister hurrying forward. Amelia was only thirteen, but she fully believed that she ought to have the same freedom as her older sisters.

A prickle of anger nudged at her, but Margaret forced it back. "It's going to rain. Are you certain you want to go?"

"And miss the chance to leave the house and hear all the village gossip?" Amelia adjusted her own basket and sent Margaret a big smile. "I cannot wait."

"What about Toria and Juliette?"

"Toria won't go, you know that. There's no reason to even ask."

Amelia's proclamation saddened her, for their oldest sister had not set foot outside the house since their arrival in Scotland three years ago. Victoria was terrified of the outdoors and all their efforts to help her had been in vain.

"As for Juliette?" Amelia linked her arm in Margaret's. "*She* is having a love affair with Paul Fraser." Her eyes widened with the thrill of a delicious secret. "I saw the letter she was writing."

"You aren't supposed to read other people's letters," Margaret reminded her. "It's rude and meddling."

"It's how I stay informed," Amelia said, not one bit repentant. "*I*, for one, think they should run away together. Juliette's seventeen. That's old enough, isn't it?"

Good Lord. Margaret shook her head and rolled her eyes. "She's far too young to marry."

"Mother was only a little older than that when she wed Father. And besides, Juliette loves Paul. Paul loves her. They're perfect together."

Amelia went on to list all the reasons why the two of them ought to elope, but Margaret heard none of it. For she understood why Juliette kept her letters a secret. All of them knew the truth—that their own family was struggling. With Father at war and Mother trying to pay the bills with money they didn't have . . . their only hope was to wed titled, wealthy gentlemen.

And considering that there was no money for them to have a Season, that hope was dwindling.

The burden fell upon Margaret's shoulders, to wed a lord with money. If she did, she could save her mother and sisters from the threat of poverty. It didn't matter whether she loved the man or not. She had the training to be an appropriate wife, and surely good manners and breeding were worth something.

Before they reached the crofters' homes on the Earl of Strathland's property, a rider approached them. Margaret shielded her eyes and saw that it was Lord Strathland himself.

"Give me your basket," Amelia said. "I'll go and deliver the food." Before Margaret could tell her no, her sister had snatched the basket and hurried over to the first house. It seemed that Amelia had no desire to speak with the earl and had seized the first opportunity to escape.

Of course. She should have known Amelia would do something like this. With a sigh, Margaret waited politely until Lord Strathland reached her side. He was an older man, a widower only a little younger than their father. He wasn't particularly tall, and his brown eyes sometimes held a hard edge. The earl was a man who expected obedience and usually got it.

But today, he smiled at her. He dismounted and tipped his hat. "Good morning, Miss Andrews."

"Good morning." Margaret returned a strained smile, wondering what it was he wanted. Though she ought to be kinder to him, the man made her feel uneasy. He might be wealthy and have a title, but she didn't like the way he treated his tenants. Raising their rents when the people were barely able to feed their children was not the mark of a charitable man. He didn't seem to care that her family was offering food and supplies to the crofters while they could barely pay their own expenses.

"I know we've been introduced before," he said, "but this is the first time I've had a moment to speak with you."

She didn't believe that at all. He could have come to call on her at any time, and she wondered what had provoked his sudden interest. "What was it you wanted to say?"

"Only that I find you quite lovely. And I wondered if you and your family might enjoy attending a supper party at my home."

Logic reminded her that he *was* a wealthy earl, exactly the sort of man whom she should appreciate. And yet, the thought was abhorrent to her. He might be affluent, but his money had come from depriving his tenants.

No, she didn't want a miser for a husband. And yet, her upbringing prevented her from responding truthfully. "You'll have to speak with my mother, Lord Strathland."

He nodded, but it didn't seem that her answer had satisfied him. "What of your wishes?" he asked softly. "Would you enjoy spending more time in my company?"

No, no, and once again, no.

But she dug deeply for an appropriate response. "I don't know what to say, my lord." And wasn't that the truth?

"Think upon it, Miss Andrews." He reached for her gloved hand and raised it to his lips. "I should enjoy seeing you and your sisters again."

I'm certain you would. Now she wished she had followed Amelia's example and fled. "Good day to you, Lord Strathland."

After he'd left, she started to walk toward the house where Amelia had disappeared, but her sister was already returning. Cain Sinclair strode alongside her, and it was clear that he'd seen Lord Strathland kissing her hand.

Something about the intense expression on his face made her pulse quicken. She tried to steady herself, but a blush rose to her cheeks.

"Is Lord Strathland finished with his conversation?" Amelia whispered loudly, staring back at the departing earl.

"Yes, he is." Margaret tried to behave as if nothing were amiss, but her wayward heart was beating all too fast.

"Thank goodness. When I saw him, I thought I should fetch Mr. Sinclair," Amelia explained. "I knew *he* could defend us."

The innocent look in her sister's eyes was an act, Margaret knew. Heaven help her, but it appeared that Amelia was matchmaking again.

"Aye, that's true," Sinclair answered with a smile. He wore a brown-and-green kilt and plaid like the other crofters, but there was a restless energy about him, as if he were a Highlander of old, fighting to slash down an enemy. Even when Margaret cast her gaze at the ground, she knew he was watching over her. They had known each other for years, but in the past few months, something between them had changed.

She sensed his attraction, even though he'd never said as much. And although she ought to put it from her mind, she couldn't deny her own rise of interest. It had to be the allure of the forbidden, for she knew there could never be anything between them.

"Stay away from the earl, lass." The warning held more than mere concern. It sounded as if he intended to personally shield her from the man's interest, and her traitorous heart warmed to hear it.

"I don't like Lord Strathland," she admitted. "Something about him seems wrong."

"Aye. Verra wrong, and you shouldna ever be alone with him." Sinclair walked alongside her, and she didn't miss the way his hand rested upon his dirk as if to guard her from harm.

"I don't intend to be alone with any man," she informed him. "You needn't worry."

But his eyes held a gleam of amusement. "You're alone with me, lass."

And sure enough, it was true. Her sister had secretly hurried on ahead, and Margaret hadn't even noticed.

"Now why would Amelia leave?" Margaret wondered aloud.

Cain sent her an amused look. "Because she thinks we are—what was it she said?" He paused and raised his voice in mimicry. "Desperately meant to be together."

Margaret groaned. "There are days when I should like to murder her." With an apologetic smile, she added, "I really should catch up to her so she's not walking alone."

"She did go to a great deal of trouble to put us together," Cain pointed out. "Why should it matter if I walk back with you?"

Her cheeks warmed at that. "I suppose you're right." It wasn't so very far to her house, after all.

Cain sent her a knowing smile. "Of course I'm right." Offering her the crook of his arm, he continued, "I'd ne'er lay a hand upon you, lass. No' unless you wanted me to."

A strange prickle ran through her at his words. Cain Sinclair was a wildly handsome man, but she wasn't at all certain it was a good idea to welcome such attention. "Thank you, but no." Even so, she took his arm and allowed him to guide her farther along the pathway.

"One day you might change your mind." When they reached

the path leading toward her house, he paused. "There's something I'm wanting to show you, lass. If you could spare a few minutes."

She wasn't so certain that was a good idea, but Amelia was waiting for her at the doorway. Undoubtedly she would want to gush over them, embarrassing Margaret even more. This was her chance to hold fast to a few more moments of freedom. "All right."

He led her across the glen, not far from the village, but toward a different part of the earl's land. Though she kept her face forward, she caught a sidelong glimpse of his face. His black hair was longer than the typical fashion, falling lower than his shoulders. His jaw held the prickle of a darker beard, and his mouth was firm.

But it was his eyes that she found most intriguing. Sometimes they were a blue so vivid, they held her spellbound. At other moments, they turned a silvery gray, like a brewing storm.

"We're here," he said at last. But the moment she saw where he'd brought her, goose bumps rose over her skin. It was the place where Lord Strathland's men administered justice. Men had been hanged upon Eiloch Hill—including Paul Fraser's father.

"I don't think I want to be here, Mr. Sinclair." Though she didn't believe in ghosts, she was unnerved by the haunted past that lingered here.

"Neither do they." Cain pointed in the distance, and she saw wooden stocks on the far side of the hill.

It wasn't hardened men who were locked there. Instead, she saw children, hardly more than eight or nine years old.

"Why are they there?" Margaret glanced up at the sky, knowing that soon enough it would pour down rain. These children would be soaked, their bodies shivering in the cold air.

"Their parents stole food a few days ago. This was their punishment."

Margaret frowned. "He locked up their children?"

"Aye. Strathland thought it would be a punishment that would hurt their parents more. He doesna care that they did naught to deserve it. A man like him would ken that it hurts a man to see his children locked away."

Margaret stared at the children in disbelief. How could anyone do this? These were innocents, who had done nothing wrong. "I should do something."

"Nay. They've already spent one night here. They'll be set free in a few hours, and that will be the end of it. But I wanted you to see what sort of man was courting you."

Margaret had already suspected the worst, but this was more than she'd imagined. She took off the shawl she'd worn and walked toward the children. "Here," she told them, placing the wool over their shoulders and heads. "It might help with the rain."

The young boy and girl muttered their thanks, and she told them they would not have to stay for much longer. But the words felt hollow. No one should treat children in this way.

She walked with Cain back along the pathway, understanding why he had shown her Eiloch Hill. It wasn't jealousy—he only wanted her to see the truth.

"Lord Strathland invited my family to a supper party," Margaret said aloud, not really knowing why she was telling him this.

"Don't go."

She didn't want to, but it would be impolite to refuse, particularly since they were close neighbors. "If he asks my mother, I may not have a choice." Since they were neighbors, how could Beatrice possibly decline?

Sinclair offered his arm and escorted her back the way they had come. The summer sky was laced with the storm clouds that were blowing in. Margaret hastened her step, hoping to avoid the rain before it fell.

"Then if you do go, be more *proper* than you usually are." He sent her a sidelong glance, and she understood his meaning.

"You mean I should be so prim and disdainful, he'll want nothing to do with me." It was a perfect way to avoid the man's attention, and her mother could not fault her for rudeness.

"Aye, lass."

The idea of it was rather devilish, but she knew it would work. "All right."

No sooner had they reached the glen than fat droplets began to spatter over her bonnet. Cain raised his plaid over his head, pulling her closer to share in it. "Come this way. There's a small copse where we can take shelter."

She followed, hurrying with him toward the trees. The rain was pounding hard, and it was at least another mile to her family's home. By then, she would be fully drenched.

They ran together, his arm around her waist, until they reached the grove. An older oak shielded them from the worst of the downpour, and Cain kept his plaid over them. "We'll wait here until it stops."

Margaret leaned back against the tree, and beneath the woolen wrap, she grew fully aware of him. The warmth of his body kept her from shivering, though inwardly, she was questioning the wisdom of taking shelter in his arms.

"Don't be looking at me like that, lass," he warned.

"Like what?" She kept her question calm, though she already suspected what he meant. His blue eyes were watching her, filled with such longing, she couldn't move.

"Like you're wanting me to kiss you."

The moment he spoke the words, her mind conjured the image of his mouth upon hers. It was a heady temptation, simply thinking of it. She ought to be kissed by the man who would become her husband, a gentleman who might steal that kiss on the night of a ball.

Not a Highlander who was staring at her as if she was his reason for being alive. Cain lowered the plaid, his knuckle grazing her cheek. The heat of his touch burned through her, and she might as well have been made of stone. She couldn't move or speak, particularly when he bent his face toward hers.

"Last chance, Miss Andrews," he murmured.

When she said nothing, he claimed her mouth in a soft kiss. It was the first time any man had taken such a liberty. Margaret was fully conscious of the taste of his mouth and the way he was coaxing her to kiss him back. She'd never expected to feel the urge to open herself to him. It was both alluring and terrifying.

He guided her hands to rest upon his chest as he continued kissing her, his mouth slightly open as her knees melted beneath her.

Dear Heaven, Cain Sinclair was quite good at kissing. His mouth tempted her in a silent invitation to push back the boundaries of friendship and allow him to become something more.

"I shouldn't let you do this," she whispered, before the second kiss he stole. "It's not right at all."

"I'll stop any time you ask," he said. "But if you don't speak, I'll kiss you as long as you're wanting me to, lass."

All afternoon, her reckless body pleaded. She tried to gather her scattered thoughts, even as she lifted her face for another kiss. She wanted him, and in his blue eyes, she saw a glimpse of what it meant to surrender to a man. If he tried to seduce her, she would go willingly. And it would ruin her life.

"It's wrong," she whispered.

"Is it?" he asked. He didn't seem to care as his mouth claimed hers, nipping at her lower lip.

Margaret forced herself to pull back, inwardly trembling at what there was between them. Now she understood the temptation her mother had warned her about. She had a wanton side buried within her, and this man knew exactly how to coax it from the shadows. He was utterly dangerous, no matter that they'd once been friends. Cain Sinclair's name spelled out *R-U-I-N*, no matter how she looked at it.

"I'm sorry," she murmured. "It won't happen again."

He tilted her head back, his eyes burning with desire. "Aye, it will. And one day you'll ken what I have all along. You were mine from the moment I saw you, Margaret Andrews. No man will ever have you, save me."

His assurance shocked her. He really believed that, didn't he?

And why wouldn't he? You were all but throwing yourself at him. You wanted him.

Her cheeks were burning, and her thoughts slid into turmoil. Not because of his predictions, but because of her own response. Never in her life had she imagined that a shameless side lurked within her.

She'd always believed she was a responsible, obedient daughter. Her mother had enough to worry about with Father away at war. Margaret was supposed to marry a nobleman with a title, someone who would help rescue their family from financial ruin. Her own desires didn't matter, and she certainly had no choice.

If she behaved like this, allowing Cain to kiss her openly, he had every reason to believe that she might one day marry him. But that could never happen, for they were so very different. How could she keep him at a distance, to protect herself?

She lowered her gaze, wondering what she could possibly say to him. The answer came, though it bothered her deeply.

Cain Sinclair had already told her how to drive men away, especially those like the Earl of Strathland—by behaving in an overly proper manner, with arrogance.

She could do the same with him. And the truth was, she *had* to put aside her feelings and place an invisible wall between them. He was far more dangerous than any man she'd ever met—not because he'd ever threatened her. But because he made her care deeply. If he'd tried to seduce her, he would succeed because she was powerless to resist him.

Margaret took a step backward, steeling herself. "It will *not* happen again. I made a mistake coming here with you. I must return home before anyone finds me gone."

"I'll walk back with you," he offered.

And if she permitted that, undoubtedly he'd share his plaid with her, holding her close. She couldn't allow that, not if she wanted to push him away.

Despite her unease, she forced herself to speak words that would make her decision clear. "You may walk with me. But after today, I cannot see you again."

The expression on his face held disbelief. "Why? Because you're angry that you kissed me back?"

"It's for the best," she insisted. "We both know that you could never become my husband. It would be unfair to let you think otherwise."

Her stomach twisted, hating herself for using the words as weapons. He'd received her answer clearly, and she suspected he would one day grow to hate her. Her eyes welled up, but she held her ground.

"You're afraid," he predicted.

And oh, he was right. But what else could she say? Instead, she stepped away from him and began the walk home, never minding the rain. The downpour soaked through her skin, but it was not the terrible weather that sent a chill down to her bones. It was the knowledge that she would have to maintain this pretense for many years. She had to become the good girl her parents wanted her to be. She could never, ever let herself ignore a rule, for behind her propriety lay a woman who delighted in wickedness.

If she let her guard down for even a moment, she might fall into ruin.

Chapter Eight

1815

"Forgive me, Mr. Sinclair, but I have my doubts that you are Miss Andrews's cousin," Lewis Barnabas began without preamble. He poured Cain a glass of brandy, which he accepted. "I understand that you may have had to invent a story for the sake of propriety, but I strongly suspect that you are not a member of the family."

The man's look of discomfort said that he believed Cain was incapable of proper behavior. Which was likely because of the way he'd behaved at the dinner table. The truth was, it had been a good deal of fun to see their horrified reactions when he'd eaten with his fingers. Aye, he knew what he should've done. And yet, he'd felt the sudden desire to break free of the rules.

"I would have remembered a Scottish relative," Barnabas continued. "Lord Lanfordshire is as English as I am."

"Is that what you think?" Cain countered. The brandy was smooth and fiery against his throat. "You're wrong, Barnabas. Say what you will, but Margaret and I are family."

Or at least, they would be, if he could ever convince her to wed him. He knew his words had come out steady with the ring of truth. Cain knew exactly how to lie, how to say what people wanted to hear. He took another swallow and added, "No one will harm her under my protection." He wanted Barnabas to hear the hinted threat. *Especially against any man who seeks to hurt her.*

There was something about this nobleman that bothered him—a sense that all was not right. The servants were tentative, and that said a great deal about their master.

"You watch her in a different manner than a cousin," Barnabas continued. He stood before the fireplace while sparks flew up against the wood. "Are you . . . together?"

Cain didn't like the man's assumptions or his insinuations against Margaret. He took a step forward, using his height to intimidate the man. "You willna speak a word against her. She's a lady."

Lewis Barnabas shrugged as if he didn't truly believe that, but he said, "I am glad to hear it. Perhaps Miss Andrews and I can become better acquainted in the next few days."

Cain wasn't about to let that happen, but he decided to soften their disagreement by feigning indifference. "The lass is going to Ballaloch, as I said. If you're wanting to court her, you should call upon her father. Lord Lanfordshire would have to give his permission."

"Then of course, I shall do so." Barnabas's voice held an air of arrogance. "That is, if Miss Andrews would enjoy my companionship."

When I'm dead and buried, Cain thought. The man behaved as if it was a privilege for Margaret to have his interest.

"There willna be time to speak with her. We're leaving," Cain reminded him.

Barnabas only smiled. "Are you?"

Cain didn't know what he meant by that, but he set down the glass of brandy. He sent the man a dark look, letting him see that he would not stand down. "Aye. And while I ken that she's grateful to you for a place to spend this night, I willna let you threaten her. 'Tis Margaret's choice to leave whenever she wants."

Were it up to him, he'd leave this moment. But he knew Margaret wouldn't understand his reasons. "Now, if you wouldna mind, I should like to get some rest." Which meant he planned to visit Margaret and ensure that she was safe, with a means of barring her door.

Barnabas signaled to the maid who had accompanied them earlier. "Give Mr. Sinclair his room for the night. I'm certain we will talk more in the morning."

Not if Cain could help it. His instincts had never failed him before, and he sensed trouble brewing. He planned to awaken Margaret before dawn and take her far away from this place.

***

"Let me in, lass," came the voice of Sinclair from behind her door. Margaret paused, for she was wearing only a cotton nightgown she'd found in a dresser drawer.

"What do you want?" she whispered.

"I need to talk with you for a moment."

She hesitated, not knowing whether it was wise to let him into the bedroom. Cain Sinclair had made no secret that he desired her, and she worried that he would attempt more than a conversation. But worse, she feared that she could not turn him away if he dared to reach for what he wanted.

"Come back in the morning," she whispered. "It's late, and you should not be here."

"Open the damned door, lass, or I'll break it down."

His words weren't exactly encouraging, but she had no doubt that he would do precisely what he'd threatened.

She yanked open the door and glared at him. "What is so important that you must steal into my bedroom at this hour?"

Cain said nothing but closed the door behind him. Then he lit a candle and began examining her room. He ignored her presence but went straight to the window and locked it. A moment later, he dragged a heavy dresser over toward the door.

"What are you doing?" she whispered. "This isn't necessary. You act as if you expect me to be attacked by someone in the middle of the night."

His eyes turned cold. "Aye, lass. I wouldna put it past him."

She couldn't believe he would think such a thing of Mr. Barnabas. The man had impeccable manners and had not once behaved in an inappropriate manner. Furthermore, he'd opened his home to them.

"Nothing is going to happen," she insisted. "Now if you would kindly leave my room . . . " She let her words trail off, waiting for him to go.

He moved forward and looked down upon her. His dark hair hung down over his shoulders, and the look in his eyes reminded her of the way he'd touched her before.

"I would never harm you at all, lass. You ken that, don't you?" His voice was husky, filled with unspoken promises.

She managed a nod, caught up by his close presence. He touched her shoulders, running his hands over her arms, until his hands rested at her waist. "If I could sleep outside your door, I would."

"I'll be fine," she insisted. Her skin rose up with nerves, and she was so afraid that he would begin touching her again. She was sensitive to him in a way she didn't understand. Images rose up in her mind, of him taking her back to bed . . . of him running his hands over her flesh and tempting her toward sin.

Don't do this, her conscience warned. Now was not the time to fall prey to any man.

"Push the furniture in front of your door after I go, lass," Cain told her.

But the dresser was so heavy, she didn't know if she was capable of it. "I have a key to this door," she pointed out. "I can lock it from inside." If it would make him feel better and convince him to leave, so much the better.

"Do that," he insisted.

She waited for him to go, but Cain remained standing where he was. His hand moved up to her hair, and he ran his fingers over the long blond strands. "I like your hair this way, lass. You're no' so proper now."

She caught his hand, trying to ignore the way her heart was beating faster. "You must go, Mr. Sinclair. Now, please, before anyone discovers you here."

"What do you care if anyone finds me?" he demanded. "We're leaving in the morning."

"It matters to me." She *did* care what others thought of her, while it might be foolish. She didn't want Mr. Barnabas or his servants to discover her lies, not when they were reliant upon the man for transportation. Margaret took his hand and guided him toward the door. "I will be fine, I promise you."

But the way he was watching her went beyond attraction. He was staring as if he wanted to take her back to the bed and have his wicked way with her.

"It's no' safe here, lass. And don't be allowing that Mr. Barnabas to turn your head. He may be wealthy and have better table manners than me. But there's a darkness in him."

She didn't know what to believe. Mr. Barnabas had opened his doors to strangers, giving them food and a place to sleep. Outwardly, there was nothing to suspect.

But she had allowed herself to be led astray once before, by Lord

Lisford. She'd been caught up by his handsome face and the way he'd spoken all the words she'd wanted to hear. It wouldn't happen again.

"I will be fine, Mr. Sinclair," she told him. "You needn't worry."

"Get some sleep, then." His voice was deep, as if he wanted to sleep at her side. Once again, she faltered at the tone of his voice. "We'll be traveling early." Cain sounded as if he intended for them to continue on horseback. She'd had her fill of that, especially when Mr. Barnabas had offered another means of transportation. If they borrowed his driver, they could continue their journey in comfort, and she would pay the servant well for his trouble.

"I thought we would use Mr. Barnabas's coach. He *did* make the offer." She couldn't understand why Cain was in such a hurry to leave.

"He willna offer us a coach," he countered. "Mark my words, there will be something wrong with the vehicle in the morning. We won't be leaving in it."

"You're being ridiculous, Mr. Sinclair." He made it sound as if Mr. Barnabas intended to keep her prisoner here, when that wasn't the case at all.

"He'll be finding a reason, lass. He wants you to stay. And damned if I'll let you become his prey."

She was convinced that he was overreacting out of jealousy. "Perhaps you're the one I should be afraid of," she murmured. "Seeing as you're the one in my bedroom."

"Say the word, Margaret, and I'll keep you warm."

A rush of heat slid over her at the thought of his hard body beside hers. She remembered what it was to feel him pressed against her, his hands moving over her skin.

But that would be a grave mistake. She could not let herself succumb to the wild longings that kept creeping nearer. She knew that her reputation was tarnished and what others would say about her. Yet somehow, she thought she could bear the gossip more easily if it wasn't true. If she remained innocent, despite all that had happened, it would bring her comfort.

"No," she whispered. She crossed the room and opened the door. "Good night, Mr. Sinclair. I promise I'll lock the door after you're gone. In case anyone tries to come inside."

Like you, she thought.

⚘

Henry Andrews was slowly losing his wife. She sat in a chair beside the window, staring into nothingness. Rarely did she speak, and each time he'd tried to coax her back into the world of the living, she'd ignored him. It was as if she had retreated inside herself and no longer wished to live.

He walked slowly toward her and rested his hands on the back of her chair. "I wondered if you might like to go for a walk."

She didn't look at him, but he knew she'd heard him. "What I want is to go back to Scotland."

Her answer startled him. "Why do you want to go to Ballaloch?" It had been weeks since Margaret's disappearance, and his wife was behaving as if their daughter was dead.

At last she stood from the chair and turned to him. "Because I think those men you hired are lying to us. They know that the longer it takes to find her, the more money we'll pay. I can't believe that in all this time, no one has found her. Something is wrong."

He agreed with her on that point. Which was why he'd joined with Castledon, both of them hiring men to search all the roads leading from London.

They had found the coach Margaret and Sinclair had traveled in. It was overturned, badly burned by fire. A man's body had been found nearby, presumably the driver.

Beatrice worried that Margaret had been seriously wounded in the accident or worse, that she was dead. She hardly slept at night anymore, and she'd stopped eating meals with him. Over the past few days, he'd watched her grow even more fragile. She needed news to bring her hope, not news that would devastate her.

He strongly believed that Margaret would be found. It was *that* news he wanted to give his wife—not more cause to worry.

There was a fire in her eyes now, of a woman determined to find her daughter. He was glad to see that she'd emerged from the shadows of grief and was willing to leave London. After the weeks of her suffering and sadness, he would do anything to bring back her smile. If that meant traveling together across England, so be it.

"When do you want to leave?" he asked.

Her cheeks flushed, and she appeared startled that he'd agreed so readily. "Tomorrow," she whispered. In her eyes, he saw a hopeful light, as if she could bring Margaret back by fervent wishing.

"I'll make the arrangements," he promised. "In the meantime, why don't you have the servants pack our belongings? We can reach our estate in a week or two, and hopefully we'll find her on the way there."

Beatrice ventured a step forward. Her face held a wistfulness, and he wanted so badly to hold her close. He wanted to feel her arms around him and breathe in her scent. Although both of them were older, she was as beautiful now as she was on the day he'd met her. The lines around her eyes showed the marks of happiness and sadness over the years.

A fierce hope beat within him that he could mend the breach

and get his wife to love him again. He opened his arms slightly, hoping that she would move forward and embrace him.

But she didn't. Instead, she turned away, pretending she hadn't seen his invitation. Her rejection bruised his pride, but he said nothing, letting his hands fall to his sides.

"In the morning, then," was all he said as he walked away, ignoring the shard of frustration. He'd been married to Beatrice for many years. And yet, on days like these, it seemed that he didn't know her at all.

Margaret walked into the dining room, searching for a glimpse of Cain. He'd claimed they would leave early this morning, but so far she had not seen him.

"Did you sleep well, Miss Andrews?" Mr. Barnabas inquired, while she took her place at the dining room table. He wore a blue morning coat with a cravat and cream-colored trousers. His dark blond hair was neatly combed, and he was clean-shaven. She detected a slight scent, rather like bergamot. He offered a warm smile, but his gaze fixed upon her body in a way that made her feel uncertain.

Outwardly, the man was exactly the sort of man she might have wanted, a few years ago. He was wealthy, in command of a large estate, and kind. In fact, nothing appeared to be wrong with him, which made her wonder why he hadn't married sooner.

"I slept very well, thank you," she answered. "We were most grateful for your hospitality last evening." It was true. She'd fallen into a deep, dreamless slumber. It had been wonderful to sleep beneath covers, safe and warm within four walls.

The footman offered her sausage and toast, but while she ate, it struck her that this was the first normal morning she'd had in many days. It was like dining with her family in the morning—only this time, there was a gentleman smiling at her.

"I wondered if you might consider staying for another day, before you set off for Scotland," he ventured.

He wants you to stay. And damned if I'll let you become his prey. Cain's words rang in her memory, along with his warnings. But Mr. Barnabas had never threatened her—this was only an invitation.

The footman poured her a hot cup of tea, and Margaret used the distraction to think for a moment. "Thank you for your offer of hospitality, but we really do need to go."

"I am hosting a supper party tonight for some of my friends and neighbors." Mr. Barnabas sent her a kindly smile. "I thought it might be an enjoyable way for you and your cousin to spend an evening. There will be dancing."

The thought of Cain attending a party with dancing almost brought a smile to her face. He had attended many *cèilidhs* over the years, but he wouldn't know how to join in the formal dancing sets she was accustomed to.

"Also, I fear that I have relied too heavily upon my mother and sister over the years, when it comes to making arrangements," Mr. Barnabas apologized. "Although my cook is preparing the food today, I've no idea of the proper seating. I would welcome your assistance, since I imagine you know the etiquette better than I. And then you and your cousin could stay for the gathering. It would be my way of saying thank you."

Margaret hesitated, though she knew Sinclair would refuse outright. He was determined to reach Scotland quickly.

And yet, she did feel a slight obligation toward Mr. Barnabas. He *had* given them shelter and food, when they were strangers to him. If she stayed a few hours longer, she could easily look over the seating arrangements and adjust them accordingly. After so many years of training, she could plan elaborate gatherings in her sleep, for it was a skill she had mastered.

"Since you were so kind to offer us a place to stay last night, I'd be happy to help you," she began. "I fear we cannot stay for the party, but I can indeed look over the plans you've made."

"I would be most grateful." His smile was warm, and she redirected her attention back to her tea.

"It's the least I can do, since you've been so kind as to offer your coach for traveling." Her voice came out rushed, revealing her nervousness. "But it won't take days to set everything to rights. I can manage it in a few hours."

His sheepish smile grew. "I know you could. But I must confess, it's an excuse to ask you to stay," he admitted. "It's rare for me to have visitors, much less a woman of such beauty as yourself. I'd like to know you better."

"I'm certain you would," interrupted the voice of Cain Sinclair. The Highlander's dark hair was damp, hanging below his shoulders. He looked as if he'd just splashed water on his face, and he'd worn the same brown-and-green kilt from yesterday. His chiseled face sent a warning toward Barnabas, as if to say, *Leave her alone.*

"We must be on our way," Cain said to Margaret. "After your meal, we'll go." He stood behind her chair, with both hands on the curved edge of the mahogany. It was a blatant show of possession, and she didn't appreciate it at all. Why was he behaving like this?

She decided that now was not the time to mention Mr. Barnabas's request. Something had provoked Sinclair's anger, and she sensed that there was a strong reason why he wanted her to go. To pacify him, she said, "You haven't had anything to eat yet. Why don't you join us?" Perhaps food would put him in a better mood.

Instead, Cain picked up her fork and stabbed a sausage, eating directly off her plate. "This is enough for me, lass."

She could hardly believe what he'd done. It went beyond bad manners, as if he were staking his claim upon her. Uneasiness rippled through her, for he'd well overstepped his bounds.

To the footman, she asked, "Please fetch Mr. Sinclair a plate. Since he appears to be so hungry that he cannot wait for his own food." She turned and glared at him, but his eyes were fixed upon Mr. Barnabas. A moment later, Cain chose the chair beside hers, as if guarding her.

What on earth was the matter with these men? It was as if they were competing for her favors—Mr. Barnabas by using good manners and Cain Sinclair by behaving like a barbarian.

She straightened and said, "Mr. Barnabas, please forgive my cousin's behavior. I fear that he tends to be rather outspoken at times."

And domineering, she thought. Stubborn and demanding, too. He presumed too much and she didn't like the way he was ordering her around.

Their host behaved as if nothing had happened and offered, "If you would like to join me in the parlor within the hour, I will bring my list of guests attending, and we can discuss the best seating arrangements for the supper party."

"What supper party?" Cain demanded.

"Mr. Barnabas has asked for my assistance, since he is hosting a gathering here tonight. He invited us to attend." Margaret raised her napkin to her lips and took a sip of hot tea. "I told him we could not stay, but I will help him with his seating arrangements."

Beneath the table, Cain pressed his knee against hers, as if in warning. She nudged him back, in her silent demand, *Leave me alone.*

"There won't be time for that, lass."

"Then I shall *make* the time. After all, were it not for Mr. Barnabas's coach, we would be traveling on horseback again," she pointed out. "It won't take long, I promise."

Although Cain wanted to remain on horseback, *she* did not. Margaret saw no reason not to borrow the private coach when it had been offered to them.

Mr. Barnabas's face held amusement at the small victory. "Do feel free to finish your breakfast at your leisure," he said. "I have a few matters to attend, and then I will meet with you in the parlor."

As soon as he was gone, she turned to Sinclair. "Why are you behaving as if you're angry? Mr. Barnabas only asked for a few moments of my time. It means nothing at all."

"He wants you to stay," he pointed out.

"Yes, he said that. And I told him I could only spare a few hours."

"A few hours?" He sent her an incredulous look. "Why would you agree to that? Don't you ken what he's trying to do?"

She was growing more and more annoyed with his high-handed jealousy. "Will you stop acting as if you expect him to accost me? *What* has he done wrong except to show interest in courting me?"

"If you walk into that parlor, he'll do everything he can to coax you to stay longer," Cain insisted. Beneath the table, he reached for her right hand.

"You are being entirely too suspicious," she chided.

"My instincts have no' failed me yet. Have you seen the way the servants are acting?"

She shook her head, not understanding.

"They're being careful, lass. Too careful. There's no one gossiping in the servants' hall, no smiling. No laughter."

She hadn't really considered it, but he was right about the atmosphere being more serious. "Perhaps they keep their conversation to themselves."

Cain's voice was a whisper over her skin. "Any man who has such tight command over his staff is a dangerous person." He stood up from the dining-room table and said, "Come with me, and we'll see what sort of man he really is."

She took one last bite of breakfast and followed him. "I still believe you're being foolish."

In answer, he raised a finger to his lips and beckoned for her to follow. She wanted to tell him no, but he took her hand and led her from the room. They kept their backs to the wall, and Margaret wasn't entirely certain where Mr. Sinclair was going. He passed the parlor and made his way toward the library. The door was slightly ajar, and Cain pressed her back into the shadow of a grandfather clock.

Although they weren't hidden, it seemed forbidden to be skulking about, eavesdropping upon poor Mr. Barnabas. Cain pulled her close, and she half wondered if he was inventing all of this as an excuse to spy upon the man.

But a moment later, she heard Lewis Barnabas speaking in an entirely different tone.

"Why was I not informed that he left London?" Barnabas was asking the butler. His voice held unmistakable frustration. "Did I, or did I not, hire men who were supposed to tell me if he ever left?"

"You did, sir, and that is why we received the letter—"

"It was because of *me* that these estates prospered. They were given into *my* care, and I will not allow him to run them into the ground again."

Margaret gripped Cain's shirt, uncertain that they should be overhearing any of this. His arms curled around her, and she heard the steady beat of his heart. She was about to suggest that they go, when the door suddenly slammed shut and the room went silent.

"What's happening?" Margaret whispered.

Cain's mouth moved to her ear. "He's killing the butler."

Appalled, she turned back, only to see the glint of teasing in his eyes. Whispering back, she responded, "No, he is not!"

"He might be. 'Tis verra quiet."

But within a few moments, the butler emerged from the library. His face was pale, and in his hand, he clenched a letter. He didn't appear to see them, and after a moment, Cain led her from their hiding place. "Are you still wanting to help Barnabas plan his supper party?"

She shrugged. "Just because we overheard him being angry doesn't mean that he's dangerous." Anyway, they would be leaving and it didn't matter at all. If she could make the adjustments quickly, they could be on their way, and that was that. Margaret started to walk toward the library when Cain caught her arm. "What are you doing, lass?"

"I am going to meet with him, as I said I would."

"No' without me," he insisted. "We stay together."

She didn't argue with him, but she was questioning the wisdom of staying here. "I'll ask him for the coach, and we can go."

"He's no' going to give it to us," Cain said, beneath his breath.

She didn't believe him, but she pressed onward and knocked upon the door. When there came no reply, she opened it and found Mr. Barnabas seated, staring out the window.

"Is everything all right?" she asked.

Mr. Barnabas spun, his fists clenched. As soon as he saw her, he relaxed his hands. "Forgive me, Miss Andrews. You startled me."

From behind her, Margaret felt Cain's palm pressing against her back. "There's no need for us to stay any longer," he told Barnabas. "It seems that you have enough troubles without us."

The man stood from his desk, his face softening. "I must beg your pardon. I received some bad news about . . . a family member who is in trouble. I spoke rashly, and I am sorry if you overheard that."

He appeared distinctly uncomfortable for the outburst. Margaret wondered if the family member had been gambling or spending a great deal of money. She frowned a moment, wondering if he was somehow related to Lord Lisford. Such had not occurred to her, but she knew Mr. Barnabas was only caring for the estates—he was not the heir.

Curious.

"I understand," Margaret said smoothly. "I won't bother you any further, but I thought I'd ask if we might still borrow your coach before we go."

His expression turned apologetic. "Regrettably, I must take it myself in the morning when I travel to . . . see about matters. I am terribly sorry that I can no longer lend it to you."

He crossed the room and added, "But if you would stay another night, perhaps I can atone for it. I will not be leaving until tomorrow morning, and my invitation to attend the supper party stands. There will be music and dancing, as well as good food." His gaze passed over to Cain. "However, I understand if such a gathering would be uncomfortable for you, Sinclair."

It was not an insult, to be precise, but he'd implied that Cain might not conduct himself appropriately. She also recognized it as a means of declining the invitation.

Behind her, she felt Cain's hand tighten against her waist. She waited for him to agree that they did need to leave. But instead, he surprised her, asking, "What is it you want to do, lass?"

Never had she imagined that he would even consider such a thing. She'd half expected him to refuse and haul her back to their horse.

Instead, he'd offered her a choice. It was all she could do to keep her mouth from dropping open.

Margaret discreetly reached back for his hand and squeezed it.

Though she already knew what the outcome would be, she was grateful that he'd not made demands. To Mr. Barnabas, she gave a polite excuse. "I fear I haven't a proper gown," she apologized, "and undoubtedly, we would be outsiders among your neighbors." Not to mention, there was a slim chance she might be recognized by someone.

"Have you a gown she could borrow?" Cain asked Barnabas abruptly. "Your sister's, perhaps?"

What was he doing? One moment he was demanding that they leave, and now he was considering staying?

"There might be a leftover gown," Barnabas answered. "Though since I have no brothers, I cannot say if there would be any clothing that would fit you, Mr. Sinclair."

"I've no need of them." Cain dismissed the idea, but Margaret wanted to know why on earth he was even thinking of attending the gathering.

"May I speak with you alone, *Cousin*?" she asked, though it wasn't truly a question. "We need to discuss a few things."

With a nod to Barnabas, Cain led her outside the library, closing the door behind him. He crossed his arms over his chest, looking for all the world like he intended to have his way.

"I don't understand," she blurted out. "One moment you insist that we leave, and now you're asking if I can borrow a gown? For what reason would you want to stay?"

His gaze passed over her, and he gave a light shrug. "You said you would be shut away from the world, after you return home. That you wouldna be able to attend any gatherings at all."

A hard lump formed in her throat, but she nodded. "That is true." She could live with her parents, but there would be no invitations for her to accept—not after this scandal.

Cain took her hand, his thumb drawing imaginary circles over her skin. "I wondered if you might want to attend one last night of dancing, before it all ends. Before we go home."

It hadn't even occurred to her, that this might be the only chance she had to make merry, before the walls closed in on her. But *he* had thought of it.

"You would do this for me?"

He shrugged. "I willna do much dancing myself, but if you're wanting to go, I suppose one more night willna make much difference."

"And what about Mr. Barnabas? I thought you didn't trust him."

A sly smile crossed Cain's face. "Nay, I don't. But I'll be there to pound him into the floor if he looks at you wrong, lass."

Chapter Nine

Jonah eyed the bed longingly, but MacKinloch shook his head. "You'll take the floor, lad."

They had been forced to share a room with other travelers, and there was no space for him. The room itself was sparse and cold, his breath forming clouds in the night air. It didn't matter that it was the middle of summer—it was always cold in Scotland.

He curled up against one wall, wishing he had a blanket. Anything to bring warmth to his half-frozen feet and hands. But sleep wouldn't come. Instead, tears rose up in his eyes.

Damn it all, he wouldn't cry. He was nearly a man, and he couldn't be so foolish as to weep like a girl.

The truth was, he missed Cain. Aye, his older brother had always told him what to do and was unforgiving about it. But he'd never gone hungry or cold. He'd had a pallet of his own near the fire and a woolen blanket that Grania had woven for him.

Cain hadn't left him alone often, he admitted to himself. His brother had arranged for him to stay with Grania and Rory whenever he'd had to travel for Lady Lanfordshire and her daughters. Grania had treated him like a son, and though she could never take his mother's place, she'd been good to him.

Why had he journeyed this far? He'd never known hardship like this. His body was shivering from the cold, his teeth chattering. The wooden floor was hard against his back, and no matter what he tried, he couldn't get warm.

No longer did adventure have the same appeal. He wanted to be back home at Eiloch Hill, where he had a warm bed and enough food to eat.

Silently, he got up from his place and went over to Joseph MacKinloch. The older man was sprawled across the bed, snoring. He couldn't be fully asleep, Jonah reasoned, so he tugged at the man's shoulder.

MacKinloch's eyes flew open, and he swung his fist toward Jonah's face. Cursing when he realized who it was, he muttered, "Leave me alone, lad."

"I want to go back," Jonah said. "I don't want to go to London anymore."

At that, MacKinloch yawned. "If that's what ye're wanting. In the morning, go where'er ye like, lad. I'll go my way and ye can return."

That wasn't what Jonah had meant at all. "But I don't ken how to get home, Joseph. I couldna find Ballaloch if I wanted to."

The man rolled over and opened his eyes again. In them, Jonah saw the ruthlessness of a man who didn't care. "I'm no' returning to Ballaloch. If ye want to go back, it's yer choice. But don't be asking me to help ye."

A sinking dread took hold in his stomach. He realized now that MacKinloch had his own purpose in this journey, and though he'd allowed Jonah to come along, he didn't care what happened to him. He was truly alone, with no money, and he'd given his father's pistol away.

"Or ye can continue our journey and find yer brother," MacKinloch offered. "That is, if he's still in London."

It seemed he had little choice. Jonah believed Cain had to be in London, since Margaret Andrews was there. His brother often found reasons to be around the baron's daughter, though Miss Andrews would never wed a man like Cain.

Jonah had to stay with MacKinloch. Otherwise he'd be abandoned here, lost and alone. "I'll stay," he told the man, returning to his corner of the room.

The damn tears came back again, but this time Jonah let himself cry quietly. He'd made a mistake in coming here, but with any luck, he'd find his brother again. Cain might have told him what to do at every waking moment, but at least he cared. Jonah knew that MacKinloch wouldn't care at all if they parted ways.

With his knuckles, he swiped at his face. Silently he prayed that he would find his brother again. And when he did, he knew just what he'd say to Cain.

I'm sorry.

⚘

The sapphire gown was rather tight across the bosom, and it revealed entirely too much skin. Yet, Margaret eyed herself in the looking glass, feeling as if she were staring at a stranger.

The maid, Annie, had used tongs to curl her hair, and Margaret couldn't look at her own reflection without remembering the last ball she'd attended, on the night Amelia had been taken. Though outwardly, she could pass for any lady of the ton, now, she felt like a different person—a survivor.

Annie helped her put on long white gloves, and Margaret was thankful that the hem of the gown was long enough to hide her shoes. Unfortunately, Mr. Barnabas's sister had smaller feet, so Margaret had no choice but to wear her own.

"You look perfect, my lady," the maid pronounced.

"Thank you." Margaret managed to smile, but inwardly, she was worried about Cain. He'd agreed to stay tonight for her sake, but he'd never said anything about attending the supper party himself.

Before she left her room, she went over the guests' names in her mind. She had helped Mr. Barnabas rearrange the seating, but she had not placed herself or Cain at the table. It occurred to her that he had invited eight guests, along with himself. There was one seat remaining at the table, and she questioned whether he'd purposely left Cain out.

Perhaps she could find a footman and discreetly ask him to set another place. With that thought in mind, she continued down the stairs until she found Mr. Barnabas waiting for her. His face lit up at the sight of her, and he offered his arm.

"You are the most exquisite lady I have ever laid eyes upon," he said, and his gaze lingered briefly upon Margaret's bosom. She pretended she hadn't seen that, and took his arm, allowing him to lead her inside. Soon enough, it became clear that he intended for her to act as the hostess, greeting the guests while remaining at his side.

Cain, in the meantime, was nowhere to be found.

Worry knotted inside her, even as she slid into the role she could perform without thought. She greeted guests, made polite conversation, and memorized the names of people she would never see again. And all the while, she was searching for a glimpse of *him*.

As minutes turned into an hour, she longed to go in search of Cain. A footman passed by, and winked at her.

Winked?

Margaret frowned, wondering why on earth he would do such a thing. She saw him disappear through one of the doorways. Before she could follow, she found herself speaking to an elderly man who appeared quite fascinated with the tight lines of her bodice.

My face is up here, she wanted to tell him, but of course that would be rude.

"The weather has been ghastly, as of late, wouldn't you agree, Miss Andrews? We've had so much rain, I imagine Noah and his ark might appear at any day now."

The older man let out a barking laugh, and she sent him a vacuous smile. "Quite."

"Nothing like a bit of sunshine, eh?" He was still chuckling over his own humor, and Margaret's smile was strained.

Actually, there's something to be said for being caught in the rain with a handsome Highlander.

"Barnabas told me that your father is Lord Lanfordshire and that you have estates in London and in Scotland."

Oh for goodness' sake. The man was practically salivating at the thought of her potential dowry. What he didn't know was how ruined she was.

"He does, yes." In the corner, the dancing was about to begin, and Mr. Barnabas asked her if she wanted to be his partner.

Margaret agreed, but she was already searching for a means to escape. Although there was nothing outwardly wrong, she was beginning to realize that, without Cain, this supper party wasn't enjoyable at all. She wanted to share the gathering with him, to bring him into her world and teach him how to be a part of the merriment.

After the third country dance, she saw him standing at the doorway. He was wearing the green-and-brown kilt, but it appeared that he'd borrowed a clean white shirt and a cravat. He also wore a black coat with brass buttons, and his head was bare. His long black hair was pulled back into a queue, and more than one young woman noticed him.

"Who is *that*?" the lady beside Margaret asked. Her eyes gleamed with interest.

"*That* is my cousin, Cain Sinclair," she answered, tamping down her own surge of possessiveness.

"Will you introduce us?" the lady pleaded, but Margaret ignored her and crossed the room to greet him.

"I am glad you came, Mr. Sinclair."

He bowed slightly and sent her a secret smile of his own. "The gown suits you, lass."

Instead of feeling exasperated that he, too, had noticed the tightness of her bodice, she felt a flush of awareness. "Thank you."

She placed her arm in his and guided him toward the others. A glimmer of excitement took hold, that she could finally show him what it was like to attend a supper party and enjoy an evening of dancing. He had never been permitted to be a part of this society, and she wanted to give him the experience for the first time in his life.

Keeping her voice low, she told him the names of the guests and which ones were of the nobility. Thankfully none of them were acquainted with her family, which meant it was unlikely that she'd see them again.

"If you would like to dance with me, before we go in to supper, I think there's another set left," she hinted.

Cain reached for her gloved hand. "This night isna about me, lass. It's about you. Go back and enjoy yourself."

He believed that, didn't he? She shook her head. "No. I've already danced. I merely thought we could . . . have a dance together." Then again, the steps were rather intricate. Likely he wouldn't know what he was doing, and it would only make him uncomfortable.

His hand squeezed hers. "Another time, lass."

She acceded to that, but she had the sense that he intended to remain in the background. "Shall I introduce you to the others?"

"They willna care who I am."

His stubbornness was beginning to frustrate her. "At least try, won't you?" She wanted him to enjoy himself, to find a bright moment in this evening.

"I am here, Margaret. But I came only to guard you. No' to play a part in this."

"Then why did you wear the clothes?" She studied the black coat he was wearing. "Where did you get them?"

"The butler, Mr. Merrill, loaned me a coat and a shirt." There was an uncomfortable look on his face, as if he didn't like being beholden to anyone. "I think they might have belonged to the former master of this house."

"You look handsome," she informed him. "And without the kilt, you would look like any of the men here."

"Without the kilt, I'd be half naked, lass." He sent her a charming smile, and she bit back a laugh.

"Well, then. I suppose you *would* be noticed." She was glad to see that his humor had returned.

After supper was announced, Mr. Barnabas began leading a countess inside the dining room. The guests lined up by rank, and Cain squeezed her hand. "I suppose now I'm to disappear into the kitchens."

"You will not." Margaret led him in. "As the acting hostess, it is my responsibility to lead you inside." She linked her arm in his and saw that the footman had indeed arranged an extra place beside her. Margaret took the chair at the farthest opposite end from Mr. Barnabas, and Cain sat to her right.

He said nothing, but she sensed that he would have preferred the kitchens. The young lady on his other side was the same one who had begged an introduction earlier. She was flirting shamelessly with him, and Cain answered her questions. All the while, he mimicked the table manners of those around him.

As the dinner progressed, Margaret conversed with the people around her, but she felt like a shadow of herself. Though she could behave as if this were an entertaining evening, it felt as if she no longer belonged here. What did she care if others spoke about Parliament or the weather? What did it matter if the fish was a trifle overdone?

Cain turned to her and remarked, "Have you been enjoying yourself, lass?"

She kept her voice low. "Only when you came to join me."

Cain didn't know why he'd bothered to come to this gathering. He knew nothing of these people or what was expected of him. He should have listened to his instincts and stayed back in his room.

And yet, he'd wanted to catch a glimpse of Margaret. Her hair was bound back, with a few teasing strands curled against her cheeks. She was wearing sapphire blue, and the color of the gown brought out her green eyes.

And damn him if the gown didn't fit her like a second skin. It was tight against her shoulders, revealing the curve of her breasts. It made him remember touching her, arousing her on horseback. He wanted nothing more than to peel back that silk and reveal her delicate flesh, tasting her until she moaned.

She blushed, as if she'd guessed his thoughts. From beneath the table, he took her hand. She squeezed it, and he kept her palm in his.

At the other end of the table, Barnabas was smiling at the older woman beside him, and there was a strain around his eyes. He might've decided to host this supper party, but it was clear that his thoughts were elsewhere. Cain wondered exactly what family matter was distracting him, but undoubtedly it had to do with the estate.

"I must say, Barnabas, you've done very well with Hempshire," one of the gentlemen remarked. "I believe we should call you the Phoenix now, for you've brought this estate out of the ashes."

Barnabas gave a deferential nod. "I've worked very hard to make it prosperous." He met Margaret's gaze at the other end of the table. "All I need now is a wife and helpmate." As a courtesy, he also smiled at each of the other young women, but it was clear where his interest lay.

No' bloody likely, Cain thought. Aye, the man had wealth and good manners. But Margaret was his.

"You're hurting my hand," she whispered, and he realized then that he'd been clenching her fingers.

"I'm sorry." To atone for it, he stroked her fingers lightly.

The next course arrived, and the guests appeared delighted when the footman revealed a dish of tiny birds. Cain stared down at his plate, appalled when the guests began slicing the fowl and crunching their bones.

"What in the name of God is this?" he demanded of Margaret in a low voice.

"Ortolan buntings," she explained. "It's a French delicacy."

"Why would anyone want to eat those?" The idea of crunching through a songbird was revolting. "I'm no' touching it."

Margaret didn't appear thrilled by the dish, either, and in a low voice, she whispered, "It's not exactly in good taste, considering we've been at war with France. I can't imagine why he served this, unless he was hoping to impress his guests."

She sliced through the bird and moved it to a different part of her plate. It was an illusion, designed to make others believe that she'd eaten it.

"Don't you just love ortolan, Mr. Sinclair?" the woman beside him was asking. "It's such a rare dish."

"Here. You can have mine," he said, pushing the bird onto her plate. The other guests stared at him, as if he'd committed an unforgivable sin. Why would they care?

Margaret said nothing at all, and he supposed he'd embarrassed her. She was pushing her bird all around the plate, and her lips were pressed together. At a closer look, he realized that her shoulders were trembling.

"Are you all right, lass?"

She covered her mouth with a napkin and shook her head. When he tilted his head to look at her closer, he realized that she was laughing. Honestly, what had come over the woman?

"Were you wanting the bird, instead?" he demanded.

She choked back a laugh, gripping her napkin as if her life depended on it. "N-no. I'm fine."

"Well, I, for one, do not want your castoffs," the young woman said. Her sour expression made it seem as if he'd spit upon her plate.

"As you like." Cain speared the bird with his fork and dropped it onto Margaret's plate. The feet stuck straight up in the air, and at that, she broke down with laughter.

"Forgive me. I shouldn't laugh, but honestly—" A snort escaped her, and a few of the others smirked as well. Barnabas's expression darkened, and it was clear that Cain had offended him. So be it. He didn't care what any of these folk thought of him. They could take their ridiculous foods, and he'd play no part in it.

"I'll leave you to your supper, then." He stood up from the table and tossed his napkin on the chair. The other guests regarded him with fascinated horror, but Cain was ready to be gone from all of them. He didn't belong here with men and women like this. He'd come on Margaret's behalf, but it was clear that he couldn't even dine among them without making a fool of himself.

He strode away from the guests, not even bothering to apologize to Barnabas. But worst of all was knowing that he'd made *her* laugh at him.

He had more pride than to endure an evening like this with strangers. And it only reminded him that they came from different worlds—and this was one that he wanted no part of.

As he crossed through the hall, toward the staircase, he caught a glimpse of a small boy carrying a bucket of coal. The lad was far younger than Jonah, but he had the same dark hair that looked as if it hadn't been combed in a few days.

Seeing the boy reminded Cain of his purpose. He wasn't here to let Margaret pull his strings, teaching him how to behave among the gentry. He had his own family to protect.

And he remembered, too well, the dangers he and Jonah had faced together.

※

FIVE YEARS EARLIER

"But . . . we can't leave, Cain." Jonah stared up at him, his nine-year-old face shocked. "This is our home."

Cain had begun throwing clothes, food—whatever he could find—into a bundle. He didn't stop to look for anything but kept adding as much as he could carry. When he glanced up, his brother was still staring at him, frozen in disbelief.

"Don't stand there, lad. We have to leave within the hour." He knew what would happen to the crofters who refused to leave their homes. Strathland had ordered them all to go, and there was no choice in it.

"He canna do this," Jonah protested. "We've always lived here. How can he make us leave?"

"Because the earl owns this land." His younger brother didn't understand that Strathland's men were riding even now, torches in hand. Those who had not yet abandoned their homes would be forced to leave when the flames struck the thatched roofs. Cain had seen the fires in the distance and heard the screams of the folk whose belongings were going up in smoke. It was only a matter of time before they reached these dwellings.

"Take everything you can carry," he commanded. "We've no time left."

His brother didn't seem to understand the urgency but kept staring at the walls as if he couldn't decide what to leave behind.

"Now, Jonah," Cain said softly. "Or you'll no' be able to carry any of it."

When his brother turned, his face was stricken with fear. He picked up a handkerchief that had belonged to their mother, crumpling it in his hand. "Where will we go?" This was the only home he'd known, and Cain could see how close Jonah was to tears.

"To Lady Lanfordshire," Cain said. "We'll ask to set up our shelters there until we can find another place. Near the coast, maybe." He reached for the pistol that had belonged to their father, tucking it in at his waist. At least they could have a few things that would remind them of their parents.

Jonah was already shaking his head. "I won't go, Cain. I canna leave."

The sound of horses drew nearer, and there was no choice but to seize as many of their clothes as he could gather.

"Jonah, get out!" he shouted.

A lighted torch landed upon the thatched roof, and it caught fire immediately. The flames took hold, the black smoke thickening the space.

Cain grabbed his brother by the hand and jerked him outside. Only moments later, a bundle of charred thatch and bits of the roof fell inside where his brother had been standing. Hatred darkened the boy's face when he saw their home go up in flames.

"We did naught to Strathland," he told Cain. "It wasna our fault."

No, but they were at the mercy of a man who had decided they were no longer useful to him.

"Our fault was in living upon his land," was the only answer Cain could give. Then he led the boy away from the blaze of fire, pretending a confidence he didn't feel.

He'd built a new home for his brother, though not so large as the one their father had built. The winter had been freezing that year, and food was scarce. Although they'd survived the winter, he'd struggled to earn a living. Until Victoria Andrews had asked for his help in acquiring fabric for Aphrodite's Unmentionables.

During the war, it had been all but impossible to find silk and satin. Cain had never told any of them how much of the fabric he'd had to steal. He'd let them believe that he'd bought it secondhand or from the shops in London.

The truth was, he'd taken some of the silk off a ship that had come in from China. It hardly mattered what the color was—all

Victoria cared about was texture. He'd lied, cheated, and stolen from the wealthy . . . all to feed the hungry men and women of his clan.

And he didn't care that he'd done it. If breaking the law meant that he could get food for his brother, so be it. Aphrodite's Unmentionables had given the crofters' wives sewing work that brought in more money and supplies. It had given them hope. He'd have stolen silk from the Prince Regent if necessary.

Now, he could buy the fabric honestly, but he saw no reason to regret the past.

It also had given him a means to see Margaret, both in Scotland and in London. He'd found reasons to be near her, to tease her and watch indignation make her blush. And he'd savored the stolen moments.

Just as he'd enjoyed the time they'd spent together over the past few weeks. He'd always been fascinated by her—but now he knew her far better. The prim and proper behavior was a carefully constructed act. She used it to keep men away and to protect herself from anyone who dared to see the truth.

For there was far more to her. She might have protested when he'd claimed a kiss or two . . . but she'd kissed him back. There was a passionate side to her, one she kept hidden from the rest of the world.

Cain walked up to the second floor of the house, counting doors until he found Margaret's bedroom. He pressed his ear to the room but heard nothing. When he opened the door a fraction, the room was empty. Margaret's belongings were still there, and he chose the wardrobe as a place to hide.

He kept the door slightly open, waiting for her to return.

She'd made such a mistake by laughing.

Margaret knew what Cain believed, but the truth was, she wasn't laughing at him. She was laughing at the shocked expression of the young lady. And, in a way, she was laughing at herself for ever believing that good manners and proper behavior were necessary to social survival.

These people were dining like barbarians, and honestly, she'd never liked ortolan buntings, though she'd been trained in the proper way to eat them. One was supposed to consume the songbird whole, with a napkin over one's head. Likely the other guests had never eaten them before, but their incorrect manners had made it far easier to disguise her lack of appetite for the delicacy.

Though she remained for the duration of the dinner, she fully planned to find Cain and apologize. He would be angry, but she felt certain that she could make him understand that she'd been laughing at the idiocy of eating songbirds.

It had been the worst supper party of her life . . . and at the same time, the best one. For now she realized that frankly, she didn't care about any of it.

When the gentlemen retired to their cigars and port, she slipped away from all of them. She hurried up the stairs, planning to find Cain and apologize in her own way.

She went to his room and knocked, but there was no answer. Inside, the room was cold and dark, though his belongings were still inside. She didn't know where he'd gone, but at least he hadn't left.

Margaret returned to her own room and asked Annie to help her dress for bed. The maid unbuttoned her gown and unlaced the corset, helping her change into a linen nightdress.

"Will that be all, miss?"

"Yes, thank you." Margaret dismissed the young woman and stood for a moment in the room. Her thoughts were tangled up like a skein of yarn, but above all else, she wanted to find Cain and talk to him. Perhaps she could go to him later, if he returned to his room. She should have asked Annie if she had seen him, but even if she had, the maid might not confess the truth.

Until then, she turned the key in the lock, knowing she had to keep everyone out. The dark emptiness stretched before her, and Margaret tried to decide what she would say in her apology to Cain.

She closed her eyes a moment, wishing she'd never laughed. He'd saved her life, protecting her at every turn. He'd teased her and tempted her into casting off her prim ways, making her feel alive again.

And now he believed she had mocked him.

With a heavy heart, she walked back toward the bed, trying to stave off the worry. She had nearly made it to the bed when she heard a creaking sound coming from behind her. Fear roared through her, and she stumbled forward, seizing the fireplace poker.

"Who's there?" she managed to whisper.

"Don't be killing me, lass," Cain interrupted, pushing the wardrobe door open.

Relief rushed through her at the sight of him, and Margaret let the poker fall to the floor. Without thinking, she ran to him and threw her arms around him. He embraced her hard, and she blinked back the tears, so thankful that he was here with her now.

He stroked her back, letting his hands move down to her hips. His blue eyes stared at her with undisguised longing. "I like what you're wearing, lass."

Oh dear. It meant that he'd watched as the maid had undressed her. Mortification burned her cheeks, and she blurted out, "You didn't have to spy on me, Mr. Sinclair."

He moved forward, his presence shadowing her. "I didna see verra much. Does it bother you that I watched?"

It should have. And yet, her body flushed with the thought of him watching. Why on earth would such a thought cross her mind? "Of course," she lied. "You shouldn't have done such a thing." She closed her eyes, thankful that she'd had her back facing the wardrobe. "I want to apologize to you for laughing earlier. I wasn't trying to insult you—it was simply that I realized how appalling the food was. I don't know why he believed that such a dish would honor his guests. It was terrible."

He said nothing but stepped back. "It was, aye. And if you're wanting to apologize, you ken the best way to do that."

A kiss, she remembered. Her skin warmed at the thought, and she let her hands rest around his waist. He kept his posture erect, so tall, she had to stand on tiptoe. "I can't reach you."

In answer, he lifted her up, his arms beneath her hips. She was trapped in his embrace, forced to hold on with her arms around his neck.

"I'm sorry," she breathed, pressing a light kiss against his closed mouth. Cain kept her body close to his, letting her slide down until she stood before him. "I never meant to wound your pride."

His hands framed her face, caressing her temples. "In the morning we'll go." But there was no mention of accepting her apology. Though he'd accepted the kiss, he hadn't returned it.

She wanted to talk to him more, but it appeared that he wanted to leave. And she didn't want him to go—not yet. "Will you stay a little longer?" She kept her voice calm, as if it meant nothing at all for a man to be inside her room. But her hands were trembling.

Cain's blue eyes turned hooded, and he murmured, "For how long, lass?" The hunger in his gaze made her question the wisdom of her request.

She didn't know what to say. Only that the idea of him leaving her alone sounded terribly wrong. She was torn between the desires of her heart and proper behavior. "A little longer," was all she could tell him.

"You're afraid of me," he predicted.

She was about to deny it, but then the words came bubbling out. "I *am* afraid, yes. I shouldn't want you to be here—even though you're a trusted friend."

"Is that what I am?" he asked. "A friend?" He bent to her mouth, taking her lips in a soft kiss. And with that one motion, she felt her inhibitions falling away.

No, he was far more than that. Margaret wanted this man desperately, wanted to feel his kiss and the welcome weight of his body upon hers.

"You are," she agreed, trying to gather the shreds of composure that remained.

"And you trust me, aye?" His wayward mouth moved to the soft part of her throat, her body weakening beneath the onslaught.

Shivers broke over her skin. "I trust that you would never hurt me."

His wicked hands moved downward, and the seductive touch made her ache for more. "Nay. I would only love you, lass."

Something inside her cracked apart at his words, like a physical caress. Her breasts tightened beneath the linen nightdress, and she could almost imagine his warm mouth closing over her nipple.

The shock of heat and dampness between her legs caught her unawares, and she sat down on the bed, trying to collect herself. Sinclair had always been a dangerous man, but she felt like the ground was shifting.

"I don't know what to say or do anymore," she whispered. "But I will say this—I'm glad you are here with me now."

Her heartbeat quickened, and she grew aware of Cain in a way she hadn't before. He was so very tall, and every time she was near him, she felt the dark strength of his presence. It was as if he could see past her prim and proper rules to a very different woman.

Her words seemed to intensify his response, pulling her deeper beneath his spell. His hand reached out to cover hers, and she didn't pull away. The weight of his palm seemed to push her past a breaking point she hadn't known was there.

"I want to be with you. You ken that, lass." His hand laced with hers in a silent promise. The air between them was charged with heat, and she was torn by the desire to reach out to him, to feel the strong warmth of his embrace. To rest her cheek against his heart and let everything else go.

"I . . . was afraid you would be angry with me," Margaret admitted. Yes, Cain was an outspoken, brash Highlander who did as he pleased. But his rebellious ways had awakened a wilder side of her. With him, she could say anything she wanted, reveling in the freedom to be another woman.

For a while, the silence descended between them as she considered what to say now. If she allowed him to touch her, there was no going back. But the thought of lying alone in her bed, with only the cool sheets, brought another sense of despondency.

There was a light knock at the door and a male voice said, "Miss Andrews, are you all right? When you left early, I thought you might not feel well." It was Mr. Barnabas, who had apparently felt the need to come and see about her welfare.

Abruptly Cain dropped her hand and moved toward the door. Although it was already locked, he shoved a small table under the knob. He raised a finger to his lips and shook his head.

"I was about to retire for the night," she called out. "I found that I was more tired than I'd thought."

"Might I have just a few moments of your time?" Mr. Barnabas continued. "We needn't have this conversation with a door between us."

Oh yes, we should, Margaret thought. She didn't doubt that the man had come with the hope of courting her.

Cain crossed his arms and rolled his eyes. Then he walked over to Margaret and caught her by the hand, pulling her toward a wing-back chair. Now why was he doing that? To protect her in some way?

She cleared her throat, answering Mr. Barnabas. "It would be inappropriate for me to open the door, since I was about to go to bed."

Especially wearing only her nightdress. But it was even more inappropriate to have Sinclair within her room while she was wearing so little.

The Highlander sat down, pulling her back to sit on his knee. Immediately, she tried to get up, but he locked his arms around her waist. What was he doing?

Margaret wanted to protest, but he pressed his hand over her mouth to prevent her from making a single sound. Every part of her body went rigid being this near to him. Not because she was afraid of what he was doing . . . but because she feared her own response.

His masculine scent caught her, and the feeling of his hands upon her waist was dizzying. She didn't know what his intentions were, but a rush of heat poured over her.

"I am sorry that I cannot lend you my coach in the morning," Mr. Barnabas insisted. "But I thought we could perhaps make other arrangements. You could stay here a little longer until my return."

The man's words blurred in her mind, for she was incredibly conscious of Cain's presence. He pulled her nearer, his mouth at her throat. Shivers of need coursed through her, and she wanted so badly to turn her head to accept his kiss.

"Miss Andrews, please consider delaying your journey," Mr. Barnabas asked again. "I should hate to think of you traveling on horseback for such a great distance. Not when I can be of assistance."

Cain's hands moved to her rib cage, his heated breath causing shivers to break over her flesh. Her body was aching for him, wanting so badly for his hands to move higher.

Touch me, the wanton side of her wanted to beg.

"Good night, Mr. Barnabas," was her shaky answer. "We will speak again in the morning."

The sound of the knob turning startled her. Thankfully, it was still locked with the table shoved beneath it.

Cain set her aside and moved toward the door, poised to fight. He waited a moment, and Margaret held her breath. Barnabas wouldn't try to force the door open, would he?

There was a long pause, and at last he muttered, "Good night, Miss Andrews."

She listened to his retreating footsteps, not daring to speak a word, for fear he would come back. Her heart was racing, and she returned to sit at the foot of her bed. Cain didn't move from his position by the door. His deep blue eyes studied her, and she felt a blush rise over her skin.

She reached for a wrapper, hiding herself as much as possible. Cain hadn't moved from his place by the door, and she questioned what he would do now. She didn't move for long moments. If she went to bed, would he stay where he was? Or would he try to join her?

Her hands were still shaking, so she clenched them together as she approached the coverlet, not looking at Cain. She pulled back the covers and climbed into bed, bringing the blanket up beneath her chin.

And waited.

He stood against the small table, behaving as if she weren't there. He leaned his head against the wall, as if he were listening to the hallway. Long minutes passed before she realized that he wasn't going to touch her anymore. His earlier kiss had been a way of provoking her, while Mr. Barnabas was on the other side of the door. It was almost an act of possession, reminding her that no one could ever affect her the way Cain did.

She rolled onto her side, cooling her burning cheeks against the pillow. He would sleep over there, she suspected. Far away from her, close to any threat. He would keep her safe.

Just as he always had.

Her mind twisted in turmoil as she realized that, although he'd stolen a kiss or two over the years, never once had he harmed her. He'd been her steadfast shield, with the quiet strength of a man who didn't belong in her world.

Shame darkened her cheeks even more. She'd used him, knowing that there would never be anything between them. And when she'd surrendered to temptation, allowing him to kiss her, she'd only fueled his ardor.

He wanted her still, and she didn't know why. After all the years she'd spurned him, why had he stayed? She didn't like the woman she had become. All her life she'd obeyed the rules, doing what a good girl should. And she'd pushed aside the one man who had loved her, who had always protected her.

Slowly, Margaret sat up in bed, drawing up her knees. Her movement caught Cain's attention, and he turned back to her.

She'd mistreated him so badly. Worse was the realization that, if he had been a duke, she'd have accepted his proposal years ago, without a moment's hesitation. Did that mean she had valued wealth and a title over another person's feelings? What did that make her?

Selfish. That's what she had been. And the more she looked back on herself and the way she'd treated Cain Sinclair, the worse she felt. He had always put her needs before his own.

Without really understanding what she was doing, she swung her legs to the edge of the bed and pulled back the coverlet. She didn't know what to do right now, but she had silenced the prudish young woman who had lived her life in ironclad rules. It had brought her nothing but spinsterhood.

Cain didn't move from his place by the door, but he never took his eyes from her. Margaret removed her wrapper and set it upon the back of the chair, walking toward him in her nightdress.

"What is it, lass?" he whispered.

"I've been unfair to you." Her inner sense of propriety was raging, but she couldn't have moved away if she'd tried. "All these years, you watched over me. Even when I was engaged to wed Lord Lisford."

"I did try to talk you out of it," he reminded her.

She nodded, but the right words wouldn't come to her. Her mind and heart were caught in a state of confusion. She was so weary of all the rules, of all the years of obedience.

"When I go back home . . . when my parents learn about all that I've done, they'll want to lock me away."

"What do you want?" His hand moved up her spine, and the touch was so light, a shiver rocked through her.

She lifted her face to his, wanting to close her eyes and shut out all the reasons why this was wrong. The desire to lash out at her former self was growing stronger. She wanted to rebel against the rules, to break every last one of them.

"I want something I shouldn't have." Her arms slid around his neck, making her invitation unmistakable. "Before I have to face the outside world."

Cain muttered a curse in Gaelic, drawing her against him until she felt the hard outline of his body. Her skin grew sensitive, her body awakening against his touch.

"I'm no' a saint, lass." He drew his hands down to her hips and his arousal rocked against her legs. He tempted her beyond measure, and she hardly cared about anything else.

No matter what she said, no matter what choices she'd made, not a single person would believe she was untouched.

And the truth was, she *did* crave Cain's touch. She wanted to cast out the prim and proper miss, becoming someone else. Someone who didn't care what others thought of her.

"You'd best be certain about what you're asking," he warned. "For once we begin, I won't stop."

Margaret laid a finger against his lips, bidding him to be quiet. Then she lifted her mouth to his and kissed him hard.

Chapter Ten

Never in a thousand years did Cain believe Margaret Andrews would try to seduce him. Something had pushed her over the edge, and she was trying to ruin herself. He couldn't be certain of her reasons, but like the sinner he was, he didn't care.

Her mouth was closed, and he angled his kiss, coaxing her to open for him. She softened, and he slid his tongue inside her warmth.

She let out a sudden gasp, but he covered the noise by claiming her mouth, trapping her arms against her sides. The sweet taste of her was honey to his mouth, and he didn't hesitate to take her further, palming her hips. He wanted to show her the pleasure there could be between them, but he didn't want her to be afraid.

Against her ear, he murmured, "I want to touch you the way I've dreamed of, lass."

"Please," she whispered. The softness in her voice was an invisible caress.

"Is this what you want?" he asked, daring to move his hand slowly up the side of her breast. He didn't touch her nipple, but from the way her face tightened, he sensed her need deepening.

"Yes." A sigh mingled with her words, and she closed her eyes.

Cain reached for her hand and forced her to touch her own nipple. Using her hand, he guided her to caress herself. He kissed her earlobe, asking, "Does this make you feel good, lass?"

"It makes me ache," she confessed, her face blushing.

It made him ache, too, his erection taut against his kilt. But he shoved back the primal reactions, knowing he had to go slowly. "Best no' to talk much, lass," he warned, keeping his voice low. "Someone might hear us."

She obeyed, then startled him when she rose up on tiptoes to kiss him again. It was as if she craved him, as if all the years of desire had reached the breaking point. And Cain couldn't think of anywhere else he'd rather be than in her arms.

He reached down and picked her up, carrying her over to the bed. She was light in his arms, making him wish he'd fed her more on this journey. Gently, he laid her down on the pillow, marveling at her. Her dark blond hair was loose around her shoulders, framing an angel's face. Her green eyes held secrets she would not say, and he wondered if he ought to step back.

He sat beside her, his arms on either side of her shoulders. "Are you certain, lass?"

Her answer was to reach for his palm and place it upon her breast.

❧

The touch of Cain's hand upon her body was overwhelming. Margaret closed her eyes, letting herself experience the unfamiliar pleasure of a man's caress. Through the linen of her nightdress, she felt the sensations and the sweet abrasion of her nipple against the fabric. His thumb circled over it slowly, and there came an answering echo in the aching between her legs.

Then he dared to touch her other breast, both of his hands moving over them. It was a sweet torture, knowing how forbidden this was.

But Margaret was tired of obeying the rules. Tired of being the good girl, so prim that a man would hardly dare to hold her hand. She pulled Cain's mouth down to hers, wanting the sharp rush of the world falling away at his kiss.

He ravaged her mouth, making her want so much more. Her legs scissored against the coverlet, and he broke away, his mouth traveling down her throat.

No, that wasn't what she wanted. She tried to guide him back, but he pinioned her hand at her side, his mouth moving to the buttons at the top of her nightdress. He flicked open the first button with one hand, his mouth finding her bare skin.

Then he drew out the tip of one breast, rubbing the nipple between his forefinger and thumb. Her breathing grew uneven, and she tensed when he undid another button. His mouth drifted lower still, his palm claiming her breast.

He wasn't going to—ohhh . . .

The explosive gasp of air couldn't be stopped when his hot mouth covered the nipple he exposed after the last button. She bucked against him, her hand moving to his hair.

Between her legs, she felt a burgeoning sensation of desire deepening. It was nothing like she'd expected, although her sisters, Victoria and Juliette, had warned her. She didn't know what she'd thought it would be like—simply lying back and letting her husband do as he wanted to. Submitting meekly as a good wife should.

But this was more than submission—it was seduction.

"Are you all right?" he whispered against her breast. The stubble of his beard pricked her skin, but the roughness stimulated her even more.

"Don't stop," she managed. It occurred to her that he was touching her, but she'd not done the same to him.

She lifted her hands to his hair, smoothing it back. She'd always thought his long black hair was terribly uncivilized, but here, against her skin, it felt silken.

"Do you ken what happens when a man makes love to a woman?" Cain whispered.

She went motionless, shaking her head. No words would come to her, for she was utterly stunned that he was speaking in such a way.

"He spends all night touching her, taking her body apart until she cries out with the pleasure of it." He leaned in, his hand brushing her erect nipple as he traveled lower. "That's what I'm wanting to do to you, Margaret. I'm wanting to feast upon your skin and take you down until you're so wet, you're pleading for me to come inside you."

He reached toward the hem of her nightdress and touched her calf. "You hold all the power, lass. Tell me what it is you're wanting."

Her conscience was screaming at her to cease this madness, to retreat back into the shell of the woman she'd been. But she ignored the spinster, no longer caring about anything else but Cain. "Just don't stop."

His eyes turned so blue, they were like the hottest part of a flame. "Good."

She wanted to bind him to her this night, to embrace the fervor that had always been between them. His hands moved up her legs, beneath the nightdress. She grew shy, tightening her legs together when he drew closer to her intimate space.

"Are you wet, lass?" he asked, his hand moving against her center. There was no need to ask. The moment his fingers slid against her, he had his answer. She was throbbing, her body crying out for something she didn't understand.

He began to stroke her, and she tilted her hips upward, welcoming his touch. There was a primal rhythm to the motion, and deep inside, she felt herself rising to his call. Higher still, he took her, and she moved against him, straining for more. His thumb edged her hooded flesh, circling and filling her with need. She was tremulous, aching to be filled with him, and her nipples grew erect. He licked at the tips, teasing her with his tongue while his hand caressed her.

She was beyond all conscious thought, so aroused that she grasped his hair and pulled him up to kiss her again. At that very moment, he slid his finger inside her wetness. His tongue invaded her mouth, while his hand did the same, and the sensation took her beyond all control. Without warning, her body spiraled apart. Aching heat shuddered against her, and she felt her body drawing his finger deeper inside. Against her mouth, he murmured, "That was faster than I thought. You must have been close."

She didn't know what he was talking about, but she bit back a moan when he stroked her intimately. Her body was alive in a way it had never been, and she couldn't get enough of him. She kissed him again, and her nails dug into his skin when he continued thrusting his hand inside her. Steadily, he kept up the rhythm, and she clenched him, moving her hips.

"I want you to come again for me, lass," he told her. "Only this time, I'll make it even better."

She wasn't certain how that was possible. It was already as if she'd been unlocked, her body open to an ecstasy that she'd never imagined. But he wouldn't stop touching her, his fingers drenched in her wetness. This time, he kissed her bare breasts again, his tongue teasing the edge of her nipple. He pushed a second finger within her, and her fist clenched the coverlet when his thumb began to circle the hooded flesh above her opening.

She could imagine having him inside her. Thick and hard, she envisioned him thrusting, in the same way he was moving two fingers. He'd stretched her, making her want so much more.

Then he stopped moving, his own breath growing unsteady.

"Please don't stop," she begged. With his fingers buried inside her, she was craving the intrusion. She pressed her hips close, trying to mimic the thrusting he'd done.

"I need a moment," he said, closing his eyes.

But Margaret didn't want that at all. She was too close, poised on the edge of another release, but she didn't know how to seize it.

She reached out to touch him, trying to encourage him to continue. His body was rigid, his face against the pillow.

Was he hurting?

She reached out and encountered the wool of his kilt. Without warning, he moved atop her, still fully clothed.

"Take off your clothes," she murmured.

He stilled at her command, but eventually, she heard him remove the coat and shirt. Then there came the light shush of his kilt as he removed it. In the darkness, she couldn't see him, but she took a moment to remove her nightdress.

This time, when he leaned his weight atop her, she felt the shocking heat of his naked body against hers. The sensation of his thick length against the seam of her opening was enough to bring back the intense longing. She knew that all of this was wrong. She would undoubtedly regret it in the morning.

But for now, she didn't care.

Her lips were swollen from his kisses, her body demanding more. Without asking, she reached out to touch him. His thighs were tightly muscled from years of running and riding horses. She marveled at his strength, learning his body with her hands.

A low growl resounded from his throat when she caressed his

hips. "No' there, lass," he gritted out. He rearranged his position and guided her hand to the front, pressing her palm against his erection.

She'd never seen a naked man before, much less touched one. But she found him beautiful. There was indeed a power in touching him, encircling his velvet shaft and giving him pleasure.

"Careful," he warned, when she squeezed him. He taught her how he liked to be touched, how to stroke his length, and how to make the head of him wet.

As she pleasured him, the feelings of uncertainty grew. He'd asked her to wed him twice before, and she'd said no. All because he'd lacked a title and lands.

And all he'd ever wanted was to be with her.

Her eyes filled up with tears, and she closed them to keep from weeping. He was as hard as stone within her fist, and as she touched him, he renewed his own assault upon her flesh.

Giving him the same pleasure was deepening her own. As he invaded and withdrew with his hands, she imitated his motion with her palm around his shaft. Cain moved her to the side, then rubbed his length between her thighs. He was riding her core, not inside her, but tempting her in a way that made her shudder.

Suddenly she realized that she would not want another man as her husband. She could not imagine a proper gentleman or a titled lord doing this to her. There was only one man she wanted in her bed—Cain Sinclair.

He took both breasts in his palms, rocking his hips against her, until the ache intensified to the point where she released the tears she was holding back. She trembled against him, moving her leg up until she could guide him inside. The head of him entered her, and the thickness stretched her tight.

"Lass," he whispered against her, "this wasna part of the plan. I was ne'er going to take you."

"This is my choice," she whispered. "If you want me. And I don't care what happens afterward."

If she was well and truly ruined, what did it matter now, that she took pleasure for herself? Her cheeks were wet with tears as she silently cried for the woman she had once been. And the woman she was becoming.

Cain let out a low curse but caught her around the waist and thrust slowly. There was a little pain as he took her innocence, but she bravely ignored it until he was sheathed deep inside her.

He didn't move at first, and the soreness began to abate. Then his hand came back between her legs, gently stroking at the hooded flesh above the place where they were joined. Her body responded, and she couldn't help but clench against him.

"That's it, lass. Relax for me," he ordered, touching her and gently sliding and withdrawing. He kept the pressure of his fingers upon her while he created a slight rhythm. She didn't know what he was doing, but he was gliding in and out with no resistance.

"I didna think I'd ever be with you like this," he admitted. "It was only a dream for me."

He seemed to know exactly how to move, how to draw out the aching pleasure until she started shaking against him. Like a blossom unfolding, she strained against his thrusts, welcoming the intense flood of sensation. It was here, oh sweet God, he was going to take her under again.

The release exploded inside her, and she cried out, unable to stop herself from spasming against him. Cain gripped her waist and pressed her to her back, continuing to thrust as she shattered in his arms. He let out a single hiss and jerked against her, finding his own pleasure as he flooded her.

It was the most exquisite sensation she'd ever known, with him buried inside while the aftershocks claimed her. And though there would be consequences for what she'd done this night, right now she refused to think of them.

They were intimately joined, and Margaret reveled in the closeness. She felt like melted candle wax, unable to form a coherent thought.

But then he spoke against her skin. "I'm taking you away from here on the morrow, lass. And when we find a minister, you're going to be marrying me. You willna have a choice."

⚔

Cain lay against Margaret's soft body, but sleep would not come. It had been hours since he'd taken her innocence, and now it was nearly dawn. Though it had been her decision, he couldn't help but feel guilty about it. Aye, he planned to wed her. But after that, what sort of life would she have? A woman like Margaret Andrews would be miserable dwelling in a one-room thatched cottage, like the one he shared with Jonah. She couldn't live like that, and he didn't want her to.

She hadn't answered him when he'd told her his intentions. The only sign that she'd heard him was the touch of her hand over his heart.

He leaned against her hair, breathing in the scent of her. She was going to regret this in the morning. And though he knew marrying her was the only choice for either of them, he hated the thought of bringing her down to his social class. If her father, Lord Lanfordshire, learned of this, the man would want Cain taken out and shot.

He stayed beside her for the rest of the night, savoring her skin against his. An ache caught him, for he had craved a night like this one, a chance to show her how much he desired her. But now that it had happened, his own regret made it impossible to sleep.

He'd stolen a piece of Heaven and made an angel fall. If that didn't make him a devil, he didn't know what would. Marriage wouldn't solve the problem of her ruin, for he was well beneath her. But it would protect her if there came a child from their union.

A strange ache touched his heart at the thought of a son or a daughter with Margaret's green eyes. He almost smiled, imagining how she would teach them good manners. She would be strict and proper, giving them the education he'd lacked.

And after the children were in bed, he'd unlace her and spend the night hours loving her.

As if in answer to his dream, Margaret moved her hips against him. Her sleepy motion aroused him instantly. He couldn't tell if she was awake or not, but when he reached out to touch her breast, she emitted a soft gasp. Her nipple was taut, and he rolled it between his fingers, adjusting his erection until it was pressed at her opening. He didn't move against her, but continued giving her breasts attention, waiting to see if she would welcome him inside her. She might be too sore.

Against the tip of his shaft, he felt her opening to him. She pressed against him, and she was indeed wet and welcoming.

God above, he could spend every day for the rest of his life with a woman like her. He began steadily thrusting inside, and she met his penetrations, pushing back as he took her from behind. He made love to her until her breathing transformed and he knew she was close to breaking. It took only a few more strokes for her to arch against him, trembling as she found her release. He took his, only after he knew she'd been fully satisfied.

For long moments, he remained buried inside her. He kissed the soft skin of her shoulder, then nibbled at her throat. But he didn't speak. Any words he said would only remind her of the choice she'd made.

"It's almost morning," Margaret whispered in the darkness. "You'd better leave the bed, before the maid comes in."

He knew it, though he didn't want to leave. Instead, he ran his hands over her bare skin, making a memory of her. Then he withdrew from her body and gave her back the nightdress. He got dressed in the darkness, but it bothered him to be sneaking around like this. He preferred to simply take her away from here and damn the consequences.

Margaret pulled on her nightdress, then her wrapper. Her hair was tousled around her shoulders, and in the faint morning light, he saw that her lips were swollen, and her eyes were bright. She crossed the room toward him. "I know I should regret what I did with you last night. But I don't."

He took her mouth in another kiss, one that she met with enough passion to make him want to drag her back to bed. "Neither do I, lass."

And after he sent her a smile filled with promises, he slipped outside her room.

ꞏꙨꞏ

Margaret walked down the stairs, wearing the gown she'd arrived in. The maid had informed her that Mr. Barnabas wanted to dine with her at breakfast. She had also offered a new morning dress, but Margaret had declined to wear it. She knew, too well, what that would imply.

When she arrived at the dining room, Mr. Barnabas was reading a letter. As soon as he saw her wearing the old gown, he set the letter aside and frowned. "Did you not receive my gift, Miss Andrews?"

"I did not feel it was appropriate for me to accept it, when I only met you a few days ago," she explained. After his remark, that he was seeking a wife, she'd needed to dissuade him of any ideas. "I borrowed the gown last night out of necessity, but I've left it with Annie to be cleaned."

"A woman of your beauty should not be forced to dress like a housekeeper," he said. "I would have thought you'd prefer to wear clothing that befits your station."

"I do not wish to be beholden to you," she said quietly, "when I shall be leaving this morning."

His expression tightened, as if he didn't wish to hear it. "Be that as it may, if you would prefer to remain here and send word to your family, it would be more comfortable than a journey on horseback with your . . . *cousin.*"

She gave no response to his jibe, for his opinions didn't matter. While a footman served her breakfast, she noticed Mr. Barnabas studying a letter. A dark frown deepened the lines around his mouth.

"Was there bad news?" she inquired, though it was none of her business.

He folded it up and shrugged. "As I said before, it's family troubles. I must leave today and hope that I can intervene before too much damage is done." But though he kept his tone casual, she sensed frustration beneath his voice.

While Margaret dined at breakfast, she let her thoughts drift back to last night. Cain's touch had been searing, her body responding to his with unbridled passion. Never before had she experienced anything like it. The unabashed joy of giving herself to him was unforgettable.

There was freedom in breaking the rules, in embracing a wilder side of herself. It was intoxicating to know that she held power over a man as strong as Cain Sinclair and could drive him past the brink of sanity.

But his marriage demand had caught her unawares. She understood his reasons for wanting to protect her—but his domineering command had made her falter. She might be a fallen woman now, but she was hesitant to marry a man who took it upon himself to order her around.

Mr. Barnabas folded up the letter and set it aside. "I shall deal with my cousin's situation immediately and return within a few days." His face softened, and he told her, "My offer stands, should you wish to remain."

"She doesna plan to stay," Cain interrupted, striding into the dining room. To Barnabas, he added, "We thank you for your hospitality, and 'twill be repaid."

Lewis Barnabas rose from his seat immediately. His expression grew troubled, and he said, "That won't be necessary, Sinclair. Miss Andrews gave her assistance at the supper party last evening, and she was an excellent hostess. Perfect in every way."

She felt the man's eyes upon her, along with his silent plea for her to stay. But she could not. "Thank you, Mr. Barnabas. And I hope that you are able to help your cousin when you find him."

He nodded and gestured toward the food. "Eat, if you wish, before you go."

There was strained tension between the two men, but Cain declined. "We must leave, and Margaret will come with me." He rested his hands upon the back of her chair and added, "You were right, that Margaret is no' my cousin. She's going to be my *wife*."

She bit her tongue at that. He was behaving like a barbarian, as if he intended to haul her over his shoulder and carry her off. She was tempted to interrupt, but Barnabas met Cain's stare with his own disdain. "I suspected as much. I had hoped that Miss Andrews might reconsider marrying a man so beneath her."

Cain didn't rise to the bait. "She was with me from the beginning, Barnabas. She was ne'er going to be yours."

Barnabas raised a hand to gesture for the butler, Mr. Merrill. "Escort Mr. Sinclair out and help him prepare to leave."

"Why don't you go and prepare our horse?" Margaret suggested to Cain. "I will pack a little food for both of us."

"I'll gladly go," he said, "but you are coming with me." He gripped Margaret's hand, and she didn't at all like the direction this conversation had turned. Nor did she appreciate the way he was behaving.

"No," she said calmly. "As I said before, you may see to it that our belongings and the horse are prepared. I will see to the food."

Anger blazed in his eyes, but she stood from her chair and faced him. She would not allow him to treat her like a child, commanding her to obey his wishes. She was a grown woman and expected to be treated as such.

Without another word, he turned and walked away.

After Cain was gone, Mr. Barnabas rose from his seat, resting his hands upon the linen tablecloth. "Do you truly wish to travel with a man who treats you thusly?"

"He doesn't normally," she said, making excuses. "It's only jealousy."

"But what is it *you* want, Miss Andrews? A baron's daughter can have her choice of suitors, and you would not have to suffer orders from me."

She didn't know how to answer him. Yes, Cain was behaving in a domineering manner. But it was only because he wanted to protect her.

"Thank you for your concern, Mr. Barnabas. But I intend to go home to my family. Whatever decisions I make regarding my marriage are my own choice."

He moved to the other side of the table and took her hand, raising it to his lips. "If ever you reconsider, know that you are always welcome here. I have worked for five years, bringing this estate into prosperity, and when the day comes that I inherit my cousin's title, I can give you everything you've ever dreamed of."

Margaret knew he believed that. But she was no longer the same woman who would have valued a title and lands over her heart's desires.

The question was, what sort of life did she want now? A life with a gentleman? Or a life with a Highlander?

✦

"There's been a slight change of plans, lass," Cain informed her, when he saw Margaret walking outside, followed by her lady's maid. He pointed behind him to a farmer's wagon, hitched to their mare, along with a second horse.

"Where did you find that?" Her face was startled, but she appeared pleased.

"The butler, Mr. Merrill, arranged for it." He gestured toward the older man, who stepped forward. In the meantime, Cain began taking bundles from the maid, loading the wagon with food and supplies.

"We made an agreement, my lady. I would provide the wagon and another horse, if Mr. Sinclair agreed to take me and my daughter with you." He sent her a pleading look. "I do hope you will allow us to come."

Margaret appeared curious, and she asked, "Why do you wish to leave?"

Mr. Merrill signaled for the maid to come forward, answering, "Annie has been approached by Mr. Barnabas on more than one occasion. I do not want her working in a household where she is in danger of unwanted advances."

Cain agreed with the man on that point. Whether or not Margaret was aware of it, Barnabas had revealed his true nature, even on the night he'd come to her room. He didn't doubt that if the door had been unlocked, the man would have forced his way inside.

"Of course you may come," Margaret agreed. "And I thank you both for the use of your wagon and the extra horse. It's very kind of you."

The servants helped her inside, but when Cain was about to take the reins, Merrill took them instead. "After all that you've done for us, sir, you should ride with Miss Andrews. Annie and I will sit in the front."

He deferred to their wishes, but it did seem strange to be treated as if he were a gentleman. Cain gave orders to Merrill to travel in a northwestern direction, and once they had begun their journey, he sensed Margaret beginning to relax. He spread a blanket over her lap to offer warmth, and beneath it, he took her hand.

Though she held it, he sensed tension in her grip. "I do not like the way you've been ordering me around," she said in a low voice. "I am a grown woman."

"Aye, that you are, lass." He knew he'd been pushing her hard, but then again, every time he'd asked her to wed, she'd refused. It was a matter of honor now. He'd taken her virtue, and he wasn't the sort of man to abandon her.

She leaned in to whisper in his ear. "Then you will understand that I do not intend to simply wed you, because of last night."

"And what if there is a child?" he whispered back. "I am no' the sort of man to walk away from you."

She was silent for a moment, but then she leaned in. "All my life, I've been told what to do and when to do it. I've been told what to wear, how to eat, how to behave, and what sort of man I should marry. The last thing I want is another man to order me around."

It wasn't like that at all. This was about sheltering her from scandal, about offering her the protection of his name. "You're no' being reasonable, Margaret. What choice do you have but to marry me?"

"Can you not ask?"

You'd say no, he wanted to respond. She'd always said no, no matter that he'd asked her to wed him in the past. Why would he set himself up to be spurned again?

No, he wasn't going to yield on this. He would never sire a bastard and walk away from her.

"I already told you," he said quietly. "I'll no' ask you again to wed me. We're past that now. You *will* become my wife, and that's the end of it." He didn't care that his words were harsh. She needed to know that he would never, ever leave her. Aye, she was a stubborn lass, but she'd sealed her own fate when she'd invited him into her bed.

The wagon rumbled along the road, and in time, it began to rain. "There's an oilcloth in one of the bundles," Annie called out to them. "You can use it to shelter Miss Andrews from the rain."

"What about you and Mr. Merrill?" Margaret asked.

Annie smiled. "I've brought an umbrella for my father and me to share."

In this, Cain was glad that the maid had thought of nearly everything. He found the oilcloth and pulled it over Margaret and himself to shield them from the rain. With a covering over their heads and a blanket to warm them, it was far more comfortable. Cain drew her closer, but Margaret remained stiff in his arms. In a low voice, he asked, "What troubles you? Is it that you're no' wanting to marry me or that I havena asked you properly?"

She created physical distance between them, shifting to the left. "I don't know if I want to marry you or not. But right now, it feels as if my life has been shaken inside out. I'm not the lady I was, and I can't go back to the way things were."

"You weren't happy in that life," he reminded her. "Don't be forgetting that."

She didn't answer him, though her demeanor seemed to suggest it was true. Her knees were curled up under the blanket while she huddled beneath the oilcloth.

She'd said that she wanted him to ask her, instead of making demands. And though he still intended to wed her, he did ask. "What is it you're wanting, lass?"

"My freedom," she whispered. Turning toward him, her green eyes met his. "I want to be treated as if I have a brain in my head. If I marry, I want my husband to treat me as an equal, not someone to decorate his life and host parties." Her eyes lowered, and she added, "I always thought that marrying a wealthy man would give me that freedom. And now it seems that any marriage is only an extension of those chains."

"Don't be asking me to walk away from you," he said softly. "Or did you forget the way it was between us?"

"N-no." Her voice was thick, as if she was fighting back tears. He didn't want her to cry, and he knew when to step back.

"We'll return to Ballaloch first," he told her. "There's no need to be making decisions before then."

His hand remained upon hers, and for a long time he didn't speak. The wagon rumbled through the meadows and over the hills, the rain continuing to fall. He didn't know what to say to her or how to convince her that marriage to him would not be a prison. It would be different from the life she'd known, aye, but he saw no reason why she could not enjoy it.

He released her hand, staring off into the distance. The only worry was how to give her the wealth she'd had as a baron's daughter. If he could find a means of supporting her, he felt certain that he could make her happy.

He had to try.

Chapter Eleven

Night came, and Margaret was well aware that Cain's frustration was brewing hotter. They stopped at an inn, and he arranged for two rooms. She mistakenly believed he intended for her to share a room with Annie, but after the maid fetched her belongings, Cain said good night and shut the door in the young woman's face.

"What are you—we shouldn't share a room," she protested.

In response, Cain reached behind her and locked the door. "There's more that we need to talk about, lass. And I'm no' wanting us to be interrupted."

A sense of uneasiness crept over her. Why would he expect that he had the right to stay here? To stall a moment, she asked, "How did you pay for two rooms? I thought we didn't have enough money."

"Mr. Merrill paid for his own room, lass. And I did save enough coins for this."

Margaret swallowed hard and turned away. She was beginning to realize that he'd kept more secrets than she'd ever imagined. "I didn't realize."

"There's more to me than you ken, lass." He moved in closer, then he reached into his pocket. "You might believe that I've no' a tuppence to my name. But you'd be wrong." He withdrew her strand of pearls and held them out.

Margaret stared at the white pearls, shocked to see them. "How did you get these?"

"I got them back from the vicar's wife and paid her instead. Were you thinking I stole them?" He turned her to face the wall, his hands resting upon her shoulders while he held the pearls.

"I don't know what to think," she admitted. "You never said anything."

"I wouldna let you give up your pearls for me." His hands unfastened the top button of her gown. The moment he did, she went motionless, all thoughts fleeing her mind. Cain unfastened a second button, then a third.

Another flush darkened her cheeks, and she ventured, "What are you doing?"

When he didn't answer, Margaret pulled away, clutching her gown. "You said you wanted to talk to me. This isn't talking."

"I talk better with my hands than my mouth. And I want you to ken all the reasons you should be marrying me."

His blue eyes were smoldering, and she saw how badly he wanted her. "First, I have enough money to take care of you, lass. I'm no' the sort of man to throw away five years of good wages."

Aphrodite's Unmentionables. Of course that was where he'd obtained the money.

She closed her eyes, remembering that they'd paid him a great deal over the years. Not only for his deliveries, but also for secrecy. He'd kept his word and had earned every penny.

"Second, you seduced me last night. I'm a fallen man now."

Her lips curved in an unexpected smile, and she allowed him to move in closer to unfasten the remaining buttons. "Are you suggesting that I compromised you?"

"Aye. And you owe me compensation for it."

His charm was seductive in and of itself. She warmed to him, fully aware that her gown was sliding off one shoulder. "What sort of compensation were you hoping for?"

"Time, lass. Years of waking up beside you."

The teasing was gone now, and in its place was all seriousness. She could almost envision it, and a slight thrill ran over her skin.

Cain removed his shirt and went to pour a cup of ale. His back was bared to her, and she saw the healed burns. Though his skin would always be marred, she was glad to see that the open wounds were now closed up. He'd suffered on her behalf, and these scars were her fault.

Without speaking, she crossed the room and touched her fingers to his bare back, examining him. "Does it still hurt you?"

She ran her fingers over his skin, and he brought her around to face him. "The only thing that hurts is no' being inside you right now, lass."

Heat flushed over her skin, but she made no protest. Tonight was about something else. It was about choices.

She could choose to leave this room and sleep with the maid, letting all the confusing doubts cloud her mind with sleeplessness. Or she could choose to spend the night in Cain's arms, a night where he would love her.

No, she didn't know what she would do after this. He was demanding marriage, but she didn't have to accept his dictates. Though he wanted to protect her from gossiping tongues, she also knew that he wanted to keep her to himself. And she simply didn't know what would happen to her now.

He took both of her arms and drew them around his neck. "I think you need to be reminded of why we're meant to be together, Margaret Andrews."

"I fear I've committed so many sins, I can hardly face anyone." A rush of need flowed over her when his hands moved down against her breasts.

"The only person you have to face right now is me, lass." He bent and captured her lips, pulling her hips against his. The scalding heat of his mouth shoved aside all of Margaret's inhibitions. From the moment he kissed her, she melted into him.

It wasn't a forced seduction. She knew that as she answered his kiss, giving back to him all the desire that roared within her. Cain Sinclair had always been able to reach past her boundaries.

He'd recognized the truth—that she wasn't at all a good girl. She was good at pretending to be the perfect lady, but after all these years of attempting to wed a nobleman, she realized that her reasons weren't the right ones. She'd wanted to wed a duke to win her freedom. She wanted to have enough money to never worry about food or shelter . . . and she wanted a man who would be so caught up in his own duties that he'd leave her alone.

Lord Lisford had led her to believe that he possessed all the qualifications she'd wanted. She'd believed his lies that he had feelings for her. Only after he'd abandoned her did she realize that he'd made a fool of her. His estate was debt-ridden, and his only asset was a silver tongue that had spoken the words she'd wanted to hear.

She'd been selfish, and it seemed that Fate had taught her a lesson. Wealth was an illusion, easily lost. And the one man she cared about had no title and hardly any wealth.

After all they'd endured together, she wanted to be with him again, damning the consequences.

Margaret kissed him back, her own hunger rising. Against her throat, she felt him fastening the pearl necklace, in a tangible reminder that she should have held more faith.

Cain's hands moved over her corset, his hands warming her skin as he unlaced her. "Just once, I'd like to see you in a scandalous undergarment, lass." But he removed the simple buckram corset, revealing her linen chemise. "Something red with lace."

"I would be too embarrassed," she admitted, drawing her arms around his neck. "It's not who I am."

"You're wrong." He bent to her breast and took her nipple in his mouth, through the linen. Shock and desire seized her, and she gripped his hair. "I ken your secrets, Margaret Andrews. And you like a bit of wickedness."

She did. All of this was wrong, but she wanted to steal one last moment with Cain. There was time enough for her family's disapproval and the knowledge that she'd thrown away her virtue. Time enough later to worry about the choices she'd made. But for now, she wanted to give back to him a taste of what he'd given her. She wanted him to be mad with desire, and she wanted to give him the same release he'd granted her.

He reached down to lift her up, and she drew her legs around his waist. "Will you do something for me?" she whispered, knowing that he was already deeply aroused. His hands moved against her bottom, beneath her chemise.

"What are you wanting, lass?"

She took his face between her hands. "I want to touch you. And I want to be in command of you."

The incredulous look on his face was replaced by a searing look in his eyes. "You can do anything you like, lass. So long as it ends with me inside you."

Her body responded with an aching between her legs. Margaret caressed a path down his shoulders, and he lowered her to stand before him. Then she took him by the hand and led him to the bed, ordering him to undress and lie on his stomach. His back was still red, but the burn marks were healing. She left him there for a moment, while she searched her belongings for the healing salve the apothecary had given her.

This time, she dipped her fingers into the salve and moved it over his back, working it into his skin. He flinched at a few tender spots, but she continued massaging him, moving her hands toward his shoulders and arms.

She paused a moment to remove her undergarments, and it felt utterly wicked to be naked and touching him. He let out a harsh groan when she sat with her legs on either side of his waist. Skin to skin, her palms traveled over his spine, and she reveled in the power of this.

It was as if he'd unlocked another side of her, and she ordered him to roll over. She adjusted her position until she was seated against his rigid erection. Her hands were slick from the salve, and she slid them from his shoulders to his chest. There was a light dusting of dark hair, and she caressed his chest, touching her thumbs to his own flat nipples.

Cain moved his hands behind his head, watching her with those blue eyes. His black hair fell beneath his shoulders, and she pushed it back, lowering her mouth to his heart.

These past few weeks had been otherworldly, almost as if she had been a different woman. The old Margaret had died in the coach accident, while she'd found a strength she hadn't known she had. And that new woman wanted to savor the last few moments of being with Cain.

She caressed his ribs, moving lower until her hand reached his shaft. Though she was slightly afraid of touching his thick length, she knew it would drive him over the edge. Slowly, she curled her hand around him, watching his response. His hands moved down to the tangled sheets, gripping them hard. She fisted him, watching as his eyes flared and his hips moved in counterpoint.

"Is that all right?" she asked, wondering if he liked it.

"More," he ordered. He brought his hand over hers, showing her how to find a rhythm, how to stroke him, until her palm grew slick.

The longer she touched him, the more her own desire grew. She wanted to feel him deep inside her, to thrust and become one with him.

She felt herself transforming into someone else, a woman who abandoned the rules to do as she wanted. And regardless of what unknown future lay ahead, she did want more time with Cain Sinclair. But only if he treated her as an equal, not a woman to be commanded.

When he reached between her legs, she couldn't stop the gasp that spilled forth. "You ne'er said I couldna touch you, lass." He caressed the sensitive skin surrounding her opening, rubbing until she grew wet against his hand.

"You're distracting me," she accused, clenching her palm against him when he slid a finger inside.

"Challenging you," he corrected. "To see which of us loses control first." He kept one finger inside while he used his thumb to rub her hooded flesh. "And I'm going to make you come so hard, you willna remember your own name, lass."

"You can try." Margaret gripped him, moving her hand over him from the end of his shaft to the wet tip. Increasing the friction, she heard a growl emit from his throat.

She felt him stroking her from inside, finding a place that made her tighten against his fingers. And without warning, her body began to tremble, the shimmering sensations building higher.

He was right; she was going to lose this battle. But not before she brought him to the edge. She lifted the thick head of him and sat down, sheathing him fully inside her. It was an exquisite tightness, being so filled by him. And his hands moved to grasp her hips.

"No," she said. "You are mine to take."

Margaret rose up on her knees, sliding back down in a slow, torturous rhythm. His face tightened as if he were fighting the feelings she'd kindled. She rewarded him by hastening the tempo, rising up and down. Closer, she brought him toward his release, feeling his body grow even harder within her. Her own breathing was ragged, and when he sat up, he grasped her hips. He bent to suckle her, and the sensation of riding him while he tormented her breasts was an exquisite torture. He moved his hand between her legs, and the first release swept over her, causing her to spasm against him.

"You win," she murmured, slowing the pace once more.

"I always do," came his response. Then he began thrusting against her as she moved. With his hands, he forced the rhythm to go faster, their bodies pounding while he seized her hips.

"Every night," he swore. "'Twill be like this."

She said nothing, unable to agree to his demands. Not yet. In the past two days, she had let go of her inhibitions and rules. No longer was she a woman who lived in a glass house where every choice was made for her.

She had chosen to give herself to Cain, to experience this rush of pleasure. And though he wanted marriage, she was hesitant to agree. She didn't want to wed a man who believed it was his role to tell her what to do. And Cain was a stubborn Highlander who would undoubtedly have his own ideas about a wife's place.

No, she preferred to hold on to her freedom a little longer, before she had to face the reality of what she'd done.

She continued riding him, feeling herself moving closer to another release. But before her body could reach another climax, Cain withdrew and turned her around, facing in reverse. Then he guided her hips down and plunged inside once more. The new position drew his shaft against her most sensitive place, and she ground against him, growing even more excited.

The pleasure of being taken like this was more than she could bear. And then he let out a hoarse cry, slamming against her. Again and again, he thrust until she convulsed against him and he found his release.

He held her waist, and she lowered her head, suddenly realizing that he was right about the danger. She could easily bear his child, and likely would, if she continued to lie with him over the next week. It was a sobering thought, one that troubled her.

Her eyes burned, but she forced the words out. "We need to be careful, Cain."

"If we wed, it willna matter, lass." His hands moved over her bare breasts, stroking the tips. Her body reacted violently, an aftershock claiming her while he was still buried inside.

Cain withdrew from her, pulling her to lie on her side. The candlelight in the room covered the bed sheets with a golden haze. "You're going to stay with me each night, lass." He fingered the pearl necklace around her throat. "And trust that I'll keep you safe."

She wanted to believe it could be that easy. But if she wed him, his life would remain the same while hers irrevocably changed. In her heart, she believed that Cain would take care of her. But was it right to bind herself to this man when the two of them were from such different worlds? Would he grow to despise her over the years because she wasn't the sort of wife he'd imagined? She was a terrible cook, and she knew nothing about keeping a house. The young lady's education she'd received was utterly useless for a man like Cain.

Her heart was heavy as she tried to sleep beside him. For she could not give him an answer when she didn't know it herself.

✦

ONE WEEK LATER

The green hills of Ballaloch should have been a welcome sight. After all the traveling they'd done, Margaret wasn't certain if her family was still in London, but she knew their servants would be there—especially Mrs. Larson, their housekeeper.

"We should go to your house first," she told Cain. "Jonah will want to see you." Her nerves were raw and she felt as if her sins were written upon her face. Mother knew her so well, Margaret feared that if Cain brought her home, he would be blamed.

"Soon," he agreed. "But first, I'll take you home." The stony resolution on his countenance made it clear that he would not argue with her on this. He directed Merrill where to drive them, and Margaret steeled herself for what lay ahead. If she was fortunate, her parents might still be away.

But the moment she spied the manor house, she knew they were here. Her father's carriage was outside the house, and a servant was tending to one of the horses.

"Leave me now, and go see about your brother," she bade Cain. "I'll be fine."

"I won't leave you to face the storm alone," he insisted. "We've been gone well over a month now."

She knew he was trying to protect her, but she didn't want him caught in the middle of her ruin. "If you come inside, they'll believe

208

the worst," she insisted. "If I go alone, they will rejoice that I am safe. We can discuss the rest later."

Cain remained unconvinced, but she insisted. "Please. I know my family, and this is the best way."

"One hour," he relented. "And after that, I'll speak with them."

If he did, her father would insist upon pistols at dawn. Never in a thousand years would Lord Lanfordshire allow his second-eldest daughter to wed a Highlander.

"I would rather speak to them without bloodshed, Cain," she said. "Let me come to you later. Besides," she said, offering a slight smile, "I want to see that your brother is all right."

He didn't look happy about the idea, but he agreed to let her go. "If you don't come, I'll return for you."

Margaret didn't doubt that for a moment.

When the wagon came to a stop, Cain helped her out. He drew out the pearl necklace around her throat, and her skin warmed beneath the gesture. "Go, lass." Before she could walk up the winding path, he caught her mouth in a light kiss.

She blushed fiercely. "You shouldn't do that in public, Mr. Sinclair."

"I do many things I shouldn't, lass." He watched as Merrill and Annie accompanied her to the house. When she glanced back at him, he met her gaze before driving the wagon back toward the land where the crofters dwelled together.

His house stood upon land between Ballaloch and Eiloch Hill. Cain drove the wagon toward the small wooden house with a peat roof. He drew the horses to a stop and got out, expecting to find smoke curling from the chimney. But there was nothing.

Unease caught him low in the stomach. Though it was summer, there should have been a cooking fire. Cain opened the door and called out, "Jonah?"

The house was cold and silent. His younger brother could have gone out hunting or fishing, logic told him. But his instincts warned that this was more than that. He knelt by the cold hearth and saw that there had been no fire here for days. There were hardly any ashes at all.

Cain crossed the space and saw that his brother's belongings were missing. His clothing, all the food . . . and their father's pistol.

Jonah was gone.

A curse rose to his mouth, out of fear that the boy had run away. He'd threatened to, more than once, but he'd always had Grania MacKinloch to talk him out of it. Grania had been a foster mother to the boy, along with her husband, Rory. Grania had died in the spring, but Rory would know where the boy had gone. Cain couldn't imagine that the man would leave Jonah alone. In the past, Jonah had spent his days with them and his nights in their own house. Had something changed?

He uttered a silent prayer that his brother had gone to live with Rory, that he was somehow safe.

Cain walked among the crofters' houses, and several folk greeted him on the way to Rory's cottage. None knew what had become of Jonah, nor had they seen him in weeks. The dark worry caught hold and grew.

When he knocked at Rory's house, it took several minutes before the older man answered. His hair was shot with gray, his eyes reddened. In one hand, he held a bottle of whisky.

"You're looking for Jonah, then. About time you came back for him. But he's been gone nigh a month, I'd wager."

"Where is he?" Cain demanded.

"Oh, hither and yon. He said he was wanting adventure. That you wouldna allow him to go anywhere."

"He's four-and-ten," Cain shot back. "Why would I let him go somewhere alone?"

The older man shrugged, his balance weaving back and forth. It was clear that he'd spent most of the night with the whisky bottle. "He wasna alone. MacKinloch went with him."

Cain's jaw tightened. "*Which* MacKinloch?"

"Joseph, I think it was. Aye, I'm fairly certain 'twas him."

Cain stilled at that. Joseph had once been a footman for Margaret's family. His sister had been taken by Lord Strathland's men, and after Strathland had ordered the girl killed, Joseph had vowed to avenge his sister's death. Cain didn't want his younger brother involved with the man in any way.

"Where did they go?"

"Let me think." The man took another drink of whisky. "I canna remember wha' he said."

"Were they going to Strathland's estate?" He knew that Joseph had been responsible for some fires, in retaliation against the earl. Now that Lord Strathland was locked away in an asylum, they might have tried looting the house.

"Nay. They were going on a longer journey. To find you, I think." Rory nodded and leaned against the doorframe.

Cain felt as if someone had slit his throat. He'd never expected his brother to run away—not like this. And if Joseph MacKinloch had accompanied him, it would only drag Jonah into more trouble.

He mumbled a thanks to Rory and walked blindly toward his house. Never should he have left his brother alone. After Grania's death, it was clear that Rory was more interested in getting drunk than caring for a boy who wasn't his.

MICHELLE WILLINGHAM

The burden of guilt weighed on Cain's shoulders as he unhitched the horses and led them to the stream to drink. He had to go after Jonah, find him, and bring him home safely. Which meant leaving Margaret behind.

One action had torn apart his plans. He would have to leave, first thing in the morning, after he'd gathered enough supplies for the journey. The thought of riding away didn't sit well with him, but what choice was there? Margaret would understand what he had to do.

He only hoped it wouldn't take long to find Jonah.

🦎

Her mother was weeping and hugging her tightly. "Thank God you're all right. Oh, my darling, you don't know how happy I am to see you alive." Tears dampened her cheeks, and Margaret didn't know if they were hers or Beatrice's.

Her father stood back a little, and sheepishly admitted, "I want to give you a hug of welcome, but I don't think your mother is going to let go of you."

Margaret smiled and held out her arm so he could embrace both of them. The scents of home surrounded her—the soft floral tones of her mother and the darker sandalwood of her father.

When at last they allowed her to step back, she asked, "Is Amelia all right?"

"Yes, very," Beatrice said. "She married the Earl of Castledon after he saved her from abduction. They are quite happy together."

Then it seemed the viscount hadn't lied. In spite of all the mishaps, Margaret was glad to hear that her sister had been rescued. She gestured toward Annie and John Merrill, introducing them. "Mr. Merrill loaned us the use of his wagon and an extra horse to get here."

A strained look came over Beatrice's face. "You were escorted home by strangers?"

Time to admit the truth. "No, Mother. Cain Sinclair was my escort, both in leaving London and returning home."

"And where is he now?" her father asked. Though his words were calm, Margaret recognized the silent threat beneath them.

"I sent him to go and see his younger brother, Jonah." She clutched at her skirts, hoping neither of them would see the telltale flush on her cheeks. "Anyway, Mr. Merrill and Annie are both very good servants, and I thought they could help us for a time."

Her mother recognized Margaret's change-the-subject tactic, and sent her a warning look. "Perhaps. Mrs. Larson has been away visiting Amelia, so extra help would be welcome." Glancing toward the servants, she added, "Provided you have experience, of course."

"They do, and I will vouch for their character," Margaret said. "Now, if you don't mind, I would love a hot bath and one of my own gowns."

"What happened to yours?" her father asked. His voice held a trace of murder within it, as if he believed Cain had torn it from her body in a frenzy of lust. Which wasn't entirely far from the truth, given the nights they'd spent together.

"It was damaged," was all she said. "I'll tell you about it later."

"I will accompany you upstairs," Beatrice announced. "And Henry, why don't you speak with Mr. Merrill and Annie and see if they would be of help to us until Mrs. Larson returns."

Her mother placed her hand upon Margaret's back and guided her upstairs. When they reached the landing, Beatrice stopped. "Are you all right?" she murmured. "In every way, I mean. Sinclair protected you, didn't he?"

Margaret shielded her emotions. "I am fine, Mother. Mr. Sinclair kept me from harm."

And he thoroughly seduced me, she thought. Never before had she imagined that she would welcome such carnality. She turned away so her mother would not see her burning cheeks.

"But you traveled with him for weeks," Beatrice continued. "Are you certain?"

"I am, yes." She squared her shoulders and faced her mother.

A pained expression came over Beatrice's face. "I cannot understand why you would leave London, with an unmarried man, in search of Amelia. It's not like you, Margaret."

She followed her mother inside her bedroom, and when Beatrice closed the door, Margaret admitted, "I wasn't thinking clearly. I know you're right."

Her mother began searching through Margaret's gowns, discarding one after the other, until she found an embroidered cream morning gown with a prim neckline and long sleeves. Then she lowered her head, as if to gather up her feelings. "You don't know how I worried about you. I was so frightened you were dead. We never received word from you."

A sense of guilt clouded over her for that. "I was frightened, too." Margaret took the gown, folding it in half. "But everything will be fine now."

"Will it?" Beatrice asked quietly. She stood behind a chair, studying her.

"My life isn't over," Margaret reminded her. "I made mistakes, but time will heal them."

"I hope so." Beatrice crossed the room and took her into another embrace, stroking her hair. "But you'll have to stay in Scotland for a while. Even then, I don't know if the ton will ever forget what happened. You will have to learn to ignore the gossip."

"I survived, Mother. And in the end, isn't that more important?"

Her mother nodded. "I just don't want your chances at happiness to be ruined. Perhaps we could wed you to a foreigner or a titled lord who can look past all this."

She made it sound as if Margaret had to be traded to another country. No, she was in no haste to decide her future—not yet.

"We will speak of it later," Margaret said. "In the meantime, I've been traveling for so long, I want a hot bath and a chance to sleep in my own bed."

Beatrice ventured a smile. "You've nothing to worry about. I'll let no one speak ill of you, and I promise we'll set everything to rights. Now let me see if I can arrange that bath for you."

She hurried out, and after she'd closed the door behind her, Margaret sat down, feeling like a traitor. Not once had she spoken of Cain's marriage offer. She'd behaved as if nothing had happened . . . when the truth was, he'd taken her life apart.

Inside this room, every piece of furniture was artfully displayed. The linens were pressed, the cream drapes bordering tall windows that let in a great deal of light. Nothing was out of place.

And yet, she felt a sense of being imprisoned here, closed off from the outside world.

You'll have to stay in Scotland for a while, her mother had said. It would be like a seclusion, Margaret guessed.

Her sister Victoria had done the same, never leaving this house for years, out of fear. She'd wept when anyone had tried to lead her outside.

Did her family intend for her life to be the same as her sister's? Would they shield her from the world like a forgotten book? Placed upon a shelf where no one would ever desire her?

A ball of hurt caught up in her throat at the memory of the last time she'd lain in Cain's arms. With him, she felt more alive than she'd ever been before. He'd changed her.

This room felt colorless and empty now, like an eggshell. She couldn't imagine remaining in isolation here, not when she could spend those days living with Cain. Even if they lived in utter poverty, she could imagine him coming home and kissing her until she couldn't breathe. She strode toward the window, tugging at the sash until she brought fresh air into the room. From the second-floor room, she could see the green land stretching before her for miles. Across the hills lay Eiloch Hill, where the crofters dwelled.

Cain might be there now with his brother. She had promised to go to him, and she would keep that promise.

Her hands moved to her stomach, wondering if there would be a child from the nights she'd shared his bed. She had fallen so far in the past few weeks, surrendering to temptation from a man who was little more than an outlaw.

But none of it seemed to matter anymore. For already she missed him. And she wondered if she had the courage to reach for another life.

⚜

It didn't surprise Cain that Margaret had not yet come to see him. But with Jonah's disappearance, he had to begin his search as soon as possible. And he couldn't go without speaking to her first.

He stood in front of the manor house, uncertain of how Lord and Lady Lanfordshire would react to his presence. The door swung open, and Cain saw Mr. Merrill standing there. It reassured him to know that he wouldn't be thrown out right away. "I see you've found a position with the family, Merrill."

The older man gave a slight smile. "A temporary one, sir. The family has been kind to Annie and me, granting us a place to stay. Even if it's only for a short time, at least we may earn references here."

Cain was glad to hear it. "I've come to pay a call upon Miss Andrews," he told Merrill.

The older man opened the door wider. "Of course, sir. Come in, and I'll let her know you've returned."

Before Cain could set foot in the house, Lord Lanfordshire saw him standing at the entrance. He moved forward, blocking the hallway. "I think you've seen enough of my daughter in the past month."

From the man's tone, it was clear that Margaret had told him very little. "I brought her home safely to you," Cain reminded the man. Before he could repeat his request to see her, the baron's expression narrowed.

"And you're wanting a reward for it, I suppose. How much did she promise you?"

The man honestly believed he'd come here for money?

Of course. He would think that, wouldn't he? The assumption was a blow he should have anticipated. But Cain met the man's gaze and said, "That isna why I've come, Lord Lanfordshire. I came to tell Miss Andrews that I'll be leaving Ballaloch again. My brother has gone missing."

"You presume she would care where you've gone?" The baron's expression was cold. "Go on your way, Sinclair. Your business with my daughter is finished."

The soft sounds of footsteps caught his attention, and Cain spied Margaret standing at the top of the stairs. Her hair was damp and hanging down across her shoulders, as if she'd just bathed. The old Margaret would never have dreamed of appearing before anyone in such a state, but she'd rightfully understood that her father was about to make him leave.

She called out, "No, Father, it's all right. I will speak with Mr. Sinclair."

Lord Lanfordshire's expression turned rigid. "You will not, Margaret. Remain upstairs, and I will ensure that Sinclair does not bother you."

Her father's words were meaningless, for Margaret hurried down the stairs, ignoring him entirely. "Has something happened, Mr. Sinclair?"

"It has," he agreed. "Jonah is gone."

Her eyes widened with dismay, and she moved closer. From this distance, he could smell the floral aroma of the soap she'd used. It made him want to pull her nearer.

"Do you have any idea where he might be?" she was asking.

"Nay. But I'll have to go and find him."

Her eyes met his, and she nodded faintly, to show that she understood. But he didn't want her to think he was abandoning her.

Lord Lanfordshire stood between them, trying to keep Margaret from coming any closer. And yet, it was as if the baron weren't there at all.

"Of course you must go," she murmured. "I will pray that he's found safely."

Will you be all right? he asked silently. He didn't know how long his search would last, and he was torn by wanting to protect her . . . and knowing he couldn't.

He wasn't the sort of man to leave a woman behind, not like this. She shouldn't have to suffer shame because of choices they'd made on the journey.

"I'll be leaving in the morning," he told her. "I'll have to gather supplies for the journey beforehand." He held her gaze, wanting her to come and see him one last time.

She glanced at her father and then looked back at him. Worry creased her green eyes, and he suspected she couldn't leave. "Be careful."

There was nothing more to say, and he started to turn away when Margaret called out, "I'll walk out with you, Mr. Sinclair."

"No, you will not." Her father caught her arm and pulled her back. "I allowed you to speak with him, but that is all."

"Henry, you're being ridiculous." Lady Lanfordshire came downstairs and put an arm around Margaret. "Our daughter is a grown woman, and I hardly think Mr. Sinclair intends to accost her at the front door."

Anger flared in the baron's eyes. "We are not having this discussion here, Beatrice. I've said what I intend to say, and that's final."

In response, the baroness took him by the hand and started to lead him away. "Go on, Margaret. Say your farewell, and I'll manage your father."

"I am not a child to be managed," Lord Lanfordshire gritted out.

"Then stop behaving like one." She gripped his hand and nodded to them. "You may have two minutes."

The warmth in the woman's eyes caught Cain by surprise, like an unexpected ally. He bowed to her and smiled in return. Was it his imagination, or did the baroness actually wink at him? Surely, he was seeing things.

Margaret smiled gratefully at her mother and hurried forward. She closed the door behind her, and took his hand. "Thank you for telling me about Jonah. I'll pray that you find him quickly."

"Come to my house tonight, lass," he said beneath his breath. "One last time before I go."

"I can't. It will be too hard to slip away."

He'd expected her to say that. "I'll wait for you."

She hesitated, and he knew her beautiful mind was coming up with all sorts of reasons why this was improper.

"We need to talk," he said. "Say you'll come."

"I can't make any promises," she protested. "But I hope you find Jonah quickly and return."

"Aye. That I'll do." He took a step backward and walked down the stairs. It felt as if he'd intruded upon enemy territory, but he didn't care. Aye, Lord Lanfordshire would sooner kill him than allow him to see Margaret again. In the end, it was her decision. And the fact that she'd defied her father to speak with him held a promise of its own.

"Tonight," he repeated.

Chapter Twelve

Margaret trudged along the path leading toward Cain's house. Although she'd worn a hooded cloak so that no one would see her face, it wasn't a good idea to walk alone. Her heart was pounding at the thought of being discovered by anyone—especially her father.

But thankfully, she'd managed to slip away.

After another mile of walking, she reached Cain's house. The wood frame was a few years old, and the peat roof held an earthy smell. Was this the sort of house she would share with him, if they did marry? She studied it for a moment, touching the rough exterior. At one time, she would have been horrified to live in a house such as this.

But now . . . she saw that it wasn't the house that mattered. It was the people inside. And she didn't want to turn away from the man who had kept her safe during these past few weeks.

Her father had made it clear that he wanted her to have nothing to do with Cain. He would do everything in his power to prevent them from being together. No, Cain wasn't the sort of man her parents would approve of. But neither was she ready to walk away from him.

Confusion muddled her thoughts as she stood before his door. Did she want to marry Cain? She tried to imagine what it would be like if she never saw him again, and an aching emptiness took root in her heart. Perhaps it was better to be with him than without him. But if she dared to accept his proposal, it would tear her family apart.

Margaret stared at Cain's door, wondering what she should do. Her parents would pressure her to wed a gentleman quickly, but in the end, she held all the power. She could do what *she* wanted to do, not what they believed was proper. But the longer she held off, the more it would push her toward a real marriage with Cain. And perhaps that might be what she wanted after all.

She pushed open the door and found herself staring at a sharp blade. Cain let out a breath and lowered the dirk. "You should've knocked, lass."

He pushed the door closed behind her, and she moved into his arms. The scent of him filled up the space, and she rested her cheek against his heart. It felt good to be in his embrace once more with his strength surrounding her.

"I'm so sorry about Jonah," she said. "Did you learn anything else?"

His hand caressed her hair, and he shook his head. "Nay. He was gone before we got to Ballaloch."

Idly, she traced her hands down his chest until she wrapped her arms around his waist. He said nothing, but drew his hands over her face as if he were learning her features in the dark. "I don't ken when I'll be back."

"But you will return." The ache within her sharpened at the thought of him leaving. She'd never expected to feel this way for him, but it was right. He had somehow pushed past the edges of her proper ways, weakening the barriers of her heart.

"Your father wants me to stay far away from you." He released her, and the grimness in his tone spoke of a man who understood the distance between them. Then he lifted her chin and asked, "But what is it *you* want, lass?"

"I don't know," she whispered. "If I choose to marry you, my family might turn away from me. I'll lose everything I've ever known." Her hands moved up around his neck. "But I don't know if I could bear to be away from you."

She stood on tiptoe and touched her mouth to his. He kissed her back gently, and the warmth of his mouth reminded her of all the reasons why she was powerless to resist him. In moments like this, he made her feel beautiful, as if he lived for her.

"Wait for me, lass," he urged. His eyes held a dangerous glitter, and he pressed her back against the wall. "Don't give up on us." Her heart stumbled a beat, and he framed her face within his hands. "I may no' be able to give you a fine house with servants or a title. But I can give you all that I have."

She covered his hands with her own. Once, marrying a titled, wealthy gentleman had been her dream. Now, that life was out of reach. Even if she had the chance to wed a lord, she wasn't certain that was what she wanted anymore.

"Find your brother," she said, "and when you return, I'll give you my answer."

He drew her close, holding her body to his. His hands moved down her spine, until their bodies were fitted together. "Can you deny that this is where you belong?"

She didn't argue with him, but a sudden impulse made her say, "Convince me, then."

His hands moved down to the buttons of her gown, lightly teasing her nape. But she caught his hands and said, "Wait."

His blue eyes burned hot, and he gripped her hands. "I canna speak the fine words you're wanting, lass. I walked through fire for you. What more do you want?"

He spoke the truth, for he'd suffered on her behalf. But she was torn between the woman she'd intended to be and the woman she was. Cain Sinclair had seen through her proper manners. She wasn't at all a prim miss who would scream and faint at the sight of danger. She was a woman who survived, no matter what the cost.

And what she wanted was a man who saw her as an equal.

On that point, she reminded him, "I walked through fire for you, too."

The air between them was tense, for he looked frustrated that she wasn't ready to hand over her life to him. "Why do you fight what there is between us?"

She brought his hands to her waist. "I'm not fighting you, Cain. I'm fighting myself. I don't know who I am anymore or what sort of life lies ahead."

"It doesna have to be a life like this," he said in a low voice, turning her to look at his house. "I could change everything for you."

She didn't understand what he meant by that. "I don't think—"

"Listen, lass." He cut her off, bringing her back to face him. "Had you thought about Aphrodite's Unmentionables? What if I began delivering the garments again? We earned a great deal of money over the years. It could happen again."

She studied his blue eyes, turning it over in her mind. For so long, she'd resisted the idea of any involvement in the business, leaving it to her sisters and the crofters' wives who dwelled on Eiloch Hill. In the past two months, they'd virtually abandoned it, and she knew that the Scotswomen needed those profits. Someone had to resurrect it, and Cain was right. It *could* bring in tremendous profits.

"I could give you more than this," he insisted. "You'd have a better life."

"But I'd never see you, if you traveled that often," she reminded him. "What sort of life is that?"

He stopped talking then and took possession of her, claiming a kiss. She kissed him back, knowing that she could not refuse him any more than she could walk out the door. "I would do whate'er I had to, lass. You belong to me, and you'll wed me one day. If I have to chain you to my side, this I swear."

His tongue entered her mouth, sending a thousand ripples of desire floating through her. With him, her inhibitions vanished, making her into a woman who bloomed beneath his touch.

"I don't use words to get what I'm wanting. I'm a man of actions." He lifted her up so that her legs were wrapped around his waist. Then he pressed her against the wall, supporting her weight easily. Gently, he lowered her until she could feel his rigid erection pressed between her legs.

"Tell me you don't crave my touch. That you don't want to feel me here." His hand moved beneath her skirts, above her stockings, to her bare skin. His palm caressed between her legs, and she was already wet for him. "Your body doesna lie, does it?"

"No," she breathed. He murmured endearments to her in Gaelic, fumbling with his clothes until she could guide his erection inside her. It was exhilarating, being joined with him like this. Both of them were fully clothed, and yet he'd claimed her intimately.

"You aren't a good girl, Margaret Andrews," he breathed against her throat. He lifted her slightly, sheathing himself inside her wetness. "You might behave like a lady, but deep inside, you want to be wicked."

He was right. She loved the way he touched her, unraveling her senses. "And deep inside, you want to be a man of honor. You would die for someone you loved." Just as she'd abandoned all principles to fight for her sister.

"I would die for you." He took her hard against the back wall, and she understood this was his way of making her understand. He wasn't a gentleman and never would be. A life with him would be wildly unpredictable.

And as if in answer to her reckless thoughts, he fumbled with her bodice, unlacing her with one hand. All the while, he continued to penetrate her body. She was caught up in the storm of feelings, and when he freed a breast, she shuddered. His mouth was upon her, sucking and drawing even deeper sensations.

It was like being conquered by a barbarian, powerless to do anything except ride out the fury of his aching thrusts. The first release struck her hard, and she gasped, her fingers digging into his shoulders.

"That's it, Margaret," he murmured against her nipple. "Feel what it is I'm doing to you."

When the first wave ended, Cain kissed her hard, bringing her to his bed. He guided her knees up, never ceasing the rhythmic thrusts. He was like an iron rod, hard and unrelenting as he forced her to take him.

And God above, it felt good.

Abruptly, he stopped, and rested his weight on his forearms. "There's no man who will ever make you feel like this."

Margaret was trembling violently, unable to think or breathe as he remained buried inside her. She was dying on the edge of pleasure, and he rested his hand upon her breast. While he was still motionless, he plucked at her nipple, drawing out the sensations.

She wrapped her legs around him, her body helpless but to ride out the intense surrender. Cain held her wrists, his mouth sucking hard against her breast until she was unable to breathe or speak. A hoarse cry broke forth from him when he seized his own release, and she held him tightly as he shuddered.

"I have to leave and find Jonah," he told her. "I'm all he has." There was regret in his words, but she understood that there was no choice.

"I know." She stroked his back again, kissing him lightly. "But promise me that you'll come back." Flesh to flesh, she ran her hands over his scarred back, as if to heal the wounds he'd suffered for her. The fireplace filled the small house with warmth, and she relaxed under the caress of Cain's hands upon her skin.

"When I return, I'm going to marry you, lass. Because we're meant to be together."

TWO WEEKS LATER

Cold rain sliced through the wool of his plaid, making Jonah feel as if he'd never get warm again. He'd traveled across the Highlands with MacKinloch, but even after they'd caught a ride in a farmer's wagon, they were nowhere near London.

Having an adventure apparently meant being half frozen and starving to death. Aye, MacKinloch had brought him some food, but it wasn't enough to satisfy him. He was ready to begin gnawing on grass if they didn't get meat soon.

"Where are we?" he asked Joseph, when they stopped for water. "How many more days, 'til we're there?"

MacKinloch took a drink from his water flask. "Another week, lad. But we'll stop in a village. We're actually no' far from Falsham. If you look there—" he pointed to the thatched roofs on the distant horizon "—you'll see where we'll bide this night."

Jonah didn't ask how they were going to pay for their lodging.

While he hoped that MacKinloch had coins, the man hadn't mentioned anything before.

"Why are we so close to Falsham?" It was all the way on the opposite side of the country. Why hadn't they gone south? It made little sense.

"I thought we'd stop and see Dr. Paul Fraser. You remember him, don't you, lad? It might be he could loan us his coach or horses at the very least. 'Twould take too long to reach London otherwise."

Jonah relaxed at that. Dr. Fraser had been a friend of their clan, and he'd married Juliette Andrews. They had later learned that Paul Fraser's father had been the younger son of a viscount, and Fraser had inherited the estate.

Often, Jonah wondered what it would be like to suddenly learn that his parents were wealthy and that he should have been living in a palace. He dreamed of waking in a soft bed with a pillow. And food—oh, but the food would be a taste of Heaven. He imagined roasted beef dripping with juices, cakes and tarts with berries and cream . . . even a cup of chocolate. Never before had he tasted it, but he'd heard that highborn ladies often drank a cup in the morning.

His feet were blistered from walking, but Jonah hastened his step to keep up with MacKinloch. It would be sunset soon, and he was eager to rest for the night. His clothes were sodden from the rain, and he was eager to stand near a fire.

As they entered the village, Jonah saw a group of men talking and pointing toward the road. At first he wondered if they were eyeing himself and MacKinloch. But the men paid little heed to their arrival.

"Wait here, lad," MacKinloch ordered. "I'll go and find out where we can stay for the night."

While he went to talk with the others, Jonah moved toward one of the thatched cottages. He'd tried to eavesdrop on their conversation, but the men had kept their voices to a low whisper.

"Who are ye?" a voice asked from behind him. Jonah turned and saw a girl with long black braids standing there. She was slightly taller than him, and he felt his cheeks redden, for the girl was fair of face.

"I'm Jonah Sinclair," he mumbled. "From Ballaloch." At the girl's curious look, he added, "We're going to visit a friend, Dr. Paul Fraser."

She brightened at that. "He's a good man, that Dr. Fraser. I've met him a time or two." Eyeing him, she added, "Are ye traveling there tonight?"

Jonah shook his head. "In the morning." On a whim, he asked, "We're looking for a place to stay this night. Do you ken where we might find an inn or a room?"

"I'll ask my mam. She might let ye stay with us." Her eyes were the color of dark ale, and her skin was creamy and clear. When she smiled at him, Jonah backed up and struck his shoulder against the frame of the house.

Words tangled up in his mouth, and he couldn't find a single thing to say. Instead, he glanced back at MacKinloch. The men were still talking, and the girl added, "Ye are no' the first visitors today. A coach came up from London a few hours ago. Two men and a woman were traveling together. They're wanting to know who it was."

Jonah shrugged, for one coach was much the same as the next. Why would they care who the travelers were?

"Did you e'er find out?" Jonah asked. His stomach growled, and he hoped that MacKinloch would help him find supper this night.

The girl shook her head. "We only heard the name Brandon. He was an earl, and that's all we ken."

Jonah froze in place, wondering if he'd heard aright. "Did the coach have a family crest?"

The girl nodded. "There was a red star and a lion."

"Strathland," he whispered. It had to be. Yet he didn't know how that was possible. The earl had gone mad and had been in a lunatic asylum for years. How could he have escaped? But the man's name was Brandon Carlisle, and Jonah knew that crest well. He'd seen it often enough, when he'd gone to steal food from the earl.

"Have ye heard of him?" the girl asked.

"Aye. But I thought he was in London." *Locked away where he'd do no more harm,* Jonah thought. But then, why would Lord Strathland have traveled all this way to Edinburgh, even if he was free?

The answer struck him hard—Juliette Andrews. The earl had been in love with her long ago and had been furious when Paul Fraser had won her heart instead. This was about vengeance, Jonah didn't doubt. Strathland would want to kill Fraser and steal Juliette for himself.

God help them both.

There was no child. Margaret was sure of it now.

Her eyes blurred, and she didn't understand why it upset her so badly. Perhaps it was worry over Cain's absence. That, and the letters her sisters had sent. Juliette and Victoria had written of their thankfulness that she was safe, and both had mentioned amusing stories about their children.

Margaret was the second-born daughter, and she was already twenty-five. Though she knew of women who had borne children at that age, most were having a fourth or a fifth child. Whereas she didn't even know if she was capable of having one.

She swiped at her tears, knowing it was ridiculous. Without a marriage, any child would be illegitimate. It was something to be ashamed of, not a reason to rejoice. Why, then, had it upset her so badly? A part of her had prayed that her courses would be late, for she did want children.

Her sister's letter rested beneath her fingers, and she eyed a sketch Victoria had sent, of a new corset design. It was similar to the ones they had already created, but Margaret began drawing her own changes. All the while, she mulled over Cain's suggestion, that they should resurrect the business and continue selling the undergarments.

For so long, she had resisted the idea of designing and selling sensual corsets and chemises. But now, she was beginning to reconsider. If she took full ownership of the business, it gave her a purpose. And that was what she needed most to move forward in her life.

She continued to draw adjustments to the sketch, and this time, she fashioned the corset into a design where a lady could dress herself.

Her cheeks warmed, but it occurred to her that a woman who indulged in a secret tryst might require unmentionables that she could fasten on her own. It might also allow wealthy merchants' wives or even middle-class women to buy Aphrodite's Unmentionables. They could afford them if they were made of linen, but perhaps fashioned in a more sensual design.

Margaret sketched out a few more ideas to send back to Victoria. Wouldn't that shock her sister, if she took command of the business? It was a possibility, though she was less certain about Cain making the deliveries. If he was constantly traveling, he wouldn't have a true home or a life with her. It was a troubling thought.

Amelia's letter rested upon her desk, and she tore it open. Her sister had written of her difficulties adjusting to the earl's household and of her stepdaughter's loathing.

Christine unfortunately believes that I am a horrid stepmother who intends to lock her away, Amelia had written. *And though David has been a wonderful husband, there are days when I wish I could lock myself away.*

Margaret understood that feeling, especially now. Her family had forbidden her to pay any calls upon the crofters or to leave the house in any way. She'd overheard whispered discussions about what they should do about her. It seemed that she had now become a problem to be solved.

Hardly.

She straightened in her chair, feeling a twinge of resentment. It wasn't as if she were an innocent girl of eighteen. No, she'd been placed upon the marital shelf years ago. Though it might indeed bring scandal upon her family, she hardly cared what they thought anymore.

The last letter was written in an unfamiliar script. It looked as if it had been scrawled by a child, and she wondered if Victoria's son had written it. But when she opened it, there were only three words.

Wait for me.

She closed her eyes, knowing Cain had sent it. It was a promise that he *would* return. No matter what happened with his brother, he would come back for her. It gave her hope, filling up the emptiness within her.

A knock sounded at the door, and her mother opened it without waiting for a reply. "Margaret, darling? I've a surprise for you." Beatrice opened the door wider to reveal Victoria standing there. "Look who has come to visit us."

Joy filled her heart, and she found herself crushed in her sister's arms a moment later. Whether Toria was crying or whether it was her own tears, Margaret couldn't know. But it made her loneliness so much more bearable.

"Your letter just came this morning. How is it possible that you're here so fast?" Margaret asked.

"Jonathan and I had planned to visit Eiloch Hill anyhow, and I wrote back the moment I got Mother's letter." Her sister took her hand and started to lead her from the room. "We should go for a walk, and you can tell me all that's happened."

The weather was fine this morning, the sunlight gleaming over the hills while white puffy clouds floated overhead. "I know what it's like to be trapped inside the house," her sister admitted, after they stepped outside the doors. "It's like a prison."

Margaret took a deep breath and nodded. "It has been. Mother means well, but I am weary of staying inside."

They walked together until they reached the bottom of the hillside. Toria linked her arm with Margaret's.

"What really happened while you were gone?" her sister asked. "I promise I won't tell Father or Mother."

She risked a glance at Victoria, and decided that there was no reason to keep any secrets. "Cain saved my life, and we spent over a month together." A month that had been both dangerous and thrilling. "He kept me safe."

"Did you . . . ?" Her sister left the question unfinished, but Margaret knew what she meant.

"Yes." She couldn't stop the blush, but she forced herself to meet Toria's gaze openly. "And it was wonderful. He asked me to wed him."

Her sister gaped at that. "Did he? Is that . . . what you want?"

"I don't know." She hastened her pace, her steps crunching along the gravel pathway. "Honestly, I never imagined any of this would happen." But the longer Cain was away, the more she missed him. His roguish smile and the way he teased her had brought a lightness into her existence. Despite his demanding personality, she'd enjoyed the moments she'd spent with him.

And at night, she was lonely. She'd grown accustomed to sleeping beside him with his arms around her.

"Cain is a good man—that I'll agree with," Victoria said. "But you and he are so different. You're so proper and he's not at all a man you could mold into a gentleman."

Was that what Toria thought? That she intended to reform Cain Sinclair into another man? "I don't see the need to change him."

"Then how would you attend family gatherings? If Mother and Father host a supper party with guests, how will he know how to behave?"

"He knows how to behave," Margaret countered, remembering the supper party at Mr. Barnabas's house. "He may be poor, but he's not a barbarian."

"You sound as if you've already made your decision," Victoria said.

And it startled Margaret to realize that she had. After these weeks alone, she'd come to know how much she cared about Cain. He might have been overbearing and demanding, but as he'd said— *I've walked through fire for you.*

Victoria's expression grew worried. "Are you in love with him?"

Was she? If love meant that it hurt not seeing him each day, then yes. But Margaret couldn't quite bring herself to voice the words. She took her sister's hand and started walking back toward the house. "We fit together in a way I never expected."

Over the years, Cain had always been there for her. Even when she'd been betrothed to Viscount Lisford, he'd tried to protect her. "He might not be a gentleman, but he's always been good to me."

"How will you live, if you do marry him?" her sister asked. "I doubt if Father will let you have your dowry."

"I have Aphrodite's Unmentionables," she countered. "We can continue the business, and if we're discovered, I will take full responsibility so that none of the scandal harms any of you." Thus far, she had remained confined within the house, and she'd had no means of filling her days. It was no life at all, and Margaret had grown weary of it. She could not deny the fierce need to break free and do as she pleased.

Her sister started to laugh. "I would love to see the look on Father's face when you tell him that you plan to marry a Highlander."

Margaret kept a serene smile upon her face. "So would I."

⚘

"Where are you going?" Jonah demanded. He'd believed they were going to see Viscount Falsham, the former Dr. Fraser. But now it seemed that MacKinloch had another quest in mind. He had continued tracing Lord Strathland's path over the past few days, though Jonah didn't know why.

"I'm going out to play cards," the man replied. "It's late, so ye should stay in our room and get some sleep." He tucked a pistol into his belt, the one Jonah had given to him. It had been his father's favorite weapon, and the wood was polished to a high sheen with his initials carved upon it. MacKinloch hid it inside a fold of his plaid, and Jonah's worry intensified.

The man had been following Strathland's path ever since they'd heard his coach was here. Jonah suspected MacKinloch was seeking revenge for what had happened to his sister.

"Why are you taking my father's pistol if you're playing cards?" Jonah asked.

The man crossed his arms. "It's for protection, lad. Now go to sleep and stay here."

"You're no' playing cards at all," Jonah guessed. "You're trying to find Lord Strathland, aren't you?" When MacKinloch didn't answer, his suspicions were confirmed.

"Wait here," the older man said. "And don't be doing anything stupid."

But Jonah strongly suspected that MacKinloch was the one about to do something rash. And with his father's weapon, no less. No, he couldn't stay behind. He had to try and stop the man. Especially since Strathland would likely kill MacKinloch if he dared to threaten him.

"I'll go with you," Jonah said. "I promise I won't interfere. I'll stay hidden in case you have need of me." And perhaps if he was brave enough, he could stop the man.

"You're four-and-ten," MacKinloch reminded him. "You're of no use except to get in the way. Stay behind, and that's final."

"What will you do?" he asked.

"I'm going to talk with the earl about what his men did to my sister."

Jonah didn't know what to say, for it sounded like he most definitely intended to kill Lord Strathland. "You're no' going to—"

"Why do ye think I was going to London?" MacKinloch demanded. "For him. I wanted to make sure Strathland was suffering the way I suffered. And now that I find out he was set free?" He shook his head. "Nay, the man won't breathe another breath, if I've anything to do with it."

No' with my father's weapon, Jonah thought. He couldn't allow that to happen. "You willna be able to find him," he protested. "It's too dark." It was a last, desperate plea for the man to see reason.

But MacKinloch sent him a thin smile. "There's only one road, lad. And a nobleman like the earl is no' likely to go on horseback. I'll find him, rest assured of it."

Her family was falling apart before her eyes. Beatrice had never seen Henry so furious. Though it had been many years since he'd served as a colonel in the British army, he appeared ready to wage war this afternoon. He'd held his anger back at first, until Margaret had given orders for her belongings to be packed. Both of them were certain she intended to follow Cain Sinclair, since he had not returned in over a fortnight.

The moment their daughter walked down the stairs, he rounded the corner. "Where do you think you're going, Margaret?"

Beatrice suppressed a sigh. Her husband's temper was on edge, and it wouldn't take much to ignite his fury.

"I am going to Falsham to visit with Juliette," she said calmly. "Is there something wrong with that?"

Henry reached out and took Margaret's hand. Without asking, he guided her into the parlor. Beatrice followed, closing the door behind them. There was no need for the servants to witness the storm about to happen.

"You're going after Sinclair, aren't you?" he said.

Oh dear. This wasn't going to go well at all. And yet, Margaret didn't seem to care about his bluster. There was a soft glow to her, of a woman in love.

"I am going to stay with Juliette," she answered. "And I don't know if I will see Cain. It all depends on if he is there." She lifted her chin as if she weren't a bit ashamed of it.

"I don't believe you're visiting your sister at all," Henry said. "You're trying to find *him*."

Margaret merely raised her eyes to her father's in open defiance. When she didn't deny his insinuation, Beatrice's heart sank.

"Don't you care what others will say about this family?" Henry demanded. "They will believe the worst of you. And how will you ever find a proper husband then?"

There was a secretive smile on her daughter's face. "I don't need to find a proper husband, Father. Cain already asked me to marry him."

Was she honestly considering a marriage to Cain Sinclair? Beatrice felt the blood draining away from her face. No, it wasn't possible. Margaret was a good girl, a young woman who had always intended to marry a man of noble blood. "You're not serious, are you?"

Margaret adjusted her gloves, her expression serene. "Indeed I am. And if I choose to visit my sister or if I visit Cain, it is my right to do so."

"No," her father intervened. "This, I will not allow. You may have had an," he paused to find the right word, "an *infatuation* with Cain Sinclair. But you certainly will not go chasing after him. You've been under a great deal of duress, and I know you are not thinking clearly."

Margaret let out an exasperated sigh. "I am not a child anymore, Father. And it is my decision to make, not yours."

"God help us all," Henry muttered.

Beatrice agreed with her husband. She couldn't even imagine such a situation, where her proper-minded daughter would conceive of such a marriage.

"I've known Cain Sinclair for years," Margaret continued. "I trust him, and I believe I could be happy with him." Once again, a wistful look crossed her daughter's face.

Beatrice leaned back against the wall, watching Margaret surreptitiously. Regardless of what Henry thought, there *was* a difference in their daughter. She had the quiet confidence of a young woman who had endured hardship and had overcome the worst.

"Do you feel that you *have* to marry him?" she asked her daughter, wondering if Margaret had been seduced by the Highlander. Although Cain Sinclair was rough-mannered, he was wickedly handsome. Beatrice didn't doubt that a man like him knew how to pleasure a woman in her marriage bed. Was that why her daughter was considering him?

"I am not with child, if that is what you're asking," Margaret answered quietly. But from the way her daughter held herself, Beatrice no longer doubted that the two of them had been lovers. The old Margaret would have insisted up and down that she was virtuous and had never allowed Sinclair to lay a hand upon her.

But her daughter's cheeks were flushed, revealing a different story. Beatrice eyed Henry. He'd not shared her bed in a very long time. Ever since he'd gone off to war, the distance between them had heightened. And when he'd returned, he'd been so outraged that they had begun Aphrodite's Unmentionables, that it had driven another wedge between them. After her daughters had worked so hard to earn money for the family, Beatrice was proud of their success. She wasn't about to order them to stop, simply because Henry was embarrassed by it.

Then, after Margaret's disappearance, they had grown so far apart, she had only pieces of her marriage remaining. She thought back to the days when she'd been so buried in melancholy, she could hardly get out of bed each day. Henry had tried to console her, and she'd pushed him away. As Beatrice studied her husband, she questioned whether or not they could rebuild their own marriage.

Right now, he was in the midst of lecturing Margaret, his face tight with anger. And their daughter was blithely ignoring every word.

"If I choose to marry Cain, I will do so," she said. "If you would like to host a formal wedding with guests, I'm certain we can arrange that, once Cain and his brother have returned."

"I won't stand for it," her father said. His face was red, and Beatrice rather thought he might explode with anger.

"I do not require your permission," Margaret pointed out. "We can marry at any time in Scotland. With or without you."

"It sounds as if he ran away and left you." Her father rubbed at his chin as if seeking wisdom from a higher power. "Margaret, why would you do something so impulsive? You're behaving like Amelia."

Their youngest daughter was known to act first and regard the consequences later. But Margaret didn't seem to care. She sat down and smoothed an invisible wrinkle from her gown. "Am I? That's refreshing."

"It wasn't a compliment." Henry sat across from her, and Beatrice guessed that he wanted her beside him, in silent support. He reached for her hand and held it. Beneath his bluster, she knew that he was trying to do what was best for Margaret.

"I . . . I don't want you to suffer a life you don't deserve," he said slowly. "You could have had any man you wanted. Why would you choose a common Highlander with no money at all?"

"I couldn't have anyone I wanted," she said. There was a fragility to her voice, as if she was still hurt by it. "If you'll recall, I've had Season after Season with no man to offer for me. Oh, except for Viscount Lisford, who asked me to wed him because of a wager. We cannot forget him." She sat up straighter and added, "And then there is the man who has loved me ever since I set foot in Scotland. He's been there all along, and I was too blind to see it."

Henry was about to speak, but Beatrice squeezed his hand tightly in warning. She didn't want him to speak words that he would later regret.

"Cain is the man I want to be with," she said slowly. "And since he hasn't returned with Jonah yet, I believe he needs help finding him."

"Haven't you caused enough scandal?" her father demanded. "Why would you seek another reason for people to talk about you? You've brought embarrassment upon our family, and I will not allow you to become involved with such a man. It simply isn't done."

The stiffness in his tone wasn't disapproval—Beatrice recognized it as worry. He was afraid of losing Margaret or watching her descend into poverty.

But their daughter crossed her arms and faced him down. "I will stand by his side and offer whatever assistance I can." To Beatrice she asked, "I should like to borrow your coach, if I may."

Before she could respond, Henry asked, "When do you intend to return?" His expression was pained, as if he had swallowed a packet of razors.

"It depends on when Jonah is found. I hope within a fortnight."

With a heavy sigh, he said, "Are you certain you wish to marry a man like Sinclair, Margaret? All your life, you wanted to be a princess. Or a duchess at the very least."

"A title isn't important to me any longer."

Beatrice could hardly believe the words she was hearing. Henry was right. Margaret had always wanted to wed a nobleman. Why would she sacrifice her dreams for a Highlander?

"And how will you live?" her father demanded. "He cannot give you a good house or servants. You'll be working from dawn to dusk like a scullery maid. It's impossible."

"No," Margaret said slowly. She reached among her packed belongings and pulled out a crimson silk chemise. "I will take responsibility for Aphrodite's Unmentionables. With those profits, Cain and I can be quite successful."

Beatrice could not have been more surprised. *Margaret* wanted to own the business? The same young woman who had protested about how terrible it was that they had earned so much income from naughty unmentionables? Her daughter had bemoaned their efforts at every turn, never wanting to acknowledge how much the business had changed their lives. And now she intended to manage the affairs?

"I don't understand," Beatrice said. "Not that I hold any objections, but I would like to know what changed your mind."

Margaret met her gaze evenly. "I remember, many winters ago, how hard the crofters struggled to survive. We used to bring them food and clothing, but often they died anyway. How many have died since we began the business?"

"None," Beatrice admitted. It was true that the men and women had benefited greatly from Aphrodite's Unmentionables.

There was a light in Margaret's eyes as she continued. "We've changed their lives for the better because we brought sewing to the women. They have so much to offer, and why shouldn't they continue?" She straightened and regarded her father. "Cain and I will have our own prosperity, and it will be ours to manage."

"It will bring shame upon everyone," Henry protested. "Your sisters will not be able to hold up their heads in society."

"*I* may not be able to attend the same gatherings," Margaret agreed. "But it should not affect them. I will bear the scandal, if it comes to that."

Her husband looked appalled by the idea, but Beatrice understood the sort of courage it took to accept the responsibility. And Margaret needed her support.

She walked over to stand beside her daughter. "It's not a shameful endeavor, Henry. And if it keeps Margaret from living in a hovel, I understand her reasons for doing so." She reached out to touch her daughter's shoulder. "My darling, I know I've reacted badly to this news. But answer me this. If it had been another man who had rescued you, would you have agreed to marry him?"

Tears filled up her daughter's eyes. "No," Margaret admitted. "I wouldn't have."

And that was the answer she'd guessed. Pressing further, Beatrice asked, "Do you have . . . feelings for Sinclair?"

"I miss him terribly," she admitted, "and I believe it's the right choice." She mustered a smile. "It may take a few years for us to earn enough for a larger house and more land, but one day it will be possible."

"If you marry Cain Sinclair, I will not support you," her father said. "He will not take advantage of you, Margaret."

"I don't need your money," she said. "But I wouldn't mind having a true wedding celebration with my family."

"There is nothing to celebrate about you being wedded to that Highlander," Henry insisted.

Beatrice resisted the urge to sigh with frustration. Of course, he *would* see it that way. But she suspected that if he persisted in this attitude, he would lose Margaret. She sent her daughter a sympathetic look.

"I am sorry you cannot see the sort of man he is," Margaret said. "He possesses more honor than any man I've ever known. And I won't turn my back on him."

She stood and walked to the doorway. Then she added, "Annie will bring my belongings to the coach and accompany me. In the meantime, I'll bid you both farewell. I shall see you upon my return from Falsham, and perhaps we can have my wedding then."

Henry started to go after her, but Beatrice pulled him back. "Don't you dare, Henry. Let her go."

"Didn't you hear what she said? She intends to run away with that wastrel. I'll not have it."

She kept her grip firm upon his hand. "And if you go against her, she'll grow to hate you. Neither of us wants that." Beatrice knew, too well, how stubborn Margaret could be. When her daughter decided upon a course of action, nothing would sway her. And that trait had come directly from Henry. If she didn't stop him now, he would go barreling after their daughter like a charging bull.

"Perhaps Mr. Sinclair isn't so bad," she reasoned, leading her husband out of the parlor and bringing him toward their own bedroom. Right now, she wanted privacy with him, to make him see that he was overreacting.

"And what in God's name would a young woman as sensible as Margaret see in a man like that?"

A warmth suffused Beatrice's cheeks, but she led Henry inside their room and turned the key in the lock. "Can't you guess, Henry?"

His face was troubled, as if he saw himself as a failure. "No, not really."

She leaned back against the door, studying her husband. Though she'd brought him here to deter him from berating Margaret, a sudden rush of nerves took hold. He rested his hand upon the post of their bed, his gaze downcast. Instead of the stoic colonel and baron, she saw a man who was utterly bewildered by his daughter's behavior.

Beatrice's heart quickened, and she pulled the pins from her hair, letting it fall around her shoulders. It was a strange feeling to behave like a seductress, but she wanted to make a point of her own. "Sometimes two people might seem very different . . . but they are a great deal alike."

Her husband's attention was firmly caught, and she set the pins down. Slowly she walked forward and stood before him, turning her back. Henry's hands moved to her shoulders and she drew his arms around her, moving his hands down to graze her breasts.

"I remember the first night we spent together," she whispered. "I was terrified of you, so afraid I wouldn't please you."

"I felt the same."

He lowered his mouth to her throat, and the moment he did, anticipation coursed through her. It had been so long since she'd been touched, Beatrice hardly remembered what it was like.

"A woman sometimes dreams of being stolen away," she whispered. "Of being ravished by a strong, handsome man." She turned around and his eyes were heated. "She wants to be adored, her body cherished."

There was tension in her husband's arms, as if he was aching for her. Henry had tried several times to make amends with her, to heal the distance the years had wrought. And she'd continually turned him away.

He was a stubborn, strong-willed man . . . but he did love their daughters. His anger at Margaret was a desire to protect her, she knew.

"Our Margaret is a grown woman," she said to Henry. "She's old enough to make her own decisions."

"I don't want her to act in haste and later regret it," he admitted. "She has a home with us for as long as she needs it."

She leaned back, her heart softening toward him. This was the true side to Henry, the man who would do anything to keep them all safe. His hands rested at her waist, and she sensed that he wanted to touch her, but was afraid it might bother her.

"Henry, do you hold any regrets?"

In his eyes, she saw an unnamed emotion. "Many."

Her heart began to tremble within her chest, but she asked, "What do you regret?"

His hands moved to her hair, stroking back the long length. "I regret leaving to fight in the army, when you were alone with our daughters." He took her face between his hands, stroking her temples. "I regret giving you doorknobs for your birthday a few years ago."

She couldn't stop her smile. "The sapphire bracelet was much better."

"And I regret that I wasn't the husband you needed me to be."

Her eyes filled up with tears. Not of unhappiness, but because she could not hold back the feelings growing inside her.

"You tried," she said in a thick voice. "And I was at fault, too. I didn't welcome you back as I should have, when you returned from war. We were both changed, and I couldn't see that you were still the same man I once loved." A tear spilled over, and he wiped it away. "Then I let my grief over Margaret come between us even more."

"I missed you, Beatrice," he said, his hands moving down her spine. "You'll never know how much."

The ache inside her intensified, until she felt the need to open herself to him. She wanted to push back the years of hurt and replace them with new memories. "Show me."

His hands moved over the buttons on her gown, unfastening them one by one. He fumbled against them, and when her shoulder was bared, he kissed it.

"I want you to remember the nights when you were away at war," she said, helping him remove his coat. "The nights when you were lonely for me."

"I was lonely for you every night," he said.

She unfastened his waistcoat and loosened his shirt, sliding her hands up his bare skin. Unlike other men in their forties, Henry's body wasn't at all soft or stout. She touched the scar over his ribs where a bayonet had grazed him.

"Sometimes I wondered what it would be like if a handsome soldier carried me away," she whispered. "If he loved me until I couldn't breathe."

Henry's mouth came down on hers, crushing the air from her as he kissed her hard. There was no hesitation, only a man starving for her.

And as he took her down on the bed, her clothes falling away beneath his hands, Beatrice murmured, "I made the right choice when I married you, Henry. We have to trust Margaret to do the same."

Chapter Thirteen

Cain had lost track of the days, hardly eating or sleeping. But several innkeepers had confirmed that a boy of Jonah's description had been traveling alone with a man who answered to the name MacKinloch. Thank God, MacKinloch had stopped at several villages along the way.

There had been a few wrong turns, but Cain believed they had been traveling southeast toward Edinburgh. It wasn't clear why, for the men who had spoken with MacKinloch had said they'd planned to travel toward London.

Let me find him, he prayed. His brother had never taken a long journey before. Jonah had no idea of the hardships involved, and Cain blamed himself for leaving. He should have found another way to earn an income, a means that didn't require so much traveling.

He rode toward the last village, his mind and body weary. To take his mind off the endless road ahead, he thought of Margaret.

She had more courage than he'd believed possible. Though he'd always admired her beauty and spirit, she'd proven that there was more beneath the surface. She wore her proper manners like a suit of armor, hiding the passionate nature within.

He missed her. Though he'd had to leave, he didn't like the prospect of her having to face her parents alone. They would make her feel ashamed of what she'd done, when the truth was, she was trying to protect a loved one.

Now he had to do the same.

He rode into the village and saw flickering lights in the public house ahead. There, he could get a meal and find out more. After tending to his horse's needs, he opened the doorway and the sounds of conversation, laughter, and music filled the room. At first, he didn't recognize anyone . . . but then a hand touched his shoulder.

He turned and saw his friend, Dr. Paul Fraser. "What are you doing here, Fraser?"

The man's face was grim. "I ought to ask the same, but I already ken the answer, Sinclair. Join me, and I'll buy you a drink. You're going to need it." He raised his hand toward the innkeeper, signaling for the man to bring two drinks.

Now what did he mean by that? Cain's instincts sharpened as he sat down beside the man. "Why will I be needing a drink?"

"Because I saw your younger brother, and I assume you didna ken that he was here."

"I've been tracking him," Cain said. A sense of uneasiness came over him. "Where did you find him?"

Paul traced the rim of his own cup. "He's been arrested for the murder of Lord Strathland. They're holding him in the Tolbooth at Edinburgh."

Disbelief and fear caught him low in the gut. Jonah had been arrested for murdering Strathland? It wasn't possible. His brother could never do such a thing. Moreover, how had Strathland managed to leave the London asylum?

Though he knew Paul wouldn't lie, he couldn't quite grasp it. "Tell me everything that's happened."

"The magistrates questioned Jonah, and he was caught fleeing with the murder weapon. There was enough evidence to lock him away while he awaits the trial. Because he was accused of murdering an earl, he'll be tried at the High Court of Justiciary."

God help his brother. Jonah would be terrified, alone in the dark. And the Tolbooth was a place reserved for the worst criminals of all. Cain had visited Edinburgh as a boy, and the horrifying smell of the prison only hinted at the nightmares inside.

"What kind of evidence would they have on a boy of four-and-ten?" Cain demanded. "The lad can barely wake up in the mornings. He's no' able to plan something like that." He shook his head and stood up. "I'm going to Edinburgh. I need to see him."

"You won't get there until morning," Paul said, gesturing him to sit back down. "And we'll go once we've hired a solicitor for him. Naught will happen before the trial."

"He's a boy," Cain said quietly. "Imprisoned with murderers and thieves. And you think naught will happen?" His blood ran cold at the thought of a young lad locked away with hardened criminals. Being starved and forced to endure the filth was the kinder side of prison. The boy could be faced with far worse threats from the men chained up with him.

Paul let out a heavy breath. "I'll do whate'er I can for him, Cain. And I'll send word to Duke Worthingstone. He might be able to help us even more."

Margaret would want to give her assistance as well, Cain knew. And though he didn't want to trouble her, it had been over a fortnight already. It could be months before he returned to Ballaloch, and he didn't want her to think he'd abandoned her.

"I want to send word to Miss Andrews," Cain admitted. "She should be told about this so she willna worry."

"You and Margaret, eh?" Fraser lifted his cup in a silent toast. "I heard from Juliette that the pair of you spent a month together, stranded in the Highlands."

"Aye." His knuckles whitened over his cup. "But don't be speaking any words against my Margaret, or I'll have to break your bones, Fraser."

"Nay, my friend. I've always thought the two of you made a good match." Paul took a sip from his cup.

Cain relaxed at that. "I don't want her thinking I've turned my back on her."

"I'll send a letter, don't fear." His friend added, "Come and stay with me at Falsham. Juliette will want to see you."

Cain nodded his agreement, and the two men rose. Though he knew his friend would do everything in his power to help, there was no way to know how much trouble Jonah was in.

TWO WEEKS LATER

The Edinburgh Tolbooth was a stone outbuilding that reminded Cain of the Tower of London. Even outside, it held a stench so vile, it bordered on violent. Cain covered his face with his hand, following the guard inside. Though he'd been to visit his brother every day during the past two weeks, he couldn't get used to the conditions of the prison, with no privy and no drainage. He had to get Jonah out. No one could survive living in a place like this.

When the guard led him inside, Jonah was sitting against a meager pile of straw. There was hardly any light in the cell, and his brother's wrists were chained to the wall.

"Good morning, lad," he greeted the boy. His brother shrugged, saying nothing in return.

Jonah's hair had grown longer and was hanging over his eyes. His clothes were tattered and worn, and Cain doubted if the boy had slept at all. Seeing him like this, hardly caring about the world around him, was even more frightening than the prison. Gone was the outspoken, rebellious lad. In his place was a boy who was resigned to this fate.

"Are you hungry?" Cain asked. At that, there was a faint spark of life from Jonah. He withdrew a piece of bread from his sporran and handed it over. The moment he did, Jonah snatched it from his hands and crammed it into his mouth.

"I'm going to get you out of here, I swear it," he told the boy. They had hired a solicitor, but the man admitted that the prosecutor had a strong case against Jonah. Unless they found other witnesses or evidence, the outcome didn't look good. It wasn't fair and it wasn't right. He needed to understand all of it so he could help his brother.

"I want to hear it again," Cain said quietly. "Tell me everything that happened to you."

Jonah chewed the bread, but his face was hollow, his eyes locked in a glassy stare. "I'm going to be hanged, aren't I?"

"Nay. I willna let that happen, lad." The very thought of his brother going to the gallows chilled his blood. Cain couldn't understand how anyone could imagine that Jonah was capable of murder. He blamed himself for the lad's troubles. He shouldn't have trusted Rory to look after him. The man had lost everything when his wife had died and wasn't able to care for Jonah.

Cain wished to God that he'd gone back to Scotland earlier. If he'd somehow reached Ballaloch, he might have stopped his brother from leaving with MacKinloch.

"Why will they no' believe me?" Jonah asked. The hopelessness in his voice made him sound younger than his fourteen years. "I didna kill him."

"I ken that," Cain insisted. "But tell me everything that happened. I want to hear if there's aught we can investigate. We might've missed something." He didn't care how many times he heard the story. Surely the answers were there.

"I've told you. MacKinloch went out that night and took our father's gun."

"Go on." Cain was trying to piece together the story, looking for reasons why MacKinloch had not been more thoroughly questioned.

"After MacKinloch left that night, he didna come back. I got scared and I went looking for him. I just . . . followed the road and kept walking. That was when I found the coach."

"And the body," Cain prompted.

"And his body, aye. MacKinloch blew his brains out." Jonah closed his eyes, his hands shaking. "I'd ne'er seen a murdered man before, Cain. I knelt down to see if he was dead and I didna see that his blood got on my shirtsleeves. I—I took Father's pistol back and ran away as fast as I could, back to the inn. Then I saw the men gathering together. I was so afraid, I hid."

Though he understood why Jonah had hidden himself, it had likely added to the illusion of guilt. "Where was MacKinloch?"

"He was already there. He told the police he'd been playing cards all night, and the men he was with said that was true." Jonah's voice was toneless, and a faint smile touched his mouth. "They came to ask me questions and found the pistol. I tried to run away, but they caught me."

"And they didna keep MacKinloch in custody." That was what he didn't understand. MacKinloch was the man with a true reason to kill Strathland—not Jonah. Why hadn't they detained him?

"They asked him questions, but they believed the other men who said he was there all night. I told them it wasna true, that I'd gone to follow him. But since I had Father's gun, and they believed that was the weapon, they took me."

Cain let out a slow breath. The other men had clearly lied, but for what reason? Was there a bribe involved?

"Where is MacKinloch now?" Somehow, he had to find the man and get him to confess.

"They let him go," Jonah admitted. "There was no evidence against him."

It didn't seem possible that it could be true. All the evidence they had on Jonah was coincidental. But if he was the only suspect they had, Cain understood why they had taken his brother prisoner.

"I'm afraid," Jonah whispered. "They executed a woman yesterday. She was here because her husband had been beating her. She killed him to make it stop." His brother's face had gone white, but Cain said nothing, waiting for him to continue. "They burned her. I—I thought they'd hang her, but they burned her alive. I heard her screaming."

He knew all too well what that was like. The memory of the fire came back to him, and the agony of the burns. Margaret had spent weeks caring for him. And not once had she been disgusted by the sight of his back.

He remembered the way she'd touched his scars, and the vision only made him more determined to go back to her. Nay, she wasn't his wife by law. But one day, she would be his.

When he returned to Ballaloch, he intended to pursue her relentlessly. From the moment he'd laid eyes on her lovely face, he'd been struck down. Her proper ways had entertained the hell out of him, for he'd known that beneath the primness lay a woman of fire.

Even now, he couldn't stop thinking about the Heaven in her arms or the way it felt to fall asleep with Margaret beside him. God, he loved her. And somehow, they would be together when this was all over.

Cain reached out and took his brother's hand, trying to reassure Jonah. "I promise you, I willna let you die. We'll find MacKinloch and force him to confess to what he did."

"What if he's gone?" His brother's voice held dread. "What if we ne'er find him?" A moment later, tears filled his eyes. "I ken that I made mistakes, Cain. When they questioned me, they were so angry, I got confused."

He stilled, for his brother had not spoken of the examination before. "Tell me what you said."

"They asked if the gun was mine. I told them nay, that it was Father's. Then they asked if the blood on my shirt was Strathland's. I said it was, but I didna kill him. A few days later, they asked more questions. I hadn't eaten or slept, and I hardly could tell what I was saying."

Which had likely been done on purpose, Cain realized. The investigators would not spare him, merely because Jonah was four-and-ten.

"They said they knew about the fires I'd set. MacKinloch must've told them about the wool I burned that belonged to the earl—I swear to you, I didna say a word about it. And they knew I hated Strathland for forcing us out of our home." His brother broke down weeping. "They made me sound like a murderer, Cain. But I couldna do such a thing."

Cain pulled his brother into a hard embrace, regardless of the chains. "I will find MacKinloch. And when I do, I'll get you out of here. I swear it on my life."

⚔

Please let him be here, Margaret prayed. There hadn't been enough time to send word to her sister beforehand, so she could only hope that Cain was staying at Falsham. His best friend was Paul Fraser, Juliette's husband, so it was possible that he would seek help from the viscount.

After the footman opened the door and allowed her inside, Juliette caught sight of her and hurried forward. "Margaret!" She crushed her sister in her arms, talking rapidly. "I'm so glad you're safe. Mother wrote to us and told us that you came to Ballaloch. And Mr. Sinclair told us, of course, that you were all right." Juliette drew back and asked, "Whatever are you doing here?"

Margaret accepted the warm embrace of her sister and smiled. "I'm glad to see you, too, Juliette. I came to see Cain, if he's staying with you?"

"He is, yes. He's at the Edinburgh Tolbooth right now," Juliette said, "but he should be home by nightfall."

"The Tolbooth?" Margaret couldn't imagine why Cain would have gone there. "Did something happen with Jonah?"

Juliette led her into the drawing room. "He and Paul have been working together, trying to help clear Jonah's name." She began telling Margaret the details of the arrest. "Lord Strathland is dead, and they think Jonah killed him."

Oh goodness, no. Not the boy. Her heart sank at the thought of what both Jonah and Cain were enduring at this moment. It made sense now, why he'd been gone for so long. His brother's life hung in the balance.

"When will the trial be?"

"Within a fortnight," Juliette said. "Cain and Paul have been searching for the true murderer."

Which meant that Cain had likely spent every waking moment trying to help his brother. He was a man who never gave up, and he would turn over every stone to find the answers.

"Two weeks isn't long at all." Trials at the High Court of Justiciary often took months before they were held.

"Unfortunately, yes," Juliette agreed. "Jonah has been imprisoned for several weeks now, and the prosecution has a strong case against him. And there's no sign of Joseph MacKinloch, the man who traveled with him this far." Juliette bade her to sit down and rang for tea. There was unrest in her sister's voice, and she appeared pale. "I am not sorry that the Earl of Strathland is dead."

"I know he caused you and Paul a great deal of trouble."

A shadow crossed her sister's face. "Yes. And I can only give thanks that Strathland was already dead when Paul went after him. Or it might have been my husband in the Tolbooth."

"I didn't know that Paul went after him, too. What happened?" Margaret was aware that the two men had always been enemies, but there was a new fear in her sister's voice.

"Lord Strathland left the asylum and he began hunting the members of our family. He wanted to kill all of us, starting with Amelia." Juliette's hands were clenched together, and she steadied herself. "She's all right, but her husband was shot." Before Margaret could react, Juliette reassured her, "He is recovering, thank goodness."

Relief filled her to hear it, for Margaret had always been fond of Castledon. A shiver crossed over her to learn that their family had been in such danger. "And Paul went after Strathland to stop him?"

"Yes," Juliette answered. "But when he caught up, the earl had already been shot by someone else." She closed her eyes and took a slow breath, as if steadying herself.

"Are you feeling all right?" Margaret asked.

"I'm just tired." There was a slight hint of emotion on her face, and she added, "I think I may be with child again."

Margaret smiled at Juliette and squeezed her hand. "I'm happy for you."

"I am, as well. Except that the smell of most food makes my stomach toss. I never had that with Grace or with—" She paused a moment as if changing what she'd wanted to say. "That is, I was never sick before. It's terrible."

"I hope it passes quickly," Margaret said. Their tea arrived, and she poured a cup for her sister. "Drink this, and it might make you feel better."

Her sister nodded and took a sip. Then she asked, "Does Cain know you are here?"

"No." Margaret rested her hands upon her lap. "But I had to come." A sudden shyness came over her at the thought of seeing Cain again. Would he be glad she was here? Or did he not want her to come this far?

Juliette waited a long pause, and Margaret admitted, "I told our parents that I am going to marry him."

Her sister nearly choked on her tea. "What? Is it true?"

"Yes," she said. "I-I want to." The sudden giddy feeling took hold in her stomach, and she confessed, "I don't know quite how it happened, but it feels right to be with him. I couldn't stay away any longer—I was hoping I would find him here."

Her sister positively beamed. "If Amelia were here, she'd be dragging you off to the nearest church." Shaking her head, she added, "I imagine our parents were appalled."

"Horrified, more like." But it felt so good to admit the truth to her sister. "Father threatened to cut me off. He said it would bring embarrassment to them."

Juliette set down her cup and went to sit beside her. She reached out, and Margaret clasped her hand. "It's going to be all right, Margaret. I'll help you in any way I can."

Her sister's support meant a great deal to her. Juliette had wed Dr. Fraser before learning that he'd inherited his uncle's title, so she knew well enough what it meant to defy her family. Cain would never possess a title. And somehow, Margaret had reached the point where she didn't care anymore.

"I've another favor to ask," she told Juliette. "Cain thinks we should take control of Aphrodite's Unmentionables. If it's all right with you, I'll manage the business from now on." It was the easiest way to increase their income and provide enough for her and Cain to live on.

Her sister shook her head in disbelief. "I never thought I'd see the day you'd become a merchant."

Neither had Margaret. Particularly when it involved selling seductive unmentionables. But she was beginning to understand why a woman might want to draw attention to herself. Cain had voiced his own appreciation for the color red. She imagined his reaction if he saw her wearing red lace over bare skin.

A flush of memory pressed over her, as she thought of him lifting her up against the wall and claiming her then and there. Beneath her gown, her skin rose up with anticipation.

Stop this, she warned herself. *He's not even here yet.*

"I'll become a business owner, not a merchant," Margaret corrected. "It's slightly more respectable."

Although, given what she was selling, it would never truly be respectable.

Juliette's green eyes met her own. "You really do love him, don't you, Margaret?"

"I do, yes." A lightness filled her up inside with the giddy sense of rebellion. "And whether or not he'll ever admit it, Cain needs me." She released her sister's hand and said, "We don't have to be poor, not with the business to run." She straightened and added, "If anyone ever discovers the truth, I will say that it was always my idea. That you and Toria and Amelia had nothing to do with it."

"We'll stand by you, in whatever way you want us to," Juliette said. Her sister faced her and said, "You'll always be our sister, and nothing will change that. If our secret is revealed, let the others say what they will about scandal. It doesn't matter."

In that moment, the decision felt right. No, she wouldn't be married to a duke or a prince. But she would have the man she loved, she could bear his children, and with the profits of the business, they could live comfortably.

The sound of men's voices interrupted their conversation, and Margaret stood. She heard Cain arguing with Paul, and the moment she heard him speaking, her heartbeat began to quicken. The urge to run into the hallway and throw herself into his arms was far too strong.

But he entered the drawing room with Dr. Fraser, and she caught the end of their conversation. "We're going to hire men to search for MacKinloch. He has to be found within the next two days. Then we can—" His words broke away the moment he saw her.

She expected him to smile or to pull her into his arms. Instead, his expression darkened. There was no sense of surprised welcome, and her spirits sank. He didn't look at all glad she was there.

"Why did you come, lass?"

Chapter Fourteen

Cain didn't know why Margaret had traveled here, but the sight of her filled him with a blend of joy and fear. In her violet traveling gown and bonnet, she reminded him of a lilac in spring. He wanted to embrace her, to breathe in the scent of her hair and give thanks that she was with him. Right now, he couldn't touch her, for the stench of the Tolbooth was still upon him.

But he was afraid of the real reason why she might be here—if she were with child. The very thought sent a wave of terror over him. He couldn't possibly be a father. Not now.

Damn it all, he needed to speak with her alone and find out why she had come to Falsham.

"Come with me, and we'll talk," he ordered. Without waiting for her to agree, he gestured for her to follow him. Fraser started to protest, but thankfully his wife pulled him back.

Cain didn't turn around, but walked up the stairs to the third floor. He'd chosen a room only slightly better than a servant's, though Paul had tried to put him in one of the guest rooms. It hadn't felt right, and he'd admitted that he wouldn't sleep well in such a place.

The moment he opened the door, he waited until Margaret was inside. She started to move forward, but he held up a hand. "Don't be touching me, lass. I've been with Jonah, and I stink like a ruddy pig." He poured water into a basin and began stripping off his shirt. It mattered not that she was standing in front of him, for she'd seen his bare chest before.

"Tell me why you're here, lass." Cain lathered up his arms and chest, rinsing himself with the water in the basin. Though it was cold, it felt good to wash away the filth of the prison. Even after visiting his brother every day, he couldn't get accustomed to the harsh conditions.

Margaret didn't speak at first. When he turned to her, there was a faint blush on her cheeks, as if she were choosing her words. "I missed you, and I wanted to help you find Jonah. I'm sorry for what happened to him." She drew closer and added, "We'll do everything we can to clear his name."

Cain wanted her nowhere near the Tolbooth. He could hardly bear to be there himself, and he wanted to shield her from such a place. Though he admired her courage, there was a darker side of life that he never wanted her to see.

"It's naught to do with you, lass," he said. "Visit with your sister, if you wish, but leave Jonah to me."

"You think I'm not capable of helping you?"

He felt the touch of her hands upon his bare shoulders, and it burned through him. It took every effort not to seize her and hold her tightly. Though she was capable of anything she set her mind to, this wasn't a trial in the House of Lords. She needed to understand what would happen to Jonah if they couldn't find the true murderer.

"My brother was accused of shooting Lord Strathland in the head," he said, stepping back. "If they find Jonah guilty, they'll hang him." Seizing a towel, Cain dried the water from his face and torso.

She paled but nodded. "Have you hired a solicitor for him?"

"I have, aye. But the evidence is strong against Jonah." Cain strode forward until he was standing before her. Though he'd washed away the filth of the Tolbooth, he still felt unclean. He reached for a new shirt, acutely aware of her eyes upon him. There was an intimacy between them, as if she had seen him this way a thousand times.

And though she shouldn't be here, her presence did comfort him. He could imagine her as his wife, sharing in a private moment together. He thought of drawing her in for a kiss, of laying her down upon his bed and caressing her until she sighed with pleasure.

Margaret's expression turned serious. "Why would anyone think a boy could possibly murder a man like the earl?"

"Jonah admitted he was there that night. And the gun used to kill Strathland was my father's." Cain didn't know why his brother would have taken the weapon back with him, but it undoubtedly gave the impression that he'd planned to seek out and murder the earl.

Margaret sat down, frowning. "It's still too coincidental. Anyone could have stolen the gun."

"I think it was MacKinloch who blamed Jonah to hide his own guilt."

"Surely Jonah denied any wrongdoing," Margaret said. "If he told the truth, why would they not look for other suspects?"

"I've no idea why." Cain paced across the floor. "But I suspect they confused him in the questioning. He was scared and might've said anything." Tension knotted his muscles, and he added, "He tried to run, and it only made him look guiltier."

"How long has he been imprisoned?"

"A few weeks. After they took him to the Tolbooth, the questioning got worse." He met her gaze, and she understood what he meant.

Margaret exhaled softly and went to stand beside him. She drew her hands over his shoulders and down his back as if in memory of the burn wounds. "You'll protect him. Surely there's not enough evidence to convict him."

"I hope there's no' enough. But I canna say what they'll do. We have to find MacKinloch."

"And if we can't?"

He couldn't let himself think of that. Cain closed his eyes and reached for her gloved hands. "I won't let my brother die, Margaret. I'll do whate'er I must to save him from the gallows."

Her hands moved up his chest in a gentle caress, an offering of herself. He wanted so badly to kiss her, to take comfort in her arms. But he hesitated, not knowing if he should make the first move.

It was Margaret who did. She moved closer, resting her head against his heart. "I'll help you save him."

The ache within him intensified, shoving past the voices that insisted he didn't deserve her. He knew that. But he held her tightly, savoring the warmth of her arms.

"Nay, I'll handle it myself," he told her. Then he drew his hands down her back, moving to her stomach. "And what of you? Are you all right, lass?" He let his touch linger, asking her without words if there was a child.

Her face flushed at his question. Without him having to voice the true question, she shook her head slowly. "I'm fine. There's no reason to worry."

He breathed easier, knowing she wouldn't suffer the consequences of their actions. But there was a glimpse of sadness in her green eyes, as if she had wanted a bairn.

Margaret would make a good mother, he didn't doubt. But he didn't know if he would ever be ready to become a father. After all the mistakes he'd made with Jonah, he questioned whether he was any good at it.

"I am glad that all is well," he said at last. "I suppose you'll be wanting to visit with your sister." He started to walk with her toward the door, but Margaret didn't follow.

"I came to visit with *you*, Cain." She folded her hands and squared her shoulders. "I can help you to hire good men to represent your brother in court. Or we could hire more investigators to find the right evidence against MacKinloch."

Though he knew she didn't mean to offend him, her insinuation was that he couldn't afford to defend his brother. "I don't need your help, lass." What he needed was more time. He had to locate Joseph MacKinloch and demand a confession from him.

Her expression remained dire. "This is his life, Cain. Don't let your pride get in the way of that."

It wasn't only his pride. If he allowed her to help, she would be pulled into the middle of this nightmare of investigations. He wanted her safe from harm, and if she became involved, it would taint her reputation. Ladies were never associated with murder trials—even *he* knew that. "I will take care of my brother. I've done it ever since our parents died."

"And you've done well," she started to say. "But—"

"Nay. If I'd been there for him, he'd ne'er have left," he shot back. "I'm the reason he's locked away in there."

"You're not," she said. "And you mustn't believe that. You did the best you could."

"Nay." A shadow of frustration darkened his mood. "I left him with Rory and Grania far too much. He couldna depend on me."

A softness stole over Margaret's face. "You were busy earning a living for both of you. And you took care of him."

She didn't understand the truth. He'd done what was expected of him, but he'd resented every moment. "I provided for Jonah and

made sure he had a place to live. But I didna want to be a father."
He knew it made him sound like a selfish bastard, but he didn't want
her to view him as a saint. He was a damned sight far from that.

"What happened to your parents?" Margaret asked softly. "I
know they drowned, but how did it happen?"

"I don't want to speak of it." It had been a long time ago, and
there was no reason to dwell upon the past. What was done was
done. Naught could change it.

"All right. If that's what you want." She lifted her chin and
waited. Like a schoolteacher, she sent him an unspoken lecture. But
the longer he remained silent, the more he felt her knowing gaze
upon him.

He should have been watching his brother that day. His lack
of attention had caused the disaster. "It was my fault Jonah wan-
dered off that morning and got into the river."

There was a slight change in her expression, but her tone
remained calm. "Did you swim in after him?"

Cain shook his head. "I canna swim. Ne'er could." He'd waded
in as far as he dared, but the current had swept his brother away.

"So your mother went in the water?" she predicted.

"Aye. She couldna swim either, but she tried. It was too deep
for her to reach him." The memory of his mother's screams dug into
him, even after all these years. "I went to fetch my father."

She seemed to guess what had happened after that. "You don't
have to tell me." Slowly she stood and crossed the room, taking his
hand in hers.

But now that he'd begun, he saw no reason not to reveal the
rest. "My father tried to save them both. He got Jonah to the shore
and went back for my mother." A tightness sealed off the emotions
within him. He hadn't cried that day, and he'd not shed any tears
since. Tears were a weakness he would never allow.

Taking a breath, he finished, "It was too late for her. When he learned she was dead, my father stopped swimming. He just held her and didn't fight anymore. I suppose he didn't want to live without her."

Margaret squeezed his hand, and she offered, "I'm sorry you saw it happen."

Cain didn't acknowledge her words, not wanting any part of that memory. It had been one of the worst days he'd ever known, with his brother sobbing and both parents gone. He'd been numb with grief, holding his brother and wanting so badly to shut his eyes and pray that it was naught but a nightmare.

"I hated my father for leaving us. He was a coward." To this day, he'd been unable to let go of his hatred. Any man who would abandon his sons wasn't worth the grief.

"Jonah was my responsibility after that," he told her. He'd done what he could to raise the boy, but he'd made so many mistakes.

Her fingers stroked his, and she faced him. "Were you angry at your brother?"

It was a strange thing to say, and he started to deny it. "Nay. He was hardly more than three years old. I was angry with myself and angry with my father."

"And you've been trying to atone for it ever since, haven't you?" Margaret rested her hand against his shoulder. She was right. There was never peace for him, never a moment when he could forget his parents dying before his eyes.

"I've done a poor job of it," he admitted. "I let another woman raise Jonah, when it should've been me."

"You never asked to become a father." Margaret stepped back, eyeing him closely as if trying to see beneath the surface. "But you did the best you could. You had to earn a living for both of you." She framed his face with her hands. "There's no reason for guilt."

"Jonah's just a boy," Cain said. A boy who was locked away in a prison, suffering every hour. The bleakness of his brother's fate hung over him like a shadow. "He's no' guilty of murder, and I willna let him hang for it."

Her green eyes met his with honesty. "I know you won't. And neither will I."

He pulled her hands from his face, holding them. "This isna your battle, lass."

"You've spent your life fighting for others. For the crofters, for your brother. For me," she murmured. "Isn't it time someone fought for you?"

Sitting around and waiting for evidence to emerge was not a productive use of a woman's time. For that reason, Margaret had hired an investigator a week ago to find more evidence to help with Jonah's case. Mr. Julian had arrived this morning with his first report.

"Thank you for coming to call," Margaret said, pouring the man a cup of tea. He eyed her uneasily, though he accepted it. "Have you or your men located Joseph MacKinloch?" She offered him a plate of biscuits, and he accepted one warily.

"Not yet, Miss Andrews," he answered. The man looked as if he didn't quite know what to do with the refreshments.

"It is imperative that you locate MacKinloch. The sooner you do, the greater your reward," Margaret reminded him. "Now tell me what progress you have made."

"We have tracked him to the west," Mr. Julian admitted. "My men will not stop searching until they've brought him back."

"Good. But the trial is next week. If he is not found in time, there is no reason to continue the search." She drank her own tea, trying to remain calm. Cain had spent each day at the prison, and at night, he traveled in search of MacKinloch. She'd hardly seen him at all.

"I understand." He quickly finished his tea and biscuit, then stood. "If you'll excuse me, I'll see if any of the runners have returned."

"Thank you."

As the man rose to leave, she heard a slight noise of footsteps approaching. Cain walked into the parlor and dropped his hat upon the settee. He glanced back at Mr. Julian as the man was departing. "What was that about, lass?"

"Mr. Julian is an investigator I hired." She gestured to the seat beside her. "Why don't you sit and have some refreshments?"

Cain appeared haggard and weary from his visit to the Tolbooth. "I'd be glad of a biscuit. But first, I'm wanting to hear what he learned."

"Unfortunately, not as much as I'd hoped. His men tracked MacKinloch to the west, but they haven't found him yet."

Cain's expression didn't change, his exhaustion undeniable. Margaret held out the plate of biscuits, and he sat down across from her, devouring six of them. It occurred to her that she hadn't seen him at her sister's table in the last day or so. "When was the last time you ate, Cain?"

"Yesterday, I think. I canna remember."

It bothered her that he wasn't taking care of himself. Though it was past luncheon, she pulled the bell. "I'll have a meal brought to you. If you want to look after Jonah, you'll have to keep up your strength."

He didn't argue, but the tension in him was so taut, she felt the need to do something. "How is he?"

Cain only shrugged, as if her question was foolish. Margaret prompted again, "Have they found any new evidence?"

"Nothing."

"What does his solicitor think? Have any new witnesses come forward?"

"Nay."

She was beginning to get frustrated by his terse responses. After she gave the order to the footman to bring Cain a light meal, he rested his forearms upon his knees. "I don't ken why you're here, Margaret."

"Jonah is your brother," she said. "Why wouldn't I want to help him?"

"This doesna involve you. It's no' your problem to solve." There was a finality in his voice as if he didn't want her here. She said nothing, waiting until the food arrived. After the footman served him the fish and roasted vegetables, the silence grew even more strained between them.

"You want me to go back to Ballaloch," she said.

"Aye. That would be best." He ate hungrily but hardly even looked at her.

"Why are you pushing me away?" She couldn't understand why he had become so distant. It was as if he wanted nothing to do with her anymore.

"I want you to be safe, lass. You don't need to be a part of this."

It was as if he didn't think she should witness any unpleasant moments. Margaret leaned closer and said, "I came here to lend my assistance. Once your brother is free, we can go on with our lives. We can . . . marry if you still want to." It embarrassed her to bring it out into the open, but he needed to know her intentions.

He picked at his food and finally set the fork aside. "I've had to spend every penny on a good solicitor for Jonah." The heaviness in his voice suggested that he had nothing left.

"Of course you had to," she agreed. "I would expect nothing less." She braved a smile. "You needn't worry about money, though. I have funds of my own that I'll gladly use to help you."

His blue eyes held a stony pride. "I don't want your money, Margaret. I ne'er did."

"I know." She held out a hand. "But there's no reason not to use it for the sake of your brother. His life is worth that."

Cain closed his eyes and shook his head. "'Tis more complicated than that, Margaret. I'm afraid they're going to find him guilty."

"They won't," she reassured him. There was still time before the trial, and she had every faith that the investigator would find something. "Don't give up."

"I ne'er said I was giving up. He'll live, no matter what the cost." The finality in his voice frightened her even more than the prospect of Jonah's hanging. What did he mean, *no matter what the cost?*

"Are you planning to help him escape the Tolbooth?" she asked, feeling an icy chill overtake her skin. Though Cain might manage it with difficulty, he would become a wanted man, running from the law enforcers. He would become an outlaw in truth.

He stood from his chair, resting his palms upon the back of it. "Edinburgh is too heavily guarded for me to escape with him."

"Then what do you plan to do?" She couldn't imagine how he would save his brother if Jonah was found guilty.

The bleakness upon his face held a regret so strong, she couldn't stop the trembling of her fingers.

"What do you plan to do, Cain?" she repeated.

He said nothing, but took her face between his hands and touched his forehead to hers. "I hope it willna come to that, lass. But if it does, you must take care of Jonah for me."

She felt as if she were falling into an endless abyss, her words frozen inside. She *knew* his plan, without him having to speak the words. He was going to confess to a crime he hadn't committed, in order to save his brother's life.

And Cain would be the one who would hang for murder.

Chapter Fifteen

Cain wasn't prepared for the devastation on Margaret's face. "No," she insisted. "I won't let you confess to a crime you did not commit." Her posture straightened, and although every inch of her was neatly pinned and pressed into place, she looked as if she were about to explode. "I won't let you hang."

A hanging wasn't quite what he had in mind. If he lied and said that he had been involved with the murder, they would have to take him into custody. Even if they imprisoned him within the Tolbooth, Cain believed he could get himself out. But Margaret's reaction was so violent, he realized that she cared more than he'd thought.

"If we find MacKinloch before the trial, I won't have to." He kept his voice even, but her green eyes flared with fury. She looked ready to seize a sword and run him through for even suggesting that he take his brother's place.

He rather liked seeing this side to her. She was filled with fire and passion, like a warrior.

"And if we don't find him? You'll give yourself up and let them hang you when you did nothing wrong?" She closed her eyes, as if seeking patience from a higher power. "You've lost your wits. I don't know what's happened to your brain, but clearly it has gone on holiday."

Her fury was born of fear, and it warmed him to know that she was so upset about the idea of anything happening to him. He wasn't planning to be hanged—not at all. He was confident in his ability to escape a prison like the Tolbooth.

"Trust me in this," he told her. "I ken what I'm doing."

"I highly doubt that." She was chewing on her lower lip, and the nervous gesture made him want to kiss her. She was pretty enough when she wasn't angry. But when she was furious, her face held a flush and her green eyes were fiery. A more beautiful woman he'd never seen.

She spun away from him, aghast at what she'd heard. "Are you trying to be a martyr? Do you think I'll be glad to help your brother at the cost of your life?"

Martyr was not a word in his vocabulary. "I'm going to save him," he said again. He had little faith in the jury. It was likely that they were looking for someone to shoulder the blame. The death of an English earl could not be taken lightly, and there was enough questionable evidence to convict his brother.

"Do you really feel that your life has so little value?" she murmured. "Why would you give it up for nothing?"

Her hands moved around his neck, and his attention was entirely fixated upon her mouth. He wanted to taste her lips, to hear her sighs of satisfaction as he took her again and again.

"It's no' about my life. It's about my brother's life. And it's worth a great deal."

"And what about me?" she whispered. "Are my wishes worth nothing?"

He pulled her tightly against him, as if he could merge her body into his. "I would do the same for you." He stole a taste of her lips, kissing her softly. "If I had to go to the gallows for a single night with you, I'd gladly go, lass."

Margaret stood on tiptoe, her hands moving over him. His arousal was painful as she drew his hips to hers. He was nestled against her, and the gentle pressure of her body set his senses on fire.

"I will not let you sacrifice yourself," Margaret insisted. "Not for anyone."

The flare of anger in her eyes made it clear that she intended to fight for him. "What do you plan to do?"

She touched his face with her hands, and he slid his hands to her bottom. The rush of desire made him inhale sharply. She knew exactly how to arouse him, driving him toward madness.

Before he could steal another kiss, she pulled back. "Have faith in me, Cain. I'll make sure your brother gets a fair trial."

She was talking about witnesses and hiring investigators, and before he realized what was happening, she opened a writing desk and took out a piece of paper. She dipped a quill into ink and began scribbling out a list of men's names.

"Take this and ask if any of these folk have seen MacKinloch. We will find him, if we have to turn over every stone in Scotland." He had no time to react before she shoved it into his palm. Her clever mind was working quickly, and he saw her brow furrow.

"What is it?" he asked.

She shook her head, crossing the room. "Just a strange thought I had. It doesn't matter. I'll have the investigators look into it, and that will determine if it's even possible."

Before he could stop her, she threw open the parlor doors and ordered one of the servants to bring the carriage around.

"Where are you going?"

"We are going to put an end to this. We will retrace your brother's footsteps and do all that we must to find MacKinloch." She straightened her bonnet and adjusted one of her white gloves. "Now do you want to come, or do you intend to begin planning your funeral?"

Cain leaned in and kissed her lightly, not caring that any of the servants might see. "You aren't afraid of anything, are you?"

"To the contrary," she said, meeting his gaze evenly. "There is something that terrifies me. And I will not allow you to make that sacrifice."

Margaret was as good as her word. The thought of losing Cain was unthinkable, and she was scared to death that he would make a confession to save his brother's life. She hadn't slept at all last night, and it was only now that she realized how much she loved him. This man had come to mean everything to her—and she would not rest until she had saved them both.

After she and Cain traveled back to the town where Jonah had been arrested, she spoke with as many people as she could. They eyed her strangely, and she could only suppose it was because they found it unusual for a lady to be asking questions.

The coroner was even more reluctant to speak with her. "This isna meant for a young lady's ears," he argued. "I've already given my testimony on the means of the earl's death."

Margaret softened her tone and pressed Cain behind her. "Sir, I know you have a very difficult task, one that few men are strong enough to endure."

The coroner nodded, "It is indeed most trying. But I've a strong stomach for wha' would make most men sick."

"And I am certain there is no one better," she soothed. This man was a proud one, and she chose her words carefully. "We want justice as much as anyone. Perhaps more so."

She lowered her gaze, feigning a demure personality. "I've only one question for you, sir, and then we'll be on our way."

"What is it, then?" He wasn't at all eager to be helpful.

"When the earl was shot, was it a direct shot or did the bullet enter at an angle?"

The coroner frowned at that. "What does it matter? The man's dead. The boy who shot him blew his brains out."

"At such a close range, wouldn't you agree that it would be easy to tell where the exit wound was?"

"At that range, the head was nearly blown apart." He shook his head and opened the door. "I'll have to ask you both to leave."

"One moment, sir." Margaret paused at the door. "If the bullet wound went straight across, then that would suggest that the man who killed the earl was nearly the same height. An angle would mean that the shooter was far shorter."

His expression held wariness, and he shook his head. "Not necessarily. Good day to you both."

And with that, the door was closed in their faces. Cain took her hand and led her away. There was a glint in his eyes that she didn't quite understand. He was hurrying toward the coach, and when he gave directions to the driver, she understood that they were going toward the place where the earl had been shot.

But the moment Cain closed the door, he hauled her to him and kissed her hard. She didn't know what had prompted it, but the moment his mouth claimed hers, she opened to him. His tongue slid inside her mouth and she met his kiss with her own.

It was a last, desperate need to show him that she would never turn away from him. Time was running out, and she intended to stand by this man, no matter what happened.

His hand cupped her breast, and he murmured against her ear, "I want to take this gown off you, lass. And I want to taste every inch of your skin." His words sent a jolt of heat between her legs, and she straddled his lap. Amid the tangle of her skirts, she felt his hard length.

"No matter what happens, I need you to stay with me," she pleaded. "Don't give up until we have the answers we need. We'll find the man who did this and bring him to justice."

His hands moved beneath her hem, stroking her stockings. Higher still he moved, and she let out a gasp when he pressed his palm against her intimate opening.

"You're an intelligent woman, Margaret Andrews," he said against her mouth, kissing her again. "I wouldna have thought to ask about the bullet."

His fingers rubbed against her folds, and she grew utterly wet. "I—I had to ask. Jonah is so much shorter and—" She couldn't speak another word, for he was stroking her in a way that made it impossible to grasp a coherent thought.

"And what?" he prompted, never ceasing his torment. She went pliant against him, her breathing shifting as he pleasured her.

"I don't know. I can't think whilst you're touching me."

He withdrew his hand and she wanted to moan with frustration. But then, the coach had come to a stop. They were here.

Although her body was quaking with unfulfilled desire, she forced herself to settle down. There might have been something the authorities missed that night, and she wanted to believe that they would be able to trace MacKinloch.

"Lass." Cain caught her hand and pulled her back a moment. "Thank you for being here. And for what you've done." He kissed her softly, and the touch brought the taste of regret to her lips.

If they didn't find the evidence they needed, he would surrender himself and either disappear or die. She would not see him again, and the thought made her angrier than she'd ever imagined.

"Don't give up. Not on Jonah and not on us," she warned.

Cain released her hand and she stepped outside, not waiting for him. She didn't know what she hoped to find. Something. Anything that might save the life of a young boy and the man she loved.

The evening air was cool, the sun low in the sky. She trudged through the grasses where they had found Strathland's body. One area was flattened with darker stains. "I think this was where he was shot," Cain guessed.

Margaret stood, turning in a circle, trying to imagine how it had happened. The coach had stopped on the road, and Strathland had disembarked. Moments later, he'd been shot in the head and left behind.

"Look for hoof prints in the grass," she ordered. "Or footprints. We need to know how the murderer traveled here."

They walked through the area, searching every inch of ground. At one point, Cain was on his hands and knees, examining the dirt. As she joined him, her gaze fell upon the wheel ruts upon the road from Strathland's coach.

"Do you see those?" she asked, pointing to the ruts. "It looks like there was another coach there that night."

"Aye." He shrugged, as if it meant nothing. "But it's a public road, lass. Anyone could have traveled this way."

"These tracks run over Strathland's." She studied them closely, wondering whether there was any meaning in them at all. "And how many coaches travel on this road? Not many, I'd say."

He shook his head. "There's no way to tell, lass. And it doesna seem that there's anything else here for us."

Margaret let out a sigh. "I feared as much. But I thought we should look." She held out her hand to help him up, but he remained down on one knee.

Cain held her hand while he looked up at her. "It was always like this, you ken?" He stroked her gloved hand, a twisted smile on his face. "You were far above where I dared to reach."

Margaret knelt down, bringing herself to his level. "There's no difference between us now, is there?"

"Only because I've brought you down. It was ne'er where you were meant to be. I led you into your own ruin."

"No." She braved a smile. "This is where I want to be, Cain. Right here, with you." She kissed him and took both of his hands, guiding him to stand beside her.

"For now," he agreed. The words left their mark of fear within her. She sensed she had to hold fast to these moments between them.

For they might be the last memories she'd have of this man.

It had been a long day of searching. Cain brought Margaret home, and both of them were exhausted. Her hair was knotted back beneath her bonnet, the strings resting against her throat. He held her hand and was grateful for her presence. Though he'd never wanted her to be caught up in this trial, each day with her was a gift. She gave him strength, even in the darkest of days.

They walked inside the house, and the butler informed him, "Mr. Sinclair, you have a caller. Mr. MacKinloch is waiting in the parlor."

MacKinloch was here? Did the man have a death wish? The man responsible for the earl's death had the gall to arrive at Falsham as if he had a right to be here?

Cain bit back the curses he wanted to utter and thanked the butler, following him to the parlor.

"I don't want you here while I question him," he began, but Margaret would have none of it.

She raised her hand to cut him off and declared, "You won't stop me, Sinclair. We will speak with him together, and that's final. Joseph was our family's footman for many years, if you recall."

There was war brewing in her eyes, and she stepped in front of him. "We're going to need his testimony. So don't you dare kill him."

"If he murdered Strathland and let my brother take the blame, he'll answer for it, Margaret." Cain wasn't about to allow the man to escape his fate, and he was convinced that Joseph MacKinloch had committed the crime. No doubt the man wanted vengeance, after Strathland and his men had raped and killed his sister. Who could blame MacKinloch for wanting the earl's death?

But not at the cost of Jonah's life.

When they opened the door, MacKinloch was seated in a chair, holding a cup of tea. Seeing him sitting there so calmly made Cain want to seize the man and let the cup shatter. Instead, he gripped Margaret's hand to gain control from her.

"Joseph," she began. "We have been searching for you for some time now."

He set down the cup and stood. "So I understand." He spread his hands out slightly. "I am here. What do ye want from me?"

"I want you to confess what you did. Jonah's been suffering in the Tolbooth for weeks now." Cain's fingers clenched into a fist and it was only Margaret's presence that kept him from beating MacKinloch into a bloody heap.

The man stared back at Cain. "My sister endured a far worse fate than yer brother. I'm glad the earl's dead, for the bastard deserved it." He crossed his arms and regarded Cain. "But I'm no' the man yer looking for. I did naught to Strathland."

Liar. He'd been there that night and had taken Jonah's pistol. "I don't believe you."

"Please sit down, Joseph," Margaret bade him. "I want to discuss a proposition with you. One that will suit all of us."

Cain wasn't sure what she had in mind, and curiosity kept his mouth shut. Whatever it was, Margaret had said nothing of it before now.

She sat across from the man and folded her hands neatly. "You had good reasons for . . . what you did. However, to blame a boy for your actions is reprehensible."

MacKinloch leaned forward, a startled smile on his face. "As I said, I didna kill the earl, Miss Andrews. The reason I came here was—"

Margaret cut him off and continued, "If you give testimony to prove that Jonah was innocent, and if he is freed, we will work with the authorities to reduce your punishment. Instead of a death sentence, you will be sent to a penal colony in New South Wales. You will serve out those years there, and you will never set foot in Scotland or England again."

He sent her an incredulous look. "And why would I be admitting to a crime I didna do?"

"You ran away and hid for many weeks," Cain reminded him. Of course the man was guilty.

MacKinloch shrugged. "If I stayed, they would suspect me, even if I did naught wrong, ye ken? Best to go away for a while and let matters die down."

"You son of a bitch," Cain growled, seizing the man by the throat. He hauled MacKinloch against the wall, not caring if he crushed the man's skull. "You set my brother up to die."

"He set himself up," MacKinloch argued. "When he took back the pistol and ran away."

"He's a boy. Too scared to say or do aught." Cain shoved him back, and MacKinloch stumbled before he righted himself. "You're going to come with me and offer yourself up." He glared at MacKinloch. "If you don't make a confession, we'll find the evidence. And you'll hang for this." He wasn't about to let the man go free—not after all that had happened.

But Margaret had gone pale. "What if he's telling the truth, Cain? What if he *didn't* kill the earl?"

He dismissed the idea. "MacKinloch had the most reason of anyone."

But the man only smiled. "I would've killed the earl, if I'd reached him first. But he was already dead."

Margaret studied the man and asked, "Then who *did* kill him, Joseph?"

He straightened his collar. "That's why I came, Miss Andrews. I may have wanted Strathland dead, but I wasna going to let a boy hang in my place. Jonah's a lad with a taste for adventure, but I don't want him to die. And I ken who went after Strathland that night."

Cain went utterly still. He didn't want to hear it, but he already knew the name Joseph would speak.

"Who?" Margaret asked.

MacKinloch set down his cup and admitted, "Ye're living in his house, Miss Andrews. There's no man who wanted Strathland dead more than Paul Fraser."

Chapter Sixteen

I need to talk with you, Juliette," Margaret said.

Her sister was busy playing with her daughter, Grace, pouring imaginary tea as they sat at a table in the nursery. "Would you like to join us?" Juliette smiled, offering her a place at the table.

"I think we should speak alone," Margaret said. "Perhaps in Grace's bedroom." From there, they could keep watch over the little girl.

Juliette kissed her daughter on the top of her dark hair. "Mummy will return in a moment, darling. Why don't you offer your dolly a biscuit?"

Grace pretended to feed her doll while Juliette joined Margaret in the bedroom. Her face revealed her curiosity, making Margaret dread the question she had to ask.

Lowering her voice, Juliette said, "I know Joseph came to pay a call on you earlier. Is that was this is about?"

Margaret nodded. MacKinloch's insinuation, that Juliette's husband had committed the murder, was even worse than she could imagine. She didn't want to believe any of it, for if Paul was responsible, there was no good outcome. Either an innocent boy would hang . . . or her sister's husband would die.

She steeled herself, knowing that she had to tread carefully. "Juliette . . . you said that Paul went in search of Lord Strathland after he shot Amelia's husband. Did he leave right away?"

Her sister nodded. "Of course. Strathland fired at Amelia and missed, hitting Castledon instead. They're both fine, but Paul went after him, hoping to bring Strathland to justice for what he did."

"And he went on horseback," Margaret predicted. "So he could ride fast and catch up to the carriage." She hoped that was true, given the second set of coach wheels she'd seen. Her instincts told her that Paul couldn't have been the killer—she knew him too well for that.

"Yes." Her sister's eyes narrowed, as if she was wondering why Margaret would be asking about it. "Did you want to ask Paul yourself? Perhaps he saw something that night that could be relevant to the case? I know he and Cain went over it already, but it's possible you might think of something else." Her sister's demeanor was helpful, not the actions of a woman trying to hide something.

"Paul said the earl was already dead when he got there." She studied her sister, praying that it was the truth.

"Yes, that's right." Juliette peered over at her daughter, who was singing to herself.

At the sight of the young girl, a pang of reluctance caught Margaret's heart. She shouldn't even be questioning her sister. Whatever had happened, Paul Fraser was not a suspect in the murder.

Her sister seemed to guess why she was asking. "Margaret, Paul didn't kill the earl. He couldn't have." There was not a trace of doubt on Juliette's face—only impatience at the conversation.

"I agree." More and more, Margaret believed that there was someone else there that night. "But Joseph MacKinloch claims he is innocent of the murder. He implied that Paul killed Strathland."

"Don't be ridiculous. Of course a guilty man would put the blame on someone else." Her sister reached out and took her hands. "My husband did nothing wrong."

Margaret squeezed her palms. "I know that." And she truly did believe that was true. Paul was a good man and a doctor who had spent his life saving others. There was no reason to suspect him. "My only worry is, what if MacKinloch accuses him in court? There's no evidence against Paul, is there?"

"Paul told me himself that when he arrived, the coroner had already taken the body away," Juliette said. "The coroner himself can bear witness to that."

Margaret let out the breath she'd been holding. "Good." She reached out to hug her sister in apology, but Juliette barely returned the affection.

"Listen to me," Margaret insisted, drawing back to meet her gaze. "Someone killed Lord Strathland, and I need to find out who it was. I have another suspicion, but I'll need your help in sending a letter immediately with your fastest rider." A sudden wash of fear came over her, but she forced it back. If her instincts were correct, she had no choice but to pursue this.

Her sister squeezed her hand. "I'll do everything I can."

🏃

"Jonah." Margaret spoke softly within the prison cell. The young boy was curled up on a pile of dirty straw, and the stench of the room was so strong, she held a scented handkerchief to her nose.

He turned, squinting against the dim light. "Miss Andrews?"

"Yes. I've come to speak with you for a little while before the trial tomorrow morning." She gingerly stepped across the stone floor, trying not to think of what sorts of scurrying animals shared the room with the boy. It had cost a great deal to arrange for a private cell, but she had spoken with Paul and insisted upon it. Jonah was suffering enough in this place—he didn't need to worry about other criminals attacking him.

"What do you want?" His voice held a grim finality, as if he'd already abandoned hope.

"Joseph MacKinloch came to see us. He implied that someone else shot the earl. I wondered if you might know who it could have been."

The boy sighed. "It doesna matter, miss. I'm going to hang for it. And I suppose I deserve to die."

It seemed that he'd given up after so long. Margaret eyed him sharply. "Don't say that, Jonah. You didn't kill the earl."

"Nay, but no matter wha' I say, they'll believe the worst of me." He drew up his knees, his attention focused on the ground. "I shouldna have disobeyed him. Cain warned me no' to leave. But I thought I'd go and have an adventure." His face held a bleak expression. "This wasna what I'd hoped for. If I'd ne'er left the inn, I wouldna be here now."

"We'll get you out," she promised. "Did you see anyone else that night, after you returned? Any strangers?"

Jonah lifted his shoulders in a shrug. "Nay. I was only looking for MacKinloch when I left. After I came back, I got my things and ran."

"What time was it when you left the inn?" Margaret asked.

The boy shook his head. "I've no idea. After dark. There were only a few men talking to the innkeeper when I left."

And those men were likely MacKinloch's alibis, Margaret thought. "Did they see you leave?"

"Aye." Jonah stood slowly, wincing as if he was in pain. "The sheriff questioned them later, and they told him I left in secret. They wouldna believe I was only looking for MacKinloch. They told the sheriff they were certain I was the one who had shot the earl."

When Jonah turned back to her, she saw the streaks of tears down his cheeks. Margaret sympathized with him, for he was still just a boy. True, he'd made many mistakes, but he didn't deserve to die for them. She handed him her handkerchief, but he refused it.

"I couldna touch something so fine, Miss Andrews. No' here."

She ignored him and moved closer, wiping his tears away with the handkerchief. "Keep it, Jonah. And know that your brother and I will do everything in our power to prove your innocence."

"It's too late," he muttered.

"No." She held his face between her hands and smoothed away a rough lock of his dark hair. "Your solicitor has been going over the testimonies, and many of them aren't the same. If the witnesses disagree in their statements, then they cannot prove you guilty." She pressed the handkerchief into his hand. "Don't give up hope."

His blue eyes were a mirror of Cain's, and she could see that he was terrified. But he took the handkerchief and held it tightly. "Thank you, Miss Andrews."

She nodded and turned to leave. On her way out, she nearly collided with Cain, who had been standing at the door. Behind him was Jonah's solicitor, Mr. Dawson.

"You could have come inside," she told him. "I know you have much to discuss with Jonah."

Cain leaned down and kissed her openly. "You didna have to visit him, lass. No' in a place like this."

She met his gaze. "Yes, I did need to come. Especially to a place like this. He needs to know that we haven't given up on him."

There was a flare of emotion on his face, and he gripped her hand. He was watching her with an expression that made her even more worried. It was as if he were savoring a last moment, as if he would never see her again. "You're a good woman, Margaret."

"Will I see you tonight?" Her heart quickened, for she saw the heaviness in his expression. Cain gave her no answer, but touched her chin before he walked inside his brother's cell, followed by the solicitor. Whatever he'd meant, he had no intention of telling her.

Margaret walked outside the Tolbooth, feeling despondent. The calm resignation in Cain's voice made her worry that he was going to do something rash.

She couldn't let that happen. The trial would begin soon, and she was afraid of what he would do if things turned out badly for his brother.

"Jonah Sinclair, prisoner of the Tolbooth of Edinburgh, you are hereby indicted and accused of feloniously murdering Brandon Carlisle, the twelfth Earl of Strathland, by firing a pistol with the intent to cause malicious harm."

Cain sat across from the advocate panel, where Jonah remained in custody. While the Advocate Depute droned on with a list of the charges brought against his brother, the boy's face remained resolute, as if he'd come to accept an unjust fate. The only trace of fear he showed was his hands clenched together.

Cain's blood felt as if it were frozen. It was a strange experience, as if he were standing outside of himself. He wanted to shelter his brother from this fate, but he was helpless to do anything except listen to the advocates.

Margaret was seated next to him, dressed in a somber indigo gown with a sprig of heather tucked inside her sash. Her bonnet was trimmed with dark ribbon, and she held her posture erect as if she were a queen presiding over her subjects. Though outwardly she appeared controlled and calm, he knew she was as tense as he was.

He hadn't slept all night. He'd paced the floors, and he imagined that he looked like an unshaven beggar. Certainly, he wasn't fit to sit beside a lady.

Margaret reached out to take his palm. Her gloved hand was warm against his, and she squeezed gently, murmuring, "Jonah has a good solicitor and a barrister to argue his case. Too much of the evidence is circumstantial." Lifting her chin, she added, "Trust in that, Cain."

She might be right, but he couldn't bring himself to share in that faith. Jonah stood before the Lord Justice Clerk, and it was then that Cain noticed the boy trembling. He had reason for it. If they found him guilty of Strathland's murder, he might pay for his mistakes with his life.

". . . and that you, according to His Majesty's laws, may endure the just punishment for this crime," the Advocate Depute finished.

Just punishment meant hanging for a boy of four-and-ten. Cain rubbed at his chin, praying that somehow the rightful guilty person would emerge.

He fully believed that Joseph MacKinloch was responsible, regardless of the man's claims. But would the truth come out?

A list of evidence and witnesses was presented to the Lord Justice Clerk, after which time the panel pleaded on Jonah's behalf, "Not guilty."

The first witness, Peter Walker, was sworn in, but the man exchanged a glance with the Lord Justice Clerk. There was a connection between the two men, though Cain didn't know what it was. But it soon became clear that this was a witness who had seen Jonah leaving the inn that night.

"Tell the panel what you observed on the night the accused was seen leaving the inn," the Advocate Depute, Mr. Newman, began.

Walker cleared his throat and admitted, "I was traveling south, meeting friends at the Grouse Inn. I spent the evening playing cards, and around midnight, I saw Jonah Sinclair leaving. He stood against the wall, moving as if he didna want anyone to see him. Looked as if he were afraid."

"Why do you say that?" The Advocate Depute kept his voice neutral, as if he already knew what the witness would say.

"It was late, and he was alone. He returned a few hours later, still before dawn. Blood was on his hands, and he was carrying a pistol. He tried to hide, and we asked him what had happened. He tried to run out the door, but we caught him and alerted the sheriff."

"And what did the accused say to you?"

"He said, 'The Earl of Strathland's dead. Oh God, he's dead.'" Walker leaned back, his gaze holding satisfaction.

"That's no' all I said!" Jonah blurted out from his seat. His face was white, and the barrister forced him to sit down, speaking rapidly to him in an undertone.

Margaret's fingers laced with Cain's, as if she needed him. He understood her worry and stroked her gloved palm. Having her here beside him was a comfort that gave him strength to endure this. And he prayed to God that the truth would come out, so he would not have to leave her.

The trial only got worse. The prosecution continued to draw out the witness, the evidence mounting against Jonah. When his brother's agent began to cross-examine the same witness, the barrister took a different approach.

"When you saw the accused leaving the inn, was he carrying a pistol at that time?"

"Not openly, nay," Walker answered. "He might've hidden it away."

"Then you did not see any weapon on the defender?"

The man only shrugged, and the barrister continued, "He was not the only person who left the inn that night, was he?"

"Many people came and went," Walker admitted. "But there was only one other man who arrived by coach, before MacKinloch left."

Beside him, Margaret gripped his hand. She turned and met Cain's gaze, and he knew what she was thinking. She seemed convinced that there was another coach that night, but even if it was true, there was no way to know who the other gentleman was or whether he had anything to do with Strathland's death.

"Isn't it also true that Joseph MacKinloch departed first that night? And that he was acting as the boy's guardian?"

"They were traveling together, aye," the witness agreed. "But shortly after the boy left, Joseph MacKinloch returned to the inn. He played cards with us the rest of the night."

Cain's stomach sank, for it was clear that MacKinloch had somehow convinced these men to act as his alibis.

"Not true," Margaret whispered. Her face was tight with unrest, and she grimaced as the questioning continued.

"You said MacKinloch left for a time," the barrister continued. "How long was he gone?"

"Less than an hour."

There were more questions about what time they played, who the other players were, and what the stakes were. The number of questions was dizzying, and more than once, Cain wondered why the agent was switching from one topic to another. Perhaps he was trying to make the witness accidentally reveal a truth during the testimony.

Hours crept on, and with every witness who continued on the stand, his brother appeared even more despondent.

"Why haven't they called Jonah to the stand?" Margaret whispered. "Do they not want him to defend himself?"

"The prosecutor would lead him into a trap. It's best that he doesna say anything. At least, no' yet."

Cain prayed it wouldn't come to that, but if all other witnesses failed, the barrister would undoubtedly call Jonah to speak.

Finally, Paul Fraser, the Viscount of Falsham, was called to the witness stand. Lord Falsham was dressed impeccably, and he strode forward with confidence.

Margaret was aghast. "Why is Paul here?"

"He offered his testimony, Margaret. This was his choice."

Paul had known how bad the case was, and since he'd been there that night, he'd spoken with both the solicitor and the agent representing Jonah.

"Lord Falsham, will you please tell the court of your findings on the night when Lord Strathland was murdered."

The viscount nodded and said, "Of course. But first, the jury should ken that the Earl of Strathland was locked away for madness," he began. "He spent nearly five years in an asylum, and medical evidence will attest to that. He escaped the asylum and began hunting our family. He fired a pistol at my wife's sister, Amelia Andrews. His shot missed, and he struck the Earl of Castledon instead. Then he fled."

"And you pursued him, did you not?" the Advocate Depute said.

"I did, aye. We were all afraid he would try to harm other family members, and I tried to follow, to protect them."

Paul met Cain's gaze from across the courtroom. "I rode for most of the night, but I had to change horses when mine threw a shoe. By the time I continued my journey, it was morning. The coroner was already examining Lord Strathland when I arrived."

The coroner, who had already given his own testimony, was already nodding in agreement. Cain felt Margaret's grip on his hand relax.

"How long had Lord Strathland been dead when you arrived?" the Advocate Depute inquired.

"Several hours."

"And would you say his death occurred sometime after midnight?"

Cain saw exactly where this was leading, but Paul only shrugged. His friend added, "I'm no' a coroner, so I canna say when the death occurred. But I will say that Lord Strathland had more enemies than friends." He turned his gaze across the courtroom and pointed. "You should ask Joseph MacKinloch what the earl did to his sister."

"MacKinloch is not on the stand," the Lord Justice Clerk interrupted. "Please answer only the questions asked of you, Lord Falsham."

When there were no further questions, the viscount finished his testimony and left the stand. Margaret relaxed beside Cain and whispered, "I hope that will help Jonah a great deal."

It might, but he suspected they would wait until the following day for MacKinloch's testimony. Cain sat through endless hours of more witnesses, the restlessness growing inside.

Jonah risked a glance at him and quietly shook his head. It seemed that his brother had already given up.

The Lord Justice Clerk adjourned the proceedings at the end of the day, and Margaret was only too grateful to leave. She had never attended a trial before, and hadn't realized how endless it would be. Throughout the day, Cain had barely spoken to her. All of his attention was locked on his brother, as if he could will the outcome to turn in Jonah's favor.

She took Cain's arm, walking out with him, but he led her toward Lord Falsham. To Paul, he asked, "Will you take Margaret home to her sister? I won't be back until late."

"Where are you going?" Margaret asked.

He wouldn't answer, but said, "Go with Fraser. He'll look after you."

A sharp suspicion made her feel as if Cain was about to do something foolish. She thought about arguing with him and insisting that he come home, but it was clear that the bone-deep weariness was troubling him.

"Come home to me tonight," she pleaded, squeezing both of his hands in farewell.

His deep blue eyes stared into hers, and he held her hands a little longer. Then he raised one hand to his mouth, kissing her farewell. "Be well, lass."

After Cain had left, Margaret summoned one of the footmen and ordered quietly, "Follow him. Tell me where he's gone."

The man agreed, and Paul offered his arm. "Shall we go home? Juliette will be fretting over you."

She joined him in the carriage for the ride back to Falsham. When the doors were closed, she regarded the viscount. "What do you suppose Cain is doing?"

"Searching for more witnesses, I don't doubt. Or he's going to talk with MacKinloch again." His face turned kindly. "Don't be worrying, Margaret. We'll do what we can to help Cain and his brother."

"I'm afraid Cain will confess to the murder," she blurted out. "Or worse, that they'll hang him, in Jonah's place." She gripped her hands tightly and tried to keep control over her feelings. "I don't know how to stop him."

"I don't think he'd do anything that foolish," Paul said slowly. "'Twould be better to discredit the witnesses who have already spoken against Jonah."

She rubbed at her temples, feeling a touch of a headache. "I don't like being left behind."

"You're no' going after him," Paul insisted. "Stay with us and let it be."

She knew that was the sensible thing to do, but the feeling of uneasiness grew inside her. "I'm afraid he won't find anything. But more than that, I'm afraid of what he'll do afterward."

"Does Sinclair mean that much to you, then?" Paul asked.

"Yes." She loved Cain and wanted to be with him, no matter what happened. Her heart bled for him, for undoubtedly he was feeling the way she had when Amelia had been abducted. The helpless feeling was wrenching, and until the trial was over, Cain would suffer with worry.

"He's my friend, too, Margaret," the viscount reminded her. "He helped my Juliette in a time of need, when no one else would. I'll do everything in my power to assist him and Jonah."

"I know you will." Yet she couldn't help but feel as if Cain was slipping away from her. All through the trial, he'd been far away in his thoughts. She knew it was his worry over Jonah, but more than that, she could feel the way he was isolating himself, as if he'd already accepted what was to come.

His guilt held him captive, and he would not see reason. Just as she'd refused to listen to him, when he'd wanted her to stay behind and allow the authorities to search for Amelia.

She didn't regret the choices she'd made. Throughout each day she'd spent with Cain, she'd lost more and more of her former self. Bonnets and gowns didn't matter a whit when it came to survival. In the midst of that ordeal, she'd come out stronger and wiser.

And she'd fallen in love with this man. Being apart from him was a physical ache, and she now realized that she'd never loved

Lord Lisford or anyone else. She'd been blinded by the outer trappings of a title and a handsome man, never seeing the truth beneath.

Cain didn't care about any of that. He was a man of honor who would lay down his life for someone he loved. He'd walked through fire for her, and he'd offered her everything he had.

She could not allow him to sacrifice himself for Jonah's sake. Somehow they would find the answers that would lead them to the true murderer.

No matter what happened, she could not let him die.

Chapter Seventeen

The public house was crowded that evening, with men drinking and singing, while others played cards. Cain had a tin mug of ale in one hand, but he remained in the shadows watching. The first witness, Peter Walker, was speaking with Joseph MacKinloch at the far end of the room. His face was dark with anger, while MacKinloch remained passive.

It might've been the card game, but for whatever reason, Walker was looking for a fight.

Cain inched his way a little closer, wondering what the pair were fighting over. He kept his back turned, until he found a table close by. Walker was arguing with MacKinloch, and his voice held hatred. "You said you'd pay. I want my damned money, you neep-headed bastard."

"Ye'll get it," MacKinloch countered.

"You never had it, did you? You lied." A moment later, Walker shoved the table aside, and the cards went scattering. "I swear to God, you'll regret cheating me."

An older man wearing an apron came forward. "Take it outside, lads. Go out and cool yer brains."

Walker reached out and seized MacKinloch by the shirt. "Aye. Let's go and talk outside." But his efforts were met with resistance.

"I'm no' going anywhere with you. I'm going to finish my drink." Though MacKinloch spoke coolly, he appeared uneasy about what was happening.

In answer, Walker picked up the mug and poured it over his head. "It looks like you're finished, now, aren't you?"

Ale dripped down the Highlander's face, and he lunged at Walker. Another man dragged him back, shoving him toward the door. MacKinloch stumbled, and Cain caught him by the arm. He kept a tight grip on the man's elbow. "We need to talk," he said grimly. "About my brother."

He wanted to know exactly what the man intended to say on the witness stand tomorrow morning. Frustration redoubled inside him, for he sensed in his bones that MacKinloch was the murderer. He'd tried to lay the blame upon Paul, but Cain didn't believe that for an instant. His best friend would never allow Jonah to languish in the Tolbooth if he'd done aught.

"Aye, then," MacKinloch agreed. "We'll talk outside. After I've finished here."

But Cain strongly suspected MacKinloch was walking into a fight to avoid him. He released the man's elbow, letting him lead the way outside. There was a risk that MacKinloch would try to run, but he wanted to know what the disagreement was between him and Walker. He suspected MacKinloch had offered to pay the man to become an alibi.

Cain made his way to the doorway, where the unmistakable sounds of fighting broke through the stillness. When he stepped outside, he saw that he wasn't the only one watching. A few men had gathered, and one nudged Cain. "I'll bet you half a crown that Walker wins."

"I couldna take that bet. My money would be on Walker, too," Cain admitted.

Although MacKinloch was older, possibly thirty or so, he was fast. What he lacked in physical strength, he made up for in speed. He ducked a punch and followed up with his own blow to Walker's stomach.

The man grunted and doubled over, but as MacKinloch tried to leave, Walker ran after him, throwing himself at the man.

The two men grappled on the ground, and Cain asked a bystander, "What money does MacKinloch owe him?"

The man shrugged. "They were playing cards. I suppose it was a debt from their last game. Although—" He paused a moment, thinking to himself. "Walker had traveled south to visit friends. It wasna here."

Cain already knew that from the man's testimony this morning, but he wondered what part Walker had played. Had he only been paid to hide MacKinloch's guilt? Or was there something else?

"Whate'er happened, MacKinloch had best pay the man. Walker's no' one to give up a fight."

Cain waited until Walker took a moment to catch his breath. He moved between the two men swiftly and asked, "You were there that night. Did MacKinloch kill the earl?"

The sly smile on Walker's face infuriated him, though the man shook his head. "I was playing cards that night. I've no idea."

Damn him. Cain needed more answers, and he knew Walker wasn't about to give them. He stepped back to let them finish the fight, not caring how badly it went. MacKinloch deserved to be beaten bloody for bringing Jonah with him and letting his brother take the blame.

But after one more blow, the Highlander went stumbling backward. Cain watched in horror as the man struck his head against a large stone beside the gate. A sickening crunch resounded and MacKinloch went motionless.

Some of the onlookers rushed forward, but Cain held back, disbelieving what he'd witnessed.

And then came a shout from one of them. "He's dead!"

☀

"Miss Andrews, you have a caller," the butler informed her. "Mr. Lewis Barnabas is here."

Though it was past the hour for callers, Margaret nodded. "I will speak with him in the drawing room."

She had sent a letter to Barnabas only a few days ago, asking him to come and see her at Falsham. Though she had filled the note with empty compliments and her thanks that he'd given them a place to stay, she had another reason for sending it.

Lewis Barnabas had departed the same day they'd left for Ballaloch, after receiving a letter about a family member who was in trouble. He'd traveled north, along the same road where Strathland had been murdered.

But her true reason for writing to him was because she'd remembered where she had heard his name before. If she was correct, Lewis Barnabas was the cousin to the Earl of Strathland—and the heir to all of his estates. It was too strong of a coincidence for Lord Strathland to die only days after his cousin had learned that he'd left the asylum.

Her heart was pounding as she entered the drawing room. She didn't know how dangerous this man was, and although both Paul and Juliette were here in the house, she was afraid of what to say to him. If he was responsible for the murder, he would never do anything to incriminate himself.

Her brain was racing, trying to come up with plausible reasons why she'd asked him to come. The easiest course of action was to behave like an empty-headed miss who had left Cain and become infatuated with him. She'd sensed his interest in her, and perhaps by encouraging that, he might reveal what had happened that night. It was for that reason she decided not to have her sister or Paul present in the room. With the doors open and servants coming and going freely, that would be enough for propriety's sake.

The moment she stepped inside the drawing room, Lewis Barnabas's face lit up with interest. "Miss Andrews," he greeted her, bowing slightly. "You are looking as lovely as ever."

"Thank you." She offered him a bright smile and said, "Although it is late for callers, I *am* glad that you stopped to see me. I presume you received my letter?"

"I did, indeed." He took her hand and kissed the back of it. Margaret ordered tea and refreshments from the footman and then gestured for Mr. Barnabas to sit.

"Is everything well with your family?" she asked, sitting with her gloved hands folded. "I understand you received troubling news, a few weeks ago."

His expression revealed none of his emotions. "I did, yes. But all has been resolved now."

Resolved? Because his cousin was dead? The utter lack of concern in his voice warned her to tread carefully.

"That—that's good to hear." She decided it was best to continue her façade of behaving as if nothing were wrong.

The footman returned with the tea and refreshments, and Margaret poured for both of them.

"You do that very well," Barnabas complimented. "But then, it isn't surprising, since you are an unmarried young lady seeking a husband."

She set down the silver teapot, trying to hide her shaking hands.

Barnabas reached for his cup and continued, "Shall we continue this falsehood, that you are pretending to desire my company? That you are a well-bred young woman wishing to be my countess, now that I have inherited my cousin's title?" He stirred milk into his tea and continued, "Or we could set aside the pretenses and discuss the real reason I am here."

"Go on," she said quietly. Her insides had turned to ice, and she knew not what this man would say or do.

"I am well aware that you have no feelings for me whatsoever. That was clear enough at my supper party when you gave your attentions to that Highlander. I also know that your reputation is ruined and that your chances of a successful marriage are over." His gaze slid over her body, lingering upon her until she felt the flush of embarrassment. "Though I might consider you for a mistress, you would never make a suitable wife."

She stiffened at the unexpected insult but said nothing. Instead, she sipped at her tea, choosing her words carefully. "Why did you come to Falsham, Mr. Barnabas?" It was clear that he had his own reasons, and she added, "Or should I call you Lord Strathland now?"

He added sugar to his cup and stirred it. "Lord Strathland will do." After he drank, he set down the cup and steepled his hands. "I came to speak with you because I am a man who prefers order with no surprises. I know why you sent for me. And, no, I did not kill my cousin."

That didn't surprise her at all. A man like Barnabas would never stoop to soiling his hands—he would hire someone instead.

"I never thought you did," she began.

But before she could voice a single question, he interrupted, "I know that Sinclair's brother was charged with the murder. And you think to accuse me instead." Barnabas leaned forward, and in his eyes, she saw a ruthless man, fully capable of killing. "Be aware, Miss Andrews, that in the past few years, the estates have prospered in my hands. I have amassed a great deal of wealth and power.

Regardless of what conclusions you may have drawn, I would advise you to keep them to yourself."

Somehow, she managed to gather up her own courage. He thought she was a meek young woman, easily frightened. She set down her tea and answered, "If you were innocent, you would not say this to me."

"What I *am* is a man with many resources. Say nothing, and the boy might have a not proven verdict."

Her heart was beating fiercely, the fear rising so strong, she felt faint. "You want me to remain silent when you hired someone to kill your cousin?"

Barnabas smiled and shrugged. "Try to lay the blame upon me, and you will regret it, Miss Andrews. The boy and Sinclair will both pay the penalty for your foolishness."

"Cain has done nothing wrong," she said, rising to her feet. "You cannot touch him."

Barnabas stood and picked up his hat. "Underestimating me is a dangerous prospect, Miss Andrews." He moved toward the door, adding, "Perhaps Sinclair could share a cell with his brother at the Tolbooth. Then he could bid him good-bye on the morning he's hanged."

His callous manner only convinced her that she had to bring him to justice somehow. "I'm afraid I must decline, *Mr. Barnabas.*" She emphasized his name, making it clear she would not recognize him as the earl. "I cannot remain silent for all the wrong reasons."

"I think you'll change your mind, Miss Andrews." With that, he bowed and walked out.

It was long past midnight when Margaret heard the sound of footsteps in the hall. She hadn't been able to sleep at all, after her conversation with Barnabas. Silently, she crept out of bed and opened her door. Cain stood with his forehead resting against the wall, palms on either side. He didn't seem to be aware of her, so she whispered, "Cain."

When he lifted his head, she beckoned for him to come inside her room, opening the door a little wider.

His steps were heavy as he went inside, and she lit a lamp. "Tell me what's happened."

"MacKinloch is dead."

Her blood turned to ice, and she couldn't breathe for a moment. "How? Who killed him?"

A strange expression twisted his face. "It's good that you don't think I murdered him."

Margaret moved behind him to close the door. "Well, of course you didn't. We needed him alive for Jonah's case. Especially since he was likely the one who shot the earl." She wondered if Barnabas had somehow made contact with MacKinloch and hired him for that purpose.

"Who would believe that now?" Cain ventured. "Without MacKinloch's statement, we've got nothing. Jonah is going to hang, and the other witnesses canna change that."

The hollow tone in his voice devastated her. She led him forward to stand by the coal hearth. He warmed his hands, but not once would he look at her. He stared at the fire for a long time in silence. Then at last, he met her gaze. "I have to save him, Margaret."

"And you will." She drew her arms around his neck, standing on tiptoe. Though she questioned whether or not to tell him of Barnabas's visit, she did not want to be threatened into silence. She pulled him close and insisted, "You will not confess to a murder you didn't commit."

"How else can I protect him?" He lifted her chin up, kissing her softly. "I canna stand back and let him die."

"Nothing is worth the cost of your life," she countered. "Nothing, do you hear me?" Margaret stood as tall as she could, kissing him ardently. Against his mouth, she whispered, "I love you, Cain. And we will fight for him." She told him then, of Barnabas's visit. But she wasn't prepared for the anger rising upon Cain's face.

"You should no' have been alone with him, lass. If he conspired to kill his cousin, he could have hurt you." He gripped her hard, resting his face against her hair.

"He came to threaten me into silence. But we need his testimony in the trial." She drew back, kissing him again. "Can you speak to the solicitor in the morning and arrange it?"

"Aye, that I will."

She moved her hands down his face, needing to touch him. Though she didn't really believe Barnabas could carry out his threat, she questioned what he would do if he was forced to testify in the trial. And what if he lied on the witness stand?

"Don't think of it now, lass. I'm wanting to share this night with you." His rough palm edged her chin, and she pushed all the worries from her mind.

Cain picked her up and took her to the bed, laying her down upon it. She tried to unfasten his shirt and plaid, but her hands were shaking too much. In the end, he stood back and undressed himself.

His skin was golden in the firelight, his muscles taut and gleaming. He was the most beautiful man she'd ever seen, and there was nothing that would make her stand back and let him sacrifice himself.

"Come to me," she whispered, removing her wrapper. Clad in nothing but a thin nightgown, she opened her arms.

He stood before the bed, wearing nothing at all, and the intensity of his gaze stole her breath. "Say it again, lass."

"I love you."

He closed his eyes for a moment, and then when he opened them, he admitted, "I've loved you from the first day I saw you."

When he lay down beside her, she moved him to rest upon his stomach. "I want to touch you, Cain." She ran her hands over the scarred skin of his back. These burns, he'd endured for her sake.

For that was the sort of man he was—the kind who would do anything to protect her. Tears stung her eyes as she struggled to think of how she would stop him from confessing to Strathland's murder. Though she could give her body freely, it might not be enough to convince him.

Her hands stroked every inch of his shoulders and back, running lower to his firm hips. "My turn," he told her.

When she lay beside him, he ordered, "Stand over there and let me watch while you undress yourself."

Her skin prickled at the idea, but she obeyed. With the firelight behind her, she lifted the hem of her nightgown and pulled it up and over her head.

Cain gave an intake of breath and said, "Unbind your hair."

She unfastened the ribbon from her braid and unraveled it until the long blond strands spilled over her shoulders and back. In the cool night air, her breasts were tight nubs, in soft anticipation of his touch.

He crooked his finger, silently bidding her to return. When she did, he renewed the onslaught of her senses. He kissed her cheeks and nose, moving down to her chin and throat. With his hands, he caressed her skin.

"I'm going to remember this night," he said. "'Twill bring me comfort if ever we're parted."

She couldn't stop the tears that broke free, and he wiped them away. "Don't, lass. Don't think of it now."

No, she wouldn't. For tonight, she had to believe that all would be well.

He cupped her breasts, and she moved atop him, straddling his erection so that his thick length pressed against her. His eyes had gone dark with desire, and he sat up to take one nipple in his mouth. She wrapped her legs around his waist, kissing his face while his tongue swirled around her breast. Dimly, she was aware of him moving forward until he was sitting on the edge of the bed. He gripped her bottom and surprised her when he lifted her hips and entered her in one stroke.

Her body was slick, and the unexpected penetration stretched her deep. But instead of thrusting, he stood, keeping their bodies joined. Gently, he turned around and laid her back on the bed. Both of her legs were wrapped around his waist while he stood, holding her in place.

"Don't move, lass," he warned.

She braced herself, but instead of making love to her, he gripped her hips with one arm, tilting her upward. The shift in the angle of penetration caused a new friction that she hadn't expected. He moved slowly, as if he were using his shaft to caress her intimately.

Her body went liquid, and he pulled out, until only the head of him was inside her. When he began teasing her hooded flesh with his thumb, her breath released in a shuddering gasp. "Cain," she moaned. The sensations poured over her, and she clenched against him, wanting so badly for him to begin thrusting.

Instead, he kept her on the edge, touching her in a rhythm that made her shudder. She was so overcome by the intensity, she arched her back and tightened her legs, trying to draw him in. But he withheld himself a little longer, setting her hips down on the bed and stroking her breasts while he was sheathed inside.

Her breath caught in quick gasps, and without warning, a shimmering release took her under, forcing her to clench around his erection. He let out a low hiss, then began to move.

"Don't leave me," she whispered. "You can't give yourself up."

"Sweet, I'm already in Heaven," he said, making love to her slowly. "What happens after this doesna matter. Tonight you are mine. As I am yours."

She moved in counterpoint to him, raising her knees to take him deeper. In this man, she saw the lover she'd always dreamed of. Wild and untamed, he would always follow his own path. And it broke her heart to think of losing him.

Her body surrendered again, rising to his call. As he plunged and thrust, she held him as close as she dared, praying that she could somehow convince him to stay silent.

"I love you," she told him again, framing his face as he took her.

He finished inside her, his body trembling as he emptied himself. Their legs were tangled together, their bodies still joined when he kissed her softly. "I was ne'er worthy of the grass you walked upon, lass. You are a gift to me, one I didna deserve." His hands moved over her bare skin, and she vowed that nothing would part them now.

She would not remain silent because of one man's threats. Despite the danger, they would uncover the truth that would set Jonah free.

Chapter Eighteen

Cain moved as if caught in a trance. Before he'd left Margaret, he'd watched her sleeping for long moments. A blond curl hung over her cheek and he pushed it back, studying her to make a memory.

Her revelation, that Barnabas was behind the murder, was indeed possible. But there was no way to know what the man would say if he were forced to take the witness stand. And without MacKinloch's testimony, there might not be enough evidence to save Jonah.

He'd turned away from Margaret and had gone outside to the waiting carriage, steeling himself for what lay ahead. The thought of leaving her wasn't at all easy, even worse, now that she'd said she loved him. He wished he could go back and lie beside her, breathing in her scent.

But he forced himself to go, knowing that he had to save his brother before he could ever reach out for his own happiness.

The carriage had hardly gone more than a mile or two, when another vehicle blocked their path. The driver pulled to a stop, and Cain got out to see what was happening. Two men approached, both armed. He recognized the first as the sheriff, a man whom he'd seen on occasion when he'd gone to visit Jonah.

"Has something happened to my brother?" he asked, approaching the pair.

The sheriff shook his head. "I'm afraid this involves you, Mr. Sinclair. I have to bring you in for questioning, since the new Earl of Strathland brought charges against you. He claims that you assaulted him after he offered you hospitality. He also said that you caused extensive damage to his house during a supper party when you were intoxicated."

Cain had no idea what he was talking about, and he was about to voice a protest, when suddenly it occurred to him that Barnabas's lies could be put to good use.

"Why don't you join me in my carriage?" he suggested to the sheriff. "I think we have a great deal to discuss, and you might as well arrest me on the way."

The man gaped at him. "Then you admit to damaging the earl's property?"

"Oh, I don't admit to a damned thing. He's trying to prove a point to my Margaret, that he can have me thrown in the Tolbooth based on his lies. But I think you ken me better than that, since we've seen each other during the past few weeks."

The sheriff gestured for the other man to move the vehicle out of the road. "That is true. But I do have to bring you in where we can gather the evidence, and—"

"Oh, that you can do, aye. But come inside and we'll have a talk. Because you've just solved a verra big problem for me." He opened the door to the carriage and invited the sheriff inside. "It's a pity you didna bring chains to lock me up. 'Twould have made it even more dramatic."

"Mr. Sinclair, I did not come to arrest you when there has been no investigation as of yet. We do follow the law, whether you believe that or not."

He joined the man inside the carriage and offered up his hand. "Aye. But today, you're going to help me save my brother's life."

⚜

Later that morning, Margaret arrived at the High Court of Justiciary, only to find that Cain wasn't there. No one had seen him, though she knew he'd left hours before her.

She tried to speak to the solicitor and the barrister, but neither one would give her their attention. No one, thus far, had seen Cain, and she was beginning to fear that Barnabas had done something terrible.

What had he done to Cain?

When the trial was about to begin, she'd had enough of the solicitor putting her off. This time, she marched up to him and said, "Have either of you seen Mr. Sinclair?"

"Miss Andrews, please take your seat," the solicitor said. "We are about to begin."

"I will, once you tell me what's happened to Cain."

He shrugged. "I have not seen him. But at this moment, my concern lies with Jonah Sinclair."

"You need to call Lewis Barnabas, the new Earl of Strathland, to the stand." Quickly, she told them of Barnabas's relationship with Lord Strathland and of her belief that Barnabas had hired someone to kill the earl.

But they both ignored her. "Please take your seat," the solicitor repeated.

She was furious with them for not listening. Didn't they realize that one man's testimony could mean the difference between life and death?

Jonah arrived a few minutes later. In the boy's blue eyes, there was only resignation and sadness. He looked around for a glimpse of Cain, and when he realized his brother was not there, his expression grew grim.

Where was he? Margaret knew that nothing on earth would keep Cain from his brother's side. This wasn't like him at all.

But just before the trial began, she saw Cain walk in with the sheriff, both wrists bound. Behind both of them was Lewis Barnabas, who had a satisfied look on his face.

Margaret longed to knock the new earl senseless. What had he done? And why on earth had Cain been arrested? She glared at Barnabas, who attempted to leave, only to be escorted to his own seat. Clearly this was his doing, but Cain's face remained stoic, not revealing a trace of his thoughts. It almost seemed that he *wanted* to be held in custody.

The barrister and solicitor spoke with him briefly, before they turned back to the boy. Though Jonah met his brother's gaze, she could not read what passed between them.

One by one, the jurors arrived, and Margaret prayed that they would find Jonah not guilty. Without MacKinloch's testimony, it would be difficult to prove anything.

The trial continued with more witnesses taking the stand, but she was hardly paying attention at all. Instead, her gaze remained fixed upon Cain. He was seated beside the sheriff, staring straight ahead at the proceedings.

She didn't know how they would prove Jonah's innocence, but she held faith that these men would discover the truth. And from

Cain's demeanor, she believed that he had used the arrest as a means of bringing Barnabas into the courtroom.

Her mind blurred with the proceedings while she kept her attention upon the man she loved. Last night, she hoped that Cain had given up any thought of surrendering himself. She had relived those moments in his arms, and she wasn't at all ready to let him go.

The coroner gave the estimated time of death and confirmed that the bullet had ended the earl's life. Another witness confirmed that the caliber of bullet could have been from the pistol belonging to Jonah's father, and that it had been recently fired. The evidence and testimonies seemed to mount higher, pointing invisible fingers toward Jonah.

Margaret waited for them to call Lewis Barnabas to the stand. But instead, the Defense called Peter Walker back. She couldn't understand why, for Walker had already given his testimony. Moreover, he'd been taken into custody for MacKinloch's accidental death.

Unless he knew more than he'd let on.

The Advocate began the questioning, and at first, there was nothing new. MacKinloch had gone out briefly and returned to play cards. But then the agent asked, "Who was the other gentleman who arrived by coach that night?"

Walker hesitated. "He never spoke his name. He was just a guest at the inn." But he appeared discomfited by the question, for he refused to make eye contact.

"This . . . guest offered to pay you that night, didn't he? What did he ask you to do?"

Walker's complexion went white, and he said nothing.

"Answer the question," the Lord Justice Clerk said.

"He asked me to run an errand for him," Walker answered.

At that moment, Cain turned back to look at her. In his eyes, she saw faith and a love so deep, she couldn't imagine it. Whatever was happening now on the witness stand, she felt certain that he had planned it. And that it would save Jonah's life.

From across the courtroom, she felt the fury in Barnabas's stare. For whatever reason, he was angry, and he was directing all of his rage toward her. A chill pricked beneath her skin, and she tried to ignore him.

"Before you fought with MacKinloch, witnesses overheard you arguing about money."

Margaret wasn't certain why the agent had changed tactics, but she held her breath. Cain, too, was leaning in.

"Was this the same money offered to you by the gentleman at the inn for this errand?"

"Nay."

"Then the gentleman did offer you money."

"He did, but I wouldna take it."

"And why wouldn't you take it?" the agent pressed. "If you were willing to fight MacKinloch to the death for the money owed to you, why wouldn't you help this gentleman? What sort of errand did he ask you to do?"

Margaret turned back to Barnabas, but this time his entire focus was upon the witness. The contempt upon his face gave the outer appearance of ennui—and yet, she saw the way his hands were clenched together. He had reason to be afraid.

Walker stared back at the Lord Justice Clerk. "Uncle, I don't think I should be answering that."

Margaret was startled to realize that the two of them were related. She wondered if incriminating Walker would anger the Lord Justice Clerk.

"You are under oath," the man reminded him.

Walker let out a slow breath and faced the jury. "I was asked to kill the Earl of Strathland. The man that night said he would pay me twenty pounds if I went out and waited for him on the road. But I wouldna do it. I'm no' a murderer."

The jury exchanged looks, and Cain's shoulders lowered as if in relief.

"If you didn't kill him, then who did?"

Walker shrugged. "MacKinloch offered to shoot him, but only if I swore that he was playing cards with us all night. He promised to pay me half the money if I did. Then he ne'er gave me my share."

Barnabas shrank down, as if to blend in with the throng of people. There was a buzz of excitement within the courtroom, and Margaret gripped her hands together. She wished Cain were beside her, so she could embrace him. This was what his brother had needed— a testimony that would clear Jonah from the accusations. Walker had all but admitted that MacKinloch had committed the crime.

"And where is the gentleman who paid MacKinloch to kill the Earl of Strathland?" the Advocate finished. "Have you seen him since that night?"

More hesitation. But then Walker nodded. "He's sitting right there." And he pointed to Lewis Barnabas, who had gone motionless, his gaze fixed ahead. The man didn't move, nor did he speak a single denial.

No longer was there any need to bring Barnabas to the stand. The testimony of the Lord Justice Clerk's nephew was enough.

Margaret let out the breath she'd been holding. Her head swam with dizziness and a strong sense of hope. Jonah might live after all. And since MacKinloch was already dead, his death sentence had been carried out.

After the Advocate Depute declined to question the witness, he addressed the jury and the Lord Justice Clerk with his closing statement. Then Jonah's Advocate spoke on his behalf, giving his own appeal to the jury members.

"Gentlemen of the jury. After the attention you have given this case, and with the great care you have heeded at examining all of the evidence and listening to the witnesses, I must discharge upon you the duty of finding the proper verdict.

"The defender, Jonah Sinclair, is a boy of fourteen. He has made mistakes, as most boys of his age are wont to do. And yet, the evidence presented to you is largely circumstantial. Had it not been for his past reckless behavior, I strongly believe he would not be sitting here today.

"What you see is a frightened lad before you. A boy whose only crime was to follow the man who he believed was an acting guardian. A man, who we have now learned, was the true murderer."

The agent continued to plead on Jonah's behalf, reminding the jury, "The only reason Jonah Sinclair took the pistol from the scene of the murder was because it was the only possession the boy had that once belonged to his father. He acted as a child, unthinking and innocent. Would a murderer have picked up his weapon and fled? I think it more likely he would have left the pistol behind, as MacKinloch did."

In closing, he said, "If there is within you, a voice of mercy, let it be heard. This boy, like others before him, had no father to guide his path. But does that make him capable of murder? Or is he naught but a lost soul, one in need of higher guidance and a family to show him the path of righteousness?"

After the agent stepped down, the Lord Justice Clerk made his own speech to the jury, reminding them of their duty. "I hold confidence that you will come to your verdict to meet the ends of justice." With that, the jury members departed the room to conclude the trial.

Barnabas tried to stand up, but the sheriff and another man moved to either side of him. Though Margaret didn't hear what was said, it was clear that the new earl would go nowhere. The look Barnabas sent her was filled with hatred. From across the courtroom, he said to Margaret, "Nothing at all has been proven. And this isn't finished, Miss Andrews."

Cain turned from his seat and stared at the man. His blue eyes held a cold rage, and he added, "Aye, Barnabas. 'Tis indeed finished. Just as you are."

Barnabas met Cain's gaze for a long moment before he sat down. And Margaret didn't doubt that the earl would be found guilty of his crimes.

In less than an hour, the doors opened, and the jury members returned. There was no emotion upon their faces, and her heart began pounding in her chest. If they'd reached a verdict so soon, it must have been unanimous.

Cain turned to her, and though he was across the room, it was as if there were no distance at all between them. She held his gaze, feeling the hope rise up within her. Regardless of what happened now, she would stand by his side and never leave him.

A representative stepped forward, and the Lord Justice Clerk asked, "Have you come to a verdict?"

The man nodded. "We have."

Chapter Nineteen

The interior of the Tolbooth was as terrible as it had always been. And yet, Cain hardly felt the cold. His senses were dead to all of it, the noises and odors unnoticed. He could only stare at the wall and thank God that it was Barnabas who was confined here instead of his brother. Now that Jonah had survived this ordeal, Cain vowed that he wouldn't let the boy be alone again. He'd become a father to him in the best way he could.

He stood outside Barnabas's cell, his hands resting against the wooden door. It was at last over, and justice would be served to the true guilty party. From behind him, he heard the sound of footsteps and voices. It sounded like Margaret approaching, along with Jonah, though he couldn't make out the words.

Cain had no time to speak before his brother barreled forward and embraced him hard. Jonah was sobbing and muttering words that were hardly understandable except for two: *not guilty.*

He hugged the boy so hard, he didn't even care that he was crying, too.

"It's over," Jonah whispered. "We can go home now." He drew back, and the happiness in his eyes blazed brightly.

"Aye, lad. That we can." He glanced up at Margaret, who was holding on to her waist, her own tears dampening her cheeks.

Cain let the lad chatter on about the remainder of the trial and how he intended to go home with them and eat until he had his fill. Then he'd take a bath in hot water until he was never cold again.

Margaret was smiling through her tears, and when Jonah finally stopped talking, she asked him to wait downstairs for her. Jonah agreed, but not before he hugged Cain as hard as he could. "Can we leave?"

"Soon," Cain promised. He'd only come to the Tolbooth to ensure that Barnabas was locked away. The man could now face his own trial for conspiring to kill his cousin.

After the boy was gone, the sheriff came up to speak with them. "Well, Sinclair, I cannot say that I've ever had a man offer himself up as a prisoner. But it did serve to bring Barnabas into the courtroom."

"Will I need to spend time in the Tolbooth?" he asked, half in teasing.

The sheriff sent him a wry smile. "Normally, we question the accused before we bring him here. You would have been released, Sinclair, since there was no evidence against you."

He'd known that, but before he could go home with Margaret and Jonah, he'd wanted to ensure that no one would ever harm them again.

"Do you mean to say that you volunteered to be held prisoner?" Margaret was frowning at both of them. "Is that why you were late to the trial?"

Cain nodded. "Barnabas was so eager to have me arrested, he didna realize where we were leading him. And once the doors were closed, he couldna leave."

"You can go now," the sheriff told him, before he walked down the stairs, leaving them alone.

Once Margaret came closer, Cain told her, "This is no place for a lady, Miss Andrews."

"Then it's a good thing that I'm not a lady anymore, isn't it?" She leaned up and kissed him, touching his cheek. He returned the kiss, claiming her with his tongue and nipping her lips. She melted against him, her arms winding around his neck.

"I want to take Jonah back to Ballaloch," he told her. *Before I marry you,* he wanted to add. The thought was bittersweet, for he missed his home . . . and yet he knew Margaret's parents would not support a marriage between them. The last thing he wanted was to tear her from her family. But in this battle, he would never stand down. Margaret belonged to him, and always would.

"For the rest of the summer," she agreed. "And in the fall, he'll go to school. I promised you that, remember?"

He'd nearly forgotten. But the idea of Jonah gaining the education he'd never had, and building a better life, was a welcome one. "I would be glad of it." He squeezed her hands and added, "Let us go home, lass."

"He looks much better, doesn't he?" Juliette said to Margaret as she led her inside the dining room. Jonah had been bathed, had a haircut, and was wearing new clothing. He was already seated at the table but immediately stood when he saw the pair of them.

"I guess I'm no' supposed to sit down before the ladies, am I?" he asked sheepishly, stepping back from the table. "I was hungry."

It didn't surprise Margaret, for he'd had little to eat in the past few weeks. "You may eat your fill tonight," she reassured him. She gestured for him to sit, and when the first course of food came, she began instructing him on the proper silver to use.

He shot her a skeptical look but obeyed. "Does it really matter?"

"It will when you dine with the duke and duchess," she said. "You should know the proper way, so you'll feel at ease."

He shot her a wry smile. "I'll ne'er eat with the likes of them."

"As they are my sister and brother-in-law, I think there's a good chance you would." Margaret didn't want him thinking that he was unworthy of sitting with them. Although she'd never been well acquainted with Jonah, she realized that she could help him to feel comfortable among the upper class.

"You'd best listen to her, lad," a voice resounded from behind her. "She's always right."

Margaret turned and saw Cain standing at the doorway. She hadn't seen him since they had brought Jonah back a few hours ago, for he'd been helping Paul around the estate. His long black hair was tied back, and perspiration gleamed upon his face and throat.

At the sight of him, she pushed her chair back and ran forward, throwing her arms around him. She didn't know what had come over her, but she needed to feel his arms around her. "Come and dine with us."

"Lass, I'm no' fit to sit with anyone right now. I've been helping Fraser with his horses." Cain extricated himself from her arms and stepped back. "I only wanted to see both of you before I went upstairs."

Margaret wasn't about to let him out of her sight. She hadn't had the chance to speak with him or learn what would happen to them after they returned to Ballaloch. "Juliette, I—"

"Say no more," her sister interrupted. "Go. And I will see to it that Jonah has his fill, as well as cake and pudding for dessert."

With a grateful look toward her sister, Margaret caught a footman and gave the order for a hot bath to be brought up.

Cain led the way, and when they reached his bedroom, he stopped her. "This is no' verra proper, lass."

She sent him a wicked smile. "I know that. And so do you." There was only a little time before the servants returned with the hot water. Even so, she found herself without the words she wanted to say. For so many years she'd kept herself apart, afraid to admit that she cared for this man and always had.

"You're beautiful," he told her, reaching out to cup her cheek. "I canna take my eyes off you."

"I love you," she whispered.

"You've always had my heart, lass. And always will." He kissed her hard, and deep inside, she felt a lightness and a sense of joy.

"I know that I've been . . . difficult over the years," she admitted. "You were always there for me, and I never saw the man you were. But now I know you are a man of honor, one whom I will always love." With a deep breath, she stared into his piercing blue eyes.

"I'm no' going to ask you to marry me, Margaret," he said. But in his voice she heard a note of teasing. "I'm ordering you to be my wife. If I have to drag you to the altar, that I'll do."

"You won't have to drag me," she said, smiling. "This time, I will come willingly."

"And I willna bring you a life of poverty," he insisted. "I will take over Aphrodite's Unmentionables and the profits will bring us wealth, even if I have no title."

"*We* will manage it together," she corrected. "Besides, what do you know of ladies' undergarments?" The moment she said the words, she realized the trap she'd walked into.

"I ken a great deal, lass. And I plan to remove yours each and every night." He kissed her, stroking the buttons of her gown.

"If you must," she teased back. But in all seriousness, she added, "I love you, Cain. And I'm glad to marry you." She hugged him tightly, feeling the warmth of his body against hers.

"But I'll no' touch you until our wedding night," he said. "We've already scandalized your sister's household enough as it is."

She'd never expected him to say such a thing. "That's not necessary, Cain. I don't think it matters." Right now she wanted to spend the night in his arms, pushing back the horrors of the last few weeks.

"It's glad I am that you're wanting me," he said. "But you'll have to be waiting a little longer."

He truly was turning her away, wasn't he? For the life of her she couldn't understand why. But he walked her to the door and opened it. "I'll bid you a good night, lass, and you can begin planning our wedding."

"You truly wish me to leave?" she asked.

"'Twill build up your anticipation for our first night as husband and wife," he promised.

Margaret shook her head in exasperation. If that was truly his intention, she decided to retaliate with a little lie. "That's too bad," she said with mock regret. "For I'm wearing red lace."

His answering groan made her smile as she closed the door behind her.

⚜

ONE MONTH LATER

"You ought to be married in a cathedral," Amelia ventured. "Wasn't that what you always dreamed of?"

Margaret shook her head. "It would make Cain feel uncomfortable, and I'd rather we were among our family and friends." Although he'd told her to do whatever she wished, she wanted him to be at ease on this day. Her greatest happiness was knowing that all of her sisters and their husbands would celebrate with them.

They would be married in a matter of hours, and Margaret had chosen a small stone chapel for the ceremony. It was an ancient location, hundreds of years old. But within the chapel there was a beautiful stained-glass window, in the shape of a rose. An old MacKinloch legend told that it was made by a woman, the chief of Glen Arrin's wife. And being there gave Margaret a sense of peace.

"You look beautiful," Beatrice admitted. There was a wistful look in her eyes as she looked down on Margaret. "And I hope you'll be happy in this marriage."

"So long as Father doesn't kill the bridegroom." Margaret sent her mother a rueful smile, knowing that the baron had been dismayed at her choice. He had relented, but with great reluctance.

"That *would* be a problem." Amelia exchanged a look with Toria and Juliette. "I do hope he restrains the urge."

"I will manage your father, just as I've always done." A blush crept over her mother's face. During the past few months it had become clear that their parents had mended whatever differences had kept them apart.

"We should worry about making Margaret look beautiful now, nothing else." Beatrice stepped back and studied her handiwork. "There."

Margaret reached up to touch the wreath of pink roses in her hair. Last night, Juliette had helped her to tie her hair in rags, and now she'd left it undone so it fell in twisted curls below her shoulders. Her gown was a soft purple, and she'd chosen a red lace chemise to wear beneath it. True to his word, Cain had left her untouched, and now she was eager to spend tonight in his arms.

"I always suspected you would marry Cain," Juliette said quietly. "You're more alike than you know."

"Stubborn, hard-headed, believing you're always right," Amelia continued. Her sister flashed her a delighted smile, and added, "It's the perfect match."

A quiet knock sounded at the door, and Toria answered it. Their father stood at the entrance with a brown paper package in his arms. He reminded them, "It's nearly time to leave. Have you finished your preparations?"

"I am ready, Father." Margaret stepped forward, and the expression on his face softened. She could almost believe that he was pleased on her behalf.

"You do look lovely," he told her. "And you seem happy." Then he looked back at Beatrice and smiled.

"I am." Margaret sent him a full smile, and the joy seemed to fill her up inside. "For Cain Sinclair *is* a noble man. And he loves me."

Her parents exchanged looks, and Beatrice took her husband by the hand. "There is nothing better than a marriage based upon love. Wouldn't you agree, Henry?"

Her father leaned in to kiss his wife. With a sigh, he nodded. "I would." Then he handed his wife the brown paper package. "This is for you, Beatrice."

Amelia tilted her head to the side. "Well, aren't you going to open it, Mother?"

"No, not here." The crimson flush in her cheeks suggested that their father's gift was from Aphrodite's Unmentionables. "But thank you, Henry."

From the sly smile rising on Henry's face, she suspected that her father did not disapprove as much as he had once.

Amelia clapped her hands over her ears and grimaced. "There are some things a daughter should never hear or know about."

Her father shrugged. "Although I'll never condone this . . . business . . . I suppose it has its benefits."

"Augh!" Amelia made a face and went to sit on the far side of the room. "Forgive me while I die of mortification."

Margaret stifled the laugh rising in her throat. It seemed that her father now recognized the appeal of Aphrodite's Unmentionables. She took the baron's arm, but silently agreed with Amelia. Although she was happy her parents had rekindled their love, there were some matters best left private.

The baron said, "Well, shall we get this over with?"

"Henry!" Beatrice swatted at him, but he winked at Margaret. It seemed that her father did have a lighter side to him, despite his serious demeanor.

"I think you do approve of Cain." Margaret placed her hand upon the crook of his elbow, letting him escort her out of the room. "You know that he'll be a good husband for me."

"He needs to be taught some manners," he grumbled. "And I suppose I can leave that to you."

They continued to walk down the hallway toward the stairs, and Margaret added, "Cain and I have chosen the land for our house. Jonah will stay in the older cottage after he finishes school."

"Where will you live?" he asked.

"Closer to Glen Arrin," she said. "We hope to have the house built by next summer."

"At least it will be better than the cottage," he agreed. When they reached the front door, he asked, "Is this truly what you want, Margaret?"

She rested her hand against the door and lifted her eyes to his. "More than anything."

Just as they stepped toward the carriage, Mrs. Larson let out a loud shout. Margaret turned in time to see an old boot thrown at her head.

"For good luck, lass!" the housekeeper cried out. "Now go before you miss your wedding!"

She took his breath away.

Cain had never seen anyone more beautiful than Margaret Andrews. She walked down the aisle like a woodland fairy, her hair twined with flowers. Her gown was the color of spring lilacs, and the smile shining on her face brought a sharp ache within him.

Jonah stood nearby, and the look of awe on the boy's face mirrored the feelings inside him. Cain didn't know how he'd ever won the heart of this woman, but he vowed to protect her with his life.

They stood before the clergyman, and as Margaret spoke her vows, Cain remembered the first morning he'd seen her in the rain. The young girl had grown into a strong, determined woman whom he loved more than life itself. He vowed to be faithful to her in sickness and in health, and that they would never be parted.

The loud cheers of his friends filled up the church, and when the clergyman announced them as Mr. and Mrs. Sinclair, he kissed Margaret before every last one of them.

With his mouth, he claimed her, tilting her head back and glorying in the taste of her lips. She was his, now and always. And the longer he kissed her, the more the whistles and applause continued.

When at last he broke free, his bride was blushing, but smiling. "You ken, lass, that you'll have to kiss every man here. It's good luck."

"And will you have to kiss every woman?" she inquired, raising an eyebrow.

He shook his head. "Thankfully, no." With a look toward the housekeeper, he added, "You may have to keep Mrs. Larson away with a broom, though. She's always liked me."

With her hand in his, they walked out of the church, followed by the sound of pipers and fiddlers. They would spend the rest of the night feasting and dancing until breakfast the following morn.

And yet, he wasn't at all intending to wait that long. He craved the touch of her skin with a thirst that would never be quenched. "I'm going to steal you away from here, lass," Cain told her.

"You can try," she laughed, darting in front of him, forcing him to give chase. The crofters and wedding guests gathered inside her father's barn. The baron had not been pleased by the idea of dancing in the barn, but Cain had insisted it was bad luck to do otherwise.

Inside, there were tables of food and countless barrels of ale and mead. The pipers and fiddlers gathered at one end while the wedding guests began the celebration. Margaret found herself in the center of the barn surrounded by everyone else. Cain spun her in a circle, kissing her as he did.

Never in her life had she imagined that her wedding would be like this. She'd always thought it would be a formal ceremony with members of the ton in attendance. They would have a wedding breakfast and one by one, the guests would come forward and speak to her.

She couldn't imagine anything more boring.

Margaret laughed as Cain handed her off to several of the Highlanders, and she learned that the only way they would let her stop dancing was to kiss them on the cheek. It was exhausting, and her husband finally claimed her again, pulling her back into the shadows of the barn.

"I love you, Margaret," he said, resting his forehead against hers. "And I promise I'll make you happy."

She took his face between her hands and kissed him. "I am happy, Cain. Truly."

In his blue eyes, her past and future merged. He was the man she wanted to spend the rest of her life with, and nothing else mattered.

"Come with me," he urged, leading her toward a small opening she hadn't noticed. It was used mainly for livestock, and he lifted the panel, helping her to slip away. Outside, a horse was tethered against the fence.

"You planned this, didn't you?" She shouldn't have been surprised to see it.

"Aye." Cain lifted her into his arms and then set her atop the horse before swinging up behind her. "I'm no' going to wait any longer for you, lass."

She didn't know where he was taking her, but throughout the short ride, she allowed herself to glory in the thrill of being stolen away.

"No one will ever make you follow the rules, will they?" she mused, as he lifted her down.

"What rules?" But he smiled as he carried her across a grassy plain toward a small copse of trees. There, within the privacy of the space, she found woolen blankets spread upon the ground, along with a basket of food and wine.

The afternoon was warm, and the sunlight haloed the darkness of Cain's long hair. She wrapped her arms around his neck, and he lifted her up, holding her below her hips.

"Do you remember this place?" he asked.

"It's where you kissed me for the first time." She bent down and took his lips again, and Cain lowered her against his body. She felt the rigid heat of his arousal, and dared to ask, "What's beneath your kilt, husband of mine?"

He took her hand and guided it beneath the wool. "Something for you."

Margaret laughed when he pressed her palm against his shaft. "So eager, are you?"

"I plan to spend the rest of the night loving you." He turned her and began unfastening the buttons. Instead of disrobing her quickly, he took his time, pressing his mouth to her back as each bit of skin was revealed.

"Red," he breathed, as he saw the crimson corset and lacy chemise. "Thank God."

He helped her lift the purple gown away, and Margaret felt a twinge of nerves. "Will anyone intrude upon us?"

"Nay. They're too busy dancing and drinking. It's only us, lass." His hands moved around to cup her breasts. She was wearing one of the most daring garments they had ever designed, one that Amelia had insisted would drive Cain wild. The chemise was entirely made of dyed red lace, and it was sheer, revealing her bare breasts.

Cain unlaced the silk corset and lifted it away, and then he guided her to sit on a large stone. He knelt before her, admiring her body.

"I ne'er imagined you'd wear something as provocative as this, Margaret." His eyes were heated, devouring her with his gaze.

"Do you . . . like it?"

"I want to tear it apart and take your breast in my mouth to make you wet for me."

His words painted a vivid picture, and her fingers dug against the stone. "I'm waiting," she whispered.

Instead of tearing the delicate lace, he leaned forward, warming her nipples with his breath. She waited for him to suckle against her, but he only flicked his tongue against the tips. With the lace shielding them, it was an arousing sensation to feel his tongue against the abrasive material.

She was dimly aware of him lifting her, discarding her petticoat and dragging up the edges of the chemise until she sat upon his lap. He pulled her legs around his waist and reached between them to touch her intimately.

As he stroked and caressed, his tongue licked at her nipple through the lace. Slowly, achingly tender, he sucked at her, and her body responded to his touch by growing even wetter. It was an easy, gliding motion when he slid his length inside her. She clenched him within her depths, feeling the echoing sensation as he tormented her breasts. The need to move was so fierce, she tried rocking against him.

He seized her mouth in a heated kiss. She was drowning in need, feeling his thick erection deep inside.

"Don't move," he ordered, stilling her hips. "Let me touch you."

With his fingers, he rubbed her body above the place where they were joined. She moaned as the feverish intensity started to take hold. The need to arch against him, to feel him in a different angle, was a desire she would not deny. Her body was quaking, and she squeezed him tightly as he pressed her closer to the edge.

"Cain, I love you," she said, her breathing uneven.

"I love you." He lightened his touch, rubbing her until she felt herself turning inside out, blossoming as he brought her pleasure. Deep inside her, she milked his length, rising up and falling as the release swept over her. He helped her, lifting her in a rhythmic motion while he impaled her with his shaft.

The need to change the pace, to go faster, only deepened the sensations. She rode him hard, her nails digging into his shoulders as he plunged deep, again and again. The shocking release caught her like a physical blow, knocking her over as she flooded with heat.

She was wild, untamed as she cast off all inhibitions and gave him everything he'd given to her. Heart, soul, and body.

And when he emptied himself within her, she covered his mouth with hers, drowning out his shout.

Afterward, he remained joined within her, laying her down and covering both of them with a blanket. The sunlight was dappled against his skin, and it seemed that even their breathing had become one.

"Did you ever imagine it would be like this between us?" she mused, tangling her hand in his black hair.

"Aye, lass. Every single night," he teased. "And I'll wager you didna dream of me at all. It was a prince you wanted in your life and in your bed."

Turning serious, she touched his cheek. "You're wrong. It took me a long time to know that it was you I wanted." She let her hands trace a path down his bare chest to rest over his heart.

"You *are* a prince, Cain. Never doubt that." She kissed his heart and added, "And the man of my dreams."

Epilogue

There was nothing that demanded whisky so much as the birth of a child.

After the grueling hours of waiting, the men gathered in the library, feeling the strain of a sleepless night.

"I'm glad all went well," Castledon said, taking a long sip of his drink. "I know Amelia never left her side for a moment."

"Nor did Victoria." The Duke of Worthingstone grimaced. "Though I've been through this before, I cannot say that it ever gets any easier."

Lord Lanfordshire was staring at the wall, as if he didn't want to think about the ordeal. Cain didn't blame the man, but at least the worst was over. It was a fine morning in Scotland, and the birth of a son was a joy to celebrate.

"Shall we go and see the bairn?" he suggested. Surely enough time had passed that the women would allow it. The men put aside their glasses and followed him out of the library and up the stairs.

Castledon knocked upon the door, and Amelia was the first to answer. "I've never seen such a beautiful boy. He's absolutely perfect." She gushed over the infant's fingers and toes, beaming at her husband as she welcomed them inside.

They entered the bedchamber, one by one. The duke stood beside his wife Victoria, who sent him a sleepy smile. "It's truly a miracle, isn't it?"

The midwife, Bridget Fraser, pronounced, "She endured every hour with courage like I've never seen. The birth went splendidly well. And now we have a wee bairn to hold." She eyed her son, Paul Fraser, who was holding Juliette's hand. "The pair of you might give me another grandchild. Two isna nearly enough."

"I just gave you another one a few months ago," Juliette protested.

"I'm wanting an even dozen," Bridget said. "No less than that."

Juliette rolled her eyes, and Cain couldn't blame her for it. Childbirth was difficult enough, and all of them had paced the floors last night.

Margaret was seated beside the bed, holding a newborn baby boy in her arms. She was cooing to her brother while Beatrice leaned back against her pillow, utterly exhausted from her labor. All of them had worried about Lady Lanfordshire, for her unexpected pregnancy was dangerous at her age.

Even now, the baron appeared stunned that all had gone well. He approached the bed warily, almost as if he could hardly believe his eyes.

"I—I'm so glad you're all right, my dear," Henry said to his wife, leaning down to kiss her. His hands framed her face as if to ensure that she was truly whole and well after the birth.

Beatrice smiled. "Meet the future Lord Lanfordshire, Henry."

The baron appeared flummoxed, uncertain of what to do. Juliette took the baby from Margaret's arms and said, "Father, come and hold your son." Teasingly, she added, "You look as if you've forgotten how to hold a baby."

"I believe I have," he admitted. Though once the baby was secure in his arms, he met his wife's gaze with a shining love. "I never imagined in all my days that we'd have another child." He sat down beside Beatrice, staring at the newborn with awe.

"It was a surprise to me, as well." But she reached out to squeeze his hand. "And an unexpected blessing."

Cain drew Margaret into his arms, holding her close. He didn't doubt that he would feel the same as Lord Lanfordshire when he and Margaret eventually had bairns of their own. But despite the risks, he wanted to watch her grow round with his child. No longer was he uneasy about becoming a parent. With Margaret at his side, it would be worth it.

Sometimes he could hardly believe the life he was living with her. The manor house they'd built near Glen Arrin had twenty-three rooms, and they had another townhouse in London, thanks to his wife's idea of expanding Aphrodite's Unmentionables into Paris.

She had a knack for earning a great deal of money. A few matrons had tried to embarrass her, when Margaret had revealed herself as the owner. But it hadn't taken long for them to apologize and retract their remarks, after Margaret's sisters had stopped inviting the matrons and their daughters to family gatherings. Victoria Nottoway, the Duchess of Worthingstone, had made it clear that any disparaging remarks against Margaret would be taken as a personal offense.

Now, they had servants and enough wealth to send Jonah to a boarding school in Edinburgh. His brother had struggled at first, but he'd eventually found his footing and was improving in his studies.

Often, it seemed to Cain that all of this was a dream. He'd never expected to have any of it, much less the woman he adored. But he was grateful for every last moment.

His wife had opened the door quietly and was guiding him outside the room. She lifted her gaze toward Cain, and in her green eyes, he saw love.

After he closed the door, Cain caught Margaret by the hand and held her back a moment. "Were you thinking we should slip away and make a wee bairn of our own, lass?"

She leaned in and kissed him. "Mr. Sinclair, now you know that isn't at all proper."

He tempted her further by kissing her deeply. "It isn't?"

"No." Margaret glanced back at the closed door and thought a moment. "But then, you *are* a bad influence on me, Sinclair."

To his shock, she grabbed him by the cravat and led him toward an empty bedchamber. He'd never in a thousand years expected her to agree.

"Five minutes," she ordered.

And as his wife proceeded to seduce him most thoroughly, Cain Sinclair decided that being a bad influence was sometimes quite enjoyable.

Author's Note

I hope you've enjoyed *Unlaced by the Outlaw* and that you'll try the other books in the Secrets in Silk series (*Undone by the Duke, Unraveled by the Rebel,* and *Undressed by the Earl*). If you want to get an automatic e-mail when my next book is available, you can sign up at my website, www.michellewillingham.com, and scroll to the bottom of the page, where you can input your e-mail address. Your information will never be shared, and you can unsubscribe at any time.

Also, please consider leaving a review at Amazon, even if it's only a sentence or two. Your feedback is always appreciated.

Acknowledgments

Special thanks to the team at Montlake for all of your help in bringing this series to life, especially Kelli Martin, Maria Gomez, and Jessica Poore. To my developmental editor, Charlotte Herscher, I owe a great deal of appreciation. You helped me to see the forest amid the trees, and I am deeply grateful for your insightful edits. And thank you to my agent, Helen Breitwieser, who always believed in this series.

ABOUT THE AUTHOR

Frank Willingham, 2010

Michelle Willingham, 2010 RITA® finalist, is the author of more than twenty-five books and novellas set in medieval Ireland, Scotland, and Victorian England. Her books have been translated into languages around the world and released in audiobook format. She has consistently received four-star reviews from *Romantic Times Magazine*, and *Publisher's Weekly* has called her stories "Genuinely funny and thoughtful." She has also been nominated for the Booksellers' Best Award and won an Award of Merit from the Virginia Romance Writers for historical romance.

She lives in southeastern Virginia with her husband and three children. Her hobbies include baking, reading, and avoiding exercise at all costs. Visit her website at www.michellewillingham.com for more details.